The
Bedr
Boardrooms!

EMILIE ROSE

KATHIE DENOSKY

MAUREEN CHILD

MILLS & BOON

First published in Great Britain 2011
by Mills & Boon, an imprint of Harlequin (UK) Limited,
Eton House, 18-24 Paradise Road, Richmond, Surrey TW9 1SR

Forbidden Merger, The Expectant Executive and *Beyond the Boardroom* were first published in Great Britain by Harlequin (UK) Limited in separate, single volumes.

Special thanks and acknowledgement are given to Emilie Rose, Kathie DeNosky and Maureen Child for their contributions to THE ELLIOTTS series.

ISBN: 978 0 263 88349 7

05-0711

Printed and bound in Spain
by Blackprint CPI, Barcelona

FORBIDDEN MERGER

BY
EMILIE ROSE

Emilie Rose lives in North Carolina with her college-sweetheart husband and four sons. Writing is Emilie's third (and hopefully her last) career. She's managed a medical office and run a home day-care, neither of which offers half as much satisfaction as plotting happy endings. Her hobbies include quilting, gardening and cooking (especially cheesecake). Her favorite TV shows include *ER, CSI* and Discovery Channel's medical programs. Emilie's a country music fan because she can find an entire book in almost any song.

Letters can be mailed to:
Emilie Rose
PO Box 20145
Raleigh, NC 27619
USA

E-mail: EmilieRoseC@aol.com

Thanks to Melissa Jeglinski for always providing a fun challenge and for letting me play with old friends.

And special thanks to Sheri WhiteFeather for allowing me to borrow Mason and Beverly.

One

Was the guy at the bar checking her out?

No way.

Men who looked like that did not look twice at women who looked like her. Pumps, a pageboy and puny breasts didn't spike testosterone in the average male. Not that he was average. Not by a long shot. But she didn't have time for fun and games.

Aubrey Holt checked her watch. She'd arrived an hour early to scope out the unfamiliar terrain, and she had forty-one minutes remaining before her luncheon appointment. That gave her plenty of time to review the questions her father wanted her to ask Liam Elliott, the financial operating officer of Elliott Publication Holdings, the chief rival of Holt Enterprises, her father's company and Aubrey's employer. Something was going on at EPH and no one could figure out what.

Normally, Aubrey would have preferred to meet on familiar turf, but she wanted the F.O.O. of EPH to be comfortable enough to let down his guard and perhaps leak a little insider information. Prying information out of a competitor under the flimsy pretext of an advertiser conflict wasn't Aubrey's preferred method of doing business, but if she wanted to prove her worth to her father, then she'd have to play the game his way. She didn't have to like it, but she'd buckle down and do her best—the way she always did.

As if magnetized, her gaze slid back to the man standing at the bar. He had his back to her and she took advantage of that to shamelessly ogle him, beginning with his polished black wingtips and working her way up the back of his crisply pleated dove-gray trousers to his tush and then over the royal-blue shirt that had to have been custom tailored to fit that narrow waist and those broad shoulders. His dark blond hair was thick and short. Cut by a stylist and not a barber, she'd guess.

And then his gaze trapped hers in the mirror behind the bar. Busted. Her cheeks caught fire. One corner of his mouth lifted and he turned. *Wow.* This man definitely wouldn't need to pick up women in a pub. They probably followed him home in droves.

Blond, Buff And Built lifted his glass in a silent how-about-it toast.

Oh, my God. Aubrey's breath snagged in her windpipe.

At twenty nine, she'd dealt with her share of come-ons. Occasionally, she allowed a gentleman to buy her a drink. But she had *never* looked at a man and wanted to get naked with him before hello. Blue Eyes made her want to get both naked and sweaty. Here. There. Anywhere. The sooner the better. He made her want to act out some of those wild fantasies she only dared think about under the cover of darkness in her lonely apartment.

Too bad she wasn't the type to act out her fantasies. Especially not with a stranger she'd met in a bar.

He headed her way, carving a path easily through the tables and around the waitresses and customers like a skier on a slalom course. Sharp, decisive, athletic. Her heart pounded loudly enough to drown out the patrons of the Irish pub. *Gulp.*

"May I join you?"

Impossible. His voice was as deep as his shoulders were wide. "I'm, um, meeting someone…in a bit."

Darn it.

"Boyfriend?"

"No."

"Then do you mind if I share your table until your friend arrives? The place is packed."

Was it? Aubrey quickly scanned the tables in the long, narrow establishment. All full. And the bar was standing room only. The tables must have filled while she'd been immersed in her list of questions.

Hello! Aubrey Holt, when are you ever going to meet another man like this?

She hastily gathered her papers and shoved them back into her briefcase. "Be my guest. I should have—" she checked her watch "—about thirty-nine minutes left."

Straight white teeth flashed. "About that, huh?"

She concealed a wince. *Could you be more anal, A.?* "Yes."

He hung the suit jacket he'd carried over one arm on the tall coatrack rising from the end of the booth and then slid onto the bench across from her. His knee bumped hers. The light contact hit her like a bolt of lightning, sending electricity storming through her central nervous system like crackling power lines.

She'd guess he was close to six feet. With that body and face he could easily model for fitness magazines. His cologne teased her nose. Cedar? Sandalwood? She couldn't place the brand, which meant nothing except that the manufacturer didn't advertise with any of Holt's magazines.

"You don't come here often." Not a question.

She could drown happily in his Caribbean-blue eyes. "My first time. Do you come here often?"

He nodded. "Best bookmaker's sandwich in New York."

"Bookmaker's?" *Not exactly a brilliant conversationalist today, are you, A.?*

"Ham, pepperoni and Havarti on Irish soda bread with a red-wine vinaigrette that will make your taste buds sing. Or you can try the Guinness Spareribs if you don't mind licking your fingers. They're tender and moist."

And so was she. Listening to the man talk was practically an orgasmic experience. His voice was low enough to make her lean forward to hear him and rough enough to raise the fine hairs on her skin. He had no detectable accent to distinguish where he'd come from. So many Manhattanites hailed from elsewhere. "I'll keep that in mind when I order."

"You do that." He winked.

One dip of those gold-tipped lashes and she considered pulling out her compact to examine her chin for drool. She settled for licking her dry lips. Did she have any lipstick left on? She looked like a lipless lady without. "Do you work nearby?"

"Not close enough that my co-workers will follow me. When I leave the office I like to *leave the office,* if you know what I mean." He grimaced. On him it looked good. But then every expression probably did with a face like that.

"I know exactly what you mean. There are days when I want to run screaming from my office building and never return." She didn't ask his name and didn't offer hers. Fantasy Man had approached her only because he wanted to sit down. After today, she'd probably never see him again.

A totally depressing thought.

"What do you do?" he asked.

Aubrey hesitated. She'd learned the hard way that men saw

her as the yellow brick road to a job with her father's empire, and she'd been burned more than once by mistakenly believing that she was the reason for their interest. "I'm pretty much a Jill-of-all-trades. I do whatever needs doing. You?"

"Number cruncher."

In Manhattan that could mean anything from a Wall Street broker to an accountant, but she couldn't fault him for his vagueness since she hadn't been forthcoming either.

The waitress appeared at the table. "Ready to order?"

Fantasy Man met her gaze. "May I buy you a drink while we wait for our dates?"

She never drank on the job, but what the hell, she'd never tried to weasel information out of a competitor either. The idea left a bitter taste in her mouth and a burn in her stomach. She had approximately thirty-two minutes before that exercise in dishonesty began. "Sure. Thank you. May I have a lemon drop martini?"

The waitress took his order for Woodford Reserve whiskey and departed.

He leaned forward, lacing his fingers on the table. She glanced at his hands. Not manicured, but no ragged nails either. And no wedding ring. How would those hands feel dragging across her skin? *Stop.*

"So, which are you? Sweet or sour?"

The question stumped her. Or was that an estrogen fog making clear thought impossible?

"Sugar on the rim. Sour drink. Sweet and sour. Which are you?" he explained.

Duh. Wake up, Aubrey. "Whichever is required at any given moment. I'm flexible."

A naughty spark flashed in his eyes. "I'll bet you are."

Her entire body flushed hot at the innuendo. "I meant at work."

"So did I." He compressed his lips as if fighting a smile but mischief danced in his eyes.

The fact that she had a business appointment in minutes and there was absolutely no chance of this going too far made her bold enough to return his brazen flirtation. "I'll bet you have amazing stamina. At work."

The corners of his eyes crinkled. "Yeah. I've been known to pull the occasional all-nighter. I'm dedicated to a good outcome. On a project."

Her heart flipped. She'd bet there'd been plenty of female "projects" to keep him occupied. The man oozed sexual confidence but not in the sleazy, slimy, synthetic way of a bar guy trying to pick up women.

The drinks arrived. While he paid the waitress, Aubrey took a healthy sip of her martini. The alcohol hit her empty stomach with a whammy.

"Morning person or night owl?" he asked.

"I like working when the office is empty, so I can be either. I'm flex—" Realizing she'd already said that, she bit off the word.

"Flexible. Yeah. I got that part. You'll have to show me sometime." This time his bright gaze slid from her face to her neck and shoulders and then over the inadequate breasts in her black camisole with its built-in shelf bra. She rarely needed more support. Darn it.

But somehow, she didn't feel flat-chested when he looked at her that way—as if he'd like to see her shed more than the blazer she'd removed when she took the booth in the overheated pub. Her nipples tightened. The flare of his nostrils indicated he'd noticed, and then his gaze returned to hers. Hot. Aroused.

The impact took her breath away and stirred a maelstrom of need low in her belly. She couldn't blame her sudden lightheadedness on her drink since she'd only had one sip.

She recalled a scene from a dreadful movie—one in which the lovers had met in the bathroom stall of a crowded restaurant and gone at it like hormonally insane teenagers. Aubrey had snorted in disbelief during the film. Today, the idea not only seemed plausible, it appealed. Even to her. A woman with too many hang-ups, according to her last lover.

She exhaled slowly. Never had she been hit with such a powerful punch of attraction, and she'd certainly never had it reflected back at her with such potency.

Why now, when she couldn't do anything about it, she railed at the unfair Fates.

It's your turn to speak, A. Be witty. Flirt. But when she looked into Fantasy Man's eyes she couldn't think of a thing to say. She was too old and too savvy to be dumbstruck by physical attraction. And yet she was.

He smiled, drawing her attention down his straight nose to the sharply chiseled line of his lips. A small white scar curved on the corner of his not-quite-square jaw. "Like it?"

"What's not to like?" And then she blushed. She *never* blushed and yet he'd made her do so twice in less than five minutes. But he'd caught her gawking. Again.

The crinkles at the corners of his eyes deepened. "The drink. Is it good?"

She wanted to crawl under the table. Of course, if she did he'd probably get the wrong idea about why she was under there, and he'd expect her to get to know him a whole lot better. She should be appalled by the shocking thought. Instead, need tightened in her midsection.

"Oh. Oh, yes. It's delicious. Strong, too." Maybe she could blame her idiocy on the bartender. Aubrey tried to gather her scattered wits before she made an even bigger fool of herself. "So, what about you? Morning person or night owl?"

He shrugged casually, but those twinkling eyes warned her

to brace herself. "Depends on the task. Some things I handle best when I first get up in the morning. Sometimes I do my best work right before I fall into bed."

If her heart beat any harder she'd need a paramedic. He was light years ahead of her in the sexual repartee department. *Aubrey, you have been without a man for too long.* Otherwise his teasing would not make her want to jump him.

"Business or pleasure?" he asked over the rim of his glass.

"Excuse me?"

"Which brings you here today?"

She cursed her slow-functioning brain. "Business. You?"

"Same."

He glanced at his watch. "In fact, my appointment's due any minute."

Wanting to smack her forehead but refraining, she looked beyond his shoulder toward the door. She should have been watching the entrance for her luncheon appointment to arrive. Not that she knew what Liam Elliott looked like, but how many men entered this particular establishment alone at one in the afternoon? Maybe she'd subconsciously blocked her assignation from her mind because she really didn't want to pry information out of the competition. By fair means or foul, her father had ordered.

She checked the time. "Mine, too."

Regret thinned Fantasy Man's mouth. "I see a table opening up. I guess I should take it."

Disappointment settled heavily in her chest. She wasn't ready to let him go. Bantering with him had been fun. When was the last time she'd had fun? She wanted his name and number. *Ask for it.* But somehow she couldn't find the nerve to do so. He was too far out of her league. "Yes, I guess you should. Thanks for the drink and for the company."

"Could I call you?"

Yes! Yes! Yes! she mentally shouted, as pleasure fizzed through her bloodstream like fine champagne, but she replied as calmly as possible, "I'd like that. Very much."

She shuffled through her leather satchel and found a pen but couldn't find anything other than her list of questions to write on. She refused to give him a business card. It would be a while before she'd risk telling him she was a VP for Holt Enterprises, assuming they were still seeing each other in "a while." But writing on a cocktail napkin seemed…cheesy. "I don't have a piece of paper."

He rose, dug into his hanging suit jacket pocket and pulled out a slim gold case. He extracted two business cards, laid both on the table facedown and slid one in her direction. "Write on the back of this. I'll give you my cell and home numbers."

While she wrote her first name and her phone number on the card in front of her he stood beside the booth and penned his numbers on the back of the other. They exchanged cards. He offered his hand, and his fingers closed around hers. His handshake was warm and firm and sent a zing of sexual awareness vibrating though her. From the widening of his pupils and the flare of his nostrils she'd bet the reaction wasn't one-sided.

"It was great meeting you…" Without releasing her hand he looked down at the card and then his gaze, shocked and wary, jerked back to hers. "Aubrey. Aubrey *Holt?*"

How did he know her name? Confused by his reaction, Aubrey flipped the card in her hand and read the embossed letters. Her stomach plunged to her pumps.

"*You're* Liam Elliott?"

"Yes."

She snatched her hand away and cursed her luck. She'd finally met an intelligent man with whom she'd like to pursue a relationship and she not only had to lie to him, but she also had to pry confidential information out of him.

Not the way to win friends or lovers, A.

She fought the urge to scream in frustration.

The sexiest man she'd ever met was totally taboo.

Damn. Double damn, Liam swore silently. Between work difficulties and his mother's battle with breast cancer he hadn't had time to look twice at a woman since January and here he was turned on by the enemy's daughter.

Confusion replaced desire in the most extraordinary violet-colored eyes he'd ever seen. "But you were early."

He stomped on his disappointment. "So were you."

"I…I wanted to familiarize myself with the establishment."

And he'd been driven to drink by this morning's disaster of a meeting between his warring family members—a battle his grandfather had deliberately started nine months ago when he'd announced his pending retirement at the family's New Year's bash. Patrick Elliott's idiotic method for choosing his replacement had pitted his children and grandchildren against each other as they vied for the top spot at EPH.

Worse, Liam suspected his grandfather had used the information Liam had inadvertently shared in devising his plan. Liam was closer to his grandfather than anyone in the family. He and Patrick ate together, golfed together and worked out side by side in the EPH gym. They talked about anything and everything, but Liam now wished he'd kept his mouth shut and had treated his grandfather more like an employer than a relative or a friend. But he'd never expected someone he loved to use his confidences to betray the family.

Why hadn't he seen this coming and found a way to head off disaster? The family counted on him to be the peacemaker. Over the past months Liam had watched his uncles, aunts and cousins become competitors instead of teammates. His grandfather continued to turn a deaf ear to Liam's prediction that the backbiting and squabbling would take EPH down instead of making the company stronger, as Patrick predicted. Liam used to enjoy working in the family business, but the current discord made him dread going to work each day.

He knocked back the last of his drink and considered his options. He could leave, but curiosity kept his feet nailed to the floor. Why had Aubrey Holt called this meeting? Option two: order another drink and join her. But he'd had two in the past hour, breaking his personal code of ethics. He rarely drank during working hours—even though the idea appealed more each day, given the current battlefield where he worked—and he never consumed more than two drinks. Ever. If he did order a third now, he'd probably say to hell with the family, work and ethics and invite Aubrey back to his apartment to see where this attraction would lead—a decision that would cause more trouble than it was worth.

"I— Well." Aubrey visibly switched gears from flirtatious woman to business acquaintance. The spark in her eyes died and determination squared her shoulders and her chin. Her lips firmed, concealing the lush softness.

The thought had crossed Liam's mind that Aubrey might have known who he was when she'd been checking him out at the bar and maybe she'd come on to him to soften him up and worm information out of him, but her obvious horror at discovering his identity erased it.

"Please, have a seat, Mr. Elliott, and let me buy your lunch."

"Liam." Damn, he repeated silently, and slid back into the booth. This time when his knee brushed Aubrey's the fire shooting up his thigh filled him with frustration rather than the heart-racing anticipation he'd felt moments ago. Nothing could come of this attraction. Nothing. Matthew Holt wasn't the kind of adversary to whom you revealed your weaknesses. That meant his daughter wasn't either.

"What made you call my office for an appointment, Aubrey?" He'd be damned if he'd call her Ms. Holt when minutes ago he'd been savoring the idea of getting her out of her clothes and exploring every inch of her long, lean body. With his hands. With his tongue.

He'd been watching her since she walked in. Aubrey might be as tall and slender as a model and not his usual type, but when she'd shimmied out of her black blazer her moves had been worthy of a top-notch stripper. Smooth. Seductive. Riveting. Not that he'd seen any strippers, but he recognized innate sexuality when he saw it.

What's more, he didn't think she'd noticed that he—along with half the other men in Ernie's Pub—had frozen with their glasses halfway to their salivating mouths to watch her wiggle out of that blazer.

She tucked a swath of straight, light brown hair behind her ear. "I, um, wanted to discuss some of our mutual advertisers."

"What about them?"

She shifted on her bench seat and focused on the papers she'd extracted from her briefcase. "There's a rumor that EPH's magazines are deliberately lowering their advertising rates and padding their rate base to lure away Holt's advertisers."

"What? That's nuts. We'd have to falsify our circulation and demographics to do that. We'd lose advertising income and credibility. Besides, you know as well as I do that there are two outside regulatory companies who track those numbers."

With each magazine shooting for maximum profit in his grandfather's contest, there was no way any of the EPH lines would turn away sales dollars. Aubrey's rumor was pure bunk, but it could be damaging if advertisers thought EPH wasn't being truthful.

"Where did you hear that?"

"I, uh, can't reveal my source." Her gaze didn't meet his. She stroked the condensation from her water glass with one finger.

Liam's gaze focused on the slow, gliding digit and sweat, like the droplet on her glass, rolled down his spine. Minutes ago he'd been anticipating her touching him. He severed the unacceptable tangent of his imagination and eyed her suspiciously. Were those seductive moves intentional?

"Has the circulation and advertising fee changed dramatically for some of your magazines over the past year? Are EPH's magazines offering additional marketing services?"

"That's confidential information."

"I know, but the pressure is on for us to stay competitive with the EPH lines."

"What Holt Enterprises does is not my problem."

"I realize that. I was hoping—"

"Hoping I'd give you insider information?" A bitter taste filled his mouth. His grandfather had used Liam's confidences. Was that Aubrey's plan too?

"I was hoping we could work together to get a fair rate from our mutual advertisers and neither company would lose money."

The only thing that kept him from walking out was hunger. That and a prickling at the back of his neck. He never ignored that warning sign. Something wasn't kosher about Aubrey's spiel, but given the stipulations in his grandfather's plan and the disruptions at EPH, it was possible that some of the advertisers had caught wind of the dissention in the Elliott ranks and become unsettled. They'd tried to keep the competition under wraps because Patrick was fanatical about guarding the family name and reputation, but leaks happened.

Liam signaled for the waitress and ordered his regular sandwich. Aubrey ordered the same, but he had the feeling it was more because she didn't want to be bothered with a menu than from any real interest in a bookmaker's special.

"I can't help you. Nothing about the way EPH does business with its advertisers has changed." Nothing except the magazines' personnel were going at each other's throats with fangs bared. His grandfather had decreed that the magazine with the highest profit margin proportionally at the end of the year would see its editor in chief become CEO of EPH. Nobody wanted to lose.

As financial operating officer Liam was in charge of tracking the numbers. The weight rested heavily on his shoulders. He'd had to take his personal feelings out of the equation, forget the people involved and deal strictly with the cold, hard facts. It wasn't easy. He worried about EPH and worried about his mother even more.

And while his extended family self-destructed around him Liam realized life was passing him by. He was thirty-one. His parents had been married and had four children by his age. Even his brothers and sister had wised up. Gannon had married in February. He and his wife Erika were expecting their first child. Liam's younger brother Tag was engaged, and his sister Bridget had recently married a Colorado sheriff and left the family business. He also had a handful of cousins and an uncle who'd recently found their significant others.

All Liam had was a long history of hooking up with the wrong women, a job in the family business, a Porsche he rarely drove—but shelled out a fortune for in parking fees—and a Park Avenue apartment he only used for sleeping. He had no one to stand by and support him the way his father had supported Liam's mother through her ordeal.

His workaholic father had risen several notches in Liam's

opinion over the past nine months by getting his priorities straight. Family first. Work second. It hadn't always been that way. It had taken almost losing his wife to set Michael Elliott straight.

The sandwiches arrived and the server departed.

Aubrey's violet eyes met Liam's and the impact hit him like a fist in the gut, knocking the breath out of him. "How is your mother? I read about her illness in the paper."

What was she—psychic? "She's improving. She's finished chemotherapy and her hair's growing back."

"Her diagnosis must have been terrifying for all of you."

"Yes." He could have lost his mother, and while she wasn't out of the woods yet and wouldn't be until she'd been cancer-free for five years, optimism was on the upswing. The doctors gave her a good prognosis.

"You're close to her?"

"Now more than ever. Are you close to your mother?"

Sadness filled Aubrey's eyes. "No. She left my father when I was eleven. She couldn't stand always coming in second to Dad's mistress—work."

"You didn't keep in touch?"

"I shuffled back and forth for a while, but then she remarried." Aubrey ducked her head and the curtain of her shiny hair swung forward. "The sandwich is good and you're right about the vinaigrette. It's delicious."

He ignored her bid to switch topics. "You didn't get along with the new husband?"

Color leeched from Aubrey's face. "He liked me a little too much."

The sandwich turned to rubber in Liam's mouth. "He came on to you?"

Aubrey abandoned her lunch. "Yes."

Anger percolated in Liam's veins. "How old were you?"

"Sixteen."

"Did your mother divorce the bastard?"

"No. Look, could we talk about something else?"

His appetite deserted him. He wanted to ask how her mother could stay with the pervert and if her father had beaten the crap out of him. But he didn't. "Sure."

"I heard Patrick is considering retirement. Any idea who will replace him?"

Liam rested his fists beside his plate. "Aubrey, I'm not going to discuss EPH."

She abandoned the pretzel she'd been nibbling. "I understand. I'm sorry I wasted your time."

He didn't understand the emotions chasing across her face. Disappointment was easy to identify, but he'd swear he saw failure in Aubrey Holt's eyes. Why? "You haven't. Until you started with the EPH interrogation I was having the best time I've had in months."

Her lips parted and color washed her cheeks. Before she could reply his cell phone rang. He unclipped it from his belt. "Excuse me. Liam Elliott."

"Mr. Elliott, this is Trisha at the Davenport Gallery. Gilda Raines has agreed to talk about parting with the painting you wanted for your mother. I'd suggest you come now. Gilda is…unique. She wants to meet you before she makes her decision."

"I'll be right there." He snapped the phone shut and signaled for the waitress. "I hate to cut this short, but I have to go."

"Problem at work?"

A wry smile tugged his lips. Did Aubrey never give up? "No. I've been trying for months to buy a painting by my mother's favorite artist. The artist has finally agreed to discuss selling. I don't want to give her time to change her mind. I'm going to meet her now."

"Which artist?"

He reached for his wallet. "Gilda Raines."

Aubrey sat up, alert and radiating excitement. "Are you serious? She's my favorite, too. And you're going to meet her! She's a recluse who never meets *anyone*." Her hand covered his on the table and sparks hopped up his arm. "May I come with you?"

Liam looked across the table at the enemy's daughter, at her pale, slender hand over his. A wise man would cut his losses and say goodbye. *Now.* Evidently he wasn't as smart as he thought he was because the shine in those violet eyes and the curve of her lips overrode his conscience's objections.

"You can ride along. But I'm not answering questions about EPH. If you ask even one I'll have the cab pull over and put you out. Are we clear?"

Her grin stole his breath. "As clear as the Hope Diamond."

Two

Aubrey wanted to get to know Liam better, but putting her hand in his lap wasn't quite what she had in mind. She hadn't hit ground zero, but she'd come close enough that he inhaled sharply and his warm thigh muscles tensed beneath her fingers.

"Sorry." She snatched her hand away and dug her nails into the armrest on the car door, bracing herself as the taxi zig-zagged around slower cars.

"Not a problem." His voice sounded tight.

Her palm continued to tingle long after it left Liam's rock-hard thigh behind, all the way down Lexington Avenue, in fact. Awareness whizzed through her veins. The cabbie drove like a carjacker evading the law, but that wasn't surprising considering Liam had offered to double his fare if he'd get them to the gallery fast.

Another swerve pitched her back against the hard-muscled, good-smelling, taboo man beside her. Their shoulders bumped and their eyes met. Liam's gaze slowly lowered to her mouth. Aubrey's breath caught and her heart raced.

How would he kiss? Soft or hard? Reserved or passionate? She'd never know. She turned to look back out the window and a disappointed sigh slipped past her lips.

The cab pulled to the curb in front of the gallery. Aubrey said a silent prayer of thanks and climbed out while Liam paid the fare.

He joined her on the sidewalk. "You said you like this artist?"

"Yes. Her paintings are very sensual."

"They're flowers," he said with a straight face.

Aubrey studied the confused frown on Liam's face. Did he not know anything about the artist? "Have you ever studied Georgia O'Keeffe?"

He shook his head. "Only enough to know vaguely who she is. Art's not my thing."

What were his interests outside of work? She'd never know that either. Disappointment weighed heavily on her shoulders.

"Gilda Raines has been compared to a modern-day O'Keeffe although she's more likely to paint the flowers and scenes from the Southeast rather than the Southwest. She's originally from Charleston, South Carolina, and she took up painting after her husband, the love of her life, died. I've heard she's quite an unusual personality."

She followed him inside a bright, open area. Oils of varying sizes graced the walls and a few pieces of sculpture stood on wide pedestals scattered throughout the space.

A chic brunette approached. "Mr. Elliott?"

"Yes."

"Trisha Evans." In Aubrey's estimation, the handshake lasted longer than it should have. "And you are?"

"Aubrey Holt."

"Ms. Raines is waiting for you in the private viewing room.

Follow me." She turned and led the way. Aubrey wondered if the woman normally sashayed that way or if she'd widened the pendulum swing of her hips for Liam's benefit. And then Aubrey rolled her eyes. What did it matter if the woman wanted to advertise her wares? Aubrey would probably be doing the same thing if Liam's last name were anything but Elliott.

A woman no more than five feet tall awaited them. Her face held remarkably few lines for someone in her late sixties. The morning glory painting on the easel beside her took Aubrey's breath away. It wasn't one she had seen before. This painting seemed to express everything she'd felt before she'd discovered Liam's identity.

"So you wanna buy my painting," Gilda Raines said without preamble in a rich southern drawl, drawing Aubrey's attention momentarily away from the mesmerizing artwork. The artist's dark eyes assessed Liam.

"Yes, ma'am." He briefly glanced at the framed oil.

Ms. Evans barely finished with the introductions before Ms. Gaines asked, "Why?"

"I explained about my mother in my letter. About her illness."

Aubrey's gaze jerked to Liam. He'd written to the artist?

"I don't get many letters begging me to sell—especially a painting someone has never seen. Anything, you said. 'I'll buy anything.' I don't part with my babies often, Mr. Elliott, and when I do it's for a good reason. I don't know that I should give up one now. Why should I?"

"Because my mother admires your work and having one of your paintings will make her happy."

Thin arms crossed over a loose-fitting paisley print shirt. Gilda remained mute, but her expression said, "Not good enough."

Even though it wasn't any of her business, Aubrey butted

in. “Because after a double mastectomy his mother needs to be reminded she’s a woman.”

All three heads swiveled toward Aubrey. “Your morning glory embodies womanhood, femininity and sexuality. I’m guessing Karen Elliott feels she’s lacking all of those qualities at the moment.”

Gaines’s eyes narrowed and she cocked her head. “How would you know?”

Memories encroached, robbing a little of the brightness from Aubrey’s afternoon. “I lost a friend to breast cancer last year. I spent time with her during her treatment. Quite a few of your paintings hang in the Women’s Health Center. *The Daylily* is my favorite, but Jane liked *The Gardenia* best.”

Jane, her father’s personal assistant for as far back as Aubrey could remember, had lost her life to the disease after a long, valiant struggle. The heartbreaking shame of it was that if Jane had gone for the mammograms her doctor had been recommending for the past two decades they might have caught the cancer in time to save her life, but Jane had been afraid the procedure would be uncomfortable and embarrassing so she’d put it off only to learn too late that the hell of chemotherapy was much worse than the slight discomfort of a mammogram.

Grief reopened in Aubrey’s chest. She pressed a hand over her aching heart and turned back to the artwork to blink away her tears. For as far back as she could remember she’d talked more to Jane than to her socialite mother or workaholic father, and Aubrey still missed Jane, her confidante and hero.

It had been Jane who’d realized something was wrong after Aubrey’s mother had remarried and Jane who’d pried the confession out of Aubrey about her stepfather’s inappropriate advances. And it had been Jane who’d gone to her boss and revealed the sordid truth. Aubrey had been swiftly removed from her mother's home and she hadn't been allowed to visit again. When her mother wanted to see her she'd had to come to the Holt apartment. She hadn't come often.

Gilda joined Aubrey beside the painting and tipped her head to indicate Liam. "Do you think he gets it?"

Aubrey blinked away the past and looked over her shoulder at Liam. The careful neutrality of his face confirmed he didn't understand the nuances behind the flower. And then she met Gilda's skeptical gaze. "I can explain it to him."

Gilda cackled and nodded. "Yes, I'm sure you can. All right, then."

And just that quickly the deal was done. Minutes later the artwork had been packaged and placed in the trunk of a taxi and Aubrey and Liam were on the way to Liam's apartment—a decision Aubrey considered both wise and foolhardy. Wise because she might be able to glean more information from Liam, but also foolhardy because she was only tormenting herself with what she couldn't have.

The cabbie drove as aggressively as the first even without the added incentive of a double fare. He swerved to avoid a bicycle messenger at the last possible second, pitching Aubrey practically into Liam's lap. Liam's strong hands steadied her.

She lifted her gaze to his. "Excuse me."

The blue of his eyes darkened and his gaze dropped to her lips. "No problem."

Aubrey ordered her muscles to move her away from the warmth and strength of Liam's grasp. They mutinied. Liam's hand lifted from her upper arm to cup her jaw. He stroked her cheekbone with his thumb and then threaded his fingers through her hair. Aubrey shivered and inhaled a shaky breath.

Why oh why did this man have to be the one to awaken every feminine instinct in her body?

Before she could force herself to retreat, Liam's head lowered. Instead of scooting back to her side of the slippery vinyl seat Aubrey lifted her chin and met him halfway.

His lips brushed hers, softly at first and then more insistently. Her pulse raced. Her lungs seized. And then his slick tongue parted her lips and she tasted him. Delicious. Aubrey covered his hand on her face, determined to remove it, but somehow her fingers threaded through his and her other hand clenched the lapel of his jacket.

The movement of the car rocked her breast against his bicep, stroking with each swerve and bump in the road and causing her nipples to tighten and warmth to puddle low in her belly. And then Liam's arms banded around her and he lifted her across the seat and into his lap. She gasped at the suddenness of the action, at the heat of his thighs beneath hers and his groin against her hip.

A second of sanity prevailed, and she drew back to gasp for breath, but she didn't go far. Her forehead rested on his. Their noses touched. His heart slammed beneath her palm and his breath swept her skin.

"What are we doing?" she whispered.

"Damned if I know." One of his hands raked up and down her spine. The other settled on her hip and stroked downward until he found skin. The hem of her knee-length skirt had ridden up to midthigh. She wasn't wearing stockings. His hot palm glided over her knee, down her calf and back up again, edging beneath the fabric.

This really had to stop…in a minute. Aubrey couldn't remember ever being so aroused so quickly and in such an inappropriate location—a cab, for pity's sake, in plain view of the driver up front. Liam kissed one corner of her mouth and then the other, and then he took her bottom lip into his teeth and gently tugged. His tongue laved the sensitive inner skin.

A sound, half-moan, half-whimper, bubbled in her throat. She struggled for lucidity. "This is not… I didn't… I wasn't looking for this today."

Liam's chest rose and fell on a deep breath. "I know."

"We shouldn't. You're the competition."

The hand on her thigh tightened before grazing upward over her hip, beneath her blazer and past her waist to rest just below her breast. "I know that, too."

Don't stop. Dizziness forced Aubrey to suck in a forgotten breath. One more kiss, she promised herself as she arched against him. Just one. She angled her head and took his mouth, savoring the taste of forbidden fruit. His thumbnail scraped over her nipple and a moan poured from her mouth into his. She twined her tongue around the slickness of his and then suckled. His chest vibrated beneath her palm in a purely masculine purr, and he shifted on the seat, pulling her closer and bringing the hot shaft of his erection flush against her hip. Heat flooded her core and moisture dampened her skin. She tingled all over as if she'd been dunked in a warm champagne bath.

"We're here, bud," the taxi driver's heavy Bronx accent interrupted. Liam's muscles turned rigid beneath her.

Shocked by her uncharacteristically brazen behavior, Aubrey scrambled out of Liam's lap and back to her side of the cab. Her face—her entire body—burned. Rather than look at Liam, she glanced out the car window and blinked in surprise. Park Avenue? Liam lived only a few blocks away from her place on Fifth. Walking distance. Her heart missed a beat. So close…and yet worlds apart because of their employers.

Liam opened the door and offered his hand. Wisdom decreed Aubrey say goodbye and give the driver her address. But she'd promised Gilda Raines that she'd explain the painting to Liam.

You don't have to. His mother will understand it and Gilda will never know.

But you promised.

And she didn't break promises.

Snatching up her purse and her leather satchel, she slid across the seat, placed her hand in Liam's and let him help her from the car. She quickly released his hold when a fresh wave of longing swept through her.

This can't happen. But her mind and body didn't seem to be speaking the same language. Turning away from temptation, she studied the gray stone building and waited on the sidewalk while the cabbie removed the painting from the trunk.

A doorman rushed from the apartment building. "Need help with that, Mr. Elliott?"

"No thanks, Carlos, I have it."

Aubrey followed the men into the building and across the marble floor past a bank of elevators to a private elevator located at the end of a short hall. Private elevators meant one thing. Penthouse. She'd had fantasies about elevators, a handsome stranger and a blackout. She'd never even considered having an elevator all to herself and not having to rely on being trapped by a power outage to pursue her naughty dream. She shouldn't be thinking that now, but knowing the man had the power to lower her IQ fifty points with a single kiss and that he had his own elevator sent her mind sprinting down a dangerous alley.

Everyone in Manhattan or magazine publishing knew the Elliotts were wealthy, but she'd had no idea Liam owned such an expensive piece of real estate. Or maybe he didn't. Maybe like her he rented a family-owned property. Aubrey loved her bright and airy apartment, but she sometimes wished for more independence. She and her father had an odd relationship. Aubrey yearned for his approval, but she wished she didn't. Being on her own… She sighed. Probably wouldn't change a thing. Her father would continue to give her everything she wanted materially, but nothing emotionally.

The elevator doors closed, leaving the doorman behind. Aubrey faced forward, but turning her back on Liam didn't help. Dark wood wainscoting covered the bottom half of the doors and walls of the elevator, but the top half was mirrored. No matter which way she looked she faced multiples of Liam's reflection. He surrounded her. She lowered her gaze to the marble floor.

"You get used to it," he said, drawing her eyes back to his. "The mirrors," he added when she lifted an eyebrow.

He rested the painting on the floor and shoved his free hand in his pocket. His relaxed pose would have fooled her if not for the intensity in the blue eyes watching her. She didn't know what to say. Evidently, her adolescent, tongue-tied stupor had returned.

The doors glided open into a small carpeted hall containing two doors, one on the left and another on the right. So the elevator wasn't exclusively Liam's. It would take a power outage to ensure privacy, after all—not that it mattered since she and Liam wouldn't be doing the deed in the elevator or anywhere else.

He unlocked the door on the right and motioned for her to precede him. Aubrey walked through the dark wooden portal. Her heels tapped across the granite floor leading into Liam's living room. The warm wood tones, scatter rugs and traditional furniture and fabrics surprised her. She'd expected a bachelor pad to look more like…well, a bachelor pad. Black leather, chrome, fur rugs. But other than the granite floor, his home had none of those I-am-man-hear-me-roar attributes. Jewel tones of emerald, ruby and sapphire dominated a decor that was surprisingly classic and very similar to her tastes. A couple of landscapes hung on the walls. Vineyards, unless she missed her guess.

The man continued to surprise her. Too bad she couldn't hang around to uncover the rest of his secrets.

"Tell me why three women just looked at me like I was a pitiful dumbass." Liam balanced the heavy frame across the arms of a wing chair.

Aubrey's grin hit him in the solar plexus. "Didn't like that, did you? Here let me do that."

She approached to help him remove the paper from the painting. Their fingers tangled as they reached for the same piece of tape. It was a wonder the sparks between them didn't ignite the heavy brown paper protecting the artwork. Liam jerked too hard and a tearing sound rent the air.

"Careful," she said. "You're going to want to rewrap this to take it to your mother." She carefully removed the remainder of the paper and then placed it on the floor beside the chair. Stepping back, she tilted her head and observed the picture. "Tell me what you see."

Liam looked at the painting. "A white flower with a magenta center surrounded by green vines."

Aubrey closed the distance between them. Her shoulder brushed his. In her heels she stood almost eye to eye with him. "Focus on the vines. What do you see?"

Violet eyes. Sleek, milk-chocolate hair. Smooth ivory skin. Her scent filled his senses. Roses? Gardenias? Something floral and heady, reminiscent of hot summer evenings at The Tides, his grandparents' estate in the Hamptons. If the kiss they'd shared in the taxi had shaken Aubrey as much as it had him she didn't show it.

Sunlight streamed through the window, heating his skin.

He shrugged out of his suit coat and tossed it over the back of the sofa and then transferred his attention from the woman who had his hormones in an uproar to the piece in question. "Curves. The vines are curvy."

"Resemble anything you've seen before?"

"Yes. Plants." His tone and expression must have revealed his frustration.

She reached out and traced a fingertip over the thickest vine. "Look again."

He felt stupid—neither a familiar nor welcome feeling. "Hills. Valleys…" And then it clicked, and it was so obvious he didn't know how he'd missed the shape before. "A woman's body. Reclining."

Each leaf and vine shimmered like wrinkled emerald-green satin sheets and the woman's form lay right in the middle. Damn, how had he missed that?

Because any man who wasn't thinking about sex would only see a tangle of vines.

"Very good." Her approving smile filled him with an inordinate amount of warmth. "Now look at the morning glory itself. Notice the dew trembling on the edge of the blossom and the curling tendrils of the shoots surrounding the flower."

Her description made it impossible for him to miss the hidden meaning. Liam's ears burned and he swore. "I bought a pornographic painting for my mother."

Aubrey's low chuckle danced down his spine. "No, you bought her a sensual one. There's nothing dirty about this picture."

"If that symbolizes what I think it does, then I can't give it to her."

"Gilda Raines paints of life, birth, femininity and sensuality. Like you said, it's just a flower to the uninformed observer, but to someone who looks deeper it's the cradle of life."

"It's a woman's—"

She held up a hand to stop him. "Liam, don't make this ugly. It's a beautiful piece. Your mother will adore it."

She turned back to the painting. The way Aubrey looked at it—with parted lips and flushed cheeks—was the same way she'd looked at him before they'd exchanged names and again right before he'd kissed her. The air in the room thickened. He shoved his hands through his hair. He should call her a cab before sexual attraction and thoughts of this...*erotic* picture overrode his good sense.

His brain and his mouth took opposite paths. "Can I take your jacket and get you a glass of wine?"

She hesitated, catching her bottom lip between her teeth. Her gaze traveled to the door and back to him as if she, too, were weighing the wisdom of staying. "Yes."

Politeness demanded he step forward and help her remove her blazer, but watching her shimmy out of the black garment impeded the blood flow to his cerebral cortex. Mesmerized, he watched one bare shoulder appear and then the other. Her camisole top with its pencil-thin straps clung lovingly to her slender figure.

He'd noticed her sensuality at the pub. Her interpretation of the painting confirmed it. Aubrey Holt was undoubtedly the sexiest woman Liam had ever encountered. He'd never experienced such strong magnetism in his life. Who she was didn't dampen his response in the slightest.

Desire pulsed heavily in his groin and tightened his rib cage, making it impossible to draw a deep breath. She extended her arm with the jacket in her hand. Liam took it. Without turning he pitched the garment in the direction of the sofa, curled his fingers around her waist and pulled her forward until her body pressed flush against his. Aubrey's breath hitched a second before his mouth covered hers.

Her lips parted immediately, welcoming and meeting the thrust of his tongue. She tasted better than the finest wine in his collection. Her arms wound around his neck, pulling him closer, pressing her breasts against his chest.

He usually dated petite women, usually had to bend himself in half for a kiss, but Aubrey rose on her tiptoes and their bodies aligned perfectly. Breast to chest. Thigh to thigh. Her feminine mound cradled his erection and when she arched her back and ground against him, electricity crackled down to his toes, up to his skull and back again to settle hot and heavy below his belt. He cupped her tight buttocks and pushed back, relishing the way her whimper filled his lungs.

Skin. He needed skin. He raked his hands upward, dragging the hem of her top from her skirt, and then he found the warm satin of her waist and the ridge of her spine with his fingertips. She shivered in his arms and drew back to gasp. He dipped his head, burying his face in the juncture of her neck and shoulder, tasting her sweetness, inhaling her heady fragrance, feeling her rapid pulse against his tongue. His heart hammered as if he'd raced up the stairs to the twenty-fifth floor of the EPH building. His lungs burned. And he ached to lose himself in the dewy center of the woman in his arms.

Desire. That's it. That's what the painting represented. A woman on the brink of desire.

A single brain cell broke through the surface of the testosterone flooding him. This was Aubrey. Aubrey *Holt.* The enemy's daughter. Liam drew back, breathing heavily, and looked into Aubrey's passion-darkened eyes. This wasn't love. It was pure, unadulterated lust. He'd experienced lust before, but never like this, never this potent, never this intoxicating. "Aubrey?"

He hoped like hell she had the strength to end this, because he didn't think he did. Her damp lips quivered. She blinked as if trying to clear the haze from her heavy-lidded, dark-lashed eyes, and then she lowered her gaze and her hands to his waist. But instead of pushing him away, she yanked his shirttails from his pants.

Liam sucked in a sharp breath. Every muscle in his body clenched rock hard as she bared his chest one button at a time. When she spread her palms and swept them over his skin, he shuddered and then quickly lifted his arms above his head to unfasten his cuff links. He pitched them onto the end table with a clatter and then his shirt hit the floor. Her fingers fumbled with his belt and he nearly lost it.

Catching her wrists, he stilled her hands and then released her and reached for her top. He whisked it over her head and groaned at what he discovered. No bra. Dark puckered tips crested her small breasts, and his mouth watered in anticipation of tasting her. She lifted her hands as if to cover herself, but he beat her to it, covering her warm flesh. Her nipples prodded his palms. He caressed her in a circular motion and the taut tips beaded even harder. Each circle coiled something achy and tight deep inside him.

Aubrey's head fell back on a moan. Her fingers tangled in his hair and she tugged. Liam didn't refuse the invitation. He bent, stroked his tongue over her sensitive tip, raked her gently with his teeth and then suckled deeply. Her nails dug into his shoulders. He transferred his attention to the opposite breast and rubbed slick fingers over the one he'd abandoned.

Her knees buckled. Liam caught her up in his arms and carried her to his bedroom. One, because he wanted to savor every inch of her. Two, because he needed condoms. He'd long since outgrown the need to carry them in his wallet. His affairs these days, though few and far between, were planned like dessert after dinner. He never had lunch and an unexpected afternoon delight. Maybe the surprise factor explained why Aubrey had hit him so hard.

The love bite she planted on his neck derailed his train of thought. He almost walked into a wall. Her teeth teased his earlobe seconds before her tongue traced his ear. Embers ignited in his gut. He quickened his stride, reached his bedroom and set her on her feet beside his bed. He hadn't bothered to open the drapes this morning, but a sliver of afternoon sunlight seeped through the gap between them, slashing across his bed like a laser pointer indicating, "Here. Now."

No kidding. The ray of light was much easier to understand than a painting about female body parts.

Liam sat down on the micro suede comforter and turned Aubrey around so that her back faced him. He strung a line of openmouthed kissed along her vertebrae while his suddenly clumsy fingers fumbled to release the back button and zip of her pencil skirt. The skirt crumpled to the floor. He vaguely registered her kicking it and her shoes aside, but his gaze was fastened on her bottom in—heaven help him—a thong and nothing else. Black. Satiny. Tiny. He traced the waistband and then the strip between her cheeks. Goose bumps rose on her pale skin. His blood rushed south, leaving him dizzy with desire and gasping for breath. Impatient, he hooked the black bands with his thumbs and pushed them down her legs.

She stepped out and turned. Like a kid with a giant ice-cream sundae, Liam could only stare, not knowing where to start or which flavor to sample first. His hands found her breasts. His mouth skimmed her belly, edging downward in sips and nips toward her tangled brown curls. She trembled. The tiny quakes traveled up his arms, through his lips. He lifted his head and met her slumberous gaze.

"Please," she whispered. "I need to touch you, too."

An offer too good to refuse. Liam rose.

Aubrey tackled his belt and then the hook of his slacks. Her knuckles dragged across his erection as she lowered his zipper, and stars exploded behind his tightly closed lids. She shoved his pants and briefs down his thighs. He distracted himself from her mind-numbing caresses by mapping her slight curves with his hands, learning her body the way a blind man reads Braille, by feel. He found the crisp curls and delved into the slick moisture they concealed.

Her gasped "Yes" encouraged him to stroke long and slow until he discovered her magic spot, and then he teased her with short, quick brushes over the swollen flesh before dipping deeper. She arched into his touch, pressed hungry kisses along his jaw, until he covered her mouth with his and mimicked the thrust of his fingers with his tongue.

She clung to his shoulders as release shuddered through her. Her cries filled his mouth and then she collapsed against him, skin to skin. Liam slowly eased his fingers from her dampness and ripped back the bedding. When he turned around again, Aubrey was on her knees in front of him, her passion-glazed eyes gazing up at him.

He ground his molars, clenched his fists and prayed she'd give him a second to recover before she touched him. If she didn't, his afternoon delight would be over in a nanosecond. He didn't have a snowball's chance in hell of lasting if she put her mouth on him.

Three

At the pub Aubrey had tagged Liam as buff, blond and built. The description didn't begin to do justice to the man in front of her. Liam hadn't developed those thick muscles sitting behind a desk. He worked out.

Aubrey skated her palms up his hair-roughened calves and thighs. His long, thick erection jerked as she brushed past the tangle of wiry dark blond curls to shove on his hips so he'd sit down. Liam sat, knees splayed but cuffed by his pants at his ankles. Aubrey debated leaning in for a taste of him, but the urgency pulsing through her veins insisted she hurry rather than linger. Judging by the taut tendons of Liam's neck, she knew he teetered just as close to the edge of control as she.

She quickly removed his shoes, socks and pants and tossed them aside. Bracing her hands on his thighs, she levered herself to stand before him. The desire in his eyes poured over her like heated oil, burning, but in a good way. An incredibly arousing, blood-boiling way. Not something she'd previously experienced.

He lifted her hands, sketched a nerve-tingling erotic kiss in each palm with his tongue and then transferred her hands to his shoulders. His satiny skin stretched tight over corded muscle. She couldn't resist tracing each swell and crevice, and raking her fingers through the coils of burnished gold spattering his chest.

Liam's hot mouth found one breast. His talented fingers teased the other. When he devoured her that way, stroked and molded her that way, Aubrey didn't feel inadequate, unwomanly. Despite the breathtaking release he'd just given her, her body tightened once again, hungry for more. "Please, Liam. I can't wait."

He lifted his head, his gaze locking with hers, and then he reached for the bedside table, opened the drawer and extracted a square packet.

Condoms. She'd forgotten. So unlike her. But then everything about today was beyond her realm. She'd never fallen in instant lust, never become intimate with a near stranger.

He slowly rose, sliding inch by inch of his hot skin against hers. For heart-stopping seconds his shaft burned against her navel and then he leaned back and ripped the packet open with his teeth.

Aubrey stroked his back, his waist, his firm buttocks, bringing her hands around to curl her fingers around his thickness and cup the heaviness below. Her thumb found a slick droplet and smoothed it over his silky skin.

His breath whistled through clenched teeth. He muttered a curse and ground out, "Enough."

He brushed her hands aside, donned protection and urged her onto the bed. With one foot still on the floor, Aubrey leaned back across the oyster-colored sheets and lifted a hand, beckoning him into her arms. The mattress dipped under his weight. His hands, hot and slightly rough, cupped her bottom and lifted as he stood beside the bed and positioned himself. Aubrey's breath caught in anticipation and then gushed from her lungs as he plunged deeply, filling her with a solid thrust.

He withdrew and thrust again and again. She arched to meet him and then reached up and curled her fingers around his nape to pull him closer. Liam planted his hands beside her head. His molten blue gaze locked with hers and his biceps bulged as he slowly lowered until his chest hairs teased her breasts. His breath stirred the fine hairs on her neck and then finally, *finally,* his lips sealed hers. She hooked one leg around his hips, drawing him back each time he withdrew and urging him to go faster and deeper as everything inside her twisted tighter and she raced toward another climax.

Ecstasy hit hard and fast, rocking her and robbing her breath. She threw her head back and cried out as Liam slammed into her and groaned as his own orgasm undulated over him.

Breathing heavily, he collapsed to his elbows and buried his face beside hers on the bed. Aubrey traced the line of his spine and he shivered against her. The weight of him, the heat of him, blanketed her in a sensual cocoon. A satisfied smile curved her lips and a sense of well-being flooded her, weighting her limbs and her eyelids. Bliss.

Her racing heart and laboring lungs slowed and then with a sudden icy shower her conscience washed away the haze of desire.

What had she done?

She'd taken the enemy to bed and in doing so guaranteed she'd disappoint her father yet again, because she couldn't sleep with Liam and then betray him.

* * *

Aubrey stiffened beneath Liam and then shoved hard against his shoulders. He forced his drained and satiated muscles into action and rolled to her side, reluctantly disengaging from the slick heat of her body.

She pressed her fingers to the pleat between her eyebrows. Regret tightened her features and flattened her luscious, kiss-swollen mouth.

Liam's stomach clenched as reality sank in.

"That shouldn't have happened," Aubrey whispered as she reached for the sheet, dragging it across her body and sliding to the edge of the bed.

"Probably not." No probably about it. This afternoon had been a mistake. They both knew it. Chalk it up to his unerring ability to choose the wrong woman.

"I have to go." She clutched the sheet with one hand and reached for her skirt with the other. The bed sheet tethered her inches short of her goal, and she didn't look like she wanted to release it and let him see her naked. Ridiculous, considering the taste of her still lingered on his lips.

He scooped up her skirt, passed it to her and then raked a hand through his hair. "Aubrey—"

Without looking at him, she held up a hand like a traffic cop. "Please. No post mortems."

What could he say? There could be no future in any relationship between them. And for the first time in Liam's life that bothered him. Until now he'd been the king of dead-end-and-damned-happy-about-it relationships.

He rolled his tense shoulders. Blame it on all the new shiny jewelry being shoved in his face at EPH. Wedding and engagement rings had multiplied like bacteria among the staff—Elliotts in particular. His grandfather's aim might have been to increase productivity with his little competition, but what he'd done was run off employees and cause a rash of romances.

"Would you like to shower first or—"

"No. No, I need to go." She shimmied her skirt over her long, lean legs and her round, tight, bare butt. Watching her move made his pulse accelerate and his groin tighten all over again.

"Can I call you a cab?"

With her arms crossed over her chest, she shoved her feet into her shoes and bolted out the bedroom door. "No. Thank you."

He yanked on his pants, ducked into the bathroom to ditch the condom and followed her into the den. She dragged on her top, shrugged on her jacket, snatched up her purse and briefcase and wasted no time hustling toward the door. She still hadn't looked at him. That stung.

"Aubrey, wait." He planted a palm on the door, holding it closed.

She paused with her hand on the knob. Her spine remained steel-girder stiff, and she kept her chin tucked as if she wanted to hide from what had just happened.

Well, didn't that make him feel like a damned prize?

Her scent, a heady floral mingled with hot sex, filled Liam's lungs as he inhaled. He battled the unaccustomed urge to smooth her tangled hair and straighten the tucked-under collar of her blazer. "We used protection and I'm clean, but if you need anything you have my numbers."

She turned and met his gaze. Panic and regret darkened her eyes. "I won't call, Liam. I can't."

"Yeah. I guess you're right. My family's in enough turmoil without throwing an affair with the enemy's daughter into the pot."

Her mouth dropped open and a wounded expression

briefly crossed her face before she blinked it away. "The enemy? That's how you see my father?"

He cursed his clumsy tongue. "Matthew Holt and my grandfather have had a few run-ins. Holt Enterprises and EPH don't always see eye to eye on how we conduct business."

"No. No, they don't. You're right. I hope your mother likes the painting. Goodbye, Liam." She yanked open his door and then quietly closed it behind her.

Liam banged his forehead against the wood and then slowly turned to face the painting. Where was his brain? The afternoon shouldn't have happened. He should have left the pub the minute Aubrey started with her prying questions. He shouldn't have taken her to the gallery or brought her home for a lesson in Art 101. He sure as hell shouldn't have taken her to bed. Because today he'd had the best sex of his life and there was absolutely no chance that he'd ever repeat the experience.

He cursed all the way back to his bedroom. Aubrey's scent clung to his skin and to his bed. Determined to remove all traces of her from his apartment, he ripped off the sheets. As he shoved them into the hamper for his housekeeper to wash, he caught sight of his watch.

Damn. He hadn't called work to tell them he wouldn't be returning after his luncheon appointment. A first. He never missed work. Hell, for the past nine months he'd practically lived in the EPH building. He headed for the phone on his bedside table. A sliver of black sticking out from under his bed stopped him in his tracks. He bent and scooped it up. Aubrey's thong. His pulse rate tripled. He should return it. But how?

Mail? Nah, he didn't think so.

In person? Hell, no. That would be stepping right back into the fire. He couldn't risk his family—particularly his grandfather, who believed appearances were everything—finding out about today.

For several seconds he studied the black satin dangling from his fingers and then he crushed the lingerie in his hand and shoved it in his nightstand drawer.

He couldn't have Aubrey, but he could have the memories of this wild afternoon to fuel his fantasies when the only lover he had was his right hand.

"Happy to have you home again, Mom. I brought a bottle of champagne to celebrate." Liam set the champagne on the coffee table and bent over the chaise in the den of the family brownstone to kiss his mother's cheek.

She had a little more color in her face than she'd had when he'd visited her at The Tides a couple of weeks ago, and she'd lost some of the gauntness hollowing her cheeks. Short tufts of newly grown hair, more gray than before, peeked from the scarf she wore over her head.

Liam nodded hello to his father. He and his father had never been close. Michael Elliott had spent too much of Liam's childhood at work, leaving Liam to rely on his grandfather for mentorship as the years passed.

"You and your wine collection. Thank you." Karen Elliott shifted her legs to the side and patted the cushion. "Sit down, Liam. It's good to be home. Your grandparents' estate is a wonderful place to recuperate, but it's time for me to get on with life. Besides, you've all spent way too much time worrying about me and traipsing out there."

"Glad to do it. I brought you a surprise." He ignored her "you-shouldn't-haves," retrieved the picture from the foyer where he'd left it and rested the bottom edge of the frame on the sofa. "Dad, could you help me with this?"

"Certainly." His father stepped forward.

With his father's assistance Liam removed the paper. The memory of doing the same with Aubrey yesterday barged front and center into his thoughts. He set his jaw and deliberately blocked the images as best he could. Which wasn't so great.

His mother's gasp was reward enough for the weeks of phone calls Liam had made to nearly every gallery in the Northeast, his pleas with gallery owners and, finally, the letter he'd written to Gilda Raines and sent along with a picture of his mother gazing at one of Gilda's paintings in the medical center. Seeing his mother's eyes light up and then fill with happy tears was icing on the cake.

She smiled up at him. "Gilda Raines never sells anything. She donates to hospitals, but she *never* sells. How did you convince her?"

He shrugged. "I wrote her a letter and told her I needed a gift for a very special lady."

"Don't waste your flattery on me, Liam Elliott." His mother dismissed his words with a wave of her hand, but color seeped into her cheeks.

He didn't mention that the artist probably wouldn't have sold him anything if Aubrey hadn't been with him. He'd seen the refusal in Ms. Raines's eyes until Aubrey had remarked about the painting being exactly what Liam's mother needed. He knew because he'd been looking at Gilda instead of the art on the easel.

Liam had a feeling he was supposed to know why the artist had selected this particular piece from her collection and what the painting signified the second he laid eyes on it, and when he hadn't Gilda's decision had been made. No sale. But Gilda had taken an instant liking to Aubrey, and Aubrey's promise to explain the meaning behind the morning glory had changed Gilda's mind. No doubt about it. He would have walked away empty-handed if not for Aubrey Holt. He owed her. Even the gallery manager had whispered her surprise over the sale—when she'd slipped him her phone number. Not a number he intended using.

His mother carefully eased forward on the cushion until she could stroke the frame. "It's beautiful. Absolutely beautiful."

Tears streamed from her eyes and she pressed trembling fingers to her lips. Those were more than happy tears this time. Liam stood by helplessly, but his father immediately took her into his arms and tucked her face to his chest. Did his mother's emotional reaction have something to do with the way Aubrey had described the painting? Liam's ears burned and he shifted uneasily. If so, then his parents deserved a moment of privacy.

He propped the frame against the back of the sofa, shoved his hands into his pockets and retreated to the opposite side of the room to look out the window at the Brooklyn Heights neighborhood where he'd grown up. Until he'd moved away, he hadn't paid much attention to the well-maintained nineteenth-century brownstones lining the shaded street, the wide bluestone sidewalks or decorative ironwork. He hadn't appreciated that he was only a short train ride from Times Square, Coney Island and Shea Stadium and a Mets baseball game.

While he'd been trapped under the weight of family expectations, his thoughts had been elsewhere. Traveling. Exploring. With his grandfather owning Elliott Publication Holdings, one of the largest and most successful magazine conglomerates in the world, it had been assumed for as far back as Liam could remember that each family member would start with EPH and work his or her way up. Liam hadn't even left the area to attend college. Instead he'd commuted to Columbia University on the Upper West Side of Manhattan and interned at EPH, working hard to climb the EPH ladder.

Liam didn't like to make waves. As a second son, he was a peacemaker not a troublemaker.

Until yesterday.

Yesterday would cause all kinds of trouble if word of his after-lunch activities got out.

"I want to hang it in the bedroom." His mother's statement interrupted his thoughts.

"Just show me where," his father answered in an indulgent I'll-give-you-anything-you-want voice. "Could you help me, son?"

"Sure."

Carrying the painting, Liam followed his parents into their bedroom. His father helped his mother settle on the bench at the end of the bed. She glanced around the room and then pointed. "I want to hang it there, so it'll be the first thing I see each morning and the last thing before I turn out the light."

TMI. Too much information. Aubrey's description echoed in Liam's head and his skin shrank three sizes. *Don't want to go there.* His parents' intimate life was none of his business and Liam liked it that way.

His father removed the landscape already hanging on the wall and replaced it with the morning glory.

"Perfect," his mother announced.

His father hooked an arm around Liam's shoulders and nodded toward the painting. "This was a great idea."

Liam glanced at his mother. She studied the art with her hands clasped under her chin and a smile on her face. And then he turned back to his father. "So do you know what it means?"

His father shifted uncomfortably and lowered his arm. "Only because your mother fell in love with one of the paintings by this artist hanging in the hospital physical therapy room. I asked what was so great about a picture of a flower and Renee explained it to me."

Renee was the social worker engaged to Tag, Liam's younger brother. They'd met when Renee was assigned to keep Tag from terrorizing the hospital staff caring for their mother after her double mastectomy.

Liam shared a sympathetic look with his father and then confessed, "I had to have somebody explain it to me, too."

His father crossed to the dresser and returned with a pair of gilt-edged tickets in his hand. "While I have you here I need a favor. There's a charity thing this weekend. Your mother and I have decided to skip it, but we need an Elliott to make an appearance. Saturday night. Black tie. You'll need a date. Can you swing it?"

Aubrey's violet eyes flashed in Liam's mind. No. Definitely not Aubrey. He'd come up with someone who had Saturday night free and a spare formal hanging in her closet. "Sure."

"Good."

"So, how about you put the champagne on ice and I dash down the street and pick up dinner at Mom's favorite restaurant?" Liam suggested.

How in the hell he'd find a date on such short notice he didn't know. He'd been out of the dating circuit since his grandfather's announcement in January. But that wasn't his father's problem. If his parents wanted an Elliott at the gala, then Liam would be there, doing his duty the way he'd always done.

Aubrey looked at the man beside her and longed for a bed, a thick pillow, a silk-covered down comforter and solitude. Not sex. Which made her immediately think of Liam Elliott.

She huffed an exasperated breath and checked her diamond-faced watch. How long had she lasted this time? Less than an hour since she'd last vowed to never again think about Liam or their afternoon of amazing, curl-her-toes sex. God, she was weak. Blame it on exhaustion. She'd had precious little sleep during the past five nights, and when she had fallen into bed, Liam Elliott had joined her, invading her dreams and tangling her sheets.

Damn him.

As if thinking about Liam incarnated remnants of that afternoon, Aubrey spotted Trisha Evans across the ballroom. The gallery employee hadn't known that Aubrey and Liam weren't a couple, but that hadn't stopped her from brazenly passing Liam her phone number along with a come-and-get-me smile and his receipt.

Witch.

The crowd shifted and Aubrey choked on her champagne when she recognized Trisha's escort. *Liam.* Well, he hadn't waited long to accept the brunette's invitation. Emotion churned in Aubrey's stomach. Anger? Jealousy? Whatever it was, it didn't belong. How could she be angry or jealous? She and Liam weren't—and never could be—a couple.

"Who's the chick?"

"Pardon?" Aubrey turned to look at the hulking football player who'd escorted her to the arts fund-raiser this evening. One of her father's magazines was doing a series of articles on Buck Parks and his recent retirement from the NFL. Her father had "suggested" Aubrey and Buck create a little buzz about the feature by appearing together at the gala.

"The brunette in the barely there red dress. You're glaring at her like you want to mash her face into the turf."

An apt description. "No one. She's no one important."

But at that moment Liam turned his head. His gaze lasered in on Aubrey from across the room and her breath jammed in her chest. He looked amazing in a tux. Suave. Sexy. *GQ*-gorgeous.

"Ah, now I get it."

Aubrey blinked and broke the connection with Liam. Looking away wasn't as easy as it should have been. She found sympathy in Buck's eyes. "Get what?"

"It's not her. It's him."

Was she completely transparent? "You're mistaken. He's the financial operating officer of Holt Enterprises' chief competitor. I can't be interested in him."

Buck grinned and dipped his head. "Who're you trying to fool, Aubrey?"

Buck was tall and built, smart and funny. He smelled good and filled out his custom-tailored tux to perfection. Why couldn't she get hot and bothered over him? But she didn't. She experienced no blip of her pulse when he said her name, no sweaty palms when he looked at her, no burning twist of her stomach when he touched her. The feeling—or lack thereof—was mutual.

Mischief danced in his eyes. "Wanna give him something to think about? Because he's on his way over here."

Aubrey's heart stopped and then slammed in a rapid jackhammer beat. "He is?"

"Yep. I can plant one on you. Long, slow, and I'll make it look deep and hot. He'll get the message."

If she weren't panicking, she'd appreciate the handsome ball player's offer, but at the moment she was on the verge of hyperventilating. If he covered her mouth with his, she'd suffocate.

Buck's big hand curled around her waist and he tugged her closer. "Last chance," he whispered against her jaw.

"Aubrey." Liam's hard voice sent a flash-fire of heat over her skin.

Gulping, she took a second to gather her scattered nerves, pasted what she hoped passed as a disinterested smile on her face and turned. "Good evening, Liam. Trisha. Are you enjoying the ball?"

Aubrey avoided Liam by focusing on Trisha's triumphant smirk. Buck's hands tightened on Aubrey's waist. She made a mental note to thank him later. He reached past her and offered his hand first to Trisha and then to Liam. "Buck Parks."

Trisha, evidently not satisfied with one big fish on the hook, fluttered her mascara-laden lashes at Buck and gushed her name and something inane about football. Aubrey's deafening pulse drowned most of it out.

"Liam Elliott." Testosterone crackled in the air as the men shook hands and then Buck's arm settled around her waist and hauled her close to his hard body. Her pulse didn't even hiccup.

Aubrey risked looking at Liam again.

"Mom loved the painting," was all he said. His unreadable expression gave nothing away.

"I thought she would."

And then his lips twitched. "She had me hang it in her bedroom. I didn't ask why. Don't want to know."

Aubrey's lips curved upward. "No. I bet not."

Then memories of Liam touching her, tasting her, filling her, wiped away her smile and set her legs to trembling. She had to get out of here or at least away from him. She couldn't leave the gala until she'd done as her father requested. *Dance, schmooze, get your picture taken by a few society reporters.*

"Well, it was good seeing you both, but I promised Buck a dance. Bye." And then she looked up at the former quarterback and silently pleaded for him to rescue her. Lucky for her, Buck was as quick with his thoughts as he was on his feet.

Getting the seats switched cost Liam fifty bucks. The fact that he'd paid money to torture himself with what he couldn't have didn't say much about his intelligence.

He deliberately stalled until after Aubrey and her date

were seated at the big, round table with three other couples before leading Trisha to their seats in the banquet hall adjoining the ballroom. Aubrey glanced up as he pulled out his date's chair. Her violet eyes widened and filled with horror and then the color and her polite smile slid from her face.

She jerked her gaze forward and sat stiffly erect. Liam settled beside her. Their shoulders brushed as he adjusted his chair, and her scent filled his lungs, bringing back a flood of incendiary memories. His thigh nudged hers beneath the crowded table and blood drained from his brain.

He recovered enough to introduce Trisha and himself to the other diners at the table and then turned to Aubrey and her date. The big lug with her had tried to crush Liam's hand earlier. Too bad it hadn't worked. Liam had done his own share of bone crushing during the exchange.

Aubrey cozying up to the quarterback is none of your business.

"You left something at my place," he whispered to Aubrey.

Her cheeks turned scarlet, confirming she'd not only heard him, she knew exactly what she'd left behind, but she didn't turn her head. In fact, she ignored him, which irritated the daylights out of him.

"Want it back?"

"No. Throw it out." Her reply was barely audible over the hum of conversation in the large room.

He waited until after the salads had been served. "Can't do that, sweetheart."

She dropped her fork. Within seconds a server had replaced it with a clean one and stepped back to hover. One bad thing about five-thousand-dollar-a-plate dinners was that the wait staff never went far. They hovered behind you, watching every move. Not that he intended to touch Aubrey—no matter how much he wanted to.

Parks stretched his left arm across the back of Aubrey's chair, clenching his fist and displaying his Super Bowl ring for Liam's scrutiny. The gesture blatantly staked a claim, riling Liam. Hard eyes met Liam's behind Aubrey's back. Liam set his jaw.

Buddy, if she were yours, she wouldn't have been in my bed.

Aubrey glanced at Liam and then swiftly turned to the man on her right. She said something, drawing Parks's attention.

Liam faced forward. *What in the hell are you doing, Elliott? Are you willing to fight for a woman you can't have?*

Belatedly he remembered his own date. Forgetting a woman who had groped his butt on the dance floor and whispered in explicit detail what she'd like to do to him later ought to be more difficult, but he'd done so easily. Trisha didn't get to him the way Aubrey did, and he had no interest in accepting Trisha's naughty invitation. On the other hand, he knew without a doubt that if Aubrey had made those suggestions—wise or not—they'd be halfway back to his apartment already.

Aubrey's off-limits. Back off.

But knowing he should back off didn't make him any less aware of the woman to his right for the remainder of the tasteless dinner and long-winded speeches. He couldn't have her, but he ached for Aubrey Holt with each pulse of his blood and each lung-filling breath. Duty had never been so onerous and desire had never been more difficult to ignore.

Four

"Are you alone? Or is the thug with you?"

Aubrey's heart stalled at the sound of the deep, slightly husky voice on the phone. "Liam."

She scrambled upright in her bed, clutching the sheet to her chest and squeezing the phone so tightly her fingers hurt. And then she recalled his question. "That's none of your business."

"You *are* alone."

"I didn't say that." She shoved the hair out of her eyes and squinted at her bedside clock. "It's midnight. Why did you call?"

"To tell you that you looked beautiful tonight."

Her lungs failed. The phone slipped in her grasp. She fumbled it back to her ear. "Thank you. So did Trisha."

She cringed at the jealousy in her voice.

"Did she? I didn't notice." His distracted tone made her want to believe him, but the man had gone out with a woman who'd been ballsy enough to pass him her number with Aubrey standing two feet away.

"You shouldn't have called, Liam."

"You wanted me to tell you how beautiful you looked with your watchdog standing by ready to stamp my forehead with his Super Bowl ring?"

"Have you been drinking?" He sounded sober. Tired, but sober.

"Haven't had a drop since that lousy wine at dinner. But I couldn't get to sleep."

She knew the feeling. "So you decided to call and wake me?"

"Did I?"

"Did you wake me?" She should lie and say, yes, she'd been sleeping dreamlessly. But she didn't. "No."

She scooted back under the covers and laid her head on her pillow. She shouldn't ask, but her mouth didn't listen to her mind. "Why can't you sleep?"

The sound of a heavy breath and the rustle of sheets traveled through the phone line. Aubrey closed her eyes and a picture of Liam naked and kneeling above her on his king-size bed filled her head. She lifted her lids and turned on the lamp. Listening to Liam's sandpaper voice in the darkness and remembering him naked wasn't a good idea if she wanted to sleep any time in this century.

"I couldn't sleep because I was thinking about you. About Monday afternoon."

Her heart would very likely sustain permanent damage from its frantic battering against her rib cage. Her fingers crushed the sheets. She bit her lip.

"It was good."

"Good?" she choked out in disbelief.

His low chuckle made her shiver. "Better than good. Fabulous."

She smiled. "That's more like it."

"Incredible. Stupendous. Phenomenal." She could hear the laughter in his voice and then another rustling sound. "And it's a crying shame that it can't happen again."

Her grin faded at the seriousness and accuracy of the last statement. "But it can't."

"I know. But I don't have to like it."

Neither did she. "No."

The silence stretched for a dozen heartbeats. "Good night, Aubrey. Sweet dreams."

"You, too, Liam. Sweet dreams." She cradled the phone, turned off the light and then rolled on her side and tucked her hand beneath her cheek.

Odd phone call. So why was she smiling?

Seeing Liam again was out of the question. If she did, her father would expect her to weasel information out of Liam about EPH and she just couldn't stomach the duplicitous role. Her father had been angry enough that she hadn't brought him anything useful after her lunch with Liam. Oh, Matthew Holt hadn't yelled. He never yelled. But he'd treated her to that same silent stare she'd come to know so well.

She couldn't continue letting her father down. She'd worked her fanny off to be the kind of employee and daughter of whom he could be proud and she'd failed. She owed him for taking her in when he hadn't wanted her. He hadn't wanted custody during the divorce from her mother, and he hadn't wanted custody after Aubrey's jerk of a stepfather had crawled into her bed and offered to keep her from getting lonely while her mother was out of town.

Aubrey had heard her father arguing with Jane after she'd revealed that dreadful secret. His bellow had carried through his closed office door. "What in the hell am I going to do with a teenage girl?"

Aubrey hadn't heard Jane's reply. In fact, Aubrey hadn't heard anything from either of her parents until hours later when her mother had stormed into Matthew Holt's office with Aubrey's belongings and dumped them on the floor. She'd glared at Aubrey and said, "Look what you've done with your lies," and then left.

Pamela Holt Curtis hadn't asked for Aubrey's side of the story. She'd chosen to believe her young husband's version. He'd claimed Aubrey had invited him into her room and that she'd been flirting with him for weeks.

Aubrey had been left with a mother who no longer wanted her around and a father who had never wanted her in the first place.

"Liam."

Liam blinked his unfocused eyes and looked up from the papers on his desk to the man rapping on his office door. Cade McCann, the executive editor of *Charisma,* EPH's high-fashion magazine, also happened to be Liam's good friend, probably his best friend.

"Got a minute?"

"Sure, Cade. Come in." Considering Liam's mind had been elsewhere since this morning's monthly meeting with the editors in chief of the different magazines, Cade wasn't interrupting anything. Liam hated the tension invading the formally congenial meetings.

This week he'd been distracted by thoughts of Aubrey and he'd barely managed to relate the pertinent facts and figures. For a split second Liam considered asking Cade how to wipe a woman from his brain, but nixed the thought. His friend hadn't been too successful on that score, a fact proven by his recent engagement.

"What brings the rooster out of the henhouse?" The

question was a running joke between them. Cade was a rare male on *Charisma's* predominantly female staff. A lesser man would have been henpecked into submission, but not Cade.

"Are you having woman troubles?" Cade asked as he settled in the chair in front of Liam's desk.

Alarm straightened Liam's spine. "Why do you ask?"

"Because I called you three times before you answered."

Liam silently swore. His mind had been on Saturday night and the phone call he shouldn't have made. Pretty damned stupid of him to throw fuel on a fire he was trying to put out. "What's up, McCann? Spit it out."

Cade's direct gray gaze said he wasn't fooled by Liam's evasion. "Okay, if you want to play it that way. You'll have to lay your cards on the table eventually."

"Cade—"

"I want you to be my best man when I marry Jessie next month."

Jessie Clayton was the *Charisma* intern who just happened to have stunned them all with the revelation that she was Aunt Fin's daughter—a daughter Fin had been forced to give up for adoption twenty-three years ago. Until Jessie had revealed that shocking secret, Cade had questioned her loyalties and suspected her of being a plant from another magazine.

No doubt about where Aubrey Holt's loyalties lay. Liam rolled his shoulders, but the knot at the base of his neck didn't ease. "I'd be honored to stand up with you, Cade. Being your best man means I get to give you one hell of a bachelor party."

"I'm all for that. Jessie might not be. But no naked women. I have the only one I'm interested in looking at."

"What about the rest of us?"

Cade leaned forward, bracing his elbows on his knees and clasping his hands. "Want to talk about her?"

Her. Cade didn't mean Jessie. "You're offering to *give* me dating advice? Last month you were *asking* for it."

Cade snorted. "And some good you were."

"Hey, I told you to go for it."

"Well, I'm telling you the same thing. Last month I was battling the current and trying not to get sucked into the love whirlpool. Looks like you might be in the water this month. Don't fight it, man. Let it pull you under. You'll be glad you did."

Love? Hell no. He'd only spent a few hours with the woman. But lust? Oh, yeah. He had a bad rash of that and it itched 24/7. "I can't."

"Why not?"

"She's—" Damn. He hadn't meant to let that slip. "Because the only problems I'm having are EPH problems. She's been a bitch of a mistress since January, compliments of Patrick and his damned competition."

Cade shook his head. "You're lying through your pearly whites, pal. When you want to talk, let me know. In the meantime, see if you can clear your calendar for the weekend after this one. Jessie's father's throwing us an engagement party in Colorado next Saturday. I'd like you to be there. I don't want to be the only city slicker on the ranch."

Liam looked at the stacks of files and reports on his desk. With his workload, dropping everything and flying to Colorado sounded insane, but it might be worth it if putting some mileage between him and a certain female could get her out of his head. "I'll be there."

"I'm heading for the cafeteria. Coming?"

"No, I have an errand to take care of." A fool's errand.

Aubrey stood in front of her father's desk, feigning calm she didn't feel. Why had he requested this late afternoon meeting?

He kept her waiting while he scanned the blueline in front of him. Checking the magazine proof was the production manager's job, but her father tended to spend a lot of time looking over everyone's shoulders—especially hers. He second-guessed each decision she made, which made the rest of the staff do the same. He claimed he hadn't gotten to the top by letting others do all the dirty work, and delegating wasn't something he enjoyed.

Finally, she asked, "You called?"

He put the blueline aside, revealing the folded newspaper beneath it. Aubrey's tension eased. She suspected he'd seen the photo in the society section. He should be pleased. She and Buck Parks had done exactly as he'd requested and garnered a little free publicity from not only the newspapers but a few celebrity magazines as well.

But that wasn't an approving smile on her father's face.

"You sat beside Liam Elliott at the dinner. What did you learn?"

She concealed a wince. Yes, Liam's face was easily recognizable in the picture. She'd hoped her father wouldn't notice. "Um, nothing. Buck was my date. I talked to him, not to Liam Elliott."

In fact, she'd done her best to ignore Liam throughout the mediocre meal and the soporific speeches afterward. Her best hadn't been good enough. She'd been hyperaware of each shift of his body. And any change in the ventilation of the stuffy banquet hall had wafted his cologne in her direction. As if that weren't bad enough, his phone call Saturday night had only worsened her preoccupation. Warmth swept through her at the memory. She bit her lip and vowed once again to quit thinking about him.

Very slowly her father lowered the paper. "You missed your chance at lunch. You could have redeemed yourself at the gala. How many times do I have to tell you? Never let an opportunity to find out what the competition is doing slip by."

A heavy blanket of failure settled over Aubrey's shoulders. "Yes, sir, I understand. But Liam Elliott is tight-lipped about EPH. You couldn't pry him open with an oyster knife. I can't—"

"There is no such thing as *can't,* Aubrey. Something is going on at EPH. Patrick Elliott runs a first-class armada."

He extracted a page of handwritten notes from one of the neat piles on his desk. "Patrick's son Michael has been out of the office more than he's been in while his wife has undergone chemotherapy. Michael's oldest son is running *Pulse.* Patrick's second son, Daniel, has stepped down as editor-in-chief of *Snap* magazine in favor of his youngest son. Patrick's daughter, Finola, suddenly has had a secret offspring emerge from the woodwork, and Elliott's granddaughter—one of the twins—has taken off with a rock star and left her ex-fiancé engaged to her sister."

He lowered the paper and focused hard eyes on Aubrey. "That's only the news my clipping service has found in the papers. For this many ships to be adrift in Elliott's port there must be a storm stirring the water. I want to know what kind of storm and when it's expected to make landfall. Find out."

Flabbergasted, Aubrey gaped at him. "I'm the VP of single copy sales not an investigative reporter."

"I've given you a direct order, Aubrey. You know Liam Elliott. Use him as your inside contact."

Use him. "I—I don't think I can help you."

"I didn't ask you to think. Do it," he commanded in an end-of-discussion tone.

My family's in enough turmoil without throwing an affair with the enemy's daughter into the pot. Liam's comment echoed in Aubrey's head. Her father's obvious disappointment in her tempted her to throw out this tidbit to prove that she wasn't a complete failure, but she was no Mata Hari who slept with men and then shared their secrets.

"I'll see what I can find out." But she wouldn't—couldn't—go back to the source. Advertising sales directors maintained high-level contacts within advertising agencies. She'd speak to Holt Enterprises' sales directors and get them to pump the clients they shared with EPH. If there was anything amiss at EPH, maybe some of the advertisers had noticed. And then she'd collate that info and report back to her father. That way she wouldn't be sharing anything Liam had told her in confidence.

Asking for the report still felt dirty, though.

Her father turned back to the proof, dismissing her without words—an all too familiar experience. Aubrey headed for her office. There were days she hated her job. This was one of them. She reached the threshold of her office and stopped in surprise. An exquisite floral arrangement in a crystal vase sat on her desk.

Roses and Asiatic lilies in the palest pink filled her office with a heavenly scent. Who would send her flowers? Other than the obligatory bouquet her father sent on her birthday, which had been months ago, she never received flowers. She hurried forward and inhaled deeply before extracting the card buried in the lush greenery. Aubrey slid a fingernail beneath the envelope's sealed flap and extracted the card.

"The color of the flowers reminded me of your dress and their fragrance reminded me of you. Thanks again for your help with the painting. L."

Liam. Her dress for the gala had been beaded pink silk. He remembered. Aubrey pressed a hand over her racing heart. She glanced at the bold handwriting and then scooted behind her desk and dug in her purse for the business card she had yet to throw away. The bold script was identical. He'd written this note himself rather than anonymously phone it in to a florist. Why that mattered she didn't know.

Don't turn this into something romantic, Aubrey. It isn't and can't be.

Now what? Should she e-mail Liam and thank him for the flowers? She didn't dare do that from here where all incoming and outgoing e-mail was saved on a huge server, but she could from her personal computer at home. Maybe she should send a polite but distant thank-you note via U.S. Postal Service. Or should she call? Again, not from here and not the wisest choice since hearing Liam's voice weakened her knees and her resolve to resist him.

Until she could make up her mind, Aubrey tucked both cards in her purse and tried to keep the telling smile off her face.

Liam Elliott had no business sending her flowers.

And she had absolutely no business being tickled pink to receive them.

Why torture yourself? Do what she said. Throw the thong out and get some sleep.

But Liam didn't pitch Aubrey's lingerie into the trash. He lay in bed staring at the black satin in his hand.

He'd gone to bed early to try to catch up on some of the shut-eye he'd been missing, but so far all he'd done was toss and turn and fight the hunger thickening his blood and tightening his skin. Her scent clung to the lingerie. He pitched it onto the nightstand and then turned out the light and rolled over. The sheet clung to his overheated skin. He kicked it off, but it didn't help. Resting one hand beneath his head, he hunkered down for another night of staring at the ceiling.

What was it about Aubrey Holt that made her so damned hard to forget? Her violet eyes? Her slender figure? Her summer-roses scent? Or the way she'd driven him wild in bed? If he could understand her allure, then he'd be steps closer to eradicating her from his thoughts.

And what was it about him that always drew him to the wrong women? In college it had been his freshman academic advisor. He hadn't known she was married until after they'd been sleeping together for a month. He'd ended the affair immediately, a little older, a little wiser and a lot more wary. His junior year he'd become involved with a woman on the rebound. He'd lost his heart when she'd returned to the jerk who'd dumped her.

For some reason attached women sought him out. His sister, Bridget, claimed it was because he was a good listener. But, hell, problem solving was what he did best. He listened to both sides, weighed the evidence and then worked out a solution. Working out the solution was his favorite part—like solving a riddle. But he'd learned the hard way to find out a woman's marital status before asking her out.

Aubrey's single.

Don't go there, man.

The phone rang, jarring him, but he welcomed the interruption. He glanced at the bedside clock. Eleven. Probably Cade calling. He picked up. "Hello."

Silence greeted him. "Hello," he repeated.

"Liam."

The breathless voice sent his pulse rate soaring. Not Cade. "Aubrey."

"I'm sorry to call so late. Did I wake you?"

"No."

"Thank you for the flowers. They're beautiful." The words came out in a rush, as if she'd been practicing them for a while.

"You're welcome. They reminded me of you."

"You shouldn't say things like that."

"Probably not." No probably about it. And Aubrey shouldn't have been the first thing he thought of when he spotted the arrangement in the florist's window during his morning run. But she'd been in his head all week. Why would this morning be any different? He'd dashed to the florist at lunch to place the order when he should have stayed at EPH and eaten in the company cafeteria with Cade.

"Well… I should go. I just called to…well, thank you."

He didn't want to let her go. He reached for the thong, brushing his fingers over the satin. "What are you doing?"

"What?"

"What are you doing? Right now."

He heard a rush of air, as if she'd exhaled into the receiver. "Getting ready for bed."

"I beat you to it."

"Excuse me?"

"I'm in bed."

"Oh. Oh my God. Are you alone? Did I inter—"

"Aubrey, you didn't interrupt anything. I'm alone. You?"

"Am I alone? Of course…I mean, yes, I am."

A smile tugged his lips. "What are you wearing?"

"Liam. You shouldn't…" Her scandalized voice trailed off.

He'd crossed the line. He wouldn't be surprised if she slammed the receiver down.

"A white satin nightgown."

The image instantly filled his head. He bit back a groan. "Short or long?"

"Long." Another pause stretched between them. "What are you wearing?"

His heart thumped harder. "It's just me and your thong." What had possessed him to reveal that?

"You're wearing my thong!"

He rocketed up in bed, his body hot with embarrassment. "Hell no. I'm holding it. In my hand."

Her chuckle, low and sexy as hell, marched down his spine. "You had me worried for a minute."

"That I was a cross-dresser?"

"Yes. Are you?"

Was she yanking his chain? "God, no."

"Good. Not that it matters, since we're not seeing each other."

"No, we're not."

"I should go."

He scrambled for a way to detain her and recalled a comment she'd made at lunch before she knew his identity. "Did you want to run screaming from the building today?"

"You mean work? Yes. I'm having a lot of those days lately."

Was she lying in bed or seated on the edge? He wanted to ask, but didn't. "Same here."

"I'm sorry."

"Ditto." For once Liam wished he had someone to confide in. In the past he'd talked his problems through with his grandfather or Cade, but both were off-limits this time. His grandfather's plan was the cause of Liam's stress, and Cade worked for EPH and was, therefore, part of the trouble. Liam felt like a bone in the middle of a pack of starving dogs. Everybody wanted something from him, something he couldn't deliver. The staff. The advertisers.

He opened his mouth and then shut it again. Aubrey worked for the competition. Not a safe sounding board.

"Any chance your week will improve?" she asked.

"Doubtful. I'll be working through lunch all week."

"Maybe next week will be better."

It wouldn't unless his grandfather cancelled this damned

contest. "Hope so. And I hope yours is, too. Good night, Aubrey. I'm glad you called."

"Me, too. Good night, Liam. I won't say, 'See you around' because I won't."

"No. Guess not." And for some reason, that disappointed him.

A rainy day had its advantages.

The inclement weather forced Liam to relocate his usual morning run to the executives' section of EPH's private gym—the one place he could be certain to find his grandfather before the workday began. Since Liam needed to talk to Patrick, he could handle the two chores simultaneously, efficiently. Privately.

Judging by the sweat ringing the neck and underarms of his grandfather's T-shirt, Patrick must have been on the treadmill for a while. It was only 5:30, but his grandfather had started early. As usual, the TV in front of the machines streamed CNN.

Liam hoped he was as sharp as Patrick mentally and physically when he hit seventy-seven. Then again, maybe his grandfather was slipping. This retirement selection process wasn't a smart move.

Liam stepped onto the treadmill beside Patrick's as he'd done dozens of times before. The room, thankfully, was empty except for the two of them. "Morning, Patrick."

"Liam." Patrick didn't slow his stride.

Liam worked up to his optimum speed. Once his muscles loosened and he'd reached a comfortable pace he decided to broach the subject that had been keeping him up at night.

The other subject. No way would he discuss with his grandfather his nonrelationship with Aubrey Holt.

"Your contest is tearing EPH apart. You have to end it."

"Not time yet."

"Yesterday's meeting was a combat zone."

"EPH will be stronger once we're done," Patrick said with conviction. Or was it just stubborn pride?

Liam made a conscious effort to unfurl his fists. "Not if the team disbands. We're fighting ourselves instead of the enemy, Patrick. It's only a matter of time before our advertisers pick up on the infighting."

Patrick turned a hard eye on Liam. "The enemy. Holt."

Liam's neck prickled. "He's not our only competition."

"Your grandmother showed me the picture in the paper. Unfortunate error, the hostess seating you beside Holt's daughter."

If Patrick found out that error had cost Liam fifty bucks, his grandfather would hit the ceiling. For Patrick Elliott appearances were everything and consorting with the enemy never looked good. Liam said nothing. Instead he increased his pace and directed his attention to CNN.

Minutes later Patrick turned off his machine and Liam did the same even though he hadn't yet reached his usual distance. "Patrick, I don't know if the family relationships will survive this contest. We're cutting each other's hearts out. Reconsider. Please."

"I've set a course. I'll see it through." Patrick wiped the sweat from his face with a white towel bearing the EPH monogram.

"No matter what the costs?"

"No matter what the costs."

"You're making a mistake."

"I don't think so, son, and I'm willing to wager the company on that."

"Good, because that's what you've done. I hope you don't live to regret it." Hoping to ease his frustration, Liam climbed back on the treadmill and set himself a mind-numbing pace.

* * *

“Your lunch is here.”

Liam looked up from the spreadsheet. He hadn’t ordered anything. Ann, his administrative assistant, must have. “Thanks, Ann. Put it there. I’ll get to it as soon as I finish this.”

She set a bag on the corner of his desk. The Ernie’s Pub logo on the receipt caught Liam’s attention, slamming his train of thought against a wall. Nobody at EPH knew about his penchant for Ernie’s—an intentional omission. “Could you close the door on your way out?”

Her eyebrows rose. He never closed the door unless he had a private meeting. “Certainly.”

As soon as the latch clicked he shoved his paperwork aside and reached for the bag and the receipt stapled to the outside. “Bookmaker’s Special,” he read. His favorite sandwich and he knew damned well no one in this building knew that.

His heart stuttered as he tore open the folded-down top and pulled out the ordinary Styrofoam container inside. The note taped to the top of the box wasn’t in any way, shape or form ordinary. He ripped it off.

“Sorry you have to work through lunch. Enjoy. A.”

Aubrey had sent him lunch.

He didn’t know what to make of the gesture, but he sure as hell knew he shouldn’t be smiling. He tried to wipe the grin off his face, but it returned. In the midst of the tension at work his and Aubrey’s secret game was pure pleasure. Forbidden pleasure. He reached for the phone with one hand and his wallet with the other, planning to dig out her number, call her and thank her. But he set the phone back in the cradle and shoved his wallet back into his pocket.

He couldn’t call her from here. He’d call her tonight.

Tonight when it would be just the two of them.

Five

Aubrey's phone rang, startling her into dropping her book into the bathtub. "Blast."

She snatched up the juicy and now soggy romance, pitched it onto the vanity, grabbed a towel and dashed for the phone extension in her bedroom. She was out of breath by the time she reached it. She glanced at the clock as she grabbed the receiver. Eleven. "Hello."

"You don't sound as if you were sleeping."

"Liam." Her knees buckled. She sank down onto the mattress, not caring if she dampened the linens. "No. I wasn't asleep."

"Are you alone?"

"Of c— Yes."

"You sound out of breath. Did I interrupt something?"

The wicked lilt in his voice made her heart blip erratically. What was he implying? "I was reading a book."

"And the book made you breathless? Must be a good one. Which book?"

As if she'd tell him that she read romances because in the stories a woman could be happy with one man forever, and love at first sight lasted for eternity—unlike her mother, who'd fallen instantly in love and married four times since divorcing Aubrey's father. The husband who'd made a pass at Aubrey had lasted less than two years, but by then Aubrey's relationship with her mother had been irrevocably changed. "I'm not reading anything you'd be interested in."

"How do you know?"

She sighed. "It's a romance, Liam."

"Ahh. A hot one?" The husky tone of his voice gave her goose bumps. No telling what he thought she'd been doing to make herself pant while reading the steamy book.

"I—I was in the tub. I had to run for the phone." Her skin flushed at the boldness of her confession.

A low groan carried through the phone line. "You fight dirty."

A laugh bubbled up her throat. He had no idea how unlike herself she'd behaved since meeting him—or at least the self she'd been since joining her father's company. It was all Liam's fault. He made her feel sexy and naughty, and he made her want to break rules for once in her life and say to hell with pleasing her father.

"Should I let you get back to your book?"

"It'll have to dry before I can finish it."

"Why?"

She cringed. "Because I dropped it in the tub when the phone rang."

"Give me the title. I'll replace it."

"You don't have to do that. I'm the klutz, not you."

"I've seen you dance. You're no klutz. Aubrey…" he said,

his voice lowering into a commanding tone that sent shivers up her spine "…give me the title."

She reluctantly relayed the information. "But you don't have to replace it. It will be fine once the pages dry out. And I can't keep receiving gifts from you at work."

"You're going to get me in trouble," he voiced her thoughts before she could.

"How am *I* going to get *you* into trouble? All I sent was a sandwich. You sent the most amazing bouquet. All the admins are talking." Aubrey absently blotted the droplets on her shoulders with her towel.

"The atmosphere at EPH is…tense, but your lunch surprise had me smiling all afternoon. The staff probably wonders what I'm up to. Thanks for sending the sandwich."

"You're welcome. I hope the rest of your week improves."

"Yours, too. Anything I can do to help?"

She gulped. *Yes, spill your guts about EPH's problems and then give me permission to share the information with my father.* "I think I have it under control."

Silence stretched between them. Aubrey didn't want to hang up, but she couldn't think of a thing to say to keep him on the line. Why did this man have the power to make her tongue-tied?

"You know where I live. How about you even the score?"

Her fingers contracted on the damp towel. "I'm around the corner on Fifth, only a couple of blocks up from you."

"That close?"

"Yes."

"We could meet—"

"No, Liam, we can't." But she wanted to. She really, really wanted to.

"Right. I should say good night and hang up, but I know if I do I'll just lie here and think about you. Tell me how to stop thinking about that afternoon, Aubrey."

Her breath jammed in her throat. "I can't. Because I'm having the same problem. Do you think it's just the taboo thing? Wanting what we can't have?"

She wouldn't know. She always dated men her father would approve of.

"Maybe. Probably. I don't know. You said I got you out of the tub. You must be cold."

Cold? No, her skin burned. It was a wonder the remaining droplets on her skin didn't sizzle like butter in a hot pan. "I'll get back in when we're finished."

"Why wait? Do you have a portable extension?"

She bit her lip. "You want to talk to me while I'm in the tub? Is this going to turn into an obscene phone call?"

His seductive laugh warmed her even more. "Do you want it to?"

Aubrey pressed a hand to the booming in her chest. "I'm not sure. I've never had one."

"Good to know."

"Have you? Had an obscene call, I mean?"

"No. But it might be interesting."

She twisted the corner of the towel in her fingers. "Maybe. If it wasn't icky and if the person making it wasn't a psycho or a thirteen-year-old boy."

"Good night, Aubrey. You'll be hearing from me soon." And then he disconnected.

She slowly replaced the receiver. What did he mean, she'd hear from him? The book? Or would he call again? She was ashamed to admit she hoped he'd call. She loved listening to Liam's voice. And she really enjoyed knowing he was having as much trouble forgetting their lovemaking as she was.

Not lovemaking. Sex. And no matter how much she wanted more, a steamy memory was all it could ever be. Her father would never forgive her for sleeping with a rival, and as long as she worked for Holt Enterprises and lived in a family-owned apartment, she had to follow her father's rules.

Twenty-nine and still following Daddy's rules. There was something pitifully not right about that.

"What a bitch of a day," Liam muttered as he poured himself a glass of wine and took a healthy sip.

Leaning against the kitchen counter, he rolled the rich pinot noir around in his mouth, savoring the cherry bouquet and smooth finish. He finished half a glass before the calming effect of the heavy red wine kicked in, soothing his jagged nerves.

This afternoon he'd fielded a flurry of calls from advertisers wanting to know if there were problems within EPH and demanding assurances Liam couldn't give them. What had tipped them off to the internal strife? Patrick had all but levied a gag order on the company employees, but there had to be a leak somewhere. Having the advertisers get fidgety could cause EPH's advertising revenues to drop. He'd have to speak to the sales managers and remind them to keep EPH's internal dissention to themselves.

The clock on the microwave revealed the late hour. Liam had worked through lunch and dinner. Cooking didn't appeal. Going out appealed even less. But he had to eat because he had plans for later that required him to keep his mind sharp. His pulse quickened in anticipation. At the same time his stomach knotted. His plan was unwise. Foolish.

Fun.

He pulled a frozen casserole from the freezer and shoved it into the microwave. An executives' catering company supplied him with precooked meals for the nights he was too tired to cook. The service provided all the benefits of having a personal chef without having anyone underfoot in his apartment. And if he had a hot date he had the option of having the chef prepare a gourmet meal and clear out before his company arrived. Not an option he'd used yet.

While his dinner defrosted he settled on a bar stool at his granite kitchen counter, sipped his wine and studied the bottle and the label. Louret Winery, a small outfit in Napa Valley, California, had become one of Liam's favorite producers since he'd discovered their wines last year. He promised himself a tour of the facility as soon as the dust settled at EPH. As far as he was concerned, that date couldn't come soon enough.

An hour later he'd eaten, showered the knots from his shoulders. Now he sat beside the phone with his heart thumping a wild beat and a different kind of tension tightening his muscles. Adrenaline flowed through his veins as the clock inched toward midnight. As soon as the hands hit twelve he punched out the number.

"Hello?"

His pulse nearly deafened him to Aubrey's soft voice. "This is an obscene phone call. Hang up if you're not interested."

He heard Aubrey gasp, but she didn't sever the connection.

"Are you alone?" he asked in as low and sexy a voice as he could manage—not difficult considering his throat had closed up.

"Yes. Are you?"

"Not anymore." A crazy answer. Of course he was alone, but having Aubrey on the line made him feel less lonely—an emotion Liam had experienced far too frequently since Patrick's contest made him all too often the unwelcome messenger bearing bad news. "What are you wearing?"

"A smile."

His brain nearly imploded. He gulped his wine. "Anything else?"

"A nightgown."

"You're a tease, Aubrey Holt. What color?"

"Black."

Liam groaned. "Details, please."

She hesitated so long Liam feared the game he'd anticipated since last night was over. "Long with spaghetti straps and a lace bodice. There are sheer bits on my—"

"Wait," he groaned. His control wavering, he took another sip of wine. "Let me savor that much before you send me into overload with more." He closed his eyes and pictured Aubrey dressed as she'd described, in a puddle of black filmy fabric lying on his cream-colored sheets, waiting for him. And he ached. His body pulsed and throbbed, growing heavy with need. A saner man would take a cold shower or take matters into his own hand. "I'm ready. Where are the sheer bits?"

"Guess."

Her answer surprised a laugh out of him. "I need a hint. High or low?"

"High."

"If I were with you, could I see your breasts? Your nipples?"

"Yes."

Liam fisted his hand in his hair and took an unsteady breath. "You definitely fight dirty."

"What are you wearing?"

"Boxers. Silk. Blue." And they'd suddenly become tight. Very, very tight.

"No thong?"

He grinned, opened the nightstand drawer and extracted the garment. He stroked the smooth satin between his fingers. "No. That's in my hand. It smells like you, but your skin is softer, warmer."

Her gasp filled his ear. "You're good at this obscene phone call business."

"I could get better with practice."

"Are we going to practice?" Was that a hopeful note in her voice?

Should he continue this insane game, continue to lose sleep and drive himself to the aching edge of need again and again? "I'd like to."

"Me, too."

If he didn't change the subject he was going to lose what was left of his sanity and the call would go from sexy to raunchy. "Was today better than yesterday?"

"You mean at work?" Her sigh carried over the phone lines. "Not really. Sometimes I wonder if I should quit and find a job where I don't have to work so hard to prove myself."

The frustration in her voice came across loud and clear. "What happened?"

Seconds ticked past. "My father assigned me a task. I called a staff meeting and explained what I needed. But no one listens to me. They all think I was given my job because of my father and not because I earned it."

"I don't have to worry about that with EPH. Patrick made each of us pay our dues by working our way up through the ranks."

"I'm sorry, Liam. I didn't mean to ruin your call by whining."

"You're not whining, and I needed to change the subject before I asked you to take off your nightgown and touch yourself the way I would if I were there."

A half-choked sound carried over the line. "And would you return the favor? Touch yourself the way I want to?"

Desire churned thick and hot through his veins. He cursed. "Yes. Anywhere you want."

"Next time, then." And then he heard a click followed by the dial tone.

Next time. The words energized him, filling him with an anticipation for tomorrow that he hadn't felt in a long time.

Aubrey floated through her workday in a cloud of excitement, unwarranted by her position as VP of single copy sales. She'd breezed through phone calls with uncooperative distributors and meetings with the other circulation department staff. None of the usual daily irritations had brought her down or driven her for a double Mocha Frappuccino, her help-I'm-losing-it drink.

If only every day could be this enjoyable. She felt a twinge of unease. It was really pitiful that she sought, from a voice on the phone, the approval she couldn't get at work.

Since arriving home she'd showered and shampooed, given herself a manicure and pedicure all in preparation for her hot date with the telephone. She'd set her alarm for midnight, but she hadn't needed the annoying beep to wake her because there was no chance she'd drift off to sleep with this overdose of adrenaline flowing through her veins. She'd been watching the clock for what seemed like hours.

She stepped into the sexy teddy she'd darted out to purchase at lunchtime, tied the ribbon bows on each shoulder and brushed her hands over the lace covering her. The regret that Liam would never see the seductive garment dampened her excitement a little.

Finally it was time to call. Her heart raced and her mouth dried. She took a sip from the bottle of water on her nightstand, settled back against her mountain of pillows and dialed.

"Hello."

Goose bumps raced over her skin at the sound of Liam's voice. "This is an obscene phone call. Hang up if you don't want to listen."

Liam snorted. "Are you kidding? Do you know any guy

who would hang up if he had a beautiful woman promising to talk dirty to him?"

A smile twitched on her lips. His comment erased much of her nervousness. "I bought something very special for you today. I'm wearing it."

"She goes for the kill on the first line," he muttered in a barely audible tone. "Describe it for me," he said in a louder voice.

"It's lacy and sheer and very brief." *I can't believe you're doing this, A.*

"Tell me more." His pitch was lower, huskier.

Her nipples beaded and desire tangled low in her belly. "It's cut very high and very low. My legs are bare. And it's sheer and red. A teddy with a bow on each shoulder. One tug on each ribbon and…"

He groaned. "You're killing me, Aubrey."

Her inner rebel relished this brief interlude of feeling sexy and desirable and wanted. She'd never have the nerve to act as brazen face-to-face. "I want to talk about fantasies tonight. Tell me, Liam, in your secret fantasies where is the one place you'd like to make love but haven't?"

"At a Mets game," he replied without hesitation.

That jarred her right out of fantasy land. She'd never attended a baseball game, but she couldn't imagine finding a private place in Shea Stadium. "A Mets game."

"You?"

She shook away the disturbing image of crowds, stale beer and peanut shells. Did she dare confess her secret? "An elevator."

She heard the whistle of his breath. "That could be arranged."

"I know, and I think about your private elevator at night when I—" no, she would not confess that "—when I can't sleep."

"Untie the bows, Aubrey."

She did as he asked. The lace slid downward, temporarily

snagging on her erect nipples and then gliding into a puddle at her waist.

"If I were there I'd kiss you, taste you until you begged me to stop," he promised in a gravelly whisper that made her lightheaded.

A quiver started deep inside Aubrey and radiated outward. "What makes you think I'd ever ask you to stop?"

"Aubrey." Her name was half moan, half plea.

Her pulsed fluttered like a hummingbird's wings and she squirmed restlessly, aching for his touch. "What are you doing right now, Liam?"

"Wishing you were here. This is insane. I need to see you."

"We can't. My father and your grandfather would never forgive us."

"To hell with them."

Regret tightened Aubrey's throat, dousing the sparks of arousal that had flared within her the moment she'd begun her evening preparations. She wished she could believe she and Liam had a future together, but even if Liam didn't consider her father the enemy, Aubrey knew from her mother's multiple marriages that love at first sight was an illusion. What she had with Liam, though breathtakingly powerful and thought-consuming at the moment, would pass.

"Liam, what we have is temporary. Our families aren't."

And then she hung up.

She had to end this and she had to end it now. If he called tomorrow night she wouldn't answer her phone.

"I have your books and I'm holding them hostage."

Aubrey nearly dropped the phone when she heard Liam's voice. She quickly glanced out her open office door and exhaled when she spotted her administrative assistant's empty chair. A check of her watch revealed it was almost six. Linda must have left for the day. "You shouldn't have called here."

"I'm using a pay phone. No caller ID will trace the call back to me, and I used the automated directory instead of going through the Holt Enterprises operator. The ransom I'm demanding for the books is dinner."

So much for her plan to ignore him. Temptation nipped at her, but guilt took an even bigger bite. The preliminary report on EPH from the advertising department lay on her desk waiting to be read, edited and forwarded to her father. Aubrey shoved it into a drawer without reading it. Whatever the report contained was common knowledge among the advertising staff. She hadn't pried and hadn't gained the information using underhanded methods.

She still felt guilty.

Just say no, A. "We can't risk meeting in public."

"My place. I'll cook."

What happened to no? "Did you say books, plural?"

"I did. I have everything ever published by the author you mentioned, including an autographed copy of her recently released hardcover. But if you want them it's going to cost you. I need to see you, Aubrey."

Common sense warred with desire. "And you accused me of fighting dirty."

"I play to win, and I promise that if you join me tonight we'll both win. I'll be waiting in the elevator at seven o'clock. Carlos, the doorman, will give you the key." The dial tone sounded.

The elevator. Did that mean what she thought it did? Aubrey couldn't catch her breath. She lowered the receiver, pressed a hand to her chest and tried to calm down to no avail. Tremors of excitement and nervousness shook her.

Did she have the courage to accept Liam's challenge? There was only one way to find out.

* * *

Liam leaned against the mirrored elevator wall and sipped his champagne. Five after seven. Would Aubrey show or had he pushed too far too fast?

You shouldn't be pushing at all. You should be walking away. But he couldn't. Aubrey Holt had taken possession of his thoughts, and he couldn't evict her no matter how hard he tried. And he had tried.

His heart chugged slower, heavier as minutes dragged past and Aubrey didn't arrive. He'd learned that she was punctuality-conscious at their first meeting. If she were coming tonight she wouldn't be late. Disappointment weighted his shoulders. He ought to pack it in and carry back to his apartment the ice bucket standing in one corner of the elevator and the bouquet of red roses lying in the other. He'd bought a dozen roses—not because that was the tradition but because they'd met and made love the first time twelve days ago.

Romantic sap. You didn't make love, you had sex. Mind-boggling, cook-your-brain sex.

The elevator jolted and so did his heart, and then the doors glided open. Aubrey stood in the foyer, with nervousness filling her wide eyes and white teeth digging into her siren-red lipstick. She held her purse in front of her waist in a white-knuckled grip. Liam couldn't stop the grin spreading over his face—one of relief, happiness—as he took in her seductive attire.

A black wraparound dress hugged her slender waist and dipped low between her breasts. Skimpy high-heeled sandals put her eyes on level with his. And her hair was rumpled, as if she'd just crawled out of bed.

"Come inside, drop your bag and push the button for my floor."

She hesitated, her gaze roving over the ice bucket, the

roses and then him in a slow head-to-toe perusal. Her breasts rose and fell on a deep breath before she did as he asked. Her scent mingled with the heavier perfume of the roses. The elevator whizzed upward, leaving Liam's stomach behind. Or maybe the woman a yard away caused the roller-coaster effect.

Aubrey knotted her fingers in front of her. The hem of her dress, which he could see in a multitude of reflections, swished almost imperceptibly with the fine tremor of her body. He poured her a flute of champagne. Their fingers touched on the stem as she accepted the glass. His pulse stuttered and her breath hitched. "I'm glad you came."

"Me too. I'm sorry I'm late. I went home to change first."

Tension eased from his shoulders. He'd feared second thoughts had caused her tardiness. "It was worth the wait. You look incredible. Sexy as hell."

She swallowed the champagne in her mouth with a sudden and audible gulp and her cheeks flushed. "Thank you. You too."

"Thanks." He'd showered, shaved and yanked on pale gray slacks and a pullover sweater in a darker shade. Same routine he'd follow for any other date, but this wasn't like any other date. Tonight he was as nervous as a kid on prom night.

The elevator stopped on his floor and the doors opened. Liam made no effort to step out. Aubrey had said she fantasized about making love on an elevator, and he intended to fulfill that fantasy tonight—if she'd let him. The doors closed.

Her violet eyes found his and the awareness of his intent widened her pupils and quickened her breath.

Liam fought the hunger that urged him to grab her, yank the tie on the sexy dress to reveal the satiny skin beneath and then bury himself inside her. Hard. Deep. He used to have more finesse, more patience, but tonight a battle raged inside him.

Slow down.

"Decent day?" he forced out even though his mouth watered for the taste of her.

She rolled one shoulder. "As decent as it gets."

The telling flatness of her voice said more than her words. "You don't like your job."

She stared into her glass, swirling the pale liquid around and then sipping. "I'm good at what I do."

"But?"

Her troubled gaze met his. "But no, I don't enjoy my job."

"Why don't you leave?"

Another swirl of champagne. Another sip. "It's complicated."

"Try me. Tomorrow is Sunday and neither of us has to work. We have all night."

Her lips parted and then her pink tongue darted out to dampen them. "My father was there for me when I needed him. I owe him."

"Family duty is a heavy cross to bear." A fact he knew well.

"What would you do if you didn't work for EPH?"

If he didn't work for EPH… Not something he'd ever contemplated. "I don't know. Maybe try my hand at making wine."

"Making wine?" Her eyebrows arched in surprise.

He leaned against the brass rail separating the mirrored upper portion of the compartment from the dark wainscoting lining the bottom of the walls. Why did he feel comfortable confessing this to Aubrey when he'd never done so with his family or friends? "Wine's a hobby. I've been studying viticulture and enology for years."

She saluted with her now empty flute. "I don't know how much you've learned about growing grapes or making wine, but may I commend you on your taste in champagne?"

He nodded acceptance of the compliment. "Refill?"

The corners of her lips turned up. "Maybe later."

Liam's pulse beat as fast as a drum roll. He wanted to make love with Aubrey. No doubt about it. But he would have been happy to just have her company. He took her glass and set it beside his on the floor, and then he straightened. The desire in Aubrey's eyes slammed into him like a subway train, knocking the air from his lungs and the ability to think from his head. He lifted a hand and cradled her silky cheek. She leaned into his palm and her lids fluttered closed. A smile of pleasure curved her lips.

"I've been thinking about this since last night," he confessed, and then he kissed her, sinking into the damp softness of her lips and savoring the taste of Aubrey, a flavor uniquely hers combined with a nuance of the champagne.

He tunneled his fingers through her soft hair to cradle her nape and banded his opposite arm around her waist to pull her flush against him. Warm and pliant, she arched into him in perfect alignment. Her breasts teased his chest and the softness of her mound cushioned his erection.

Her arms wound around his waist and her fingers kneaded the tight muscles of his back. She angled her head, granting him deeper access, and hunger inflamed him. He shaped her shoulders with his palms, traced the line of her spine and the indention of her waist, and then he filled his hands with her tight, round bottom. A perfect fit.

Need rose inside him with overwhelming, suffocating strength. He raked his hands over her hips, down her thighs and then up again, carrying the hem of her dress with him. His fingertips encountered silken hose, an elastic band and a strip of bare skin. Stockings. He groaned into her mouth and traced the line of lacy elastic across the backs of her upper thighs. He explored higher and found nothing. Aubrey wasn't wearing panties or even a thong. Gasping for air, he yanked back his head and then he gritted his teeth as sexual heat pulsed through him with an urgency he'd never faced.

"You definitely fight dirty."

A smile quivered on her damp lips and mischief sparkled in her eyes. "I like to be prepared."

He eased a few inches between them and pulled the string fastening her dress at her waist. The rustle of the fabric ties against each other seemed unnaturally loud in the small compartment. He lifted both hands to cradle her face and kissed her again, fighting desperately to get a grip on his slipping control. He mapped the shape of her ears with this thumbs, smoothed over her fluttering pulse and then traced the V of her neckline. When he reached the valley between her breasts, he nudged the fabric aside and his knees nearly buckled.

Aubrey's tiny black bra only half-covered her breasts. The puckered tips were clearly visible beneath the border of the lacy cups. His mouth watered. His heart pounded. His lungs struggled to find sufficient oxygen in the suddenly airless elevator. Liam circled his thumbs over the lace, easing it aside, and then he dipped his head to take one tight tip into his mouth.

Aubrey whimpered and collapsed against the elevator wall. Her fingers tangled in his hair, holding him in place as he sampled first one breast and then the other, sipping, nipping, lightly abrading with his teeth.

His palms glided over the hot satin of her skin, outlining her waist and hips and then parting her dark tangle of curls, seeking and finding her moisture. Her gasps filled his ears, and her fingers tightened in his hair almost to the point of pain. Liam captured Aubrey's hands in his and transferred them to the cool, brass rail. "Hold on."

He took a moment to savor the sexy picture of Aubrey with her dress gaping open, her breasts damp above the skimpy push-up bra and her long, slightly parted legs encased in those sinful thigh-high stockings and stiletto heels. An aroused flush covered her face and chest, and desire kept her lids at half-mast.

He dropped to his knees, cupped her buttocks and tasted her. He stroked her with his tongue, filled his nostrils with the scent of her arousal and savored each whimper of pleasure he heard over the loud drumming of his heart. And then she climaxed. He supported her weight as pleasure undulated through her and then he rose, dug into his pocket for a condom and reached for his belt buckle with trembling hands.

"Let me," Aubrey whispered. Her fingers made quick work of his belt and pants, pushing them down his thighs. Good thing she worked fast since each brush of her fingers sent him closer to the edge of the cliff, and going over without her wasn't an acceptable option. She took the condom from him and smoothed it over his rigid flesh. All Liam could do was lock his muscles, grind his molars and battle his raging need.

"I need you inside me, Liam."

Her husky whisper nearly unmanned him. He'd never been happier to oblige a request in his life. He lifted Aubrey, rested her bottom on the brass rail and hooked her legs around his hips, and then he drove deep into the slick, hot glove of her body. Her arms twined around his neck, holding him close. For a moment he remained buried and still, as sensation engulfed him, and then he withdrew and plunged into her again and again until his lungs burned and his legs trembled.

Her lips found his, devouring him with one ravenous kiss after another until they were both gasping, and kissing became impossible. And then her head tipped back against the mirrored wall and she cried out his name. Her internal muscles clenched him and his own climax slammed through him.

He planted his hands against the mirror on either side of

Aubrey's head and lowered his forehead to the fragrant angle of her neck and shoulder. Satisfaction thickened and slowed his blood. "You smell delicious."

Her teeth caught his earlobe. "So do you."

And just that easily desire rekindled. How did she do it? How did Aubrey Holt turn him inside out and give him pleasure exponentially more satisfying than anything he'd experienced before?

It wasn't a question Liam could answer with his pants around his ankles and his brain lost in the ozone. Later, he promised himself, later he'd figure out why and how Aubrey knocked him sideways.

But first, he'd promised her dinner and a bag of books. And he always kept his promises. Always.

Six

She'd done it again.

Aubrey leaned back against the cool, mirrored elevator wall and tried to summon the guilt and regret she *should* be feeling for consorting with the competition. But she couldn't rally the negative emotions when every muscle in her body hummed with satisfaction, her heart still raced with passion and her arms and legs still encircled the man who'd fulfilled her secret fantasy. Liam's chest hair teased her breasts each time one of them inhaled.

The first time she and Liam had become intimate had been a fluke of hormones and happenstance, but this time she'd deliberately chosen to ignore her father's animosity for the Elliotts and pursue her own personal pleasure because Liam reminded her of the person she used to be. Fun. Sassy. A little naughty. Or at least that was what her college roommates at Radcliffe had claimed. Aubrey hadn't seen that girl in a long, long time.

Liam Elliott was the first person she'd ever met who understood the pressures of the family-owned magazine business, and their crazy late night calls had de-stressed her in a way that nothing else could. Not pills, nor alcohol. But an ongoing affair with Liam could be just as destructive to her job and her relationship with her father as a chemical addiction. She'd spent her entire life trying to please her father and prove her intelligence. This illicit involvement did neither of those.

"I guess avoiding each other isn't going to work," she asked once she caught her breath.

"Not a chance." Liam eased from her body and instantly she missed him. He helped her stand and then began righting her clothing. Her legs quivered unsteadily. Watching him make love to her in the mirrors had been hotter than she could believe, but his haste to redress her was quickly quenching that fire.

"Are you trying to straighten me up so you can shove me out the door?" She winced at the hurt in her voice and pushed his hands aside to complete the task, albeit unsteadily.

"No. But if I don't cover your delectable body, you're never going to get out of this elevator or get the dinner and books I promised you."

Pleasure wrapped around her like a warm blanket. "Oh. Well, in that case, may I return the favor?"

She bent her knees, intent on pulling up his slacks, but Liam caught her elbows and lifted her back up. "Not if you want to get out of here tonight. The thought of you on your knees..." He shook his head. "Hell, Aubrey, I can barely stand as it is."

His words and the desire lurking in his eyes sent her pulse into a tizzy. "Maybe later, then. What can I do for you now?"

"A loaded question." His eyes glimmered with suppressed hunger. He fastened his clothing, scooped up the roses and her purse and placed both in her arms. "The flowers are for you."

The heady scent of the flowers filled her nostrils. "Thank you. Florist roses don't usually have this much scent."

"I special-ordered them. Twelve, because twelve days ago we first did this."

His fingers tangled in her hair and he held her captive while he kissed her deeply, hungrily. By the time he released her lips, her head spun from lack of oxygen. Clutching the roses to her chest, she sagged against the elevator wall and filled her lungs with much-needed air.

Rendered speechless by the romantic gesture and his thoughtfulness, not to mention that killer kiss, she could only stare as he gathered the ice bucket and the champagne flutes and used his elbow to push the button to open the elevator doors.

Why oh why couldn't his last name be something besides Elliott? And why couldn't they have met and slowly fallen in love instead of instantly combusting?

The doors glided open. He nodded for her to precede him. Tantalizing smells greeted her as soon as he opened his apartment door. She followed him into the dining room. "Something smells delicious."

He deposited the ice bucket on a long cherry table that had been set with ivory cloth napkins, silver and crystal. "Steak Diane. Lucky for you, I'm pretty good in the kitchen."

"I imagine you're good just about anywhere." The bold comment—shades of the old Aubrey—slipped out before she could edit it.

Mischief sparkled in his baby blues, and the corners of his eyes crinkled as he pulled out a chair. "You're more than welcome to test that theory after dinner. Have a seat."

Aubrey laid the roses and her purse on the long table and

sat. Liam's hands briefly massaged her shoulders—just long enough to agitate her breathing—and then he bent to nuzzle a kiss on her nape. "I'll be right back."

After he left, Aubrey rested her head against the back of the chair. *What are you doing, A.? This path leads to a dead end.*

What's wrong with a dead end as long as you both know that's where you're headed?

Nothing, as long as hearts and hopes and hormones don't become entangled.

Liam made her feel young, energetic and sexy instead of old, neutered and dedicated only to her job. He relieved her stress and gave her amazing orgasms. What more could a girl want? She could be happy with that, couldn't she?

Absolutely. Without a doubt.

Hmm. Why did she have trouble believing that?

Because she wanted more. She wanted a loving husband, children, a home and a minivan. Despite her parents' bad examples, she knew there was such a thing as a happy marriage. Her college friends had married and started families. Aubrey frowned. She couldn't remember when she had last spoken to her friends. In the last few years work had taken over her life. Each time one of her friends had called she'd been shackled to her desk by some urgent deadline. She'd even given up her jogs in the park for a treadmill—with her laptop fastened to the handlebars—in her spare bedroom. Voice-recognition software made it possible for her to dictate her work as she ran.

Unfortunately, she could never have the American dream of 2-point-whatever children and a house with a yard with Liam. Even if it were possible to get over their Romeo and Juliet family situation, they'd met and ignited too quickly. Love at first sight—not that she imagined herself in love yet—wasn't based on anything deep and meaningful, and therefore it burned out quickly and painfully, and it left scars behind. Just look at her mother. Pamela Holt Dean Getty Richards Curtis paid more for therapy each month than Aubrey paid in rent and utilities combined.

The swinging door opened, interrupting her dark thoughts. Liam entered carrying a tray holding two plates and a small bowl. He set a plate before her. The other dish he placed in front of the chair at a right angle to hers and put the bowl between them. He discarded the tray, pulled a bottle of wine from the crook of his arm, efficiently uncorked it and poured the deep red liquid into the waiting goblets and then sat.

From the bowl he extracted a cloth and extended his hand. "May I?"

Surprised by this consideration, Aubrey placed her palm over his. Liam wrapped the warm, damp lemon-scented cloth around her hand and then embarked on the most sensual hand washing of Aubrey's life. He dragged the cloth between each finger, massaged her palm and the sensitive inner skin of her wrist, and then he repeated the process with her other hand. By the time he finished, the desire he'd so recently sated had rekindled and her breath came in short bursts. *All because he'd washed her hands.* She couldn't get over it. How did he get to her so easily?

He lifted his wine glass. "Enjoy."

"For as long as it lasts." She touched her glass to his with a *clink* of fine crystal and then sipped. Liam definitely knew his wines. Aubrey lifted her knife and sliced into the tender beef and then paused. "If we're going to have this…affair shouldn't we make some ground rules?"

"Good idea."

"No calls at work," she offered and then took a bite. The succulent meat melted in her mouth. "Delicious."

"Thank you. You're right. Calling at work was risky even

with the precautions I took. We need to keep our business and private lives separate. *Completely* separate," he stressed.

Guilt stabbed Aubrey between the shoulder blades. She washed down the lump in her throat with a gulp of wine. She had to destroy the report from the sales department. "Okay. And when either of us wants to end this, all we have to do is say so and that's it. No further contact. No questions asked. No explanations required."

"Agreed."

"No 'I love yous' or talk of the future. We both know this is temporary."

"Got it. Here and now. That's it."

A few moments passed as each ate in silence. Aubrey couldn't imagine being ready to say goodbye anytime soon, but then her mother probably never went into any of her marriages anticipating the messy divorces that followed, either.

She met Liam's gaze. "Meeting in public is out, and we can't meet at my apartment. My father owns the building and he lives in the penthouse above me. Besides the risk of running into him, there would be too many prying eyes. But a hotel seems…" She shrugged.

"Sleazy. My place is safe. My neighbor is overseas more often than he's home, and Carlos the doorman has been here forever. He's discreet."

Aubrey paused with her fork halfway to her mouth. "You mean there was no chance of us being interrupted in the elevator tonight?"

Liam's lips curled upward. "Not unless there was a fire, and, sweetheart, you came damn close to starting one. Watching you watch us…" He shook his head and then exhaled through pursed lips.

Warmth swept her cheeks at the compliment. "You could have told me sooner. About your neighbor, I mean."

"And spoil your fantasy?"

A smile twitched on her lips. She'd never had a man ask her what her fantasies were, let alone go to such lengths to deliver one. She said a silent prayer of thanks that baseball season was over and she wouldn't be expected to play out his fantasy at the stadium. "Fantasies rarely live up to expectations, but this one did. You definitely didn't disappoint me."

"Glad to hear it."

And then Aubrey's blood chilled. "Oh my God. You don't have security cameras in the elevator, do you? I should have thought to ask before but I—"

His grin faded and he laid down his silverware. "We don't. Aubrey, you have my promise that I will never deliberately do anything to hurt or humiliate you."

Tension drained and panic subsided. That could have been a disastrous mistake. "Nor I you."

And she meant it. Her father would have to find another minion to investigate EPH.

Liam covered her hand with his on the table. His thumb stroked a trail of chaos along her inner wrist. "Do you have any idea how hard it's been for me to sit here knowing you're not wearing panties?"

Her appetite for food vanished and a hunger for Liam reawakened deep in her belly. She lowered her gaze from the fire in his eyes and surprisingly discovered her plate was empty. She barely remembered eating. "Let me help with the dishes."

She hastily snatched up her plate and his, rushed into the kitchen and unloaded them into the sink. After plugging the drain she turned on the water. Liam's arms bracketed her, caging her against the counter. He leaned forward until his chest pressed her shoulder blades and his erection rested in the crease of her bottom. His breath stirred the tendrils around her ear and she shivered. If it were possible for bones to melt, hers would be in a puddle on the granite floor.

"The dishes can wait. Join me in the shower. I want to get you wet."

She turned in his arms and pressed her hands to his chest. Her heart echoed the rapid beat of his beneath her palm. "I think you already have, but I'm willing to let you keep practicing if you insist."

For better or worse, her forbidden affair had begun.

Aubrey dropped her towel and reached for her dress. Liam snapped out of the sensual fog induced by the sight of her damp ivory skin. "Stay. Tomorrow's Sunday. No need to rush home."

She turned, chewing her bottom lip. "Are you sure?"

"Without a doubt."

Barely nine and they'd already had dinner and made love twice. She'd destroyed him, totally wrecked him, and five minutes ago after he'd come unglued in the shower he would have sworn he'd be sated for months to come. So why did hunger still gnaw at his veins? And why did the idea of waking up beside Aubrey make his body twitch to life?

She rested her palms on his chest, sifting through his chest hairs in a way guaranteed to make his soldier salute. He pressed his hands over hers, stilling her dangerous digits. Undeterred, she bent to sip a trail of kisses along his collarbone. He tangled his fingers in her damp hair and gently tugged her head back. "I thought you said you needed to rest."

Her siren's smile could tempt a saint—something he'd never aspired to be. "We'll rest awhile if you insist. You can show me your wine collection."

He didn't need to rest. His hard-on proved that, but he wanted to share his wine collection with Aubrey. No one but his grandfather knew the extent of his interest in enology. He laced his fingers through hers, led her back to the kitchen and folded back the wooden cabinet doors concealing his built-in wine refrigerator.

Her eyebrows lifted. How he managed to keep his eyes on her face when her luscious naked body was there to tempt him he didn't know. "You're a serious collector."

"I have more."

"Show me."

But instead of taking her to the cases stored in the third bedroom he led her to the library. She released his hand and strolled toward the ceiling-high bookcases. The shift of her buttocks and the swish of her long legs as she crossed the room, followed by the sight of her fingers caressing the spines of his collection of books on enology and viticulture, had him gritting his teeth on a surge of pure, unadulterated lust.

"My family has an estate in Napa. It belonged to my grandparents. Maybe you and I…" Her voice trailed off. Regret darkened her eyes and turned down the corners of her luscious mouth. They couldn't visit her family's estate without word of their affair getting out.

She sank in his leather desk chair, tucked her knees to her chest and spun the chair around. Butter-soft ivory skin on burgundy leather. Liam's fingers flexed in anticipation. If he had a condom with him he'd have her flat on her back on top of his cherry desk in seconds. He considered making a quick trip to his bedroom to retrieve protection, but a knock at his front door doused his desire like a coach's sideline shower from the water cooler after a ball game.

Aubrey planted her feet on the floor and halted the chair with a jerk. Her eyes widened with alarm and her face paled. "Are you expecting someone?"

"No." Liam tried to think but it wasn't easy with a naked lady sitting in his desk chair. "It's probably Cade. Otherwise the doorman would have called."

"Cade's a friend?"

"And a co-worker."

"Oh." A dose of apprehension flavored the word.

"Head for my room. I'll get the door."

"You might want to put on some pants first in case it's not your friend."

Where was his brain? Lost somewhere between Panic Avenue and Lust Lane. "Good idea."

The knocking continued as they raced back to Liam's room. He yanked on his pants and then closed the bedroom door on his way out. "All right. I'm coming."

He paused a second to catch his breath and then opened the door. Cade stood on the threshold. His friend immediately stepped inside, heading for the den, the way he had dozens of times before.

"I was about to give up on you. Mind if I hang out here for a while? Jessie and her girlfriends are *oohing* and *aahing* over wedding magazines. They kicked me out." When Liam remained by the door instead of following him, Cade turned and took in Liam's bare chest, the pants he'd fastened but hadn't bothered to belt and his bare feet. "Did I get you out of bed?"

Liam wiped a hand over his face and shut the door. It was pretty damned obvious from his state of undress that Cade had interrupted something. Better his buddy think he'd awakened him than have him ask questions. "Yes."

And the lie began. At that moment it hit home exactly what a relationship with Aubrey would entail. Sneaking around, lying to family and friends and keeping quiet about the only woman who'd put a smile on his face since Patrick's contest began.

Cade's gaze drifted past Liam to the champagne, roses and purse still on the dining room table. "You're not alone."

Damn. You couldn't lie with two empty champagne flutes in plain view. "No."

Cade pointed at Liam's neck. "Is that what I think it is?"

"What?"

"A hickey."

Liam fought the urge to cover his heating skin. "Possibly."

A wicked grin spread over Cade's face. "If you'd mentioned you had a hot date tonight I wouldn't have dropped in. So who is she?"

"Nobody you know."

"The gallery lady with you in the picture in the paper?"

"Good night, Cade. We'll hang out another time."

"You're not talking? She must be special."

Denial sprang to Liam's lips, but he bit it back. Aubrey special? She was, but not in the way Cade meant. There wouldn't be a wedding at the end of this affair. Liam opened the door, an unsubtle hint. "I'll catch up with you Monday."

"I knew you were having women troubles," Cade said on his way past. "You've been zoned out all week. But I guess you've worked them out."

Not good to know his distraction was obvious. "No troubles to work out."

But he lied. Liam shut the door and leaned against it. The trouble had just begun. He'd chosen a path through a mine field. One misstep and life as he knew it could be blown to hell.

What if they'd been caught?

Aubrey's heart beat a frantic *baboom* as she pulled on her clothing. With her hands trembling like fall leaves in a stiff breeze, rolling up the expensive stockings was beyond her capabilities. She wadded them up and stepped barefoot into her heels.

The low rumble of male voices carried through the door, but she couldn't understand the words. No matter. As soon as Liam's visitor left she had to go. Spending the night and brazenly waltzing outside in the morning sunshine was too risky. Better to slink home under the cover of darkness.

A clandestine affair. So over the top. So Hollywood. So not her. And yet she wasn't ready to give up Liam. Not yet. Not when she finally felt alive again for the first time in years.

The opening bedroom door startled her. She spun to face Liam. His gaze ran over her and a pleat formed between his eyebrows. "You're dressed."

"Yes. I need to go."

"Why?"

"Because staying isn't a good idea. I thought— But no. I mean I—" She was blathering. She stopped and pressed her fingers to her lips.

He cupped her shoulders. "Aubrey, it's okay. No one knows you're here."

She looked into his understanding blue eyes and almost caved. Almost. She'd love to spend the night pleasuring Liam and letting him return the favor, because he was exceptionally good at delivering pleasure, and she'd love to wake up in arms, but the stakes were too high. "I want to go home."

"Spend the weekend with me. We'll drive to the coast or upstate and find a place where we don't have to worry about anyone knocking on our door." His thumbs stroked the hollows beneath her collarbones with thought-blocking sensuality.

"I can't. My father is entertaining tomorrow night. I'm his hostess. Maybe next weekend."

He shook his head. "Next weekend I have to fly to Colorado for Cade's engagement party."

Aubrey sighed in resignation. Their time together would consist of stolen interludes, until finding time for each other became more hassle than happiness and one or the other of them would end the relationship. Had she expected otherwise? No, because she hadn't bothered to think that far in advance. In fact, thinking seemed to be an ability she lacked around Liam Elliott.

The relationship was moving too fast. Aubrey needed to step back and assess the situation. Otherwise, she'd end up in one of her mother's relationship train wrecks.

"I want to go home," she repeated.

He must have recognized the determination in her eyes, because he didn't argue this time. He raked a hand over his hair, standing the blond strands up in spikes. "I'll call a cab."

"No. It's only a few blocks."

"Then I'll walk you to your door."

"No." She bit her lip. She hadn't intended to shout.

His lips flattened. "Either I walk you to your door or you take a cab. It's better to risk exposure than have you get mugged or worse."

Once again, his thoughtfulness surprised her. Liam Elliott was truly a prize. A prize she couldn't keep.

"You can walk me to the street corner in view of the well-lit entrance to my building, but not to my door." If she wanted to protect her heart, then she had to keep the boundaries of this affair firmly in sight.

Liam's week had been a tug-of-war between family duty, his friendship with Cade and his desire for Aubrey. There had been moments where it seemed like he—the rope—would snap.

He'd spent his days at work, dodging Cade's knowing smirk and probing questions, trying to pacify antsy advertisers and attempting to alleviate the tension between the EPH staff members. Each evening he came home to Aubrey. She made the headaches disappear. He cooked dinner with her and had the hottest sex of his life. And they talked. About anything, about nothing. It didn't matter. Just being with her was enough.

He couldn't leave town without saying goodbye. Again. They'd said goodbye last night very satisfactorily. If he was a little worried that he was becoming too dependent on her, then he shrugged it off as a temporary hurdle. All too soon this sensual interval would end.

Hoping Aubrey wouldn't mind being awakened so early in the morning, he snatched up his cell phone and punched in her number. He'd programmed her as number one on his speed dial list. He tucked the unit beneath his ear and resumed shoving clothing and his toiletry bag into his suitcase.

"Hello," Aubrey answered in a sleep-roughened voice.

One word, that was all it took to reignite the sparks of hunger deep in his belly. "I called to say goodbye before I take off for the airport."

"It's only five-thirty. You're getting an early start."

He didn't want to go. The realization surprised him. He'd always wanted to travel, but he'd stayed close to EPH, fearing that if he left he'd give the impression that he didn't care about his job. In other circumstances he'd love to see Colorado and spend time with his family away from the stress of work, but the timing of Cade's engagement party reeked. Liam loved Cade like a brother and he was happy his friend had found Jessie, but watching the lovers cuddle and kiss would rub salt in an open wound. Liam and Aubrey could never have what Cade and Jessie had—an open relationship and a family celebration.

Did he want that?

"Liam?"

"I'm here. I was just recalling dinner last night."

"We never got around to eating last night, if you recall."

He grinned. "I feasted, if *you* recall."

Husky laughter filled his ear. "I vaguely remember you nibbling somewhere."

He'd done more than nibble. He'd sipped from her sweetness right there on the dining room table until she begged him to stop, and then he'd carried her to bed because she'd claimed her legs were too weak to support her. Once there she'd made him a very, very happy man.

He'd miss her, he realized. He'd miss her sassy, irreverent humor, her calming voice, her sexier-than-sin body and her amazingly talented mouth. He started to tell her and then clamped his jaw shut on the words. Their relationship rules didn't permit those kinds of declarations. No mention of the future allowed. All they had was here and now.

And that didn't bother him. Much.

"I'll call you from Colorado if I get a chance. If not, you'll hear from me when I get back. Are we still on for Sunday night?"

"I'll be there with bells on—and nothing else."

He groaned at the provocative image.

"Liam, I…I'll miss our evenings together."

His heart thumped hard against his ribs. "Me, too."

"Have fun."

"I'll try." And he would try because duty to his friend and his family demanded he give one hundred percent. And Liam always did his duty.

Seven

Pitiful, you can't even make it twenty-four hours without talking to Aubrey.

Liam itched to share everything he'd seen on Travis Clayton's ranch with her. The place was far beyond Liam's experience. He felt like a wide-eyed kid. Whichever way he turned new sights, sounds and smells inundated him. The air was clean. His lungs would appreciate a morning run here without the exhaust fumes to choke him. And he couldn't get over the lack of noise. Sure, cattle did whatever cattle do, and there were other ranch sounds, but the constant drone of noise to which he'd become accustomed was missing.

He escaped the family gathering in Silver Moon Ranch's large, two-story log house as soon as possible and found a spot in the shadows of the bunkhouse where even the moonlight didn't penetrate. He hit speed dial and Aubrey's number dialed automatically. She answered on the first ring and his pulse did its usual stutter upon hearing her voice.

"You won't believe this place," he blurted without preamble. "The ranch is so vast I can't see anything for miles, but the view of the Rocky Mountains is incredible."

"Hello to you, too," she teased. "You've never traveled west?"

"Other than L.A. and Dallas a few times on business, no. I'm a city boy, born and bred. Would you believe Cade, Shane and I are staying in an actual bunkhouse with two of the ranch hands? It's like walking onto a Western movie set."

"Your uncle Shane?"

"Yeah." Though only a few years older than Liam, Shane was his uncle, and the editor in chief of *The Buzz* magazine.

"Is the rest of the family at the ranch with you?"

The family. Family she'd never meet. The knowledge dampened his mood.

"It's primarily the *Charisma* staff," he responded. "Besides Cade and Jessie, his fiancée, there's Aunt Fin, Jessie's birth mother, my grandmother Maeve, my cousin Scarlet and her fiancé John Harlan."

"John Harlan from Suskind, Engle and Harlan advertising agency?"

"Yes. You know him?"

"Yes. He's handled a few of our advertisers' accounts and attended several Holt Enterprises receptions."

Liam's neck prickled in warning. But there was no reason for Aubrey's name to come up and no reason for John to make the connection between Liam and his forbidden lover. Liam dismissed his concerns.

"Tomorrow's the big day. Jessie's father Travis says neighbors will drive in from all over the state for Cade and Jessie's engagement party. It sounds like he has some interesting entertainment lined up for us city slickers."

She laughed. "Don't hurt yourself. I need you fully functional when you return because I went shopping today. You're going to love what I bought."

He groaned, recalling the last bagful of sinful lingerie she'd sprung on him. Her little fashion show and the resulting action between the sheets had made them both late returning to work from the lunch break they'd taken at his apartment Wednesday.

"I can't wait." His voice sounded as if someone had poured a load of gravel down his throat.

How did she do it? How did Aubrey Holt get to him through a phone line? Until Aubrey, Liam had never been one to spend a great deal of time talking on the phone unless the call was business-related. A phone was a tool. She'd turned it into an instrument of seduction. He found himself reluctant to say goodbye. "What are you wearing?"

"Bubbles. I'm in the tub."

The blood drained from his head. He leaned back, resting his head and shoulders against the rough siding of the bunkhouse. It took a few seconds to get his tongue to work. "You fight dirty."

She chuckled. "So you always claim. But you love it. Otherwise you wouldn't have a smile on your face each time you accuse me of it. I'll bet you're smiling now."

She knew him too well. How had that happened in less than three weeks? He tried to erase his grin and failed miserably. "What man wouldn't smile when he's talking to a sexy naked lady who looks good, smells good and tastes even better?"

"*Someone,*" she continued in a sassy tone, "gave me a bag of steamy romances to read, and the tub is my favorite reading spot. I expect to spend quite a bit of time here while you're gone."

An image of her slender curves, glistening wet and dotted with soap bubbles, flashed in his brain. His mouth filled with moisture, and need twisted in his belly. "You're killing me, sweetheart."

The crunch of a shoe on the hard-packed dirt made him turn. Cade stood only a few feet away in a pool of moonlight.

"I have to go. Good night." Liam barely waited for Aubrey's reply before he snapped his phone closed.

Cade leaned against the corner of the bunkhouse. "I wondered where you'd run off to. I didn't know you needed to whisper sweet nothings to your lady."

Liam didn't know how much his friend had heard, but clearly, denial would be pointless. He replayed as much of the conversation as he remembered. Had he called Aubrey by name? He didn't think so. "Did I miss anything?"

"Travis is getting ready to open the champagne you brought." He pushed off the building as Liam reached his side. "Still not willing to reveal who the mystery lover is?"

"Does it really matter? You don't know her." Liam headed for the ranch house.

"I spilled my guts to you. The least you can do is return the favor."

"No need. My 'guts' aren't going to be dragged down the aisle."

And for the first time, Liam realized that might not be a good thing.

Done. Aubrey shut down her computer, satisfied that the e-mail version of the report on EPH from the advertising staff had been deleted and the paper copy shredded. Her father would have to find someone else to do his dirty work.

"What brings you in on the weekend?" Speak of the devil. Her father stood in the doorway of her office.

She swallowed to ease the sudden dryness of her mouth. "Nothing special. I often work on weekends."

"With the way you've been bolting out the door each day exactly at five, I imagine you have some catching up to do."

She fought a flinch. Evidently, her comings and goings hadn't gone as unnoticed as she'd hoped. "I'm trying to add an evening workout to my schedule."

The lie rolled easily off her tongue. Too easily considering she never lied. But then Liam made certain she had a thorough workout each evening—just not the kind she implied to her father. She hoped the warmth of her cheeks didn't give her carnal thoughts away.

"You've had several lunch meetings this week. With whom?"

Anger stirred. Her father's tendency to micromanage shouldn't extend to her lunch hours. "Friends. I've been working so hard lately that I've lost touch with quite a few of my college friends, and I've only been out twice."

Another lie…sort of. She had lost touch with her friends, but on those lunch hours she'd met Liam, not her former dorm mates.

"Make sure your reunions don't interfere with your work."

"Yes, sir. Absolutely." The urge to stand and salute almost overwhelmed her.

He left as abruptly as he'd arrived without the courtesy of a goodbye. Aubrey sighed. Some things never changed.

Matthew Holt never said hello.

He never said goodbye.

He never said he loved her.

She'd willingly give up a lifetime of hellos and goodbyes just to hear those three words from her father's lips one time.

City meets country. Liam studied the crowd. He didn't have to be related to any of the guests to distinguish Travis Clayton's rural denim-clad neighbors from the New York crowd. Even their casual wear shouted urban.

"Great party, Travis," Liam said as he accepted a draft beer from Jessie's father. Big and blond and gruff, the man clearly doted on his only daughter. The open affection wasn't something Liam had seen often from his own father until lately. His mother's cancer had reaffirmed the value of family connections for all of them.

"I hope you're enjoying yourself."

"I am." As were the rest of his family. Liam's gaze drifted from his host to the crowd scattered across the yard of the Silver Moon Ranch. His grandmother, Cade and Jessie had gathered with several other guests near one of the bonfires scattered about the yard to ward off the October chill. While it was comfortable outside now, Liam had been warned that once the sun set the temperature would drop dramatically.

Aunt Fin stood with a group of locals on the opposite side of the clearing. Fin kept sneaking glances at Travis through eyes the exact shade of green as Jessie's. Now that Liam knew to look for it, the resemblance between Jessie and Fin was remarkable. How Jessie had hidden in plain sight as *Charisma's* intern and not been recognized as Fin's long-lost daughter remained a mystery. Cade had suspected Jessie of having secrets. No one had expected the secret to be that she'd joined EPH to meet the woman who'd given her up for adoption twenty-three years ago. The reunion between mother and daughter had been a happy one.

Liam spotted Shane chatting up a buxom blonde and smiled. Typical Shane. Liam's gaze moved on to John Harlan emptying his pockets onto a nearby table as he prepared to join the short line of guests waiting to mount the "bull," a barrel suspended between two trees. Liam's cousin Scarlet stood nearby, calling encouragement to her fiancé.

"Ready for a turn on the bull?" Travis asked.

"Why not? Giving you a good laugh is the least I owe you for your hospitality."

"I promise not to laugh too hard when you eat dirt." And then Travis turned to look in Fin's direction. Did his aunt and Jessie's dad have the hots for each other? Liam wished Travis luck. Fin was as dedicated to her job as Liam was to his, maybe more so.

Liam shook his head. Only a guy drowning in insatiable lust would recognize the symptoms in another man. The old adage "misery loves company" seemed apt. But in twenty-four hours his misery would be over. He'd be back home with Aubrey.

He headed across the yard toward the barrel and joined the short line of other men foolish enough to risk injuring themselves with the cowboy-style entertainment provided by their host. Liam set his beer on the table, emptied his pockets and laid his cell phone beside Travis's other guests' belongings. Leaving his wallet out in the open was definitely not a risk Liam would have taken in the city, but here it seemed as acceptable as leaving the bunkhouse door unlocked last night.

Liam's family members gathered to watch him, as if the possibility of him sustaining bodily harm interested them. He rested an arm across his grandmother's shoulders. "If I break my neck will you scatter my ashes on the beach at The Tides?"

"Ooh, hush with your teasing. And be careful, will ya, love?" she scolded him in the soft Irish brogue she hadn't lost in more than fifty years of living in the States. She turned to Fin, who'd sidled up between Cade and Jessie. "Why is it boys have to prove their manhood long after they've started shaving?"

"Good question, Mother," Fin replied.

Liam intercepted another one of those heated glances between his host and his aunt. *Interesting.*

John stayed on the "bull" a respectable amount of time

before falling into the deep pile of wood shavings below. The guy in line in front of Liam, one of Travis's ranch hands, climbed on board. The cowboy made riding the pitching barrel look easy. Everyone stopped to watch until he jumped off.

Travis clapped Liam on the back. "Climb on, Elliott. Let's see what you're made of."

Liam hoped he didn't embarrass himself. "How long did John last?"

"Seven seconds," the guy with the stopwatch called out.

Seven seconds. Liam psyched himself up. He could handle seven seconds. The ranch hands held the barrel steady as Liam swung his leg over the top. The cowhide blanketing the metal slipped and he nearly went over the side. Finally, he found his balance, tucked his heels under as instructed, grabbed the rope handle with his right hand and raised his left arm in the air. "Let's go."

The cowboys working the ropes to give the "bull" its motion yanked. Liam fought for balance. Riding the barrel reminded him of piloting the small Sunfish sailboat they kept at The Tides in rough seas. The barrel pitched and bucked, rose and dropped.

"Who has Aubrey Holt as number one on speed dial? I picked up your cell phone by mistake," John called out.

Oh, hell. Liam tried and failed to regain his balance. He hit the ground with a thud. The impact winded him. He shoved to his feet, brushing sawdust from his jeans and sweater. "Mine," he wheezed. "It's my phone."

"*Aubrey Holt* is your mystery lover?" Cade asked, his tone one of disbelief.

A quick scan of his family's faces revealed the same shocked expressions on each one. Denial sprang to Liam's lips, but he didn't voice it. Affirmation would set loose an unpleasant chain of events, but he couldn't cheapen the peace, pleasure and happiness Aubrey had brought him by lying. "Yes."

John stepped forward, offering Liam his phone. "I'm sorry. Yours is the same model as mine and it was next to my wallet on the table. I picked it up by mistake. When I tried to make a call using speed dial I reached the wrong number. I checked the name on the screen and saw Aubrey's. You might want to call her and explain."

As a partner in an advertising agency, John would be aware of the rivalry between Holt Enterprises and EPH. He'd understand the repercussions of the hornet's nest he'd just disturbed. But Liam couldn't blame him. "An honest mistake, John. No problem."

The compassion in John's eyes said he knew Liam lied.

In a matter of minutes someone would call Patrick Elliott and tell him that his grandson was consorting with the enemy's daughter, and Liam's problems would begin in earnest. He needed to call Aubrey and warn her that this could be the beginning of the end of their relationship.

His fingers tightened around the phone. He wasn't ready to let go of her yet, but without a doubt he'd have to say goodbye to Aubrey all too soon.

Over. The most exciting romance of her life would soon be over.

Aubrey paced Liam's apartment Sunday evening feeling slightly sick to her stomach. Liam would be home soon. She'd known from the moment he called last night to tell her their affair had become public knowledge that she'd broken her promise to herself to keep her heart and hormones separate. Liam had become too important to her. Their meetings had become the highlight of her days—not just for the sex, which was amazing, but for his friendship, the shared dinners, the conversation and the understanding she saw in his eyes when she talked about her frustration with her job.

She didn't want to lose the man who'd given her something besides work to look forward to for the first time in seven years. But what choice did she have? Liam would never choose their temporary fling—no matter how satisfying or incendiary—over his family.

Thursday night he'd given her keys to his apartment so that she could be waiting for him when he returned. He'd want them back. He'd tell her goodbye. And according to the rules they'd established that would be it. No begging for more time. No clinging. She wasn't sure she could say goodbye gracefully, with dignity.

Even if Liam was willing to risk Patrick Elliott's wrath to keep her in his life, she'd have to face the same dilemma. Maintaining her relationship with Liam meant displeasing her father. Again. It was only a matter of time before her father had enough of her disappointments and wrote her off as an employee, as a daughter. And did she really want to burn her bridges over something as temporary as an affair?

The feelings in her heart didn't feel temporary. But they were. She knew it just as well as she knew her mother would fall in love and marry again once she got over the most recent heartbreak with husband number five.

The sound of a key grating in the lock sent her heart plunging to her stomach. The door opened and Liam stood on the threshold with his suitcase in hand. Somber blue eyes met hers. Aubrey couldn't have spoken if her life depended on it. Emotion welled in her throat, blocking all sound. What was he thinking? How to say goodbye? How to tell her to get out?

"You're here." His voice was low and flat, as devoid of emotion as his face.

"Yes. I—" She dampened her lips and swallowed. "I said I would be."

Liam stepped inside and closed the door. He dropped his bag and his coat in the foyer. Without a word he crossed the room, captured her face in his palms and kissed her.

She didn't know what she'd expected, but this deep, soul-robbing kiss wasn't it. Liam devoured her mouth like a starving man would his first meal after breaking his fast, ravishing her with teeth and tongue and lips. His kiss was a little wild, a little rough and a whole lot sexy. His fingers raked through her hair, over her shoulders, down her back, and then back again. He systematically removed her clothing. Blouse. Bra. Shoes. Slacks. Panties. She stood in front of him naked, quivering and confused.

Liam kicked off his shoes and within a minute his garments lay piled on top of hers on the floor. He barely gave her time to admire the ripple of muscles beneath his skin before tumbling her onto the sofa. His hands moved swiftly, painting a trail of goose bumps over her skin, stealing her breath and her sanity and stirring a vortex of need deep inside her. He sipped and nipped from her neck to her navel and then lower. She fisted her hands in his short hair, bowing her back, lifting her hips toward his mouth and the magic he created. She crested swiftly—too swiftly—giving her no time to question his silent desperation.

He grabbed his pants, retrieved his wallet and protection, which he quickly donned. And then he knelt between her legs, cupped her bottom and filled her. He pumped deep, fast, relentlessly pounding her toward the edge of reason. He didn't try to hold back or sustain her pleasure the way he usually did. This time he raced for fulfillment as if he were afraid it would escape him, and Aubrey greedily accepted everything he gave. If anything, she urged him on, stoking his broad shoulders, kneading his tight butt, lifting her hips for each plunge.

Tension coiled tighter inside her and her lungs labored as if she raced with him, and then waves of ecstasy crashed over her. She dug her nails into his biceps and studied his face, trying to memorize the moment as Liam groaned and arched in climax. For seconds they stayed frozen, bodies locked together, gazes connected.

His eyes said it all. The end. Tonight would be their last night. And then he collapsed to his elbows, resting his forehead beside hers on the sofa cushion. That this would be their final coupling brought tears to Aubrey's eyes. They seeped into her hair. Not wanting Liam to see her emotional reaction, she hid her face in his shoulder.

Pain squeezed her chest and she could barely choke back her sobs. She'd repeated her mother's mistake of falling in love at first sight. Aubrey looked back on her mother's roller-coaster life with a flash of clarity. Suddenly, she understood the rush and exuberance of the highs and the crushing agony of knowing rock bottom waited just around the corner.

She'd broken the rules and fallen in love with Liam Elliot—the one man she could never have.

"Good morning, Liam," Ann, Liam's administrative assistant, said as he approached her desk. "Your grandfather would like to see you immediately."

Liam's Monday had started out lousy from the moment he'd awakened to the empty pillow beside him—empty except for the keys he'd given Aubrey resting where her head should have been. Apparently, his day was about to get worse.

"Good morning, Ann. Tell Patrick I'll be there in fifteen minutes."

Ann hesitated, her eyebrows arching in surprise. In the past when Patrick cracked the whip Liam had always jumped to do his bidding. Instantly. Without question. Without even going into his own office first.

Not today. Not when Liam hadn't come to terms with Aubrey sneaking out of his apartment in the middle of the night. Not when he didn't know if he could abide by their agreement and make no further contact with her. They'd made love on his couch, in his shower and in his bed last night, and then she'd left while he slept, without saying goodbye.

He wanted an explanation, damn it. How could she walk away from what they had?

"Your messages are on your desk," Ann said, breaking into his thoughts.

"Thank you." He entered his office, closed the door and then took a seat behind his desk. He robotically sifted through the pink message slips without focusing on them and finally shoved them aside and reached for the phone.

No calls at work. The relationship rule stilled his hand.

What if he wasn't ready to let Aubrey go?

What if he still needed her?

Needed her?

Yes, needed her.

He parked his elbows on his desk and rested his head in his hands. What now? Seeing Aubrey openly would cause problems for both of them. But she didn't like her job. Maybe he could convince her to quit. Patrick would never give her a job here, but there were other publishers in Manhattan—publishers Patrick didn't despise.

Liam's office door flew open. Patrick stormed in without bothering to knock. "How dare you consort with the enemy's daughter."

And the battle began. Resigned, Liam sat back in his chair.

"Holt Enterprises isn't the enemy. It's the competition. One of many publishers in the magazine market."

"Holt isn't like our other competitors. He uses underhanded tactics to get what he wants. What makes you so sure that Aubrey Holt isn't pumping you for information?"

"Because we don't discuss business." Other than in the most general sense of work frustrations. He hadn't told her about Patrick's insane method of choosing a successor. But he'd come close a few times. He needed to discuss the chaos with someone. Someone not caught up in the rivalry tearing EPH apart.

"Not good enough. End it," his grandfather ordered.

Maybe he should, but he couldn't. Not yet. Not when he still ached for her and she occupied his thoughts 24/7.

During the weekend in Colorado the story of how his grandfather had bullied Aunt Fin into giving up her baby twenty-three years ago had been repeated numerous times for Travis's guests. Fin had spoken openly of the pain, regret and anger that had followed—anger that even now strained her relationship with her parents, Maeve and Patrick.

Patrick wasn't always right. He wasn't right now.

"Whether or not I continue to see Aubrey is none of your business."

"I'm making it mine. You work for me and what you do reflects on EPH. End it with Holt's daughter or else—"

Liam rose sharply and leaned forward, bracing his arms on his desk. "Patrick, do you really want to issue that ultimatum? Because at this moment, after the year of hell you've put us—the company and the family—through, you have no guarantee that I won't walk."

The blue eyes so similar to the ones Liam saw in the mirror each morning hardened and then filled with something else. Resignation? Liam wasn't sure. "Then I suggest you take some time off until you know where your loyalties lie."

Liam's stomach clenched. "Are you ordering me out of the office?"

"Until you're ready to end your association with Aubrey Holt I don't want you in this building."

So this was it. Time to choose between family duty and his own happiness. It should have been an easy decision. But it wasn't. In fact, last night he'd intended to tell Aubrey goodbye, but he hadn't been able to say the words or let her go. For the first time Liam wanted to be selfish and put his needs above the family's, above EPH's. And for the first time, he just might.

"You don't trust me to keep my business and personal life separate?"

Patrick's mouth flattened. "It's not a risk I'm willing to take."

"Fine. I'm out of here." But he wasn't leaving without saying what had been eating at him since January. "You might want to keep in mind that *you* are the one who betrayed me, Patrick. You used what I told you in confidence about members of this family to pit them against each other with your idiotic challenge. You are solely responsible for the self-destruction of EPH."

"I'm busy, Aubrey. What is it that can't wait?" Matthew Holt asked without looking up from papers in front of him.

Aubrey stood in front of his desk, knotting her fingers, battling nerves and bracing herself for the worst. She'd decided confronting her father immediately would be better than the torture of worrying he'd uncover her secret and attack her unexpectedly.

"I've been seeing Liam Elliott."

His expression darkened and he abandoned his work. She had his full attention now. "You've what?"

"I've been dating Liam Elliott. I wanted to tell you before you heard it from someone else."

"Stop seeing him."

Very likely a moot point, but not her father's decision to make. "I'm twenty-nine, too old for you to choose my boyfriends, Dad. I'll decide when and if to end a relationship."

His steely-eyed stare had caused her capitulation too many times to count, but not this time. Aubrey held his gaze, refusing to concede.

"Are you sleeping with him?"

She recoiled from the invasive question. Her father had never been one to offer personal advice. That had fallen to Jane, his personal assistant. But the fire in her cheeks had probably already given him his answer. "Yes."

"I asked you to get information out of him, not screw him. Is that what you're doing? Using pillow talk to get what you need?"

It would be so easy to lie, to tell him what he wanted to hear and maybe, just maybe, see respect in his eyes for once. But she didn't condone her father's methods and she wouldn't pretend she did. "Liam and I don't discuss work, and I would never use or deceive him that way."

He rocked back in his chair and studied her through narrowed eyes. "You're in love with him."

The comment—more of an accusation, really—startled her because once again, it wasn't a territory father and daughter had ever covered.

"Yes." For now. But who knew how long this heady feeling would last?

He tapped his pen on his desk for twenty-two agonizing beats. Aubrey knew because she counted—anything to keep her mind off her churning stomach.

"I want you to be happy, Aubrey, and if Elliott makes you happy…" He shrugged. "But if any confidential information leaks from Holt Enterprises and I even suspect it came from you, then you will be fired. Is that clear?"

"Yes, sir." What was clear was that her father would put business before his daughter. No surprise there.

"What have you found out about the EPH situation?"

Liam had referred to "Patrick's stupid competition" on more than one occasion, but she'd share neither the sales department report nor anything else that could hurt Liam with her father. "Nothing."

"Then start digging." He dismissed her by turning back to his paperwork. Discussion over.

Telling him she wouldn't be his spy would be a waste of breath. Besides, she'd probably never see Liam again. She'd ended the relationship by leaving his keys behind, and they'd promised no further contact if either one of them walked away.

Walking out of his apartment this morning had been one of the hardest things she'd ever done. She assured herself the ache in her chest was temporary. Her mother had always recovered from her broken hearts and Aubrey would too, eventually. But it certainly didn't feel like it at the moment. At the moment it felt as if someone had extinguished the sun.

She returned to her office. A courier stood in front of Linda's desk. "There she is," her administrative assistant said. "Aubrey, he has a package for you that only you can sign for."

Aubrey signed the electronic box and accepted the flat envelope. Curious, she checked the return address.

Ernie's Pub. Liam's favorite lunch spot.

Her stomach dropped and her heart slammed against her ribs. "Thank you."

She hustled into her office, shut the door and ripped open the envelope. Inside she found an airline ticket with a small piece of notepaper clipped on top.

"Napa Valley's calling. Join me? L." She brushed her trembling fingers over Liam's bold handwriting. He hadn't followed their relationship rules, either.

Adrenaline raced through her veins, flushing her skin and shortening her breath. She collapsed into her chair and pressed her hand to her chest while she examined the ticket more closely. First class to San Francisco, departing at nine tomorrow morning.

Tomorrow.

A wise woman would courier the ticket right back to Liam Elliott with a "Thanks, but no thanks" note and let this temporary fascination with him fade. She should walk away before sustaining further—and possibly permanent—damage to her heart. They didn't—*couldn't*—have a future together. The sooner she quit feeding the habit of seeing him, the sooner her craving for him would fade.

Obviously, graduating magna cum laude wasn't a true reflection of intelligence because Aubrey reached for the intercom button.

"Linda, clear my calendar for the next two weeks. I'm taking some personal time, and I'm not sure how long I'll be gone."

Eight

He was about to give up when he spotted her. Exhilaration flooded Liam as he watched Aubrey cut a path through the tourists and business travelers in the busy terminal. Long, lean, chic and, he'd discovered to his delight, every bit as flexible as she'd promised at their first meeting, Aubrey Holt called all of his senses to attention.

Her hair swirled around her shoulders as she turned her head, scanning the area around the gate, and then her violet gaze collided with his, winding him like a blow to the solar plexus. Her steps faltered and then she continued toward him.

Alarm bells clanged in his subconscious as he rose. He shouldn't be this happy to see her.

Was he falling for her? Falling for his forbidden lover?

Impossible. He knew the relationship was temporary.

But why else would you be stupid enough to risk alien-

ating Patrick, the one man you've spent your entire life trying to please?

Liam stifled his intrusive conscience and met Aubrey at the end of the line in front of the check-in counter. He tightened his grip on his laptop case when what he really wanted to do was grab Aubrey, pull her close and hold her. The scent of summer roses drifted to him. "I'm glad you came."

A tentative smile trembled on her lips. "What made you send the ticket?"

"I wasn't ready to say goodbye. And despite the way you sneaked out, I don't think you are, either."

The tip of her tongue peeked out to dampen her bottom lip. "No. No, I'm not ready. But you broke a rule."

He gave in then to the overwhelming need to touch her, stroking his knuckles across her satiny cheek. He loved the way her pupils expanded and her breath hitched. "I'm trying to be flexible. Like someone else I know."

Laughter sparkled in her eyes, but the airline employee asking for Aubrey's ticket and ID prevented any reply.

"We'll be boarding first class in about twenty minutes," the hostess promised. "Have a good flight."

"Thank you," they said in unison.

He led Aubrey to a seat away from the crowd.

"This trip seems a bit spur of the moment," she offered, filling the silence when he couldn't find words.

How much should he tell her? Should he confess that this trip was a final attempt to get her out of his system? "Patrick kicked me out of EPH until I get my priorities straight."

Sympathy filled her eyes. "I'm sorry."

He covered her hand on the armrest between them, threading his fingers between hers. "Don't be. This isn't your fault. We both knew the risks when we continued seeing each other."

"My father wasn't overjoyed to hear the news, either."

He squeezed her hand. "I decided to take the time to see Napa Valley. I always wanted to go, but work has always seemed more important."

"Where are we staying?"

He shook his head, his mouth twisting wryly. She couldn't possibly know how out of character this trip was for him. He never took off without a firm agenda. "Good question. I made the airline reservations, but I didn't book a hotel. For once in my life I wanted to go with the flow, follow wherever curiosity led me and stop any place that looks interesting. We'll rent a car and drive around. I'd like to tour several wineries, but other than that…" He shrugged. "I'm open to suggestion."

"We could always stay at my grandparents' place. Since our relationship is out in the open we don't have to worry about the household staff reporting back to my father, and the property is centrally located and convenient to almost everything in the valley."

"If the hotels are full I may take you up on that." Wouldn't Patrick love to hear that not only was Liam sleeping with the enemy, he was housed under his roof?

"Does your family know where you're going?"

He hadn't told anyone. Not even Cade. "No. They can reach me by cell phone or e-mail if they need me, but I needed this time for me—for us—before I return to EPH and do what's expected of me."

If he hadn't been looking directly at her, he would have missed her flinch. He hated hurting her, but Aubrey needed to understand that this week would be their last. When it ended he'd go back to his life, his job, his family. His duty.

She smiled, but it did nothing to alleviate the sadness in her eyes. "Then I guess we'd better make the most of our final days together."

* * *

"Ready to admit defeat?" Aubrey asked after the fourth hotel turned them away. Liam had also tried three bed-and-breakfast inns. "It's the tail end of the grape harvest season, Liam, and everything is booked."

"Defeat's not in my vocabulary," he replied as he pulled the car back onto the highway. "How about dinner?"

"Okay. I know a good place." Wind from the open top teased Aubrey's hair, blowing away some of her tiredness. She twisted in the passenger seat of the convertible Liam had rented and studied him. Stubble covered his chin with dark golden spikes, and tiredness dragged his clean-cut features. She'd bet he hadn't slept well after Patrick Elliott kicked him out of the office. Add in an early wake-up and a seven-hour cross-country flight and Liam must be exhausted. She certainly was. An early dinner and bed appealed.

"My grandparents' house is only a few miles down the road. If you're not comfortable staying there for our entire vacation, we can move as soon as we find a hotel room."

Liam shook his head, but kept his eyes on the Route 29 traffic. "I'm supposed to be giving you a romantic vacation, not mooching off your family."

"Oh, I plan to make you pay," she teased him in as sultry a voice as she could manage after a night with too little sleep and a day of too much coffee.

His head briefly swung her way, lingering only long enough for her to glimpse the sexual spark lighting his eyes. "Oh, yeah? How?"

Bittersweet warmth invaded her. This was it. The end. Soon Liam would return to the Elliott fold and she'd be nothing more than a memory. He couldn't possibly know how much hearing his plan had hurt and she'd make sure he never did. She intended to make this a vacation he would never forget, and she hoped that one day soon she'd get past the pain of losing him.

"You'll have to wait and see, but trust me, it involves a lot of sexy lingerie. Turn left here."

The way Liam looked at her when she wore the sinful pieces of satin and lace made her feel womanly and desirable, not flat chested and too tall, so she'd packed accordingly. After this trip she'd probably never wear any of the expensive underwear again. She wouldn't be able to handle the memories attached. She curbed her maudlin thoughts. "I guess you know Napa Valley is the richest agricultural land in the country?"

"Yes, but being here..." He surveyed the surrounding acreage, the neat rows of vines and inhaled deeply. "Seeing the vineyards stretching on either side of the road beats the hell out of reading about it, and you can't smell this in a book."

She laid a hand on his thigh. "You should have come sooner."

"Probably, but I'm glad to be here with you." His fingers laced through hers. How could anything temporary feel this good? She banked the feeling of contentment so that she could pull it out later—after Liam was gone.

"Does anyone in your family know about your interest in winemaking?" They'd left the main highway and heavy traffic behind. She loved the winding back roads, the slower pace.

"Everybody knows I'm interested in wine, but only Patrick has paid any attention to my library and knows my interest goes beyond buying a good-tasting vintage."

"Turn right here. There's a small Italian restaurant ahead. We can eat in or get takeout. Why Patrick? Why not your parents or your brothers or sister?" He'd told her about his family, describing each member so well that Aubrey felt as if she'd already met them. But she wouldn't ever meet them.

"Until Mom's illness Dad was a workaholic. I spent more time with my grandfather than my father. Patrick showed me the ropes of the business. He was the one I went to when I had questions about work, about life."

"So you're close?"

"I thought we were. Now I'm not so sure. You were right about the rumor that he's getting ready to retire. His method for choosing his replacement is—" He flattened his lips and his face filled with frustration. "I don't understand what he's doing and he refuses to explain, but his plan is causing problems at EPH."

"I'm sorry." She didn't want details, because if she didn't know anything then she couldn't feel guilty about not sharing with her father. She hated being torn between the two men she cared most about. "Here's the restaurant."

The stucco building reflected the Spanish-style architecture prevalent in the area. Stucco walls the color of French-vanilla ice cream supported a red clay tile roof. Rounded archways led through an interior courtyard to the restaurant entrance. She didn't come to Napa Valley often, but whenever she did she always stopped here. "It's early and the parking lot isn't crowded. We should be able to get a table if you want to eat here and sample some local wine."

"Sounds good." He climbed from the car, circled it and helped her alight. She clung to his hand and savored the shimmer of awareness skipping up from their parallel palms to settle low in her torso.

"Tomorrow we'll check into visiting the wineries you mentioned." He released her hand to open the door and instantly, she missed the closeness, but then his palm spread over the small of her back. His warmth penetrated her clothing and her skin tingled. Would the day come when his touch didn't affect her as strongly? If she followed her mother's example, Liam would lose impact over time.

He nodded. “Louret and Ashton wineries combined at the beginning of this year to form Kindred Estate Vineyards. I’d like to tour both estates. Louret was a boutique winery that specialized in quality instead of quantity. Ashton produced good wine but in larger quantities. I’m curious to see how the two halves merged into a new whole and if I can still get a case of my favorite Louret Pinot Noir.”

“I checked into Louret after you mentioned it the other night because the name sounded familiar. One of our cooking magazines did a story a couple of months ago on Mason Sheppard, their youngest winemaker. I’ll call first thing in the morning and see if I can pull some strings to get you a private tour.” She turned in his arms and flattened her hands over his chest. “I know you said you wanted to go with the flow, but I’d like to show you some of my favorite parts of the valley. Liam, will you trust me to show you a good time while you’re here?”

His eyes glittered with humor but also sensual heat, and suddenly her appetite for food faded and her hunger for Liam increased. “Why do you think I brought you?”

“I meant out of bed as well as in.”

“Without a doubt, I trust you, Aubrey.”

She touched his cheek, stroking her fingertips over his raspy evening beard and then the softness of his lips. “There are so many things here in the valley that I’d like to share with you.”

“I’m all yours, sweetheart.”

Oh, how she wished that were true.

The irony of ending the most passionate interlude of her life in the place Aubrey had secretly fantasized about turning into a romantic couples retreat didn’t escape her.

“Here we are. Hill Crest House.”

Even before she climbed from the car the warmth and the love she'd found here as a child radiated from the two-story colonial's redbrick walls to warm and welcome her. The setting sun cast long shadows over the formal landscaping in front of the house. Her grandfather had insisted on the formality, but Aubrey's favorite place was the rambling garden in the backyard, where her grandmother's love of flowers provided one surprise after the other. As a child Aubrey had spent many hours digging in the dirt alongside Gram, planting flowers, herbs and even a few vegetables.

"Not exactly a grandma's cottage," Liam said beside her.

"No. There are eight bedrooms, each with a private bath, but the house still feels cozy to me, if that makes any sense. I haven't visited in…eighteen months. Time slipped away."

An evening breeze danced over her skin, blowing her hair into her eyes. Liam brushed the strands back with his finger. "You love it here. I can see the tension draining from you."

"Ah, an observant man. No, wait. Isn't that an oxymoron?"

He punished her teasing sarcasm with a quick, hard kiss that tripped her heart. "I'm so observant I noticed lights on in the house."

"The staff would have turned them on before they left at five. Even though the place is only occupied for a few weeks of the year, Daddy keeps a staff year round just in case he decides to fly some associates out."

"Did you notify the staff of our arrival?"

She flashed him an "oh please" look. "Since it took me until halfway through dinner to convince you to accept my hospitality, no. But I'll leave a note in the kitchen so they won't have the local law enforcement officers roust us out of bed in the morning."

"I'll get our bags." Liam extracted their suitcases from

the trunk. Aubrey let him carry the heavier luggage, but grabbed his laptop case and led the way up the brick stairs between the fat, round white columns and onto the covered front porch.

She unlocked the door and stepped inside. *Home.* No, not home. Just her favorite vacation spot. She opened a hinged door concealed by a small painting to access and disarm the alarm system. Liam stopped so close behind her she could feel his heat, inhale his scent even in the vast two-story foyer. She glanced at him over her shoulder and caught a glimpse of the exhaustion on his face before he quickly masked it.

"How about the nickel tour and then we'll take a quick soak in the hot tub before crashing? I know it's early here, but New York time is catching up with me."

"Sounds good."

She indicated the inverted Y-shaped staircase. "Upstairs first. Gram dedicated each suite to one of her favorite plants."

The two branches of stairs joined midair and led to a bridge that connected the east and west bedroom wings of the house. If she faced the front side of the house she overlooked the foyer. The back side of the bridge overlooked the two-story great room below with its massive brick fireplace.

"You can leave the bags here." She indicated the left side of the walkway. "To the right we have the daffodil suite, the wisteria suite and the fern suite."

She indicated each door as they passed. Liam, typical of a man, barely glanced inside. Home decor obviously wasn't his thing. "We also have an elevator and the back stairs on this side of the house."

"An elevator?" The sexy timber of his voice sent a tingle of awareness down her spine.

"Yes."

Mischief sparkled in his eyes. "Christened it yet?"

She struggled to catch her breath as memories pulsed through her. "No."

"Want to?"

Her skin flushed hot all over. "Yes, but not tonight."

"I take it this wasn't a vacation home?" he asked as she backtracked to the opposite side of the house.

"No. My grandparents were older and they'd given up on having children when my dad, a late-in-life surprise baby, arrived. As soon as he was old enough to take over Holt Enterprises my grandparents retired here and left my father in charge."

"They moved halfway across the country and left him to sink or swim in the shark-infested waters of the magazine publishing business?"

"Yes. My grandfather believed experience was the best teacher of all. He always claimed you learned more from failure than success."

"Tough guy."

"Great guy. He taught me that failure wasn't something to fear." The words stalled in Aubrey's brain, a forgotten lesson recalled. She'd been so caught up in trying to please her father since being foisted upon him that she'd forgotten the lessons of her youth.

She shoved the thought back in its hiding place for later examination, retrieved Liam's computer bag from where she'd left it at the top of the stairs and indicated he follow. "This side of the house contains the mint suite, the grape suite and my room, the rose suite."

She led the way into her room and set his computer on the dresser.

"Roses are your favorite flower." It was a statement, not a question.

"Yes. How did you guess?"

He came up behind her, circled her waist with his hands and pulled her against him. She leaned into his warmth, and when he touched his lips to the juncture of her neck and shoulder, she shivered. "Because you always smell like roses."

Aroused despite her long day and restless night, Aubrey turned in his arms, but the pallor of Liam's skin cooled her ardor. She lightly touched her lips to his and then drew back. "Get naked and grab a towel. I'll show you the greenhouse and hot tub. Bathroom's that way."

Liam rolled over in bed, reaching for Aubrey. He found cool sheets instead. Déjà vu. And not a pleasant one, either.

He flopped back on his pillow, surprised at the glitch in his pulse, and he realized his reaction—overreaction—to Aubrey's absence didn't bode well for his plan to say goodbye at the end of the week. His ears picked up the murmur of her voice through the open bedroom door. She was talking to someone somewhere in this huge colonial house. Relief loosened his knotted muscles.

Her voice drew nearer. "Thank you, Mason. That's great. We'll see you tomorrow at eight. Bye."

She walked through the bedroom door with a cordless phone in her hand and the skirt of her burgundy dress swirling around her legs. "Good, you're awake, sleepyhead."

"You're already dressed." He'd awakened with his usual hard-on. Her soft smile and mile-long legs instantly made him harder. He patted the bed and she glided forward and perched on the edge of the mattress.

"My body clock's still on New York time. I have plans for you today." She leaned down and gently nuzzled his lips. "Last night was nice."

Last night after a quick tour of the downstairs and a long

soak in the hot tub they'd fallen into bed exhausted and cuddled until falling asleep. A first for him. He'd never spent the night just holding a woman and surprisingly he'd liked it. Around daybreak Aubrey had awakened him with tender strokes along his spine. He'd rolled over and she'd kissed him softly, which had segued into lazy, slow sex. The gentleness of their lovemaking had blindsided him.

How can you live without that?

Guess you'll find out.

He combed his fingers through her silky hair. "Remind me how nice."

She laughed and pulled away, but a blush painted her cheeks. "Later. Get up and get dressed. I've made reservations for us on the Wine Train. It's a totally touristy thing to do, but fun. We'll begin with a wine tasting at the depot and then lunch during a slow train ride north past twenty-six wineries. In Yountville we'll disembark for a tour of a winery that produces sparkling wine, and then we'll have dessert on the return trip south. Tomorrow you'll get a personally guided tour of both the Louret and Ashton estates from Mason Sheppard. And then on Friday, I'm taking you on a tour of the local brandy distillery. I've never been there, but I've heard you can get drunk from breathing the air."

Aubrey often had that effect on him. Like now, for instance. He threw back the covers, enjoying her gasp at the sight of his erection. "You've been busy. Are you sure we don't have a few minutes?"

She dampened her lips with a slow sweep of her pink tongue and flexed her fingers as if contemplating touching him, tasting him. The need to have those long, slender fingers and those sweet lips on him right now nearly strangled him. But she stepped out of reach before he could drag her deeper into the bed.

"We have to check in by ten-thirty, Liam. Get moving. Breakfast is waiting downstairs."

"Later, then." He rose, cupped her nape and then he kissed her thoroughly, relishing the softness of her lips and the slickness of her tongue. She tasted of cinnamon rolls and coffee. When he lifted his head a flush colored her cheeks, her lips were damp and his heart thumped violently. "Good morning."

Waking up to Aubrey felt good. Too good. But the alarm bells that should have been clanging in his subconscious were suspiciously silent.

Was he in love? Couldn't be. He'd been in love twice in college and both times had been miserable, tense and angst-ridden affairs. He hadn't been able to eat, sleep or study. While Aubrey made him harder than stone on a regular basis, she was also comfortable, exciting and yet restful. He enjoyed being with her, and he didn't have to tiptoe around overly sensitive feelings.

Nah, this wasn't love. It was just a damned good time. Too bad it couldn't last.

"You've done this before?" Liam swiveled his seat on the lounge car of the Wine Train to face Aubrey's.

The only thing better than enjoying her favorite part of California was sharing it with Liam. "Dozens of times. My grandmother took me on my first train ride up the valley when I was six or seven. I try to ride each time I return to Napa, which isn't nearly often enough."

"Then you've seen all this before." His sweeping gesture encompassed the exquisite mahogany paneling, the crystal chandeliers overhead and the vineyards outside the train's windows.

"Not through your eyes. Seeing you soak up every detail of the vintage rail cars and the valley reminds me of a child on Christmas morning. Your enthusiasm is contagious."

He took her hand in his. "Having you around has been an amazing gift."

There he went again, reminding her that this idyllic period would end. Despite the depressing reminder, she realized she hadn't seen Liam this relaxed or happy back in New York. "Have you ever considered leaving EPH?"

His smile vanished. "No."

"Does anyone in your family work outside the company?"

"My cousin Bryan never worked for EPH and several of my relatives, including my sister, have left the company this year." His voice had hardened. "Patrick's selection process is driving them away, and he's too damned stubborn to admit it."

She hated spoiling his mood, and hearing the details of EPH left her conflicted. While she'd like to understand his problems and perhaps help him solve them, knowing meant piling on guilt for not relaying the very information her father had requested.

"Liam, maybe you should consider leaving, too. Estates out here aren't easy to come by because Hollywood types snatch them up in a hurry, but maybe you could find one and try your hand at winemaking. There are more than two hundred wineries in Napa Valley and most of them are privately owned."

"I can't leave EPH."

"Can't or won't?"

"Either. Both. Take your pick."

That looked like yearning in his eyes, but Aubrey decided not to push. When and if Liam was ready to pursue his dream, he'd do so voluntarily. She changed the subject. "I love the area and I have a lot of happy memories of spending time with my grandmother at Hill Crest. My father leases the acreage surrounding the house to another vineyard, so there's always some activity on the property, but the place is peaceful. It's off the main roads, but not so far off that no one can find it. When things get really bad at work, I dream about turning the estate into a bed-and-breakfast."

She bit her lip, not believing she'd just confessed her deepest secret, one she'd not shared with anyone. Liam wasn't the only one who kept secrets from his friends and family.

"Why don't you?" he asked quietly.

"Same old, same old. I owe my father."

"When will that debt be paid?"

His question hit too close to home. Aubrey had begun to believe that no matter what she did it would never be enough for her father. "When will yours? If you're unhappy at EPH, then maybe you should move on."

"Back at you."

"I can't." She hesitated. What did she have to lose by telling the truth? "My father never wanted a daughter. Not before he and my mother divorced and certainly not afterward. When he found out about the incident with my stepfather, I heard him ask his assistant what he was supposed to do with a teenage girl. And then he said, 'If she'd been the son I needed, this wouldn't be a problem.'"

Liam swore, low and succinctly. "So you've what? Been trying to be the son he wanted?"

"I've been trying to be the savvy executive he thinks a son would have been." A sad smile quivered on her lips. "We're a sorry pair, aren't we? Unhappy where we are, but unwilling to make the sacrifices to change our lot."

"Change is..." He shrugged and turned back to the window to study a palatial home as the train passed.

"Scary," she finished for him.

"Risky and selfish. There are too many people to disappoint, including myself."

Liam summed up her feelings well. She didn't want to disappoint her father and she didn't want to disappoint herself by quitting before she proved her worthiness to him.

She wasn't the son he'd wanted. So what? But she was damned good at her job. And she wanted him to notice. Just once. And then she could move on.

Nine

"It's beautiful," Aubrey said from the passenger seat.

Liam, drawn by the wistful tone of her voice, glanced at her as he guided the car down the long driveway. He didn't know whether her comment referred to The Vines, the main house at Louret Vineyards, the steeply roofed two-story winery to the west of the residence or the property as a whole.

"Absolutely breathtaking." He meant her, not the buildings or the land. Would he ever tire of looking at Aubrey, of making love to her, of just plain being with her? What if he didn't? How could he return home and pretend she didn't live just around the corner? But if he didn't, he'd be out of a job.

After yesterday's train ride she'd taken him to another out-of-the-way restaurant for dinner and then surprised him with a charter plane flight over Napa Valley. The pilot had flown the length of the wine country and then circled back over the California coast and the Point Reyes National Seashore on the return trip. Watching the sunset over the Pacific had been spectacular. It was the first time he'd seen the sunset with no skyscrapers to block the view, and he'd watched until the big orange ball sank into the deep blue ocean.

Liam parked the car and, following the signs for the tasting room and store, guided Aubrey across the winery's large porch. He stepped inside and stopped. Like a kid in a candy shop he scanned the bottles lining the walls, searching for his favorites or something new to try.

"May I help you?" asked a woman about Aubrey's height, build and coloring asked from behind a long, high counter. And then she stepped from behind the wine-tasting bar, revealing a heavily pregnant belly.

What would Aubrey look like pregnant? The shocking thought locked Liam's jaws and seized his lungs.

Where had that come from?

Aubrey shot a curious glance his way when he remained mute and then she moved forward, extending her hand. "Hello. I'm Aubrey Holt and this is Liam Elliott. Mason Sheppard is expecting us."

"I'm Jillian Ashton-Bennedict. It's nice to meet you. Your magazine's story on Mason's return to the U.S. was great."

"I'll be sure to pass your compliment on to the writer."

"I'll assist you with the wine tasting after you've finished the Louret half of your tour, because I'm guessing you're not interested in samples at eight in the morning." Her green eyes sparkled with laughter.

Liam found his voice. "No, but we will be later. I have a few Louret favorites, and I'd prefer not to leave without ordering a case or two. Thanks for working us in before your regular tour hours."

"No problem. I'll be happy to help you with your selections when you're ready. Let me call Mason and tell him you're here. He and Darby arrived a few minutes ago." She went behind the counter to use the phone.

He led Aubrey a few yards away to the racks of chardonnay on the wall. "Who's Darby?"

"Darby Quinn, former child actress and now Mason Sheppard's wife. Her story made headlines earlier this year when she and Mason moved back to the States from France."

"I vaguely remember something about that. I'm not into the Hollywood scene."

"I know. You're into sports, finance and wine." Her fingers squeezed his, but her tender smile reached far deeper inside him.

"You think we have it bad in the family lottery. Years ago Darby's mother wrote a tell-all book that painted Darby as a bitch-slash-prima-donna and ruined her acting career. Darby tried to tell the press her side of the story, but no one believed her, especially with her own mother calling her a liar. Eventually, Darby was forced into hiding. And then she literally ran into Mason on a road here in Napa, and she didn't want to hide anymore. She went back to France with him, and while Mason finished his enology studies, they worked together to convince other child stars to come forward and admit that their former manager—who also happened to be Darby's wicked stepfather and former manager—had abused them, too.

"Getting the facts out in the open was a vindication of sorts since Darby had been telling the truth all along. Those she trusted had betrayed her, but the truth set her free by allowing her to return to the States with Mason and to live openly as his wife without the press crucifying her at every turn. Now everyone is speculating about whether she'll return to acting."

Aubrey was a romantic, Liam realized. She had stars in her eyes as she told her fairy tale of a knight coming to a maiden's rescue. He wished he could be Aubrey's knight and rescue her from the job she hated and a father who didn't love her enough.

A big blond guy in jeans and a chambray shirt and a petite blond woman in a vintage-style dress, also noticeably pregnant, came toward them. "Welcome. I'm Mason Sheppard and this is my wife, Darby. Aubrey tells me you're into winemaking."

Liam offered his hand. "Liam Elliott and this is Aubrey Holt. I've read everything I can get my hands on about enology, but I've never tried it."

"Are you thinking of relocating and starting a winery in Napa?" Mason asked.

Darby smiled. "The valley's a great place for new beginnings. I started over here and look what I found."

Merry blue eyes indicated the man at her side and her hand patted her rounded belly. Mason's hand covered hers and the loving look the two exchanged brought a lump to Liam's throat.

Starting over in Napa appealed to him more than it should have. Possibly when he retired… But that day seemed far off. Too far. "One of these days."

With a sweep of his hand Mason indicated the door through which he'd entered. "Let's get started. When we finish here we'll head over to Ashton Estates for a tour of their facility. We've merged Louret and Ashton in many ways under the Kindred Estates umbrella, but because of brand recognition we still carry our old trademarks as well as the new one, and we still have our own production facilities, because frankly we need both to keep up with demand. Aubrey warned me not to hold back on the technical side of the process because she says you're up to it, so if I go too fast or if you have questions, stop me."

Surprised, Liam's gaze found Aubrey's. She'd made sure he received more than the generic spiel offered to tourists. She looked out for him, giving him more than he would have dared hope for. Here and in New York. In bed and out.

Aubrey Holt was perfect for him in so many ways.

He didn't want to let her go.

Ever.

But what choice did he have?

A crushing sensation hit him square in the chest, as if a full wine cask had fallen on him. Liam couldn't breathe, couldn't move, couldn't speak as realization dawned.

He'd fallen in love with the enemy's daughter.

Liam hadn't looked at or touched Aubrey since their tour began almost four hours ago. The absolute silence between them sent a frisson down Aubrey's spine. And the distance. She nibbled her bottom lip in confusion. They stood only a foot apart on the Ashton winery patio, but she might as well have been back in New York.

A tall, dark haired man cradling an infant in a frilly pink romper separated himself from the group gathering on the far side of the patio. Judging by the balloons, flowers and piled gifts Aubrey suspected somebody must be celebrating a birthday.

Mason extended a hand to the newcomer. "Liam and Aubrey, meet my brother-in-law Jared Maxwell. He's married to my half sister, Mercedes, and today is Mercedes's birthday. They're setting up for a surprise party."

Darby took the baby from Jared and snuggled her. "And this cutie pie princess is Chloe. When Jared's not playing Mr. Mom, he runs a string of bed-and-breakfasts in the valley. I take it you have some news of your wife's arrival?" she asked without taking her gaze off the baby.

"Mercedes and Jillian are on their way," Jared replied, keeping a possessive eye on his daughter.

His obvious attachment to the baby gave Aubrey a case of the warm fuzzies. She couldn't recall her father ever looking at her that way, as if his world revolved around her. She swallowed the lump in her throat. "The winery grounds are a perfect setting for a party."

"You should see it on the weekends. The Ashton Estate Winery is a very popular wedding sight." Darby's gaze bounced from Aubrey to Liam and back again, as if she were gauging their interest in a wedding on the grounds. Aubrey's cheeks burned and she looked away.

Darby unexpectedly placed the baby in Aubrey's arms. Startled, Aubrey adjusted her grip. She'd held her friend's children years ago, but there were some things you never forgot, like the warmth of an infant squirming closer, the fresh baby scent or the way a gummy smile and trusting blue eyes could melt your heart. "She's beautiful. How old?"

"Six months," Jared said in a proud voice. His tanned finger trailed across Chloe's downy soft cheek. "And she looks just like her mother."

"If you'll notice, there are a lot of pregnant women and new babies around," Darby said in a teasing tone. "So don't drink the water if a baby's not in your plans."

A tight knot formed in Aubrey's throat. She'd never have Liam's baby. The yearning to hold a child created by their feelings for each other swelled inside her with surprising swiftness.

"I guess I'll stick with the wine, then," she said to fill the awkward silence and then returned the baby to her father.

Liam shifted on his feet beside her. "We should go and let you get on with your party. Mason, Darby, thank you for your time, and thank Jillian for setting up the shipments for me."

Mason shook Liam's hand. "You're welcome, but frankly,

Liam, I enjoyed your visit. Your questions challenged me. You definitely know your stuff. If you ever decide to relocate and set up shop, give me a call. And, Aubrey, if you ever decide to pursue your dream of opening up a B&B, then Jared's the one to guide you. Enjoy the rest of your vacation."

Surprised, Aubrey glanced at Liam. He must have said something to Mason during the tour. "I'll keep that in mind. Thanks. Nice meeting you all."

Aubrey almost had to jog to keep up with Liam on the way back to the rental car. They drove in silence for several miles, and her nerves stretched tighter with each passing moment until finally she couldn't stand it any longer. "Liam, is something wrong?"

He kept his gaze fixed on the road in front of them. "It's a lot to take in."

She couldn't believe the winery information had overloaded him. Aubrey sifted back through the memories of the morning, trying to recall something she or anyone else could have said or done to upset him, and came up empty. The chasm between them had opened before Darby had made her teasing comments about babies and weddings, so that wasn't it.

"Mind if we head back to the house instead of visiting the geyser in Calistoga this afternoon?" he asked.

"Whatever you want. It's your vacation. Old Faithful will still be erupting next time you come to Napa Valley."

The drive to the house took only minutes, but it seemed like hours. The noon sun hung in a blue sky directly overhead, but it couldn't warm Aubrey's chilled skin.

Liam parked, and as they climbed the wide brick front steps, Aubrey stopped him with a hand on his arm. "Did I do something wrong?"

"No. I did." Liam raked a hand through his hair and then

looked at her. What she saw in his eyes stopped her world. "I've fallen in love with you, Aubrey."

So there they were—the words she'd always wanted to hear. Emotions jumbled wildly inside her. Practicality quickly stomped out elation. Judging by Liam's serious expression, he truly believed what he'd said. But this wasn't love. It was lust. He didn't understand the mechanics of tumbling head over heels into love and then falling right back out just as quickly.

And then the doubts crowded in. What if this wasn't one of the short-lived love affairs her mother practiced with regularity and Aubrey let Liam go? No, she had to go with what she knew. This idyllic period would end and she would survive it. Her lips quivered. Her eyes stung.

Before she could speak, Liam's jaw muscles knotted. "But what good is falling in love when a future together is impossible? Part of me wants to walk out and start over here in Napa the way Darby suggested. But I can't, Aubrey. I'm the peacemaker. It's my job to keep Patrick from tearing EPH and the Elliott family apart."

Liam lifted a hand and trailed his knuckles across her cheek. His touch reverberated all the way to her womb. "And I doubt I can convince you to quit your job since you still have things to prove to your father."

He didn't need to add that his grandfather would never accept her into the family fold if she wouldn't quit.

"No, I can't leave Holt Enterprises. Not yet. Maybe never." Her heart swelled, but a cloud of doom overshadowed her joy. She'd known the end was coming, so why did it hurt so much? She captured his hand and held it against her face.

"I love you, too, Liam. But we fell too fast. These feelings won't last. Love like this never does. It's based on physical attraction and not on anything more substantial. Flash-fires burn out as soon as they've consumed the limited fuel supply."

His eyebrows lowered. "Do you honestly believe that?"

"I've seen it happen too many times not to. My mother has fallen instantly and madly in love four times since she left my father. Each time she swore with stars and hope in her eyes that this time it was the real thing, and then a few months or a year later she'd call me. We'd meet for lunch and she'd cry all over me because it hadn't been everlasting love but only another case of lust and infatuation that hadn't last."

His jaw shifted. "And you think that's what this is?"

"I'm afraid so."

What if it's not?

Even if it wasn't, it wouldn't matter. Their duties to their families would keep them apart.

Change her mind or you'll lose her.

Liam stared into the absolute certainty in Aubrey's beautiful violet eyes and knew arguing would be a waste of time. He had to convince her that what she felt for him was more than infatuation.

Lust? There was plenty of that, but his feelings for Aubrey went deeper, and he was damned certain hers for him did too. Hindsight revealed the subtle differences between his college affairs and this. He'd been in lust not love before.

Love meant wanting to give pleasure—in bed and out—and not just take it. Love meant talking, wanting to know his partner's thoughts not just her body. He'd found unbelievable physical pleasure with Aubrey, but he'd also found peace. She thrilled him, but she also soothed him.

Love meant wanting his partner's happiness more than he wanted his own.

Love meant forever, not for however long it lasted.

Lesson one in loving started now. *Give her the time and space she needs to accept what's between them.*

"Then we'd better take advantage of the time we have," he finally replied.

Liam cupped Aubrey's face, brushing her silky hair out of the way and caressing her cheekbones with his thumbs. The pulse at the base of her throat quickened, and his heart kept pace. Her eyes darkened and her lips parted. He wanted to devour her on the front steps of Hill Crest House. Only the knowledge that the staff could see them from the windows reined him in. But a kiss wouldn't hurt. One kiss. One long, slow, seductive kiss.

He sank into the petal softness of her lips, drew in the sweetness of her breath and lost his mind in her taste and in the hot press of her slender curves as she snuggled against him. He mapped her shape with his palms, and then splayed his fingers over her belly. Seeing her face soften as she'd cradled that baby had slammed him with a need to see her holding his child, their child.

But how? How could they make this work?

Her hands mirrored his, stroking, touching. Desire hit him hard and fast, knocking his train of thought off track. Aubrey skimmed her nails beneath the waistband of his slacks and he lifted his head to suck in a sobering breath. The sooner they took this inside the better. Slow wasn't on the agenda this afternoon. He laced his fingers through hers and led her up the brick stairs to the front door.

The flush of arousal pinked her cheeks and her hands trembled as she inserted her key. The door glided noiselessly open on well-oiled hinges. As Liam bent to plant a kiss on Aubrey's nape he spotted a woman—probably a maid he hadn't met yet—disappearing down the upstairs hall toward their bedroom. Maids cleaning upstairs shifted his plans. No bed.

He ducked into the library, towing Aubrey with him, and quietly shut the door. He turned the lock and then leaned against the wood and smiled in anticipation. "What are you wearing under that sexy sundress?"

Her eyes sparkled and her low chuckle teased him like a thousand feathers sweeping over his skin. "You have a lingerie fetish, Liam."

"One you induced. That lace-up top has been making me crazy all morning. Show me what you got, sweetheart." She reached for the ribbon laces, but he brushed her hands aside. "Better yet, let me do a little exploring on my own."

Winding the ends of the laces around his index fingers, he tugged the bow free, and then grommet by grommet he loosened her bodice, revealing one inch of her breast bone at a time. At the halfway point he trailed a finger through the gap.

Aubrey gasped. "There's a zipper in the back. The laces are just for show."

He considered it, but, as much as he wanted to take her hard and fast, slow had its advantages. He wanted to show her with each touch, each kiss how much she meant to him. "Too easy."

And then he lowered his head and pressed a kiss above her neckline over her pounding heart. With his tongue he traced the path his fingers had cleared and with unsteady hands he rapidly loosened the ribbons to her waist to expand his territory.

She wasn't wearing a bra. He eased the halves of her top apart until nothing blocked his view or prevented him from taking a taut raspberry nipple into his mouth. Her fingers dug into his hair, holding him close while he worshipped one breast and then the other. He raked his hands from her waist to her knees, beneath her skirt and back up her thighs until he encountered her smooth bottom. Bare. He explored further, finding a thin strip between her buttocks. Another thong.

Damn. His groin throbbed. Aubrey's sexy underwear would give him a heart attack one of these days. But it'd be worth it.

Hunger screamed through his veins like Fourth of July fireworks as he eased the satin scrap down her legs. She braced her hands on his shoulders and stepped out of the minuscule piece.

Slow down.

He leaned back to look at her, lifting the lingerie to his cheek. "Soft, but not as soft as your skin."

Her nipples were hard and damp, her face flushed and her breathing was as ragged as his. "Before Cade interrupted us at my place, I fantasized about taking you on my desk."

Her gaze darted to the desk in front of the bay window and then back to his face. Her lips parted. "Do it."

"Not worried the gardener might look in?"

"No."

Liam rose slowly. He burrowed his hands beneath her gaping bodice to cup her breasts and thumb the rigid tips. Her eyes fluttered closed and a quiet moan slipped from her lips. He covered her mouth, sipping from her softness until he had to have a taste of her. She tasted like nothing and no one he'd ever had, a flavor uniquely Aubrey's. Addictive. Her tongue met his every stroke, every dip, swirling, tangling, lingering.

Her fingers released the buttons on his cotton shirt and then she ripped the shirttails from his pants and splayed her hands over his pectorals. Her nails combed through his wiry hair with electrifying results. He was so damned hard he hurt. He clasped her waist and pulled her close, brushing his chest over hers, pressing his arousal against her mound and rubbing until he thought the top of his head wouldn't be the only thing to erupt.

Aubrey reached between them to unbuckle and unzip his pants and then she backed toward the desk, shoved a bronze statue and the phone out of the way and hopped onto the glossy surface. She crooked a finger and he gulped. He took one step toward her and then another on unsteady legs.

He loved her. Loved this sassy, confident woman who wasn't afraid to take what she wanted. And she wanted him. The knowledge swelled his heart. He'd make this work. He'd find some way for him and Aubrey to be together.

And then her fingers snagged on the waistband of his boxers, pulling him closer until his thighs bumped the desk top. She shoved the fabric out of the way and her opposite hand curled around his rigid length.

Thinking fell off the priority list. Sensation took over. The smooth stroke of her hand. The inferno of her mouth over his and then on his neck, his collarbone, his nipple. He fumbled for the condoms he now carried in his wallet. His hands shook, but he managed to don protection before pushing her back on the desk, shoving her dress up to her waist and kneeling.

Her heat, scent and moisture filled his mouth, and her cries sounded like music to his ears. He tasted, stroked and laved her until she bowed off the desk and begged him to take her as release after release rolled over her. Even then he stalled, his goal to make her want more than just here and now, to make her want more than fast and furious and out of control. Any man could give her an orgasm. He wanted her to want him. *Him.*

"Liam, please," she whispered. "I need you."

By the time he rose, his knees quaked and Aubrey was a puddle of satisfaction on the desk top.

"Me or just this?" He positioned himself between her legs and bent over her to catch her whimpers with his mouth as he plowed into her slick, tight body. Remaining still in the hot clench of her body made him gasp.

"You. Oh, my… You, Liam. Just you." Aubrey shifted impatiently beneath him.

Her words and wiggles set him on fire. He tried to slow the piston action of his hips, to draw out her pleasure, tried to make himself last beyond her next orgasm, but her hands on his butt, her mouth sipping, nipping and biting, her body squeezing his sent him over the edge far too soon. His hoarse growl of release echoed through the room.

Their labored breaths blended, and their bare chests rose and fell in unison. When the fog cleared from his brain and his lungs no longer burned like fire, he lifted himself an inch or two. He wasn't capable of more.

He met her sexy, satisfied gaze. "I love you, Aubrey. Take as much time as you need to believe this is real. I'll be here."

Worry clouded her eyes and even though she didn't physically pull away and he remained buried to the hilt inside her, he felt the mental distance widen between them. "What if this is love and not just lust—what about our families, our jobs? How can we get around that, Liam?"

"I don't have all the answers yet, but solving problems is what I do best. We'll make this work. You have my word." He caught her chin in his hand. "And, Aubrey, I always keep my promises."

Ten

Ringing jarred Liam from a deep sleep. He blinked open gritty eyes and tried to isolate the sound.

A cell phone. His. He sank back into his pillow. Let voice mail pick up.

Aubrey lay on her stomach beside him with her arm flung over his chest. Naked. Hot. He stroked a hand down her spine and caressed her smooth bottom. Smiling, she purred and snuggled closer. His pulse kicked unevenly as images flashed in his mind of yesterday on the desk and last night on the blanket beneath an apple tree on the backside of the property. Making love with someone you wanted to spend the rest of your life with was a whole different experience.

The ringing stopped. Seconds later it intruded again. Whoever was calling wasn't going to talk to a recording. "Damn."

"You have to answer?" Aubrey mumbled as she rolled to her side, revealing a soft, flushed breast with sheet wrinkles stamped into her pale skin. Once he dealt with the caller he'd trace each crease with his tongue.

"Yes. Where the hell is it?" The last time he'd seen his phone it had been clipped to his belt. They'd undressed at the foot of the bed after returning from the garden and climbed into bed. He threw back the sheet and hunted for his pants under the comforter and spare pillows they'd knocked to the floor. He found his phone buried under her dress and his shirt and snapped it open. "Elliott."

"What in the hell have you done?" Patrick's furious voice bellowed at him.

"Good morning to you, too, Patrick." Liam scraped a hand over his bristly chin and glanced at the clock. Five. Eight, New York time. "What are you talking about?"

"You released confidential financial information to the press."

What? Someone had leaked EPH info? "Wasn't me. I'm on vacation. A vacation you insisted I take, remember?"

"These are *your* files in today's *Times,* Liam, *your* numbers. Only you and I know which magazine's profit margin has dropped."

Liam's stomach plunged as if he'd gone over the hill of a steep roller-coaster. His gaze shot to his laptop on the dresser. Something about it niggled at him.

His neck prickled a warning. "What do you mean *my* numbers?"

"To have *Pulse* publicly humiliated this way is beyond acceptable." Outrage flattened Patrick's voice into monotone. Liam could picture his grandfather talking through clenched teeth. "Do you realize the damage you've done by sharing those numbers prematurely? This is potentially disastrous for EPH as well as highly embarrassing. We needed to release the data on our terms and with the proper spin or we could lose advertising dollars and credibility."

"I didn't leak the information, Patrick."

"Then you'd better ask your lover who did."

Liam looked at Aubrey sitting up in bed and clutching the sheet to her breasts. Concern and curiosity darkened her eyes. He hit the mute button on the phone. "Did you use my laptop yesterday?"

Her brow pleated with confusion. "No. When did I have the time? Why?"

Possibilities tumbled through his mind. When indeed? Aubrey had been with him all day, even when he showered. Besides, they'd been out of the house most of the day. And then he remembered the woman he'd thought to be a member of the household staff he hadn't met heading toward their bedroom yesterday. Aubrey might not have stolen the data on his computer, but one of her father's minions had both motive and opportunity.

He unmuted the phone. "I didn't leak the information, but I'm staying at Holt's house in Napa Valley. Someone here could have accessed my laptop and stolen the file."

Beside him Aubrey gasped.

Patrick swore. "That's exactly the kind of underhanded trick that bastard would try. When you sleep in the enemy's viper pit, Liam, you open yourself up to his bite. I hope like hell your choice hasn't done irreparable damage to EPH."

His grandfather disconnected with a slam. Liam closed and slowly lowered his phone and then swore.

"What happened?"

"Your father had someone steal files off my computer."

"What?" She gaped in disbelief.

"Today's newspaper printed confidential EPH accounting

files. Files I had on my laptop. I didn't submit them and neither did anyone else at EPH."

"You think my father would do something that despicable?"

"Yes."

"How dare you!"

"Yesterday morning I angled my laptop away from the window so I could read my e-mail without the early morning light glaring on the screen. Today my computer is facing the window. If you didn't use it, then somebody else did."

Doubt clouded her eyes. "M-maybe the maid shifted it when she dusted."

"You can ask, but what you're going to discover is that your father had one of his flunkies hack into my computer, steal my file and turn it over to the *Times*. The question is whether or not you knew what he planned and kept me out of the house to facilitate the process."

She flinched. Wide-eyed and pale, she climbed from the bed, dragging the sheet with her. "I can't believe you said that. You said you loved me. And now you have the audacity to suggest I'd help my father hurt you? You can't love someone you don't trust, Liam."

He raked a hand over his face. Did he suspect Aubrey? Not really, but the doubt had been planted, spreading its roots through him like a poisonous, choking vine. Was Aubrey just one more example of his habit of choosing the wrong women?

"Has your father ever asked you about EPH?" Her gulp and the nervous flutter of her lashes as she looked away gave him the answer he needed. Tension knotted his neck and dread twisted his gut. He had a question to ask, one to which he knew damned well he didn't want to know the answer. "Did you schedule our first meeting to squeeze me for information, Aubrey?"

Her hand clenched by her side and guilt filled her expression. Pain knifed Liam from all sides. Damn, he'd been a stupid, gullible fool.

"Yes, but you didn't tell me anything, and then after what happened between us, I couldn't…" She lifted her chin. "I tried to say goodbye, Liam, but you wouldn't let me. You sent flowers and you called. And then we promised to keep our business and personal lives separate. We made rules."

As if making rules kept people from breaking them. Had Aubrey played him for a fool? Had she betrayed him the same way Patrick had, by using information Liam had shared in confidence to hurt his family? Or was she telling the truth? He needed space to find the answers, and he needed to get back to New York and start damage control—if he still had a job.

"Liam, you have to believe me. I would never deliberately hurt you."

"I'm going home."

"I understand. I'll start pack—"

"Alone."

She staggered back a step, pressing a hand to her chest. Resignation settled over her features. "Fine. Go. I told you this wouldn't last, but I expected your promise to hold for more than a few hours."

She retreated to the bathroom and closed the door. Why did the quiet click feel like a nail in his heart?

Shaking with a tangle of emotions she couldn't even begin to separate and identify, Aubrey hammered on her father's apartment door.

When he didn't open immediately, she pounded again. She knew he was at home. The doorman had verified it when she'd asked on her way up. Finally, the door opened, revealing her father in his bathrobe. She'd never known him to go to bed before midnight. It was only nine.

"Aubrey, I thought you were in California."

"I came here straight from the airport." She shouldered past him and into the den. The remnants of Chinese takeout littered the coffee table, along with two glasses. Two plates. He wasn't alone. Was the woman waiting in his bedroom? Not a road Aubrey wanted to travel. She'd suspected he had women since divorcing her mother, but she'd never been confronted with the evidence. That he had someone now when she was alone seemed like a mocking twist of fate.

If she weren't furious and a little afraid that Liam's accusations might possibly have a grain of truth to them, she'd excuse herself and talk to her father tomorrow. But she'd repeatedly replayed this morning's encounter during the seven-hour flight home, debating both sides of the situation.

Liam was wrong. He had to be. She'd get the proof and then… What? Liam didn't trust her. Didn't that say it all? Love didn't stand a chance without trust. But she had to know if Liam's doubts were well-founded or if he'd just been looking for a way to end their relationship.

"Aubrey, this isn't a good time."

"Did you have someone hack into Liam Elliott's computer and steal his files?"

Something flashed in her father's eyes, but it vanished before she could interpret it. "It's late. I have company. We can discuss this tomorr—"

His evasiveness made her shift uneasily. "Did you?"

He folded his arms and set his chin in that stubborn my-way-or-the-highway expression she'd come to know so well, and Aubrey's heart sank. She silently shrieked, No!

"I asked you to get the information and you didn't. The report you requested from the sales team was a good start, but—"

"I deleted that report."

"All files are backed up on our e-mail server. You know that.

You should have brought the report to me, Aubrey. It's your job."

Her job to betray someone who trusted her? Nausea rose in her throat. Anger, pain, betrayal and guilt whirled through her like debris in a tornado. "How could you?"

"We needed the competitive edge the information could give us. It's business, Aubrey."

"It's my life! It's the man I love." As soon as she said it she knew it was true. What she felt for Liam wasn't infatuation. Infatuation wouldn't hurt this much. She wanted to crawl in a dark hole and tend to her wounds. She wanted to strike out at her father and at herself for her part in the whole sordid disaster.

How unfair that she'd discover that she loved Liam Elliott now when it was too late.

Her father's scowl deepened. "I assigned you a job. I never intended for you to get personally involved with Elliott."

"No, you intended to get what you wanted regardless of the casualties, and as usual you bulldozed over any*thing* and any*one* in your path. This time it was me, Dad."

He lifted a shoulder as if to say, "So?"

"You know everything there is to know about running Holt Enterprises, but you don't know anything about being a father."

He flinched. "This is not about being a father. This is bus—"

"No, Dad, I'm going to say my piece and for once you're going to listen. I didn't want a new sports car every two years. I didn't want expensive jewelry or designer clothing. All I wanted was time with you to prove that I was just as good as the son you wanted but never had. All I wanted was a father who loved me and one who would say so. Just once."

She hated the telling tremor racking her body. She hated the tears streaming down her cheeks even more and angrily swiped them away. Both were signs of weakness and Matthew Holt didn't tolerate weakness.

A muscle ticked in her father's jaw and he swallowed. He opened his mouth, but Aubrey halted his words with an upraised hand.

"I can't work for someone I no longer trust, someone who would deliberately use me and hurt me in some selfish quest to become number one. I quit. I'll clean out my office this weekend, and I'll be out of my apartment as soon as possible. I refuse to be your pawn any longer." She headed for the front door before she completely broke down, but then paused, took a bracing breath and turned back.

"I want Hill Crest and I want it now. Gram's will said it would be deeded to me when I married, but thanks to your greed and your lack of scruples the only man I've ever wanted to marry will probably never speak to me again."

Her father's lips thinned, but otherwise he displayed no emotion. Did he realize the wreck he'd made of her life? Did he even care? "I'll take care of it."

Aubrey's fingers closed around the doorknob.

"Aubrey." His gruff voice stopped her. "I never thought you'd be hurt."

She swallowed the sob rising in her throat, opened the door and looked over her shoulder at her father. "No, Dad, you never thought of me at all. That's what I'm talking about."

"Liam, Aubrey Holt to see you," Ann said from his open door.

Everything in Liam flashed cold and then hot and then cold again. After the weekend he'd had butting heads with Patrick, soothing family members and working with the PR team to formulate a damage control plan, the last thing he wanted was to start his Monday off by dealing with the one crisis he hadn't faced. The one he'd deliberately blocked every waking moment. But damn, Aubrey had haunted his dreams.

"I'm busy. Tell her to make an appoint—"

"Liam," Aubrey said from behind Ann's shoulder, "please."

Damn. Double damn. If somebody took a dull knife and cut out his heart it would probably hurt less than seeing Aubrey. He clenched his molars and jerked his chin, indicating for Ann to leave them. His assistant stepped aside for Aubrey to enter and then pulled the door closed behind her.

Aubrey looked like hell, as if she hadn't had any more sleep than he'd had since he'd left her on Friday. The circles smudging the pale skin beneath her eyes were almost the same deep purple as her eyes. Her black pinstriped suit and stark white shirt didn't help.

What is she wearing under there? The question struck as swift as a rattlesnake. *No longer your business, Elliott.*

He didn't stand, didn't offer her a seat. Rude of him, but he didn't owe her any politeness. Besides, if he stood he might lose the battle against the need to take her in his arms. Aubrey was part of his past. Just one more woman on his list of poorly chosen lovers.

Their relationship was over. Finished. Done.

Damn.

He sat back in his leather desk chair and folded his arms across his chest. "What do you want, Aubrey?"

Fisting her hands by her side, she inhaled slowly, deeply, and shifted in her sensible black pumps. "I came to apologize. You were right. My father did have someone go through your computer."

Hearing her confirm what he already knew didn't repair the damage. "Fine, you've apologized. Goodbye."

Instead of heading out the door she took a step closer to his desk. "When my father found out about us, he told me he wanted me to be happy. I had no idea he was setting me up so he could use me to get to you and to EPH through you. I want you to know that I don't condone what he did, and I didn't have anything to do with his plan, Liam."

She took another step forward. "You're also right about our first meeting. I did set it up to try and pry information out of you, but that job ended before we made love. Anything you told me after that I kept to myself.

"After the ball, my father pressed me to find out more about what was causing so much turmoil at EPH. I asked the sales team to milk our mutual advertisers for any rumors they may have heard about the shake-up at EPH. The advertising sales manager compiled a report and sent it to me. But I destroyed it, Liam. I couldn't forward that information to my father because I was falling in love with you. Even though it was commonly known gossip I knew it might hurt you.

"My father found the report anyway. I don't know if that's what spurred him into hiring someone to hack into your computer or if cyber-snooping was already part of his plan. It doesn't really matter. What matters is that I was trying so hard to impress him that I compromised my integrity. I'm ashamed of my part in this mess and I'm sorry you were hurt."

He steeled himself against the tremor of her voice, but it got to him and that pissed him off. "Are you done yet?"

"No. One more thing… I love you."

He sucked in a sharp breath at the unexpected jab.

"And it's not the transient kind of infatuation my mother fell in and out of on a regular basis. I *love* you. I love your smile, your patience, your enthusiasm and your loyalty to your family. I love the way you make me feel like the sexiest woman in the world and how you made me feel loved for the first time in my life." Her lips quivered. "And I'll never forget the happiness you've given me in the past few weeks. Thank you for that."

The knot in his throat nearly choked him. He couldn't speak and he could barely breathe.

"But I also know we can't get past this because of your loyalty to your family and my misplaced loyalty to mine. Goodbye, Liam. Be happy."

She left him clutching the arms of his chair in a white-knuckled grip and fighting the burn in his gut and the one in his eyes.

"Do you want to tell us why you called this 'urgent' meeting?" Gannon, Liam's oldest brother, asked as he sat down at the long table in the EPH executive boardroom on the twenty-fourth floor.

The sun shining in from the rooftop garden didn't lighten Liam's mood. He waited for Tag, his younger brother, and Bridget, his sister, to take their seats before sitting or replying. "I wanted to personally apologize for the leak to the *Times.* I screwed up."

Gannon snorted. "No kidding."

Defense surged hot and fast through Liam. He tamped it down. As executive editor of *Pulse,* Gannon had been the hardest hit by Holt's devious attack. Tag, *Pulse*'s news editor, came in a close second.

Aubrey's confession and apology from earlier that morning whirled round and round in Liam's head. "I left my laptop where I shouldn't have. I was careless. It won't happen again."

Tag leaned forward, lacing his fingers and bracing his arms on the table. "Did you suspect a setup?"

"No." Should he have? It was a question he'd asked himself over and over and over. Dammit, if only he and Aubrey had stayed at a hotel. Or would something like this have happened eventually anyway? Had Matthew Holt tagged Liam as the weak link at EPH? As Patrick said, Liam had made himself available for the enemy to use.

Tag shrugged. "If you didn't suspect anything, then I don't see how this screwup is your fault. Holt's a bastard. We all know that. Getting involved with his daughter probably isn't the smartest move you've ever made, but you're not known for making stupid moves, Liam. I'm betting there's a pretty good reason."

Liam snorted at that. Every woman he'd ever hooked up with had been a mistake. "I didn't know who Aubrey was when we met, and she…she blew me away. I've never been that attracted to a woman before. But I should have said goodbye as soon as I learned her name."

But then he wouldn't have gotten to know Aubrey, wouldn't have had the chance to find peace in her presence or ecstasy in her arms. He couldn't honestly say he regretted his time with her. In fact, even knowing the painful end, if he had to do it all over again, he would. But he'd leave his laptop at home.

"Do you love her?" asked Bridget, who had remained silent until this point.

Liam exhaled slowly and considered the question he'd refused to ask himself since Aubrey had walked out two hours ago. "Yes."

Would he get over his feelings, the way Aubrey predicted? He didn't think so.

His little sister moved in for the kill. Liam recognized the glint in her eyes and the shift in her posture. Her recent marriage to a Colorado sheriff and distance from EPH had softened Bridget in many ways, but it hadn't diminished her energetic roll-up-the-sleeves-and-dive-in personality. He was happy she was here for a visit; he'd missed her. "Do you think she knew what her father had planned?"

"At first I thought she did. Now I know better. Aubrey didn't set me up. She came by to apologize this morning." Without a doubt she'd told the truth today. He'd seen the honesty and pain in her eyes. She'd been duped by her bastard of a father, and Matthew Holt's actions had cut her deeply. Liam's heart ached for her. He knew how much betrayal by someone you loved and trusted hurt.

Is cutting her out of your life any less of a betrayal?

You promised to make your relationship work.

He stifled his conscience and dealt with the facts. "But Aubrey admitted to asking Holt Enterprises' sales reps to quiz our mutual advertisers and then report any rumors about EPH. She said she tore up the report, but that Holt found it anyway. I could never be certain that kind of encroachment wouldn't happen again. Aubrey's trying so damned hard to prove her worth to her father that I'd always have to watch my back and my tongue for fear the next time she heard insider information about EPH she wouldn't discard it."

"So you love her. What are you going to do about it?" Bridget asked.

What could he do? "Nothing."

"Nothing?" his siblings chorused in unison.

"What choice do I have? Aubrey's right. As long as she works for Holt and I work for EPH we can't get past this. We'd each be an enemy and a potential spy in the other's family camp, especially after this. We're a modern-day Romeo and Juliet, for God's sake. There is no happy ending."

Tag shook his head. "If you love her, you'll find a way to make it work. Ending a relationship because it's going to be difficult is just another form of cowardice."

Tag ought to know. His fiancée was African-American. The couple hadn't let racial differences and fear of prejudice wreck their love. It hadn't been easy.

Gannon laid a hand on Liam's shoulder. "If you really love this woman, learn from your big brother's mistakes. I let concern for what others might say break up Erika and me the first time around, and I almost lost the best woman I've ever met. Don't make that mistake. You might not get a second chance like I did."

Confused, Liam looked from one sibling to the other. "Her part in this doesn't bother you?"

"It sounds as if she was used as much as you were," Gannon replied. "As much as I hated having *Pulse*'s numbers exposed, it sounds as if we were all victims of Matthew Holt."

"Aubrey and I couldn't continue to work for rival firms, and I don't think she's willing to give up on winning her father's approval yet."

"Could you be happy working outside EPH? Family duty's always been your mantra."

Tag's question wasn't an easy one. "I don't know. Frankly, Patrick's challenge has made life a living hell around here. Most days I feel like the grim reaper. Good news for one of you is bad news for the other. It's been a lose-lose situation." He scraped a hand over his face. "Jeez, I sound like I'm whining."

"No, little brother, you sound like the pressure of being caught in the middle is finally getting to you."

Liam looked at Gannon. "Being the middle man isn't the only problem. You all know Patrick and I work out and play golf together. I have to wonder if something *I* said didn't spark his idiotic competition. At the very least I should have seen this crazy scheme coming and headed it off. Patrick swears he's doing this to make EPH stronger, but he's tearing the family apart."

Bridget rolled her eyes. "Who knows where Patrick's crazy scheme came from. But you're not responsible for his actions,

Liam, and you can't let his interference ruin your life." She held up her hands. "I know, I know, you've all heard that from me for years, but from the vantage point of Colorado, I look back on my time here and I see how hard we all tried to please him and to follow his rules. I'm over my need to embarrass him with a tell-all Elliott exposé, but the point is Patrick has had too much control over our choices and our lives. You have to do what makes *you* happy, Liam. It's *your* life. You'll have to live it long after he's gone."

Tag nodded. "I'll second that."

"I concur," said Gannon.

Bridget sat forward. "Liam, you're a great problem solver. If anyone can come up with an acceptable compromise it's you."

Touched by his siblings' support, Liam took a fortifying breath. "So all I have to do is find a solution that makes everybody happy. A piece of cake."

Not.

Eleven

Liam entered Patrick's office without knocking. "Aubrey wasn't part of Holt's scheme."

His grandfather looked up from the reports on his desk. "Are you certain of that?"

"Yes. Patrick, I'm in love with her, and I need to know if you can get past your enmity with her father or if my relationship with Aubrey will be a source of friction."

"And if I can't get past it?"

Liam took a deep breath. He'd thought long and hard since talking to his siblings. Lunch sat like a bed of hot coals in his stomach. He needed Aubrey in his life and he had to find a way to make it work. "Then I'll tender my resignation."

Patrick didn't look surprised, but, after losing three other family employees this year, maybe he wasn't. He laid his favorite Montblanc pen on his desk. His leather chair creaked as he sat back. "And do what? Start a winery in California?"

Liam drew a sharp breath. "I don't know."

"Do you think I haven't seen your books, Liam? Do you think I don't know that while your head is here at EPH your heart is elsewhere?"

Insulted, Liam bristled. "I've given one hundred percent to EPH even though I have to admit that in the past ten months I haven't enjoyed my role here."

"I know that, but I have my reasons for seeing this competition through."

Liam didn't waste his time trying to decipher Patrick's riddle. He'd done that for ten months and failed. "I want to marry Aubrey if she'll have me. If she won't quit her job, then I'll have to quit mine. If you can't accept her into the family and absolve her in this, then I'll have to quit anyway."

"Only you can make the decision about which is more important—the woman or the job."

"What kind of vague nonanswer is that?"

Patrick lifted his pen. "The only one you're going to get from me. If you'll excuse me, I have work to do."

No closer to resolving his dilemma than he'd been hours ago, Liam let himself out of the office. Something had to give. His job? Or Aubrey? Could he be happy without either?

And was it a moot question? Would Aubrey give him a second chance or tell him to go to hell for breaking his promise at the first hurdle?

Another bitch of a day. The good news was it was almost over and it couldn't get worse. Liam pulled open the glass front door to his apartment building. "Evening, Carlos."

"Evening, Mr. Elliott. You have a visitor." The doorman nodded toward the corner of the lobby. Liam whipped his head sideways, hoping to find Aubrey. Instead he saw her father, Matthew Holt, rising from the sofa.

Liam's hand tightened on his briefcase. After the day he'd had he did not need this aggravation. "Holt, I have nothing to say to you."

"Then listen."

"Forget it." Liam headed for his elevator. Holt followed.

"It's about Aubrey."

Liam's step hitched, but he kept moving. He wanted a glass of wine. Hell, who was he kidding? He wanted a shot of whiskey. Maybe three shots.

"She quit her job and she's moving out of her apartment."

That stopped him. Liam turned. His heart slammed against his ribs with the force of a jackhammer wrecking a concrete sidewalk. "What?"

"She called me a selfish bastard. And she's right."

Liam studied Holt's drawn face. The man looked decades older than the photos Liam usually saw in the paper. "Upstairs."

The elevator opened instantly. Liam waited for Holt to precede him. Seconds later he let the enemy into his home. Bad decision? Probably. Would he regret it? That remained to be seen. "What happened?"

"Aubrey came by my place as soon as she returned from California Friday night. She chewed me out for using her as a pawn and for hurting her and the man she loves."

An invisible steel band compressed Liam's chest. "She should have punched you."

Holt nodded. "I would have deserved it. She's leaving New York."

Another hit, this one winding Liam. He crossed to the wet bar, set down his briefcase and poured himself a glass of Woodford Reserve whiskey. He poured a second for his unwanted visitor. The bite of the liquor only added to the burn in his belly. "When did she quit?"

"Friday night."

Why hadn't she told him when she'd come to see him that morning? Was it because it didn't matter? Because she didn't want to be with him now? "And you're telling me all this because…?"

Holt downed half his liquor in one gulp. "Because Aubrey won't answer my calls or open her door, and because I've damaged my relationship with my daughter beyond repair. I don't want to be responsible for doing the same to her relationship with you." He knocked back the last of his drink. "I'm a selfish son of a bitch, Elliott, and I won't be a bargain in the father-in-law department, but I want Aubrey to be happy. Apparently, you make her happy."

Liam had made her happy. *Had* being the operative word. And she'd made him happy, happier than he'd ever been. But then he'd hurt her with his lack of trust and his unjust accusations. Holt's relationship with Aubrey might not be the only irreparable one.

But she loved him. Or at least she had. And God knows he loved her. Burying himself in work eighteen hours a day hadn't helped. Not a second had passed since Friday that he hadn't ached for her. He couldn't walk away without trying to salvage the bond they'd forged.

He set his glass aside. "I'll call her."

"She won't answer. I don't know how in the hell to get through to her."

"I'll find a way." He had to.

"Elliott, if you get through, would you tell her…tell her I'm sorry and that I love her?" Defeat curved Holt's shoulders.

"I'll tell her, but she needs to hear it from you."

Liam closed the door behind Holt. He had to have a plan, a

foolproof plan, to regain Aubrey's love and trust before she left New York. Before he lost her completely. If he hadn't already.

The barrier of her job no longer stood between them. That was a start, but was it enough?

"Happy Halloween, ma'am," the courier said before departing.

"You, too," Aubrey replied automatically, her gaze stuck on the envelope in her hand. The return address read Ernie's Pub. *Liam.* Her heart hesitated and then settled into a heavy *thud-thud.* She closed her door and walked blindly back into her apartment and tripped over a box.

She caught herself against the wall and surveyed the room. Packing boxes littered the floor and tabletops. Uneasiness slithered through her. Moving was the right thing to do. Wasn't it? She couldn't stay here knowing that her father was a jerk without scruples and that Liam lived just around the corner.

Liam. Her gaze returned to the envelope and a well of ache opened up inside her. He thought she'd betrayed him. That he could believe her capable of such deceit didn't just hurt. It angered her. She dumped the envelope, unopened, into a nearby trash can and returned to the kitchen and her packing.

Think positively, A. You'll finally get a chance to open your bed-and-breakfast.

Yesterday after talking to Liam she'd come home, cried until her eyes had practically swollen shut, and then she'd picked up the phone and called Jared Maxwell, the B&B owner she'd met in California. Mason's brother-in-law had generously agreed to walk through Hill Crest House with Aubrey and to guide her in setting up business. By this time next year Aubrey would be an innkeeper. The thought didn't fill her with the happiness she'd expected.

She'd miss Liam. The unexpected thought slipped through

her defenses, renewing her anger. She slammed pots and pans into a box. How could he think she'd betray him?

Because his grandfather had.

Her hands slowed. Liam had already been hurt by someone he loved and trusted, and from what little he'd let slip about his relationship with his grandfather the wound was open and raw. What else would he expect except that she'd betray him, too?

Her anger evaporated. Aubrey set the vegetable steamer on the counter and returned to the trash can. Open the envelope or not? Heartache either way. She retrieved the envelope and ripped it open. Inside she found a bright orange-and-black flier from Ernie's Pub advertising its Halloween party tonight.

"Costumes preferred, but not required. Seven to midnight, the witching hour."

Liam's handwriting in the margin caught her eye.

"I wouldn't wear this getup for anyone else. Please come. Liam."

Her heart pounded and her mouth dried. She clutched the flier to her chest and tried to tamp down the hope rising inside her like a hot air balloon. Liam wanted to see her. Why? She reread the note, looking for a clue in the short sentences, but found none.

Getup? He'd be in costume?

Should she go?

No.

Yes. What did she have to lose? She'd already lost her heart.

She glanced at the clock. Three hours to find a costume. Most likely an impossible task on Halloween night.

* * *

"You okay in there?" Pam, the waitress, asked as she set Liam's drink on the table.

"I'll never eat another sardine," Liam muttered and shifted his shoulders. The accompanying scrape of metal against metal grated on his overstretched nerves. He lifted the tumbler and then set it back down. How in the hell was he supposed to drink it through this helmet?

"Want a flexible straw?"

"I guess I need one. What time is it?" He couldn't fit a watch under his costume.

"Almost nine. You think she'll show?"

The sinking sensation in the pit of Liam's stomach said no, but he refused to give up. Aubrey had been late once before and she'd been worth every second of the wait. He shrugged and his hinges screeched. "We have a few more hours."

Pam patted his shoulder. *Clank. Clank.* "Just give me the signal when you're ready."

He peeled the paper from his straw, stabbed it into the tumbler and lifted his visor to sip. Around him revelers enthusiastically celebrated Halloween in a variety of costumes from common to absurd. His suit of armor fit right in.

He occupied the booth he and Aubrey had used when they'd first met. When he'd arrived, he'd had to bribe the guys who'd occupied it to get them to move, but he figured having the good luck seat when Aubrey arrived was worth a pitcher of beer.

The pub's door opened. His heart had quit stalling each time someone new entered about forty patrons ago. A hooker in a cheap blond wig with a red mask covering the upper half of her face hesitated on the threshold. Her minuscule red halter top cupped small breasts, and a matching miniskirt stretched low on slim hips, leaving a lot of bare skin in between. A navel ring glinted on her flat belly. She'd strapped mile-high heels to her feet.

Wolf whistles and catcalls greeted her. A couple of guys pulled cash out of their wallets and shouted offers. Her neck and the visible part of her face turned almost as red as her clothing. Liam was about to look away when the woman moved forward, looking left and right, searching the patron's faces without looking too closely or acknowledging their lewd invitations. Something about the way the hooker moved looked familiar. His pulse kicked into high gear, and his glass hit the table with a thud. Aubrey.

Sliding out of the booth was as laborious as wedging himself into it had been. He stepped in front of her when she tried to pass. The startled violet eyes looking up at him through the red mask stole his breath.

Her eyes widened in recognition and her lips parted. "A knight in shining armor. It suits you, Liam."

He smiled, but realized she probably couldn't see his mouth. Liam pried off the heavy helmet and set it on the table. "A hooker?"

"I had trouble finding a costume. I was about to give up and come without one, because this is so not me. It's—"

"The sexiest thing I've ever seen." He was as hard as steel beneath his metal suit, and hot. Oh, man, was he hot. He lifted a hand to touch her face, but stopped. The heavy glove would scrape her skin.

"I wouldn't wear this getup for anyone else," Aubrey parroted his words back at him.

"Good to know." He could spend all day looking at her. Aubrey had a body made for sexy clothing. But her delectable body wasn't the reason he'd sent her the bar flier. He gestured to the table instead. "I'm glad you came. Have a seat before I have to draw my sword and start hacking these guys down one by one."

She scooted into the booth, nibbled her siren red lip and studied his face. "I almost didn't come. Why did you send the invitation?"

He grimaced and yanked off his gloves so he could cover her hand with his. "Because I wanted to apologize. Aubrey, I'm sorry. For doubting you. For hurting you. For letting our families come between us. And I'm sorry for breaking my promise. It won't happen again."

"You had good reason."

"I had a good reason to be angry with your father, but not with you." He stroked a thumb over her palm. She shivered and her nipples beaded in the skimpy top. He drew courage from the knowledge that she couldn't be over him when his touch could still turn her on.

"Liam, you told me enough about your grandfather and the situation at work for me to figure out that you believed someone else you loved had betrayed you."

He shouldn't be surprised that she'd figured him out. Aubrey understood him better than anyone. Better than he understood himself, in fact.

"The tension at work, my mother's cancer and my brothers and sister finding someone special to share their lives with made me look hard at my life. Life was passing me by until I met you, Aubrey, and now I'm not only living it I'm looking beyond robotically doing what's expected of me." He caught Pam's eye and thumped the metal breast plate over his heart—their signal. And then he gently removed Aubrey's mask and laid it on the table beside his helmet.

"When we were in Napa you suggested I quit my job at EPH and follow my dream of opening a winery. I rejected your idea because I didn't have the courage to risk it. But you were right. Without risks there are no rewards."

Pam arrived. She slid a silver platter onto the center of the table and quickly departed. On the platter lay a single red rose and a ring box.

Aubrey gasped. Her wide gaze jumped from the tray to Liam's eyes and back again.

Liam lifted the rose and dragged the bud along Aubrey's cheek. "One rose because for one month you've excited me, soothed me and made me happier than anyone ever has. You've made me believe that dreams can come true, Aubrey."

He laid the rose back on the tray, picked up the Tiffany ring box and opened it to reveal a marquise diamond flanked by two heart-shaped amethyst stones. "One flawless diamond because you're more precious to me than anything, and my love for you is as strong and as enduring as this stone. Two amethysts hearts because our hearts belong together and because I've found my destiny in your violet eyes."

He extracted the ring from the box and held out his hand. "I want to spend the rest of my life loving you, Aubrey Holt. Marry me. Please."

His heart stalled when she knotted her fingers and lowered her hands into her lap. "How can you forgive my father for what he's done?"

"I may not ever approve of his business practices, but I'm working on forgiveness because he loves you, and anyone who loves you can't be all bad."

Aubrey made a noise of disgust. "He doesn't love me."

"He came to see me, and trust me, sweetheart, he knows he screwed up. He's sorry and he's hurting and he wants to apologize. I know you're as mad as hell at him now, but he loves you and you love him. Give him a chance to make things right. Families are forever. Remember telling me that?"

Aubrey mashed her trembling lips together. A tear slid down her cheek. "You weren't kidding when you said you're the Elliott peacemaker."

"I just like happy endings. Let me be your knight in shining armor, Aubrey. Let's live out our fantasies and dreams together. Let me make giving you a happily-ever-after my life's crusade."

"What about your job? You'll regret leaving EPH once Patrick's competition is over and life returns to normal."

"No, I won't. We both need jobs that fulfill us, jobs that reward us with more than a paycheck. We're not getting that here. I'd like to stay at EPH through the end of the year to ease the transition, but in the meantime, I want to start looking for a place for us in Napa Valley. A place where you can run your B&B and I can tinker with my grapes. Money's not an issue. I'll net a bundle from selling my apartment, and I have some healthy investments to tide us over until we make a profit."

She searched his face as if waiting for the catch and then a smile flickered on her lips. "I already have the perfect place. Hill Crest House is mine. My grandmother left it to me. There's enough land for you to build your winery, and you can keep your apartment so we have somewhere to stay when we come back to visit our families."

Liam's lungs seized and his pulse took off at a sprinter's pace. "Is that a yes?"

Aubrey lifted her hands and cupped his face. "I love you, Liam Elliott, and nothing would make me happier than being your wife."

He covered her hand with his and then pulled it off his cheek. He held her gaze as he slid the ring on her finger. "I love you, Aubrey Holt, and I swear to you you'll never regret saying yes."

The bar patrons erupted in a cheer and Liam realized they'd had an audience. He pried himself out of the booth, snatched Aubrey into his arms and covered her smiling lips with his.

Fantasies did come true. He ought to know. He'd found his when the enemy's daughter had stormed his castle and captured his heart.

* * * * *

THE EXPECTANT EXECUTIVE

BY
KATHIE DeNOSKY

Kathie DeNosky lives in her native southern Illinois with her husband and one very spoiled Jack Russell terrier. She writes highly sensual stories with a generous amount of humor. Kathie's books have appeared on bestseller lists and received the Write Touch Readers' Award from WisRWA and the National Readers' Choice Award. She enjoys going to rodeos, traveling to research settings for her books and listening to country music. Readers may contact Kathie at PO Box 2064, Herrin, Illinois 62948-5264 or e-mail her at kathie@kathiedenosky.com.

This book is dedicated to the authors of
THE ELLIOTTS.
You gals are awesome and it was a privilege and
an honor to work with you.

One

"I can't believe it's already the first of November," Finola Elliott muttered as she scanned the entries in her electronic planner.

There were only two months left before Patrick, founder and CEO of Elliott Publication Holdings and patriarch of the Long Island Elliott clan, retired and named one of his four children his successor to the magazine empire he'd built over the years. And Fin had every intention of being the indisputable winner of the competition he'd set up to decide who would best fill that role.

She'd spent her entire adult life working toward

taking over EPH, and even though her two brothers and one nephew were all equally qualified for the position, Patrick—she hadn't referred to him as her father in years—owed her the job and so much more. But when he reviewed the growth and profit margins of *The Buzz*, *Snap*, *Pulse* and *Charisma* magazines, Fin wanted there to be no mistaking that her "baby," *Charisma*, had outdistanced the others, hands down.

At the end of the second quarter, her fashion magazine had been in the lead. Unfortunately, in the past couple of months her twin brother, Shane, had pulled ahead with his show business publication, *The Buzz*. But Fin wasn't overly concerned. Everything was back on track and going her way again.

Smiling fondly, she glanced at the newly framed picture on her desk and the reason her attention had been diverted from the objective. She'd discovered that her intern, Jessica Clayton, was the baby girl Patrick had forced Fin to give up for adoption twenty-three years ago, and she and her daughter had been making up for lost time. Jessie was a wonderful young woman and they'd become quite close over the past couple of months. In fact, Fin had even accompanied Jessie to the Silver Moon Ranch in Colorado, to meet Jessie's adoptive father and see where she'd grown up.

But now that Jessie and Cade McMann, Fin's right-hand man at *Charisma*, were busy with the final preparations for their wedding later in the month, Fin needed to get back on track and regain her focus. She hid a yawn behind her hand. She just wished she wasn't so darned tired all the time.

As she switched to the month of October to review her notes on the magazine's growth projections for November, goose bumps skittered over her skin and a little chill streaked up her spine.

Something was missing. Where was the personal notation she made every month marking the start of her cycle?

Switching back to her entry in September, her heart slammed to a stop, then pounded hard against her ribs. She hadn't had a period in almost six weeks?

"That can't be right."

Surely she'd just forgotten to record the date for October. But as she thought back, she couldn't remember having had a period since well before accompanying Jessie to Colorado.

Stunned, Fin sat back in her high-backed leather chair and stared out the plateglass windows at the Manhattan skyline. The only other time in her life that she'd skipped her cycle had been at the age of fifteen when she'd gotten pregnant after her one night of passion with her sixteen-year-old boyfriend, Sebastian Deveraux. But there was absolutely no way she could be pregnant this time.

She almost laughed. For that to even be a remote possibility, she'd have to have a love life. And she didn't. She couldn't even remember the last time she'd been out with a man when the evening hadn't been business-related—either courting a potential advertising client or entertaining one of the many designers featuring his or her new line in *Charisma*.

Her social life had taken, and probably always would take, a backseat to the magazine that had become her obsession over the years. But a sudden thought caused her to catch her breath. There had been that one night at the party Travis Clayton, Jessie's adoptive father, had thrown in honor of Jessie and Cade's engagement.

Fin's cheeks heated at the thought of just what had taken place when she and Travis had gone into that charming old barn of his to check on a mare and her new foal. What had started out to be an innocent hug to express how grateful she was that Travis and his late wife, Lauren, had done such a wonderful job of raising Jessie, had turned into a passionate encounter that still left Fin feeling breathlessly weak. There had only been one other time in her life that she'd allowed herself to lose control and throw caution to the wind like that. The night she'd conceived Jessie.

She thoughtfully nibbled on her lower lip. She couldn't possibly have gotten pregnant from that one stolen moment with Travis, could she?

Shaking her head, she dismissed the idea outright. It might be possible, but it was most definitely improbable. She'd read somewhere that the closer a woman got to forty, the longer it sometimes took to become pregnant. And at thirty-eight, she was closing in on forty faster than she cared to admit.

Besides, fate couldn't possibly be that cruel. She'd conceived Jessie the night she'd lost her virginity to Sebastian. Surely the odds of her becoming pregnant again after making love with a man one time had to be astronomical.

No, missing her period had to be an indication that something else was wrong.

Swiveling her chair around, she reached for the phone to make an appointment with her gynecologist, but gasped at the unexpected sight of Travis Clayton leaning one broad shoulder against her doorframe.

"I know I'm not the best-looking thing to come down the pike, but I wasn't aware that I'd started scaring the hell out of pretty women and little kids," he said, his deep voice filled with humor.

The teasing light in his sinfully blue eyes sent a delicious warmth coursing throughout her body. If she'd ever seen a man as ruggedly handsome as Jessie's adoptive father, Fin couldn't remember when. Looking much younger than his forty-nine years, he was the epitome of the modern western man from the top of his wide-brimmed black cowboy hat all the way to his big-booted feet. Wearing a pair of soft-looking, well-worn jeans, chambray shirt and a western-cut sports jacket that emphasized the breadth of his impossibly wide shoulders, he could easily be one of the male models in an advertisement for men's cologne.

"Travis, it's good to see you again. I don't remember Jessie mentioning that you would be visiting this week." Rising to her feet, Fin walked around the desk to greet him. "Please, come in and sit down."

Giving her a smile that caused her toes to curl inside her Italian designer heels, he straightened to his full height and crossed the room with the confidence and grace of a man quite comfortable with who he was and what he was about. "When I talked to Jess the other day, she sounded a little hassled from all this wedding stuff, so I decided to surprise her," he said, settling into one of the chairs in front of Fin's desk.

"A little paternal support never hurts," she agreed, wondering what it would be like to have a father who was sensitive to his child's emotional needs. Patrick's approach to childrearing had been nothing short of dictatorial and he could have cared less how his issued orders affected his offspring's emotions—in particular, hers.

"How have you been, Fin?" Travis asked when she sat down in the chair beside him.

The warmth and genuine interest in his smooth baritone sent a little shiver up her spine. "Fine. And yourself?"

He shrugged. "Can't complain." Looking around her office, his curious gaze seemed to zero in on a stack of ad proofs on her desk. "When I asked Jess how you've been getting on, she said you're working like crazy to win this contest your dad set up."

Her stomach did a funny little flip at the thought that he'd been asking Jessie about her. "The competition and helping with Jessie and Cade's wedding arrangements have been keeping me pretty busy."

"I'll bet it has." He chuckled. "All this wedding hoopla makes me kind of glad I'm stuck off in no-man's-land until it's time to walk her down the aisle. Jess said all I have to do is go for the final fitting on my tux while I'm in town and that suits me just fine."

He wasn't fooling Fin for a minute. Travis and Jessie had a wonderful father-daughter relationship and he had to be feeling a little left out for him to fly all the way from Colorado.

"This is pretty tough for you, isn't it?"

He started to shake his head, then looking a bit sheepish, he grinned. "It shows that much, does it? I thought I was doing a pretty fair job of hiding it, but I guess I was wrong."

Fin nodded sympathetically. "I'm sure it's a difficult transition to suddenly be relegated to the number-two man in your daughter's life when you've always been number one."

"I can't believe she's old enough to get married," he said, removing his hat to run his hand through his thick dark blond hair. Replacing his hat, his expression turned wistful. "It seems like just yesterday I was kissing her skinned elbows and teaching her how to print her name for kindergarten."

A little pang of envy gripped Fin's heart. She'd been cheated out of so much when Patrick had forced her to give her baby daughter up for adoption.

They sat in silence for several long moments before Travis spoke again. "I know this is short notice, but I stopped by to ask if you'd like to join Jessie and me for supper this evening. We'll be meeting at some place she called the Lemon Grill."

He grinned. "If the name is any indication, it sounds like a place a man could get a decent steak."

Fin smiled. "I'm sure you can. It's a charming little bistro with excellent food."

"Then you'll join us?"

She should decline the invitation outright. She and Travis had absolutely nothing in common beyond their love for Jessie. But for reasons beyond her comprehension, Fin was drawn to Travis and had been since the moment they met.

"I don't want to intrude on your time with your daughter," she hedged.

He shook his head. "She's your daughter, too. Besides, I wouldn't have asked if I hadn't wanted you to join us. And I'm sure you want to spend as much time with her as you can now that you two have found each other."

Her heart filled with emotion when he referred to Jessie as her daughter, too. "You're sure you don't mind?"

When he took her hand in his much larger one, a tingling thrill streaked up Fin's arm at the feel of his work-callused palm against her much softer skin. "I'm positive." The warmth in his incredibly blue eyes assured her that he did indeed want her to have dinner with them. "What man wouldn't want to be out with the two best-looking women in this whole damned town?"

The truth was, spending the evening with Travis and Jessie was far more appealing than sitting alone in her too-big apartment eating take out and going over spread sheets filled with *Charisma*'s growth projections and profit margins. Surely one more night of putting off the task wasn't going to hurt her chances of winning the competition for EPH.

"Wh-what time should I meet you at the bistro?" Why did she suddenly feel like a teenage girl being asked to the homecoming dance by the best-looking, most popular boy in school?

"Eight." Still holding her hand, he rose to his feet, then pulled her up to stand beside him. "I guess I'd better let you get back to work if you're going to win your dad's contest."

"I suppose that would be a good idea." Why didn't she sound as resolute about it as she would have before he appeared at her door?

He leaned forward to press a soft kiss to her forehead. "Then I'll see you this evening, Fin."

Her skin tingled where his lips had been and before she could find her voice, Travis touched the wide brim of his cowboy hat in a gallant gesture and turned to walk away.

As she watched him disappear into the outer

office, she felt the need to fan herself. Dear God, the man was six feet four inches of pure sex appeal and could heat up a room faster than a blast furnace. His kiss had only been meant as a friendly gesture, but her heart had skipped several beats at the touch of his lips to her suddenly overly sensitive skin.

"Was that the model for Calvin Klein's new cowboy cologne?" Chloe Davenport asked, entering Fin's office. She glanced over her shoulder at Travis. "If so, could I sign up to be his cowgirl?"

Fin laughed at her executive assistant. "No. That's Travis Clayton, Jessie's father."

"You're kidding." Fin watched the young woman take another lingering glance before closing the office door. "He's the real deal, isn't he?"

"If by that you mean that he's a working cowboy, then yes, he's the real thing."

Chloe sighed wistfully. "If they grow them like that in Colorado, I just might have to head that way sometime."

Fin laughed. "And leave that cute little apartment you have in Chelsea?"

"Ooh, that would be a problem. I finally have it decorated just the way I want it," Chloe said, handing Fin the latest accounting reports. "I suppose

I'll just have to stay in New York and content myself with finding an urban cowboy."

Fin nodded, distracted by the report. "What's the latest word around EPH? Anything going on with the other magazines that I should know about?"

The young woman shook her head. "Not that I've heard. You and Shane are still the top contenders for CEO. *The Buzz*'s growth and profit margin is slightly better than *Charisma*'s, but the consensus in accounting is that *Charisma* could still come out the winner."

"G-good." Suddenly feeling a bit dizzy, Fin walked around her desk to sit in her high-backed chair. She definitely needed to see a doctor.

"Fin, are you okay?" Chloe asked, her pretty young face marred with concern.

Nodding, Fin gave her a weak smile. "I'm just tired, that's all."

"I'm worried about you, Fin. You've been working way too hard." Chloe frowned. "You've always been driven, but these past ten months you've made workaholics look like total slackers."

"I'll be fine, Chloe."

Her assistant looked doubtful. "Are you sure about that?"

Smiling, Fin nodded as she handed the report back to her assistant. "Now, go give these to Cade and tell him that I want to meet with him first thing in the morning to go over these figures."

"Anything else?"

Fin checked the clock. "No, I have a few phone calls to make, then I think I'm going to take off the rest of the day."

Chloe looked thunderstruck. "You're kidding. You never leave before eight or nine in the evening and more times than I care to count, I've found you sleeping on your couch when I arrive for work. Are you sure you're feeling all right? Should I call someone?"

"No, you don't need to call anyone." Smiling, Fin hid a yawn behind her hand. "I have a dinner engagement and I think I need a short nap to make it through the evening. Otherwise, I might fall asleep between the appetizer and the main course."

"That wouldn't be good for business," Chloe agreed, shaking her head as she walked to the door.

Fin didn't bother to correct her assistant as the young woman quietly closed the door behind her. Dinner this evening had nothing whatsoever to do with business and everything to do with pleasure. Her only concern was deciding which she was anticipating more—the pleasure of spending time with her newfound daughter or her daughter's adoptive father.

* * *

Travis felt like a fish out of water. The concrete and steel of New York City was a far cry from the wide open spaces he was used to and the Lemon Grill was to hell and gone from the little diner he sometimes frequented when he drove over to Winchester County for the stock auctions. Here he sat in an upscale café in the middle of Manhattan with a prissy little waiter sporting a pencil-thin mustache and slicked-back hair, hovering around him like a bumblebee over a patch of new spring clover.

"My name is Henri. It will be my pleasure to be your server this evening." The too-polished character smiled, showing off a set of unnaturally white teeth. "Would the gentleman like something to drink while he's waiting on his dinner partners?"

Travis frowned. The little guy sure spouted out a lot of words to ask a simple question. He was more used to being asked straight up what he wanted to drink instead of being referred to like he was some sort of third wheel.

"I'll take a beer."

"Would the gentleman like a domestic brand or imported?"

Unable to resist teasing the pretentious little man, Travis grinned. "I can't say what the gentleman would like, but I'll take domestic." As Henri started to leave the table, Travis added the name of a beer brewed exclusively in the Rocky Mountains.

"I'm sorry, sir. We don't carry that particular brand," Henri said, his apology as fake as his cap-toothed smile. Rattling off a list of the beer the restaurant had available, he asked, "Would the gentleman like to choose one of those?"

"Surprise me."

"Very well, sir."

As the waiter hurried away to get his drink, Travis spotted Fin entering the restaurant. She briefly spoke to the hostess, then when she headed his way, he couldn't help but marvel at what a beauty she was. With her straight, dark auburn hair stylishly brushing her shoulders, and looking like a model in her black form-fitting dress, she looked far too young to be the mother of his twenty-three-year-old daughter.

Standing when she approached, he thought his heart would jump right out of his chest when her perfect coral lips turned up in a warm smile. "I hope I'm not too late. The crosstown traffic was particularly heavy this evening."

"You drove?" He held the chair for her while she seated herself at the small table. "I remember Jessie telling me that you'd never learned to drive."

Fin's delightful laughter caused an unexpected

heat to settle in the pit of his belly as he sat back down. "Guilty as charged. I've never even been behind the wheel of a car."

"You're kidding, right?" Hell, he'd been driving around the ranch in either a truck or on a tractor since he was ten years old and he'd taught Jessie to drive when she was twelve. "You've never—"

"No. When my brothers and I lived at home, we always had drivers to take us wherever we wanted to go. Then, after I moved from the Hamptons into my Manhattan apartment, there was no need to drive. Everything I need is so close, I walk a lot. And when where I want to go is too far to walk, I use the corporate limo or take a taxi." Her eyes twinkled wistfully as she added, "But I've always thought it might be fun to learn how to drive a car."

"The next time you visit the Silver Moon, I'll teach you," he said, unable to wipe what he was sure had to be a sappy grin from his face.

Her eyes held a warmth that stole his breath. "I'd like that, Travis. Thank you."

The thought of Fin coming back to his ranch for a visit had his heart pounding like the bass drum in a marching band. But it was the slight blush on her porcelain cheeks and the warmth in her pretty green eyes that caused the region south of his belt buckle to tighten. She remembered what happened between them when she visited his ranch last month, the same as he did.

"Would the lady like something to drink before ordering dinner?" Henri asked, returning to their table with Travis's beer.

For reasons Travis didn't want to dwell on, the man's appreciative grin when he looked at Fin irritated the hell out of Travis.

"Just some water with a slice of lemon, please," Fin answered the prissy little guy. As he moved away to take care of her request, she asked, "Where's Jessie? I was sure she'd be here by now."

Travis shook his head. "I don't know. She said something about going with Cade to pick up airline tickets for their honeymoon after they got off work. But that was a good three hours ago. Surely it doesn't take that long to..."

His voice trailed off when he felt Fin's soft, delicate hand touch his. "I'm sure she's fine, Travis. I overheard her and Cade talking about a stop at the jeweler's to pick up gifts for their bridesmaids and groomsmen. Maybe it took longer than they had anticipated."

As he sat there trying to force words around the cotton suddenly coating his throat, Henri placed a glass of water on the table in front of Fin. "Sir, you have a phone call. If you'll follow me, you may take the call at the hostess's desk."

When Travis glanced at Fin, she smiled. "It's probably Jessie telling you that she's held up in traffic."

"I hope you're right." He briefly wondered why his daughter hadn't called his cell phone, until he remembered that he'd turned it off when he entered the restaurant.

Excusing himself, Travis quickly made his way to the front of the restaurant. Even though Jess had been living in New York City for the better part of a year, it still made him nervous to think of his little girl on the mean streets of a big city. He'd relaxed a little after meeting her fiancé, Cade McMann, and being assured that the man had every intention of keeping her safe and making her happy. But if something had happened to her, Travis would have Cade's head on a silver platter for not taking better care of her.

When the hostess handed him the phone, he was relieved to hear his precious daughter on the other end of the line. "Hi, Daddy."

"Where are you, angel? Are you all right?"

"I'm fine, but I'm afraid I won't be able to meet you and Fin for dinner this evening." There was a short silence before she added, "I've, um, got a headache and I think I'll turn in early. You don't mind having dinner alone with Fin, do you?"

"Of course not, princess." Travis glanced over at the beautiful woman waiting patiently at his table. He'd have to be as crazy as a horse after it got into a patch of locoweed to mind spending time with her.

"Good. I'm sure you'll both enjoy yourselves. The Lemon Grill has great food." Jessie's voice was a little too enthusiastic and she didn't sound the least bit under the weather. "Please give Fin my apologies and tell her that I'll see her at the office tomorrow morning."

"I'll do that, angel." She wasn't fooling him for a minute. Jess had been after him for the past couple of years to get out more and revitalize his social life, as she put it. And unless he missed his guess, his little girl was trying to play matchmaker between him and her biological mother.

"Oh, don't forget, Daddy. We're supposed to meet for lunch tomorrow, then go to the men's store to have you fitted for your tux."

"You're still going to make me wear that monkey suit, are you?"

"You'll be the best looking monkey at the wedding," she said, laughing. "I love you, Daddy. See you tomorrow."

"I love you too, Jess."

Handing the cordless phone back to the hostess, Travis walked over to the table where Fin sat waiting for him. “Looks like it’s just the two of us for supper tonight,” he said, settling into his chair.

She gave him a questioning look. “Jessie isn’t coming?”

“Nope.” He shook his head. “She said she has a headache and intends to go to bed early.”

“Since your other dinner partner won’t be joining you, would you care to order now?” Henri asked, suddenly appearing at Travis’s elbow. The man had obviously been eavesdropping on their conversation.

Tired of the waiter’s obtrusive presence, Travis gave him a look that had the little man quickly fading into the background without another word. “What do you say we go somewhere we can talk without old Ornery over there hanging on our every word?”

Fin looked puzzled. “Ornery?”

“Henri. Ornery.” Travis grinned. “Same difference.”

She gave him a smile that did strange things to his insides. “I think I know of a place where we can talk uninterrupted.”

“Sounds good to me.” Raising his hand, he motioned to Henri.

The little waiter was at Travis’s side almost immediately. “Would the lady and gentleman like to order now?”

Fin spoke up before Travis had a chance. "No, we've changed our minds and won't be dining with you this evening."

Leaving Henri to hover over someone else, when they stepped out onto the street, Travis put his arm around Fin to shelter her from the chilly November wind. Her slender body pressed to his side sent his blood pressure up a good fifty points and brought back memories of the last time he'd held her close. His body tightened predictably and he felt as if his jeans had shrunk a size or two in the stride.

"What's the name of this restaurant where the waiters leave the customers alone?" he asked when he finally got his voice to work.

"Chez Fin Elliott."

His heart stuttered and he had to remind himself to breathe. "We're going to your place?"

Nodding, she smiled. "If you don't mind missing out on your steak, I thought we could go back to my apartment, order in some Chinese and talk without having someone else hanging on our every word."

He wasn't wild about egg rolls and chop suey, but he'd have to be a damned fool to pass up spending the evening alone with one of the most beautiful women he'd ever had the privilege to lay eyes on.

Before she had a chance to change her mind, Travis raised his arm and waved at an approaching yellow car. "Taxi!"

Two

As Fin phoned in a delivery order to her favorite Chinese restaurant, she watched Travis glance around her cavernous Upper East Side apartment and couldn't help but wonder what he thought of her personal space. Obscenely spacious for one person, it was a study in chrome and glass, black and white, and light-years away from his warmly decorated home in Colorado.

When she'd visited the Silver Moon Ranch, she'd found the house to be roomy and pleasantly cluttered, but it was also welcoming, cozy and everything her apartment wasn't. While Travis's rustic home had the unmistakable look and feel of being lived in and enjoyed—of love and family—her apartment appeared to be stark, cold and uninhabited in comparison.

Of course, that might have something to do with the fact that she was never there for more than a few hours at a time, nor had she made the effort to add anything to reflect her own personality after the interior designer had finished decorating the place. The really sad thing was, that had been several years ago and she still had no more interest in personalizing the place than she had the day she'd moved in.

"Mr. Chang assured me the food will be here in less than fifteen minutes," she said as she ended the phone call. "Would you like something to drink while we wait? I think I have a bottle of wine in the refrigerator or I could make a pot of coffee or tea."

"A cup of coffee would be nice."

When he turned to face her, Travis's smile sent a wave of goose bumps shimmering over her skin and a delicious little shiver straight up her spine. He was, without a doubt, one of the sexiest men she'd ever met. And she seriously doubted that he had the slightest clue of how handsome he was or the tantalizing effect he had on women.

Suddenly needing to put a little space between them before she made a complete fool of herself, Fin started toward the kitchen. He was her daughter's adoptive father, the man who had, along with his late wife, raised the little girl Fin had been forced to give up for adoption all those years ago. The last thing she needed to do was complicate the fledgling relationship she had with Jessica by lusting after Travis. Come to think of it, it was totally out of character for her to be lusting after anyone.

"I'll start the coffeemaker."

"Need help?"

She stopped in her tracks, then slowly turned to face him. Even as he stood all the way across the living room, his presence made the space feel decidedly smaller than it had when they'd first walked through the door. She could only imagine how minuscule the kitchen would seem with him in much closer proximity. Besides, having him join her would defeat the purpose of her much needed escape.

"No." To soften her hasty reply, she smiled. "By no stretch of the imagination am I domestic, but I think I can manage a pot of coffee without too much trouble." Waving her hand toward the white velour sofa, she added, "I'll only be a few minutes. Why don't you make yourself comfortable?"

"I think I'll do that." His grin sent a wave of heat from the top of her head to the soles of her feet.

As if riveted to the floor, Fin watched him remove his wide-brimmed hat and shrug out of his western jacket, then toss them on the back of an armchair. Years of listening to her mother recite the rules of proper etiquette went right out the window when she turned and entered the kitchen.

The proper thing would have been to step forward, take his hat and coat and hang them in the closet. But when Travis had unsnapped the cuffs of his chambray shirt and started rolling up the long sleeves over his tanned, sinewy forearms, she'd quickly decided there was a lot to be said for the old adage about retreat being the better part of valor.

Just the memory of those arms holding her so tenderly as they'd succumbed to passion that night in his barn last month was enough to cause her pulse to race and her breathing to come out in short, raspy little puffs. Everything about that night had been pure magic and she'd spent the past month doing her best to forget that it ever happened.

"You've got to get hold of yourself," she muttered when she noticed her hand trembling as she spooned coffee into the basket.

"Did you say something?" he called from the living room.

"No, just talking to myself."

Closing her eyes, she shook her head in an effort

to dislodge the disturbing memory. What on earth had gotten into her?

She was editor-in-chief of one of the top fashion magazines in the world, a shark in the corporate boardroom and had the ability to send the most fearless intern running for cover with nothing more than a raised eyebrow. But in Travis's presence, she seemed to be continually reminded of the fact that she was first and foremost a woman who had ignored her feminine wants and needs in favor of a rewarding career in the publishing industry.

Only, in the past couple of months she'd begun to realize that her career wasn't nearly as satisfying as she'd once thought it to be. Since learning Jessica Clayton was her long-lost daughter and meeting Travis, Fin had been reminded of what she'd given up in order to devote herself to making *Charisma* the premier magazine of the fashion world.

When she'd been a young girl, she'd wanted nothing more than to be a wife and mother, to have a family of her own. But that dream had been shattered when Patrick had forced her to give her baby girl away and had forbade her to ever see Jessie's father again. She'd never forgiven Patrick for denying her desperate pleas to keep her child, nor had she ever gotten over the loss. After she'd returned from the convent her parents had sent her to in Canada to hide her and her "shameful" condition from social and business acquaintances, she'd thrown herself into her schooling, then later into her career in an attempt to assuage the pain.

But it hadn't worked. She sighed heavily. All that she'd accomplished was finding that as she approached middle age, she was alone, childless and had become a hopeless workaholic.

"Are you all right?"

The sound of Travis's voice caused her to jump. Spinning around, she found him leaning one broad shoulder against the doorframe, much like he'd done this afternoon in her office. "Of course, why wouldn't I be?"

He pushed away from the doorframe and took a step toward her. "You were standing there staring off into space like your mind was a million miles away."

Shaking her head, she turned to slide the filled basket into the coffeemaker, then flipped the switch. "I was just thinking about the latest accounting figures for *Charisma*," she lied. "If my staff and I work hard enough, we should still be able to pull ahead of my brother Shane and his magazine, *The Buzz*."

"I don't think so."

"You don't think we'll be able to win?" she asked, frowning.

He shrugged. "I can't say if you will or not. I was

talking about what you were thinking. Whatever it was, you looked like your best roping horse had just pulled up lame, not like you were worried about winning a contest."

Shaking her head, she hoped her laughter didn't sound as hollow to him as it did to her. "I've never even ridden a horse, let alone owned one. And as for roping, I'm afraid I'd be a hopeless failure."

"You've never ridden a horse?" he asked, clearly shocked.

Grateful that she'd successfully diverted the conversation, she shook her head. "Not unless the rocking horse I had as a child counts."

His promising grin sent a wave of heat zinging throughout her body. "Looks like the next time you visit the Silver Moon, I'll have to teach you how to do more than just drive."

She swallowed hard as she tried not to think of the many other things he could teach her. And not one of them involved any type of horsepower—mechanical or otherwise.

Before she could think of something to say that wouldn't give her inner thoughts away, there was a knock on her apartment door. "I think our dinner has arrived," she said, thankful for Mr. Chang's habit of always being punctual.

"Why don't you set the table while I take care of the delivery guy?" Travis asked, starting toward the door.

As he walked across the living room, he wondered what in the name of hell he'd been thinking when he'd taken Fin up on her offer to eat at her place. They couldn't be within twenty feet of each other for more than a couple of minutes without the sexual tension around them becoming so thick it could be cut with a knife. And just the thought of how responsive she'd been to his touch that night in his barn was enough to make his body as hard as a chunk of granite.

But no matter how strong the attraction was between them or how great the sex, nothing could ever come of it. Not only was she Jessie's biological mother, Fin Elliott was a sophisticated career woman. She was city from the top of her pretty red head all the way to her perfectly polished toenails. Her lifestyle was glitz and glamour and that was a far cry from the simple life he led in the wide open spaces on the Silver Moon Ranch. While she attended formal galas and went to trendy nightclubs, he was more apt to be going to a stock auction or stopping in at the local honky-tonk for a cold beer.

As he paid the delivery boy, Travis took a deep

breath. The best thing he could do for his peace of mind would be to remove himself from the temptation that Fin Elliott posed to his suddenly overactive libido. He'd take the food into the dining room, make his excuses and head back to his hotel for room service and a shower cold enough to make him spit ice cubes.

But a few minutes later, when he set the bag on the chrome-and-glass table, Fin's warm smile had him settling onto a chair across from her. As he watched her pull white cartons with red Chinese symbols from the sack, he counted at least six, plus a couple of foam containers and some small waxed paper bags.

"How much did you order?" he asked, skeptically eyeing the amount of food in front of them.

She stopped fussing over the lids on the containers of what looked to be some kind of soup to give him a sheepish grin. "For some reason, everything sounded so good." She caught her perfect lower lip between her teeth. "But I think I might have gotten a little carried away."

"It looks like you're getting ready to feed an army." Laughing, he reached for one of the boxes. "Lucky for you, I've always had a pretty healthy appetite."

"I normally try to watch what I eat, but lately, I've

been absolutely ravenous," she said, spooning a heaping mound of rice onto her plate.

They ate in silence for some time, but Travis took little notice of the flavorful food. His mouth had gone as dry as a desert when he watched Fin delicately nibbling on a barbecue rib. But when her index finger disappeared between her kissable lips as she sucked away the last traces of sauce, his heart stalled and he felt as if he'd taken a sucker punch to the gut.

"That was good," he lied when, several minutes later, they settled down on the couch to drink their coffee. Truth to tell, he had no idea what he'd consumed, let alone how it had tasted. But it beat the hell out of telling her the truth—that he'd been so caught up in watching her, he'd practically forgotten his own name.

"I'm sorry you missed out on your steak dinner," she said apologetically.

"I wouldn't have enjoyed it anyway." He took a sip of the worst coffee he'd ever tasted in his entire life. Placing his cup on the coffee table in front of them, he decided that Fin might be beautiful and sexy as sin, but she couldn't make coffee worth a damn.

"You wouldn't have enjoyed your dinner because you missed getting to spend time with Jessie?"

"Not really." Shaking his head, he grinned as he

stretched his arm along the back of the couch behind her. "I'd had about all I could take of old Ornery and his hovering. That more than anything will put a man off his feed."

"He was a bit much, wasn't he?" The sound of Fin's delightful laughter sent a wave of heat streaking from the top of his head all the way to the soles of his size 13 boots.

Travis nodded as he touched the silky strands of her auburn hair with his index finger. "Old Ornery crossed the line between providing good service and being a pain in the butt."

When he moved his hand to lightly stroke the satiny skin at the nape of her neck, he felt her tremble. It was only the slightest of movements, but there was no mistaking that she was feeling the same overwhelming pull that he was.

As he watched, she closed her eyes and leaned back into his touch. "You know what Jessie was up to this evening, don't you?"

Putting his arm around Fin's slender shoulders, he pulled her closer to his side. "Our daughter is trying to set us up."

"That would be my guess." Fin's voice was softer than usual and she sounded a little breathless.

"Jess has been after me for quite a while to improve my social life." He chuckled. "Before she moved here, she even hinted that I'd been hiding out on the ranch ever since my wife died."

Fin nodded. "I've been accused of using my career to avoid becoming involved with anyone."

"Have you?" Realizing that she might be offended by his question, he shook his head. "It's really none of my business."

"I don't mind." She opened her eyes to look at him. "I haven't been using my career as an excuse. I'm just not good at relationships." She smiled. "As long as we're being honest about it, what about you? What's your excuse?"

He wasn't sure how to answer. It had taken him a few years, but he'd finally moved past the grief and accepted that he and his wife, Lauren, had been robbed of growing old together. But getting back into the dating pool seemed a little ridiculous at his age. And to be truthful about it, he hadn't really wanted to expend the energy to try.

"Some people might call it hiding out." He shrugged. "I think it's been more a case of not knowing how to be single again. I met my wife when I was nineteen years old and we were together until she passed away a few years back. If I have any dating skills left, they're pretty rusty. And besides, the rules of the game have changed quite a bit over the past thirty years."

She smiled. "Some of us were never good at the rules to begin with."

When his gaze met hers, he seriously doubted that Fin had any problems with dating protocol or with men asking her out. She most likely had them lined up from one end of the city to the other just waiting for any indication she'd be willing to grace them with her companionship.

"You're probably a lot better at it than you think, sweetheart."

Staring into her beautiful emerald eyes, Travis couldn't have stopped himself from leaning forward to press a kiss to her perfect lips if his life depended on it. But instead of the brief, friendly peck he'd intended, the feel of her lips as she kissed him back sent a wave of longing all the way to his soul and he didn't think twice about taking the kiss to the next level.

When Travis's firm masculine lips moved over hers with such tenderness that it brought tears to her eyes, Fin felt something warm and inviting blossom deep inside of her. The feeling quickly spread to fill every corner of her being. Never in all of her thirty-eight years of life could she remember a kiss being as enchanting, as compelling, as his gentle caress.

Without a thought to the consequences or the fact

that they were playing a game that could very well end in disaster, not to mention destroy her newfound relationship with Jessie, Fin didn't so much as hesitate to move closer and wrap her arms around Travis's broad shoulders. Is was totally insane, but she wanted to feel his strength surrounding her, needed to once again savor the taste of his masculine desire.

When he traced the soft fullness of her lower lip, she felt as if the blood in her veins turned to warm honey and she opened for him on a ragged sigh. Every detail of their night together in Colorado came rushing back as he tasted and explored her with tender care, and Fin felt her body tingle to life as he coaxed her to respond.

She'd never thought of herself as a sensual being, but in Travis's arms she felt more sexy, more alive than she'd ever felt in her life, and she tentatively met his demands by stroking his tongue with the tip of her own. His deep groan and the tightening of his arms around her was her reward. Feeling more feminine and powerful than she had in a very long time, she pressed herself to his wide chest. Heat flowed through her from the top of her head all the way to the tips of her toes as he stroked the tender inner recesses of her mouth. Fin could have no more stopped the insanity than she could stop her next breath.

Desire, sweet and pure, filled every cell of her being, but when he broke the kiss to nibble a path down the column of her throat, the building passion sent waves of delicious sensation coursing throughout her body. Her insides quivered and a soft moan escaped her lips as the heat flowed through her and began to gather in the pit of her stomach.

"Tell me to stop, Fin. Tell me to get the hell away from you before this goes any further," he said, his voice raspy with the same need overtaking her.

"I don't think…I can," she answered honestly.

His deep chuckle caused her to shiver with longing. "Then we may be in a heap of trouble, sweetheart, because I'm not sure I have enough strength to do the gentlemanly thing and leave on my own."

"You're right. We have a big problem, because I'm not sure I want you to be noble," she said before she could stop herself.

His chest rose and fell as he took a deep breath. "I haven't been able to forget that night back in October when you visited the ranch."

"I haven't, either."

"I don't know how it's possible, but I want you even more now than I did then."

Her breath caught and her heart skipped a beat when he slid his large hand along her ribs to the underside of her breast. "Th-this is insane."

"I couldn't agree more," he said as he cupped the soft mound through the layers of her clothing.

"I'm not good…at relationships," she reminded him when he began to trace slows circles over the tip of her sensitive breast.

"Like I told you earlier, I'm not looking for one," he said, his lips caressing the side of her neck as he spoke. "But I know what it's like to make love to you and I'd like to do it again."

"No strings attached?"

He nodded. "We've already opened that corral gate and the horse got out. I can't see the harm in having one last time together."

Resting her head against his shoulder, Fin did her best to remember all of the complications that being with this man could cause. But for the life of her, she couldn't think of a single one at the moment. And if she were perfectly honest with herself, she didn't even want to.

Before she could change her mind, she pulled from his arms, stood up and held out her hand. When he placed his callused palm on hers and rose to his feet, the look in his incredible blue eyes promised forbidden ecstasy and dark pleasure.

"One last night," she said as she led him into her bedroom and closed the door.

Three

Fin's heart raced and her knees had started to tremble, but calling a halt to what she and Travis were about to do wasn't a consideration. She felt as if she would burn to a cinder if she didn't once again feel the tenderness of his touch and experience the power of his passion.

"I know this is going to sound like I've lost my mind, but I have to know," he said, his voice low and intimate as he turned her to face him. "Are you sure about this, Fin?"

Just like everyone else, there had been several instances in her life when she'd been uncertain about her decisions. But this wasn't one of them.

"If we don't make love, I think I'll go up in flames, Travis."

"No regrets tomorrow?"

"Maybe." She caught her lower lip between her teeth to keep it from trembling a moment before she shook her head. "But not about you or our lovemaking."

She knew he was confused by her answer, but she wasn't sure how to explain what she didn't fully understand herself. How could she put into words that if she had any misgivings at all about what they were about to share, it wouldn't be about him or their night together? It was her inability to share more of herself than just her body that saddened her.

But she'd made a decision the day her father had forced her to give up her daughter. She'd vowed to concentrate on building a career that no one could take away from her. Very few men wanted to take a backseat to a woman's commitment to her work, let alone accept it and understand why she was so driven to succeed.

Of course, with Travis it was a moot point. He wasn't looking for a relationship any more than she was, nor did he have any expectations that they would ever have anything more than this one night together. Still, it seemed rather sad to think of all that she'd had to sacrifice in order to ensure her success.

Reaching up, she smoothed the lines creasing his forehead with the tip of her index finger. "Rest assured, I don't regret that night at your ranch, nor will I regret making love with you tonight."

"Then what—"

"It doesn't matter." She placed her finger to his firm lips to silence him. "Please hold me, Travis. I need you to kiss me and make love with me."

He stared at her for several long seconds as if trying to assimilate what she'd said before he took her into his arms. Slowly lowering his head to settle his mouth over hers, Travis kissed her with a thorough tenderness that brought tears to her eyes and curled her toes inside her chic black pumps.

Her pulse sped up and her stomach fluttered with anticipation when he deepened the kiss and she tasted his undeniable hunger for her. As she surrendered herself to the way he was making her feel, every nerve in her body sparked to life and a heavy warmth flowed through her veins, settling into a delicious coil deep in the pit of her belly.

As he teased her with a light stroking touch of his tongue to hers, she was vaguely aware that he'd moved his hands from her back to her waist. But when he slid his palms up over her ribs, her heart skipped several beats and her nipples tightened in anticipation of his gentle caress.

When they'd made love that night in his barn, their joining had been spontaneous and hurried—an unplanned union with the danger of being discovered. But tonight would be different. Although neither of them had intended for the evening to end with their sleeping together, tonight they had time to explore, time for the excitement of discovering what pleased each other. And they were completely alone. There was little or no possibility of anyone interrupting the coming together of two lonely souls in search of a few hours of comfort and companionship in each other's arms.

The exquisite sensations radiating from her breasts when he finally grazed the sensitive tips through her clothes sent liquid fire racing through her veins and caused her knees to wobble. The taste of his passionate kiss and the feel of his gentle touch were both thrilling and, at the same time, extremely frustrating. She wanted to feel his hands on her body without the encumbrance of satin and lace, wanted to experience the excitement of his firm lips and moist tongue savoring her sensitive skin.

"You feel so damn good," he said, raising his head. He drew in a ragged breath as he reached to turn on the bedside lamp. "But it's not enough. I'm a visual kind of guy. I want to see your beautiful body while I'm bringing you pleasure."

Captured by his intense stare, Fin felt as if he could see all the way to her soul and knew the degree of need he was creating within her. "I want to see and touch you, too, Travis."

With nothing more than a promising smile, he pulled the tail of the shirt from the waistband of his jeans, then took her hands in his and guided them to the snap closures. "Taking off each other's clothes was one of the many things we missed getting to do the first time we were together."

Her stomach fluttered with a delightful thrill at the thought of undressing him. "What else did we miss?" she asked as she unfastened the first gripper.

"We didn't get to take our time the way I would have liked," he answered, leaning forward to nibble on her earlobe.

"How long—"

"What I have in mind will take all night, sweetheart."

A shiver streaked up her spine and her fingers didn't seem to want to work as she fumbled with the next snap. "A-anything else?"

The look in his eyes seared her. "I didn't get to kiss you in ways that will make you blush from just thinking about it."

"I—I don't blush easy." Why couldn't she get her voice to work the way it should?

When he whispered what he intended to do, a jolt of pure electrified desire shot to every part of her being and she knew exactly why her vocal cords were freezing up. He was trying to send her into sensual meltdown and doing an excellent job of it.

"Is that what you want, Fin?"

Unable to get words past her suddenly dry throat, she nodded. She wanted everything this wonderful man was willing to give and had every intention of returning the favor in kind.

When she finally managed to unfasten the last snap on his shirt, she parted the chambray to gaze at his perfectly sculpted chest and stomach. A fine dusting of downy, dark blond hair covered sinew made hard from years of strenuous physical labor. She knew several male models who would kill to have Travis's muscle definition. But his perfectly padded pecs and rippling belly were results that no amount of time spent in a gym could accomplish.

"You're magnificent," she said, deciding he definitely had a point about their missing out on several enjoyable steps in the fine art of foreplay.

His low chuckle sent a wave of goose bumps shimmering over her skin. "I've been called a lot of things in my life—most of them pretty unflattering—but this is the first time anyone's ever referred to me as magnificent."

She grinned as she slipped off her shoes. "Trust me on this, darling. Your body is quite remarkable."

"I'll bet it can't hold a candle to yours," he said as he bent to pull off his boots. When he straightened he wrapped his arms around her to pull her against him. "But I'm damned sure going to find out."

His eyes held her captive as she felt his hands begin to gather the fabric of her dress. In no time at all, he pulled the clingy knit up and over her head. Then, reaching behind her, he unhooked her bra and slid the straps from her shoulders. The scrap of lace joined her dress on the floor.

When he stepped back to gaze at her, she hoped that he missed the fact that gravity had affected certain parts of her anatomy and things weren't as pert as they'd been ten years ago. Of course, they hadn't known each other then, so maybe he wouldn't notice that, although still slender and toned, she was approaching forty.

"My God, Fin, you're beautiful." From the appreciative gleam in his eyes, she had no doubt that he meant it.

Feeling more feminine and attractive than she had in a very long time, she pushed his shirt from his impossibly wide shoulders and tossed it on top of the growing pile of their clothing on the plush white carpet. Sparks of heat rushed through her at the speed of light when he pulled her back into his arms, and she had to force herself to breathe at the first contact of sensitive feminine skin meeting hair-roughened male flesh.

"You feel as good as I knew you would," he said, his breathing sounding quite labored.

"So…do…you." He wasn't the only one having trouble catching his breath.

His large hands splaying over her back felt absolutely wonderful and she marveled at how exciting his callused palms felt on her smooth skin. Closing her eyes, she reveled in the tiny tingles skipping through her at his touch. But when he leaned back to kiss the slopes of her breasts, the coil of need deep in her feminine core tightened to an empty ache and she felt as if she would melt into a puddle.

His firm lips nibbled and teased until she thought she would go mad if he didn't take the tightened tip into his mouth. But the moment his mouth closed over her, Fin's knees gave way and she had to grasp his hard biceps to keep from falling into an undignified heap at his feet.

"Easy, sweetheart." His lips grazing her sensitive

nipple as he spoke intensified the sensations racing through her body and she barely managed to suppress a moan from escaping. "We're just getting started."

"You really meant it…when you said our lovemaking would take…all night," she said, struggling to draw air into her lungs.

He raised his head, the promise in his dark blue gaze causing her heart to pound against her ribs. "I'm going to take my time and by tomorrow morning there won't be a single inch of you that I haven't kissed or made love to." His smile sent an arrow of heat straight to the most feminine part of her. "I'm not from New York, Fin. I'm a country boy with country ways. I take my time and don't get in a rush about much of anything. And especially when I'm loving a woman."

The sound of his smooth, steady baritone and the vow she detected in his navy eyes made her insides feel as if they'd turned to warm pudding. "Th-there won't be anything left of me but a pile of ashes," she said, barely recognizing the sultry female voice as her own.

His sexy grin as he guided her hands to his belt buckle increased the heat building inside of her. "Then I guess we'll go up in a blaze of glory together, sweetheart."

Slowly unbuckling the leather strap, Fin concentrated on unfastening the metal button at his waist. She delighted in the shudder that ran through his big body when her fingers brushed the bulge straining against his fly as she reached for the tab of his zipper. But instead of easing the closure open, she decided to treat him to a bit of the sweet torture he'd been putting her through.

"I think I'm going to enjoy this slow, country lovemaking," she said as she leisurely ran her finger along the top of his waistband. She allowed her knuckles to lightly brush his skin and watched his stomach muscles contract in response.

"I don't want you get the wrong idea." He drew in a deep breath. "I swear I'm not trying to hurry things along, but these jeans are getting damned uncomfortable in the stride."

"It does appear that you have a problem in that area," she teased. Taking pity on him, she eased the zipper down. "Does that feel better?"

"Oh, yeah." Brushing her fingers aside, he stepped back and made quick work of removing the denim from his muscular thighs. "You have no idea how painful a pair of jeans can be to a man in my condition."

When he straightened and reached for her, he hooked his thumbs in the elastic just below her waist. "As good as you look in this little scrap of satin, I think you'll look even better out of it," he said as he pulled her bikini panties down.

Her legs trembled and she had to brace her hands on his shoulders to steady herself as she stepped out of them. When she finally found her voice, she reached for the band at the top of his cotton briefs. "By the same token, I think you'll look fantastic out of these."

When she removed the last barrier separating them, her eyes widened and it felt as if the temperature in the room went up several degrees. That night in his barn they'd been in the shadows and there had been little time to pay attention to anything but their hurried coming together. But now she had the opportunity to study his incredible body and the perfection that was Travis Clayton.

His long legs and lean flanks were as well-defined as his upper torso, but it was the sight of his full erection that sent a shiver of anticipation and need straight to the heart of her femininity. He was an impressively built male, heavily aroused and looking at her as if she were the most desirable creature he'd ever seen.

"You may make me out to be a liar, sweetheart," he said, reaching for her.

"Why do you say that?" she asked, feeling as if

she'd go up in flames at the feel of his body touching hers from shoulders to knees.

"I promised you I was going to love you all night, but now I'm not sure that's going to be an option." He shook his head. "Just the sight of you has me hotter than a two-dollar pistol in a skid row pawnshop on Saturday night."

"That makes two of us." Her body quivered at the feel of his hard arousal pressed to her lower stomach. "I feel as if I'm going to go up in flames at any moment."

"I think we'd better take this to bed, while we still have the strength to get there," he said, swinging her up into his arms.

Smiling, Fin draped her arms around his neck. "I could have walked. The bed is only a few feet away."

He gave her a quick kiss and shook his head. "I know. But that would have required me turning loose of you and I didn't want to do that."

His candidness caused her heart to skip a beat. He knew just what to say to make her feel special and cherished. But more than that, she sensed that he really meant what he said. He didn't want to let her go and she didn't want him to.

When they reached the bed, he lowered her enough to pull back the black satin comforter, then placed her gently in the middle of the queen-size mattress. She watched him retrieve something from his jeans, then slide it under the pillow a moment before he stretched out beside her.

He gathered her to him and fused their lips in a kiss that caused her head to spin. She tasted his urgent male hunger and the depth of his passion and marveled at the fact that she was the object of this amazing man's desire.

As he broke the kiss to nibble his way down to her collarbone, Fin drew in a ragged breath. But when he continued to the slope of her breast, then on to the hardened peak, her breath caught. At the first touch of his tongue to her sensitive flesh, she held his head to her and wondered if she'd ever breathe again.

Taking her nipple into his mouth, he gently sucked and teased as he slid his hand down her side, then along her outer thigh. The delicious tension deep inside of her increased to an almost unbearable ache, but when he moved his palm up the inside of her leg to her nest of feminine curls, a jolt of need stronger than she could've ever imagined raced to every fiber of her being.

But nothing could have prepared her for the level of excitement Travis created within her when he parted her soft folds and, with a feather-light touch, stroked the tiny node hidden there. Her heart pounded against her ribs and she moved restlessly against him as wave after wave of intense sensation coursed through her.

Travis was taking her to heights of passion she'd never known existed and she was certain she'd spontaneously combust if he didn't make love to her soon.

"Please, Travis…I can't…take much more."

"What do you need, Fin?"

Driven to distraction by his continued stroking and the feel of his warm, moist lips brushing the puckered tip of her breast as he spoke, she had to concentrate hard on what she needed to tell him. "I need you…to make love to me. Now!"

"But I'm just getting started, sweetheart," he said, stroking her more deeply.

"I'll never…survive."

"Are you sure?"

"Yes."

Reaching down between them, she found him and used her palm to measure his length and the strength of his need for her. When a groan rumbled up from deep in his chest and his big body shuddered against her, she was overcome by a need like nothing she'd ever known.

He caught her hands in his to stop her. "I get the idea, sweetheart."

His breathing was labored as he moved away from her to find the foil packet he'd tucked under the pillow earlier. When he'd arranged their protection, he rose over her to nudge her knees apart and settle himself between her thighs.

"Let's do this together," he said, smiling as he took her hand in his and helped her guide him.

His gaze held hers captive as together they became one and Fin knew she'd never experienced anything quite so sensual or erotic. But as he eased his hips forward and her body stretched to welcome him, she gave herself up to the delicious feeling of their joining and abandoned all other thought.

She watched his jaw tighten as he moved farther into her. "You feel so damn good, sweetheart."

"So do you," she said, wrapping her arms around his broad back and her legs around his slender hips.

When he was buried completely within her, his heated gaze held hers as he set a slow pace of rhythmic thrusts. The weight of his lower body pressed intimately to hers and the exquisite friction of their movements sent tingling sparks skipping over every nerve in her body and in no time she felt the coil in the pit of her stomach tighten to the breaking point.

Holding him to her, Fin fought to prolong the feeling of being one with this amazing man. But all too soon the tension inside of her shattered into a million shards of sensation and she moaned his name as the sweet waves of release coursed through her.

Her satisfaction must have taken him over the edge because a moment later Travis's big body stiffened, then surged into her one final time as he released his essence with a shuddering groan.

As the light of dawn began to creep into the room, Travis lay holding Fin's slight body to his side. After making love again sometime in the middle of night, she'd drifted off. But he'd lain awake, thinking about one of, if not the most, exciting encounters of his life.

When Lauren had been alive, their coming together had been that of two people comfortable with each other. And although their intimacy hadn't been overly passionate, it had been satisfying.

But what he shared with Fin was nothing short of explosive. Her unbridled responses to his lovemaking fueled a fire within him that he'd never imagined possible. Hell, she made him feel more like a randy teenager than a man staring long and hard at fifty.

It was a real shame that with the coming of morning their time together would end. She'd resume her life as the glamorous editor-in-chief of a fashion magazine, while he went back to being a

Colorado rancher, chasing a herd of cattle all over hell's half acre.

When Fin moaned and stirred next to him, he glanced down to find her satiny cheeks had turned ashen and her emerald eyes were clouded by a mist of tears. "What's wrong, sweetheart?"

He watched her close her eyes and swallow hard. "I think…I'm going to…be sick." She'd no sooner gotten the words past her pale lips than she was bolting from the bed and running for the adjoining bathroom.

Following her, he supported her shoulders as she sank to her knees and lost her battle with the nausea. When she finally raised her head to take a breath, he released her long enough to grab a plush terry washcloth from a rack by the shower and dampen it with cool water.

"Th-thank you," she whispered brokenly as he bathed away the beads of perspiration from her forehead and helped her into the robe that had been hanging on the back of the bathroom door.

"Feeling better now?" When she nodded, he helped her to her feet and led her back to bed. "Do you have some seltzer?"

"I think there's some club soda…in the refrigerator behind…the wet bar," she said haltingly.

Quickly pulling on his jeans, Travis hurried into the other room. When he returned to the bedroom, he found her once again paying homage to the porcelain god.

"Do you think it was something you ate that didn't set well?" he asked as he knelt beside her and helped her take a few sips of club soda.

She shrugged her slender shoulders. "I've been queasy a lot lately, but this is the first time I've been sick."

Her words slammed into him like a physical blow and he had to force himself to breathe. "How long has this been going on?"

"I don't know," she said weakly. "Maybe a couple of weeks. I've been meaning to make an appointment with my doctor, but haven't gotten around to it."

His heart raced and a knot began to form in the pit of his stomach. "Have you had a period since you returned from your trip to the Silver Moon?"

As he watched her worry her lower lip between her teeth, he knew the answer even before she managed to get the single word out. "No."

The timing was right and the fact that they'd failed to use any kind of protection that night in his barn left him with only one conclusion. Taking one deep breath, then another, Travis felt light-headed and just a little queasy himself.

"Fin, I think there's a damned good possibility that you're pregnant with my baby."

Four

When the gravity of the situation finally began to settle in, Travis's words were as effective as a dose of smelling salts to Fin's cloudy brain. For the past week, she had purposely denied the telltale symptoms of pregnancy, but it was past time that she faced the facts.

She'd rationalized the occasional light-headedness and morning nausea as the result of stress from the competition and working grueling hours to win. But apparently that wasn't the case. It appeared that history was repeating itself and she was pregnant again after only one incidence of unprotected sex.

"This can't be happening," she moaned, burying her head in her hands. "Not again."

"It's going to be all right, Fin. Until you take a pregnancy test, we won't know for sure," Travis said, his voice gentle as he lifted her to his wide chest and carried her back into the bedroom. When he placed her on the bed, he sat down beside her and took her hands in his. "If you'll tell me where the nearest drug store is located, I'll run out and buy one of those home tests. Once we get the results, we'll know what we're facing and figure out how to handle it."

She raised her gaze to meet his. "We?"

He nodded without so much as a moment's hesitation. "If you are carrying my baby, you're not going to face the music alone. I'll be there with you every step of the way and whatever decisions have to be made, we'll make them together."

His vow to lend his moral support was very much appreciated, but until the stick turned blue, she had every intention of holding out hope that she wasn't pregnant. "Let's get that test kit and find out for certain one way or the other."

Giving Travis her key to let himself back in and directions to a pharmacy close by, she waited until he left before she allowed her tears to fall.

What on earth had she gotten herself into this time? And could the timing have been any worse?

She was in a fierce competition with her family, and especially her twin, Shane, to be named CEO of Elliott Publication Holdings when Patrick retired in a couple of months. Even if *Charisma*'s growth pushed it over the top and she became the clear winner of the contest, she seriously doubted that her self-righteous father would turn over the reins of his magazine empire to the daughter who made a habit of disgracing him with grandchildren born out of wedlock. And although times were different than they'd been twenty-three years ago and it was perfectly acceptable for a single woman to bear and raise her children alone, Patrick was from a different generation. There was no way he'd hand over his precious company to a woman he considered unable to manage her own life.

Her breath caught on a sob and she squeezed her eyes shut as she thought of all she stood to lose. "J-Jessie," she said aloud.

What would this do to her fledgling relationship with her daughter? They'd just found each other. How would Jessica react to the news that her biological mother and adoptive father had been unable to control themselves and now she was going to have a baby brother or sister?

Leaning back against her pillows, Fin tried not to think of the fallout an unplanned pregnancy would cause if what she and Travis suspected was true. The implications were endless and just thinking about them made her temples throb and a heavy feeling of dread fill her chest.

When she heard Travis unlock her apartment door, she sat up and wiped the moisture from her cheeks. She was no longer that frightened fifteen-year-old girl who'd had no recourse but to go along with whatever decision her parents made for her. She was a woman now and no matter what results the test showed, she would handle the situation with dignity, grace and a strength of will that she hadn't possessed twenty-three years ago.

"Is it showing anything yet?" Travis asked as he paced outside of Fin's bathroom door.

The pharmacist he'd talked to had assured him that the pregnancy test kit he purchased was the easiest, most accurate over-the-counter indicator on the market. If the digital display spelled out "pregnant," then he and Fin were going to have a baby together.

His heart thudded in his chest like an out of control jackhammer every time he thought of Fin being pregnant. He never in his wildest imaginings would have thought that at the ripe old age of forty-nine, he'd be anxiously awaiting test results to see if he'd gotten a woman "in trouble."

When he heard the bathroom door open, he stopped pacing. The look on her beautiful face answered his question even before he got the words out. "You're pregnant, aren't you?"

He watched her take several deep breaths as if she needed fortification, then nodding, she walked over to sit on the side of the bed. "It was such a strong positive that it didn't even take the entire amount of time the directions said it would for the results to show up."

Before his knees gave way, he sank down on the mattress beside her, then, putting his arms around her shoulders, he tried to think of something to say. Hell, what could he say? He felt as if he'd just been hit right square between the eyes with a two-by-four.

"I don't know how you feel about all this, but I'm going to keep my baby," she said suddenly. Emphatically.

He shook his head. "I never doubted for a minute that you wouldn't."

She straightened her shoulders and turned to face him. The only indication of her turmoil was the slight trembling of her perfect lips. "Patrick forced me to give up Jessica, but this time I won't let anyone take my child."

Travis could understand why she felt the way she did, given that her parents had made her put

Jessie up for adoption. But the baby was his, too, and he fully intended to be part of his child's life.

Only now wasn't the time to start discussing shared custody. Fin was about as fragile as he'd ever seen a woman and she needed his support. And he'd damned well give her the encouragement she needed or die trying.

"I give you my word that as long as I have breath in my body no one will separate you and the baby," he said gently.

Tears welled up in her pretty emerald eyes. "There's no way I could bear to go through that again, Travis."

"I know, sweetheart, and I promise you won't have to." He pulled her into his arms and held her close. "I'll be right beside you every step of the way and I'll walk through hellfire and back before I let anyone or anything harm you or our baby."

They sat in silence for some time before she pulled from his arms. "If you don't mind, I think I'd like to be alone for a little while."

He could understand her need for a little solitude. A lot had happened in the past hour or so and they both needed time to sort out their feelings.

"Are you going into the office today?" he asked as he rose from the side of the bed.

She shook her head. "My absence is going to

raise a few eyebrows and generate more than a little speculation, but I'll call Cade and have him take over for me today. Aside from the fact that I wouldn't be able to concentrate, I'd like to see my gynecologist as soon as possible. Hopefully, she'll be able to work me into her schedule sometime today."

As she walked him to the door, he shrugged into his coat and picked up his wide-brimmed hat. "Will you be all right on your own or do you want me to go with you to see the doctor?"

"You really meant what you said about being there for me." Her amazed expression and the sound of her voice left little doubt that he'd surprised her.

He caught her gaze with his as he touched her soft cheek with his index finger. "I never say anything that I don't mean, Fin." Giving her a quick kiss, he opened the door. "I'll be back this evening to check on you and see that you're all right."

Stepping out into the hall, he put his hat on and closed the door behind him. The last thing he wanted to do was walk away from her. But they both had a lot to think about and things they needed to do. Fin was going to try to get an appointment with her doctor and he had to call his housekeeper, Spud, to see how the ranch was faring in his absence. Then, after a quick lunch with Jessie, he had to get fitted for that damned monkey suit she was going to make him wear when he walked her down the aisle.

While he stood on the sidewalk waiting for a passing taxi, he couldn't stop thinking about the baby Fin was carrying. He shook his head in total disbelief. Most of his friends back home were becoming grandpas and here he was starting a second family.

When he and Lauren had discovered that she was unable to have children, they'd accepted the fact they would never have a child of their own and started the adoption process. And although Jessie wasn't his biological daughter, she was, and always would be, his little girl. From the moment he'd laid eyes on her bundled up like a little doll in her light pink baby blanket, she'd stolen his heart. He loved her more than life itself and that would never change.

But the baby growing inside of Fin would be his own flesh and blood—a child he never in a million years expected to have. That was going to take some getting used to, especially after all this time. It was also going to take awhile to wrap his mind around the fact that his adopted daughter and his biological child had the same mother.

And if he was struggling to come to grips with it

all, he couldn't even imagine how hard it was for Fin. Within the past couple of months, she'd found her first child and become pregnant by that child's adoptive father with her second child.

Sliding into the backseat of a taxi, he gave the driver the name of his hotel. As an afterthought, he asked, "Would you happen to know where I could order some flowers?"

"My cousin Vinnie's a florist," the man said. "His shop is a block down from your hotel. Tell him that Joe sent you. He'll give you a deal."

"Thanks, I'll do that."

Travis wasn't certain what the protocol was, or even if there was one, for waking up to find that he'd impregnated the woman he'd just spent the most incredible night of his life making love to, but he figured a nice bouquet of flowers surely wouldn't be considered offensive. He not only wanted to show Fin that he meant what he'd said about being supportive, he also wanted her to know how honored he felt that she was giving him a second go-round at fatherhood.

"What the hell's going on, Fin?" Her twin brother, Shane, barged into her apartment as soon as Fin answered the door.

"Good evening to you too, Shane," Fin said dryly.

She wasn't surprised that he stopped by on his way home from work. His apartment was only a few floors up from hers.

When he turned to face her, his expression was filled with concern. "Are you feeling all right?"

"I'm fine."

He frowned. "Then why didn't you come into the office today? I can't remember the last time you took an entire day off and neither can anyone else. Cade and Jessie have no idea what's going on and you have poor Chloe worried sick. She said you were having some problems with dizziness and she's convinced that you've worked yourself into physical exhaustion."

Fin had known that her absence would create a stir, but that couldn't be helped. "Would you like to sit down while you're taking me to task or would you prefer to stand?"

Her question seemed to erase much of the irritation from his handsome face. "Look, I'm sorry if I came across a little strong, but you'll have to admit that missing a day at *Charisma* is completely out of character for you. Especially when we're neck and neck in the competition for CEO."

Fin could understand her twin's confusion. She'd made it clear from the moment Patrick made his announcement about the contest that she had every intention of winning. But several things had changed in the past couple of months and she was having to realign her priorities.

"I appreciate everyone's concern and I truly didn't mean to cause you or anyone else any undue worry, but I had some personal business to attend to."

He cocked one dark eyebrow. "Would you care to elaborate?"

"No."

He looked taken aback. "But—"

"As I told you, it's personal."

She could tell he was more than a little mystified by her lack of details. But as close as she and Shane had always been and as much as they'd always shared, she wasn't about to discuss her pregnancy with him or anyone else. At least, not until she and Travis had the opportunity to talk things over and decide how to spring the news on everyone.

To soften her refusal to explain further, she smiled. "I'm sure there are things about yourself that you keep private, aren't there?"

A slow smile began to spread across his handsome face. "A few."

"Shall we agree to leave the matter alone, then?"

He nodded. "Agreed." As she watched, her brother turned his attention to the beautiful bouquet of two dozen long-stemmed red roses arranged in a crystal vase on top of her coffee table. "Do those have anything to do with the *personal* part of your time off?" he asked, his smile turning to a knowing grin.

Reaching down, she snatched up Travis's card before Shane had the opportunity to pluck it from the plastic pick and read it. "That, dear brother, is none of your business."

The cad threw back his head and laughed. "I'll take that as confirmation that it does."

"Don't you think it's past time that you went on up to your apartment and left me alone?"

"Expecting the sender of those flowers to show up soon, sis?" he teased. Before she could get the words out, he answered his own question. "I know, it's none of my business."

"Give the man a prize," she said, ushering him toward the door.

"All right, I'm going." Opening the door, he stepped out into the hall and turned back to face her. "Then you'll be at the office tomorrow?"

She nodded. "Of course. Where else would I be?"

His grin turn mischievous. "In the arms of whoever sent those flowers?"

"Mind your own business, Shane. And while you're at it, have a nice evening," she said, closing the door behind him.

She'd only made it halfway across the living room before a short knock had her turning back. "What part of 'it's none of your concern' don't you understand?" she asked as she jerked the door open.

"I take it that I'm not who you were expecting to see."

Fin's heart skipped a beat at the sight of Travis. He and Shane couldn't have missed each other by more than a matter of seconds.

"I'm sorry, Travis," she apologized, standing back for him to enter her apartment. "Shane felt it was his duty to give me the third degree about missing work."

He nodded as he removed his hat and coat, then tossing them onto one of the armchairs, he reached out to pull her into his arms. "Yeah, when Jess and I had lunch this afternoon, she said that you'd put Cade in charge for the day and wondered if you'd said anything about not feeling well at supper last night."

It was completely insane, considering the circumstances, but his strong arms surrounding her made her feel secure and more at peace than she could ever remember. "What did you tell her?"

"The truth."

Fearing Jessie's reaction, Fin's voice trembled. "Y-you told her I'm pregnant?"

"No." Stepping back, he kept his arm around her shoulders as he led her over to sit on the couch. "Jess asked if you'd mentioned it over supper, which you didn't. I made it a point not to say anything about knowing that the sickness thing didn't show up until this morning."

Fin breathed a sigh of relief. "I know how close you and Jessie are, but would you mind me telling her about the baby?"

"To be perfectly honest, I'd really like it if you did." He gave her a sheepish grin and hugged her close. "When Jessie was a teenager, one of my biggest fears as a father was that one day she'd tell me some pimple-faced kid had gotten her in trouble."

"Didn't you trust her?" Was Travis more like Patrick than she'd thought?

"Don't get me wrong," he said, shaking his head. "I've always had all the faith in the world in my daughter. It was the teenage boys with more hormones than good sense trying to talk the prettiest girl in the county into climbing in the back of their daddy's pickup truck that gave me nightmares."

Fin couldn't help but smile. "You're a wonderful father, Travis."

He shrugged one broad shoulder. "As hard as it

is to believe, I was a teenage boy once." He chuckled. "Hell, at the age of seventeen, I think I was hard about seventy-five percent of the time. And if the truth is known, I probably caused more than a few dads some sleepless nights myself."

If he was even half as good-looking in his youth as he was now, she could imagine that he had worried several girls' fathers. "I suppose it is rather ironic that the very thing you feared for Jessie has happened to you now."

He put some space between them in order to face her. "I know this was the last thing we expected to have happen and you have every right to blame me for not protecting you that night in the barn, but I've spent the day thinking about it." He ran his hand through his thick hair. "Hell, I haven't been able to think of anything else."

"Me, either," she said, reaching up to cup his face in her palm. "But I don't want you to think that I'm assigning blame or that I regret what's happened."

"You don't?"

"Not at all." Placing her hand on her still flat stomach, she smiled. "This is a second chance for me. I missed out on so much when I was forced to put Jessie up for adoption. I never got to see her take her first step or hear her say her first word."

"Horsey."

"Excuse me?"

His grin widened. "'Horsey' was the first thing she said."

Fin laughed. "Why doesn't that surprise me? She's always talking about her horse, Oscar."

"He loves her just as much as she loves him." Laughing, Travis shook his head. "I've never seen a horse mope around like he's on his last leg for weeks at a time, then perk up like a new colt the minute she comes home for a visit."

Uncharacteristic tears filled Fin's eyes and she cursed her hormones for making her so darned emotional. "Thank you for giving her such a wonderful childhood, Travis."

When he wiped a tear from her cheek with the pad of his thumb, her skin tingled from the contact and a warmth began to fill her chest. "Thank *you* for having her," he said, his voice sounding a little gruff. "I know that putting her up for adoption was the hardest thing you've ever had to do, but raising Jess and watching her grow up was the best thing that's ever happened to me. I wouldn't have had that if not for you."

"That's why having this baby is so important to me," she said, nodding. "I'm going to get to be a part of this baby's life the way I never was with Jessie."

She could tell by the look in his sky-blue eyes that he understood, but she noticed an underlying shadow of concern there as well. Anticipating what bothered him, she rushed to alleviate his fears. "I want you to be part of his or her life, too. You're the baby's father and I would never deny you your child."

The doubt disappeared immediately and she could tell he was relieved to hear that she wasn't going to cut him out of the picture. "How are we going to handle this? With you living here in New York and me living in Colorado, it's going to take some work."

"I'm not sure," she said honestly. "But we have eight months to discuss it and make plans."

"With Jessie and Cade's wedding coming up, the next couple of weeks are going to be pretty busy." He drew her into his arms, then leaned back against the couch. "What do you say we postpone any serious discussion until after the ceremony? That will give us a little time to think about it and see what we can come up with."

"That sounds like an excellent idea. And in the meantime, I'll find a way to break the news to Jessie." Snuggling against his shoulder, she hid a yawn behind her hand. "How do you think she'll react?"

His wide chest rose and fell a moment before he tightened his arms around her. “Your guess is as good as mine, sweetheart.”

Five

Fin stared at the young woman seated across from her at the dining room table and wondered how on earth she was going to broach the subject of her pregnancy. To say she was a nervous wreck was an understatement.

She and Travis had hoped she'd have the chance to talk to Jessie before he left to go back to Colorado. Unfortunately, with the approaching wedding and all the last-minute details to pull together, there hadn't been enough time.

But when she learned that Cade was flying to the west coast for a few days to wrap up a lucrative advertising deal for *Charisma* the week before the wedding, Fin seized the opportunity and asked Jessie to have dinner with her.

"Fin, our relationship means a lot to me and I want it to continue to grow," Jessie said without preamble. Fin watched her lay her fork down and catch her lower lip between her teeth as if trying to gather her courage. Then, taking a deep breath, she asked, "Have I upset or offended you in any way?"

Her daughter's question was the last thing Fin expected and she hurried to put Jessie's mind at ease. "No, honey. You haven't done anything." She covered Jessie's hand with hers. "I know we've missed out on so much over the years, but you're still my daughter. I love you. You could never do anything that would change that."

"Thank God."

The relief on Jessie's face tore at Fin's heart. She hated that she'd caused her daughter any undue worry. But she wasn't sure how long the euphoria would last once Jessie learned about Fin's pregnancy and who the father was.

"You haven't been yourself since I canceled dinner with you and Dad last week." Jessie gave her a guilty smile. "I thought you might have been angry with me for trying to set you up with Dad."

Fin's heart beat double-time. This was her opening. She just hoped her announcement didn't cause irreparable damage to Jessie's feelings for her.

"I need to talk to you about that." Fin folded her napkin and placed it on the table, then rose to her feet and motioned toward the living room. "Let's get comfortable."

Jessie suddenly looked apprehensive. "You're beginning to frighten me, Fin."

As she led the way over to the sofa, Fin shook her head. "There's absolutely no reason for you to be afraid, honey." I, on the other hand, have every reason to be scared to death, she thought, dreading what she was about to tell her daughter.

Once they were curled into opposite corners of the plush sofa, facing each other, Fin took a deep breath. "If I've been a bit distracted lately, it's because something has happened—"

"Are you all right?" Jessie interrupted anxiously.

"I'm fine, sweetie." Fin hoped her smile was reassuring, but she was so nervous, she couldn't be sure. "In fact, when I saw the doctor last week, she said I'm in perfect health."

"Then what's the problem?" Jessie asked, clearly confused.

"It's not a problem as far as I'm concerned." Fin couldn't help but smile. "It was a shock at first, but

I've had time to get used to the idea and I'm actually quite happy about it." Taking a deep breath, she met her daughter's curious gaze head-on. "I'm pregnant."

Jessie's eyes widened and she covered her mouth with her hands as she let loose with a delighted little cry. "Fin, that's wonderful." She shook her head. "I didn't even know you were involved with anyone."

"I'm not…exactly." The next part of her announcement was what Fin had dreaded most—telling Jessie who the father was. "Travis is the father."

Jessie's mouth dropped open and she stared at Fin for several long seconds. "My dad? Your baby's father is my dad? My dad, Travis? Travis Clayton?"

Fin nodded slowly. She couldn't tell if Jessie kept repeating Travis's name out of shock or revulsion.

"It was that night at the Silver Moon, wasn't it?" Jessie guessed, her expression giving nothing away. "The two of you left the party to go into the barn to check on that mare and new colt."

Nodding, Fin tried to explain. "I gave Travis a hug to show my appreciation for raising and taking such good care of you and…it just happened."

"This is wonderful," Jessie said suddenly, leaping forward to throw her arms around Fin. "I suspected that something was going on between the two of you." Leaning back, she beamed. "I could see the attraction from the moment you met."

"You're not upset?" Fin asked cautiously as she hugged her back.

Jessie shook her head and sat back to give her an encouraging smile. "I'll admit that it's a huge shock, but I'm thrilled for both of you. I know how much you missed getting to see me grow up and Dad is the best father, ever. This baby is extremely lucky to have the two of you for parents."

Relief washed through Fin at Jessie's emphatic tone, leaving her feeling weak and emotional. "I'm so glad to hear you aren't upset."

"Why would I be upset? I'm ecstatic that I'm finally going to have a sibling," Jessie said, grinning from ear to ear. "And I'll bet Dad is excited beyond words." She stopped suddenly. "You have told him, haven't you?"

Fin nodded. "I discovered that I'm pregnant last week, while he was in town visiting and getting the last fitting for his tux." She purposely omitted they were together when she'd taken the pregnancy test and the fact that they'd spent the night before making love.

"I wonder why Dad hasn't said anything."

"I asked him to let me tell you about the baby because if our predicament upset you, I wanted the brunt of your anger directed at me," Fin explained. "I thought if I took the majority of the blame it would keep from damaging your relationship with your father."

Jessie reached out and took Fin's hands in hers. "That is so sweet of you. But I'm in no way upset by this." She grinned. "Far from it."

Fin felt as if a huge weight had been lifted from her shoulders. "You don't know how many times I've wanted to talk to you about this, but there was never a good time."

"Everything has been so busy with the wedding and all, I'm surprised we were able to find time to have dinner this evening," Jessie agreed, nodding. "Have you told anyone else?"

"No. We felt that you should be the first to know."

"I know I'm just full of questions," Jessie said, her expression turning serious, "but have you made any decisions about how you're going to raise the baby? Are you going to try to share the responsibility?"

"It's only fair that we do." Fin sighed. "But I have no idea how we're going to work this out."

"You have *Charisma* and I can't see Dad leaving the Silver Moon to move to New York," Jessie said, shaking her head.

"We're going to review our options while he's

here for the wedding and hopefully come up with a workable plan." Smiling, Fin reached out to hug her beautiful, understanding daughter. "Keep your fingers crossed that we find a solution and that when we make the announcement about my impending motherhood the rest of the family is as enthusiastic as we are."

Tears filled Fin's eyes as she watched Travis, looking incredibly handsome in his black tux, escort their beautiful daughter down the sweeping staircase at The Tides. Jessie was utterly stunning in her pure white satin-and-lace wedding gown and if the captivated look on Cade's face was any indication, the groom thought so, too.

Glancing over at her mother and Patrick, Fin was thankful they'd welcomed their long-lost granddaughter back into the Elliott clan and insisted the wedding be held at their estate in the Hamptons. All things considered, it was the very least they could do for Jessie.

When Travis walked his daughter down the aisle between the rows of chairs assembled in the large living room, Fin's heart went out to him as he kissed Jessie's cheek, then stepped back for Cade to take his place beside her. It had to be one of the most difficult things Travis had ever had to do—placing the care and happiness of his beloved child in the hands of someone else.

"That was tough," he whispered, his voice gruff as he sat in the seat beside her to watch Jessie and Cade exchange vows.

Unable to get words past the lump clogging her throat, Fin reached over to give his hand a gentle squeeze. She wasn't at all surprised when he held onto it as the ceremony proceeded.

By the time Jessie and Cade had been pronounced husband and wife and everyone started making their way to the heated tent that had been adjoined to the family room to accommodate the reception, Fin needed a few moments alone to collect herself. "If you'll excuse me, Travis, I think I need to freshen my makeup."

"I could use a couple of minutes myself," he said, his need for solitude reflected in his tight expression and the gruff tone of his voice. "If you don't mind, I think I'll step outside to catch my breath."

"I'll see you a bit later," she said, kissing his lean cheek.

As she stood watching Travis walk to the front door, she couldn't help but wonder what it felt like to have a father who loved his child as much as Travis loved Jessie. She'd never had that, never known what it was to have a father who loved unconditionally. Placing her hand over her stomach, she knew her baby was extremely lucky to have Travis for his or her father.

"Fin, are you feeling well? I noticed you look a bit pale."

At the sound of the soft Irish lilt beside her, Fin glanced over at Maeve Elliott. "Mom, could we speak in private?" she asked, deciding there was no time like the present to tell her mother about the baby.

A look of alarm widened Maeve's soft green eyes and Fin knew her mother anticipated bad news. "Of course, dear." Leading the way into the library, she closed the door behind them. "What is it, Finola? What's wrong?" The use of Fin's given name was an indication of the level of Maeve's concern.

"There's nothing wrong," Fin said, placing her hand on her mother's arm to reassure her. "Actually, everything is the way it should be for the first time in twenty-three years."

The worry lines creasing her mother's kind face softened into a smile and she gathered Fin into her arms. "'Tis the way I feel, too, Finny."

Fin held onto her mother for several moments before she led her over to the tall leather armchairs facing the fireplace. "Please sit down, Mom. I have something I need to tell you." When they were both seated in the comfortable chairs, Fin met her mother's questioning gaze. "I'm pregnant. I'm going to have a baby with Jessie's adoptive father, Travis."

Maeve stared at her a moment before covering her eyes and breaking into soft sobs.

A feeling of déjà vu swept over Fin. Her mother's reaction was much the same as it had been the night Fin had told her she was pregnant with Jessie. The only difference between then and now was that Patrick wasn't present for this announcement.

"I had hoped you would be happy for me this time," Fin said, sighing heavily. "But it appears that I've once again disappointed you."

"Oh, no, Finny." Her mother reached out to take Fin's hands in hers. "My tears are those of joy. You never got to hold Jessie, to watch her grow into a beautiful young woman. 'Tis past time that you got to hold and raise a wee babe of your own."

"I should have been allowed to raise Jessie." Try as she might, Fin couldn't keep her bitter tears in check. "Why, Mom? Why didn't you stop Patrick from forcing me to give my baby away? You of all people should have known what it felt like to lose your child. To have her taken away without being able to…stop it from happening." Struggling to control her voice, she shook her head. "Didn't you feel as if your heart had been ripped from your chest when Anna died?"

The emotional pain that clouded Maeve's eyes tore at Fin's heart. She hadn't meant to mention her sister. It had to have been devastating for her mother to lose a seven-year-old child to cancer, but what Fin said was true. Maeve should have known what it would be like for Fin to have her baby taken from her with no say in the matter.

"Oh, Finny, 'tis sorry I am that you had to go through that," Maeve said, her Irish accent becoming more pronounced, as it always did when she was upset or overly emotional. Wiping her tears with a linen handkerchief, she shook her head. "'Twas a sad day for this family and one I have regretted all these years since."

"Then why did you let Patrick do that to me? Couldn't you have stopped him?"

Her mother shook her head. "I did try. But your da wouldn't listen and when it became a threat to our marriage, I backed down."

"You and Patrick had problems because of my situation?" It was the first Fin had heard of it if they had.

Maeve nodded. "Your da is a stubborn man. He put his pride ahead of what was right for you and this family."

"I never knew." Fin had always thought her mother supported every decision Patrick made. "The two of you always presented a united front and I thought you let him force me to give up my child without lifting a finger to help me."

"'Twasn't for you to know," Maeve said, smiling sadly. "What happens between a husband and wife behind closed doors is no one's affair but their own."

"I'm so sorry, Mom." Letting go of the last traces of her misguided anger at her mother, Fin knelt down and put her arms around Maeve's thin shoulders. "I know how much you've always loved Patrick. It must have torn you apart to be caught in the middle of all that."

"'Tis done and past." Her mother soothingly stroked Fin's hair. "Since we are all gathered for Jessie's wedding, I think you should tell the family about the wee one you carry," she said softly as they continued to embrace.

Leaning back, Fin shook her head. "I don't think it's the right time. This is Jessie's day and I don't want to cause a scene or detract from her happiness in any way."

"Does she know?"

Fin nodded. "I didn't want her to hear it from someone else."

"Was she happy for you and her da?"

"She's thrilled."

"'Tis rare when we all gather at the same time." Smiling, Maeve rose to her feet, then tugged on Fin's hand for her to stand. "We should celebrate a new babe on the way, as well as a wedding."

Fin tried to swallow her apprehension. "I don't want Patrick ruining this day for Jessie because of me."

Maeve shook her head. "You needn't worry, Finny. Your da is different now."

"Since when?"

"Give him a chance," Maeve said, her smile encouraging.

As they walked out of the library and down the hall, Fin found Travis standing by the staircase. She needed to warn him about her mother's request, as well as find Jessie and Cade and see if they had any objections to her announcing her pregnancy.

"We'll join the reception in a moment, Mom," Fin said, waiting until Maeve disappeared down the hall before she turned to Travis. "Since everyone is here, my mother thinks we should tell the family about the baby," she said, careful to keep her voice low. "Are you okay with that?"

He nodded. "I'm fine with it. The question is, how do you feel about it?"

"I'm not sure," she said truthfully. "I couldn't be

more excited and I want to tell everyone how happy I am that I've been given a second chance at motherhood. But at the same time, I'm apprehensive about Patrick's reaction. I don't want him putting a damper on Jessie and Cade's big day."

Travis shook his head. "He won't."

"You don't know Patrick Elliott the way I do." She sighed. "And thank your lucky stars you don't."

"He's all about appearances, isn't he?"

"That's *all* he's about," she said, unable to keep the disgust from her voice.

Nodding, Travis smiled. "Then don't you think he'll keep his mouth shut to keep from airing the family laundry in front of all these people?"

The more she thought about it, the more she realized that Travis was right. Not all of the guests were family. And Patrick would never dream of saying anything in front of outsiders that would throw the family in what he perceived to be a bad light.

"You might have a point."

Touching her elbow, he guided her toward the happy sounds coming from the direction of the reception. "Let's find Jess and Cade and clear it with them."

"I want you to promise me you'll let me know if this yahoo doesn't treat you right," Travis said as he and Jessie moved around the dance floor during the father-daughter dance. "I'll hop the first plane east and by the time I'm done with him, there won't be enough of him left to snore."

"Oh, Dad, you're such a cowboy," Jessie said, laughing and hugging him close.

He hugged her back. "I just want you to be happy, angel."

"The only thing that would make me happier would be if Mom was here," she said softly.

Time had eased his loss, but he hated that Lauren couldn't have been here to see their little girl on her special day. "Your mom would have been right in the middle of all this fuss and loving every minute of it."

A tear slipped down Jessie's cheek. "I know."

They were silent for a moment before he asked, "Are you and Cade sure you're all right with Fin letting the family know about the baby here at the reception?"

She nodded. "I think this is the perfect time. In fact, if you don't mind, I'd like to have the honor of telling everyone. Do you think Fin would mind?"

"To tell the truth, I think she'd be relieved that someone else let the cat out the bag." Travis glanced over at the Elliott patriarch. "She's dreading the head honcho's reaction."

"I can't imagine Fin being afraid of anything," Jessie said, frowning.

"I don't think it's a matter of her being frightened as much as it is a case of nerves," he corrected. "She just wants this day to be perfect for you and Cade." He chuckled. "I have a feeling if old moneybags over there gets his drawers in a wad, she'll take into him like a she-bear protecting her cub."

Jessie smiled fondly. "That's so sweet of her." She paused for a moment. "I don't think Granddad will say a single word after I make the announcement. You just stick close to Fin. I'm sure she could use all the moral support she can get."

Travis had no idea what Jess had planned, but she had a good head on her shoulders. He trusted her judgment and if she said she could spring the news and keep Elliott from raising a ruckus, he had no doubt she could do it.

"All right, angel. This is your day. Do what you think is best."

When the dance ended, Travis kissed her cheek and, stepping back for Cade to take his place, walked over to sit at the table with Fin and Shane. "Jessie's going to take care of telling everyone the big secret," he said close to Fin's ear. "Any objections?"

She shook her head and her silky auburn hair

brushing her creamy shoulders fascinated the hell out of him. "I don't mind, but when is she going to do it?"

"Your guess is as good as mine." He covered her hand where it rested on the white linen tablecloth. "But if I know Jess, it won't be long."

He'd no sooner gotten the words out than Jessie and Cade walked over to one of the band's microphones. "If I could have your attention, my wife has an announcement to make," Cade said, giving Jessie a look that left Travis with no worries about how much he adored her.

When all eyes turned her way and the room fell silent, Jessie gazed lovingly at the man standing beside her. "This is one of the happiest days of our lives and Cade and I would like to thank you all for helping us celebrate our marriage." Turning her attention toward the table where Travis sat with Fin, she smiled. "I would also like to announce that we have another reason to celebrate. My dream of being a big sister is finally going to come true. Fin and my dad have just learned they're going to give me a brother or sister in the summer."

The stunned silence that followed was suddenly interrupted by a round of applause and Travis found himself and Fin besieged by a herd of well-wishing Elliotts. As Fin's brothers, their wives and what seemed like an endless line of nieces and nephews congratulated them, he couldn't help but notice that Fin's gaze kept returning to the tall, silent, white-haired gentleman standing as stiff and straight as a marble statue on the opposite side of the room.

It appeared that Patrick Elliott was none too happy about the news, even though his wife, Maeve, looked just the opposite. As Travis watched, Maeve said something to Patrick, then took the old gent by the arm and led him toward the crowd congratulating them. Putting his arm around Fin's shoulders, Travis drew her close as he met the older man's steely gaze head on, sending a clear message that Travis wasn't going to tolerate Fin being bullied or upset in any way.

When the elder Elliott approached, it was like watching the parting of the Red Sea. The family divided into two groups, and just as Travis imagined happened thousands of years ago, a hushed silence reigned. Not even the smallest child present made a sound.

"A wee babe is a grand event and we welcome another addition to the family," Maeve said, breaking the uncomfortable silence.

Stepping forward, Fin smiled and hugged her mother. "Thank you, Mom."

The crowd seemed to wait for Patrick to add his

blessings, but it never came. The man remained as stoic as ever.

Although Fin's expression never changed, Travis could have sworn he saw a shadow of pain in her pretty green eyes. But it was gone in a flash, replaced with a defiance that matched her father's.

The uneasy silence was almost deafening and just when Travis thought they'd all pass out from holding their collective breath, Maeve turned to her husband. "'Tis time you told them why you put them at odds to win the company, don't you think?"

A frown creased the man's forehead as he shook his head. "Leave it be, Maeve," Patrick said gruffly. "They'll understand soon enough." And with that, the Elliott patriarch tucked his wife's hand in his arm, turned and walked away.

"Don't let the old man get you down, sis," Shane said, hugging her.

Fin didn't look the least bit surprised by her father's reaction. "I expected nothing less from him," she said, shaking her head as she hugged her twin brother in return.

As the crowd began to recede and the band commenced playing, Travis noticed a young blond-haired woman slip up beside Shane. When she whispered something in his ear, the man let out a whoop loud enough to wake the dead, then wrapped her in a bear hug and, grinning like an old possum, swung her around in a circle.

When everyone stopped to stare at them, Travis had to choke back his laughter at the red flush creeping up from Shane's collar all the way to his forehead. The little blonde beside him was just as embarrassed and looked as if she were ready to dive under the table at any moment.

"Travis Clayton, this is Rachel Adler, Shane's executive assistant," Fin said, grinning as she made the introductions.

"It was nice to meet you, Mr. Clayton," Rachel said, her cheeks still bright red. "If you'll all excuse me, I need to be going now. I'll see you at the office on Monday, Shane."

As they watched Rachel hurry to the family room door, Fin turned to her brother. "Would you care to explain that emotional display and the huge grin on your face?"

"No."

"You want to know what I think?" Fin asked.

"No, I don't care what you think," Shane said defensively.

"Tough." As she winked at Travis, her smile caused a warmth to spread throughout his chest and he didn't think he'd ever seen her look more beautiful. "I'm going to tell you anyway, dear brother."

Shane frowned. "I'd rather you didn't."

"I don't know what Rachel told you, but I think you're to the point where you'd use any excuse to finally have her in your arms," Fin said, clearly ignoring her brother.

"You, dear sister, need to shut up and mind your own business," Shane said irritably as he turned to walk away.

"You just confirmed my suspicions, Shane," Fin called after him.

For reasons he didn't even want to begin to analyze, her delightful laughter had a strange effect on Travis's insides. "Let's dance," he said suddenly, taking her by the hand to lead her out onto the dance floor.

"I thought Jessie mentioned one time that you didn't like dancing," she said, sounding a little breathless as he pulled her to him.

"I don't." He smiled at the shiver he felt course through her when he whispered, "Your brother isn't the only man here who'll use whatever excuse he can find to have the most beautiful woman in the room in his arms."

Six

"I don't think I've ever seen a more lovely couple," Fin said, settling into the back of the EPH corporate limo for the ride back to the city. She sighed happily. "Jessie was absolutely stunning."

"She looked just like you," Travis said, reaching over to take her hand in his.

"A much younger version, maybe," she said, laughing.

His smile heated her all the way to her toes. "I don't think I had the chance to tell you how sexy you look in that slinky green dress." He lightly touched the teal silk of her Versace gown with his index finger. "You and Jessie were the two most beautiful women at the wedding."

"Well, you clean up pretty good yourself, cowboy." She placed her hand on the arm of his black tuxedo. "You look incredibly handsome in formal attire, Travis."

He grunted. "I feel like a trained monkey in a side show."

"I think you're a very handsome monkey," she said, laughing.

"Well, take a good look because I won't be wearing this thing again," he said, putting his arm around her shoulders. "I'll take it home and hang it in the closet, never to see the light of day again."

"Never say never."

"I think this is one time it's a sure bet to say never." His arm tightening around her to draw her close and his low chuckle caused every cell in her body to tingle to life. "A jackass will sprout wings and fly before you see me in this thing again."

As they left the lights of The Tides behind and the intimacy of the night closed in around them, Travis reached over and pushed the button to raise the privacy panel between them and the driver. "How are you doing?" he asked. "I know today was an emotional roller coaster for you and you have to be drained."

"I probably should be, but surprisingly I'm

feeling pretty good." Slipping off her high heels in an effort to get comfortable for the two-hour drive, she added, "Now that my pregnancy is no longer a secret, I'm more relaxed than ever."

When he gathered her close, a wave of goose bumps shimmered over her arms at the feel of his warm breath stirring the fine hairs at her temple. "I told you your dad wouldn't say anything."

"There wasn't a lot he could say after Jessie made her little speech." Touched beyond words at the enthusiasm and support her daughter had shown for her pregnancy, Fin smiled. "She's going to be a wonderful big sister."

"She'll have the poor little thing spoiled rotten."

"And you won't?"

He chuckled beneath her ear and tightened his arms around her. "I didn't say I wouldn't."

They rode along in a comfortable silence for several minutes before Travis spoke again. "Have you come to any conclusions about how we can handle your pregnancy and the distance between us?"

"With all of the last-minute details for the wedding, I haven't had time." She shook her head. "What about you? Have you come up with anything?"

"No, but we're going to have to figure out something." He touched her chin with his index finger to tilt her head back. When their gazes met, he gave her a smile that had her toes curling into the thick carpet on the limo floor. "This is all pretty new for me, but when I told you I'd be there with you every step of the way, I meant it. And I wasn't just talking about raising the baby once it gets here. I intend to be there for you through the pregnancy, as well."

Before she could respond, he lowered his head and captured her lips in a kiss so gentle it brought tears to her eyes. The soft caress of his mouth as it moved over hers had her quickly feeling as if the temperature in the car had gone up several degrees. But when he coaxed her to part for him and used his tongue to mimic a more intimate mating, a spark ignited deep in her soul and the heat flowing through her veins spread throughout her body.

Sparkles of light danced behind her closed eyes and a longing began to build in the most feminine part of her when he slipped his hand inside the plunging neckline of her evening gown and pushed the built-in cup aside to caress her breast. The work-hardened calluses on his palm chafed her sensitive nipple, sending tingling streaks of pure delight to every cell of her being. But when he traced the puckered tip with his thumb, her heart skipped several beats and her breathing became extremely difficult.

As he gently rolled the peak between his thumb and forefinger, he continued to tease her inner recesses with his tongue and her insides quivered with need like nothing she'd ever known. Heaven help her, but she couldn't have stopped a tiny moan of pleasure from escaping if her life depended on it.

"Does that feel good, sweetheart?" His smooth baritone vibrated against her lips and fed the pool of desire gathering in her lower belly.

"Mmm."

Lifting her to sit on his lap, she felt the hard ridge of his erection against her thigh, and her own body's answering need left her feeling light-headed from its intensity. The tension building inside of her was maddening and she wanted nothing more than to surrender herself once again to Travis's masterful brand of lovemaking.

His groan of frustration penetrated the sensual haze surrounding her when he tried to shift them into a more comfortable position. "It's been a long time since I made out in the backseat of a car, sweetheart." He eased her back to sit beside him on the limo's plush velour seat. "And for what I want to do to you, we'll need more room than there is in the backseat of this damned limousine."

"When are you leaving to return to Colorado?" she asked breathlessly.

"Tomorrow afternoon." He kissed his way to the hollow at the base of her throat. "Spend the night with me, Fin," he said, nibbling at her wildly fluttering pulse.

If she'd stopped to think about it, she might have thought of all the reasons they should back away from whatever was going on between them. Even though they were going to have a baby together, he lived thousands of miles away on his quiet, charming ranch in Colorado and her life was in the most exciting, glamorous city in the world.

But without a second thought, she snuggled against the most incredible, giving man she'd ever met. "Your bed or mine?"

"Why the hell can't these places have regular metal keys?" Travis muttered as he fitted the little plastic card into the lock on his hotel room door.

The ride from the Hamptons to the hotel had been the longest trip of his life. Coupled with the fact that he and Fin hadn't been able to keep their hands off of each other, he was hotter than a blast furnace in the middle of an August heat wave. And Fin wasn't much better off. Her porcelain cheeks wore the blush of unfulfilled passion and he didn't think she'd ever looked sexier or more desirable.

When the tiny light on the lock finally flashed to

green, he pushed the door open and quickly ushered her inside. The door had barely swung shut before he had the light switched on and reached to pull her back into his arms.

"You know what I've discovered about these designer dresses?" he asked as he slid the back zipper down below her waist.

"What's that?" she asked, sounding as winded as he felt.

"They're designed to drive a man out of his mind with lust."

Peeling the dress from Fin's luscious upper body, he took her into his arms as the evening gown floated down to form a green pool of silk around her trim ankles. As he pressed kisses across her collarbone, then down the creamy slope of her breast, he could have cared less that he'd just sent thousands of dollars worth of dress to lie in a tangled heap on the floor.

She shivered against him when he took her pebbled coral nipple into his mouth. Tasting her sweetness, feeling the nub tighten further, he felt his lower body harden to an almost painful state.

"You're driving me insane," she said, sagging against him.

"I'm right there with you, honey." He drew in a ragged breath. "Let's get out of the rest of these glad rags before I do something stupid and rip them off of both of us."

Fin's laughter sent a shock wave of heat coursing through him at the speed of light. "At the moment, I think you're the only one with an over abundance of clothing, Mr. Clayton."

Glancing down, he grinned at the sight of her standing before him in nothing but a little triangle of lace and silk. The dress Fin had been wearing not only had a built-in bra, it had some kind of underskirt, as well. He wasn't sure who came up with the idea of combining women's undergarments with a dress, but he'd bet his last dime that men all over the world were singing their praises.

"I think you might have a real good point there, Ms. Elliott." Tugging his shirt from the waistband of his trousers, he could have cheerfully throttled whoever thought it would be better to use studs instead of buttons on formal wear.

"Let me help you with those," she said, stepping forward.

To his relief, within no time Fin was pushing the shirt apart to place her hands on his chest. At the first contact of her soft palms on his flesh, it felt as if a bolt of lightning shot from the top of his head to the soles of his feet.

Jerking as if he'd been zapped by a cattle prod,

he shook his head and backed away from her. "I think I'd better take care of getting undressed or else the race will be over before this old horse leaves the starting gate."

"That wouldn't be good," she said, kicking out of her high heels and reaching for the elastic band that held the tiny patch of lace material covering the apex of her thighs.

When Fin tossed her panties on top of her dress, then slid beneath the covers of the king-size bed, he swallowed hard and did his best to concentrate on getting himself out of his clothes. By the time he crawled in beside her, he was breathing as if he'd run a marathon and he was pretty sure he'd just set some kind of speed record for disrobing.

As he put his arms around her and settled his mouth over hers, her eager response sent blood surging through his veins and his arousal was so intense it made him feel light-headed. He needed her with a hunger that robbed him of breath and he wanted nothing more than to join their bodies in the age-old dance of love. But what shocked him down to the core was his deep desire to join their souls—to make her his in every way.

It should have been enough to scare the living hell out of him. But the feel of her soft body pressed to his and the taste of her sweet lips as she returned his kiss made rational thought all but impossible.

As he continued to kiss her, he felt her hands slide down his chest as if she were trying to map every individual muscle. But when her fingers touched his puckered nipple, Travis broke the kiss as he struggled for his next breath. Falling back against the pillow, he clenched his back teeth together so hard he figured it would take a crowbar to pry them apart as he tried to slow his runaway libido.

"Does that feel as good to you as it does for me when you touch me like this, darling?" Fin asked.

"Oh yeah." The blood rushing through his veins caused his ears to ring and sent a flash fire straight to his groin.

If he'd had the presence of mind, he would have stopped her before things went any further, but her hands on his body felt so damned good he didn't even consider it. Then, when her hand drifted lower to trace the narrow line of hair that arrowed down to his navel and beyond, he couldn't for the life of him force words past his suddenly dry throat.

But as her talented little fingers closed around him to measure his length and girth, then teased the softness below, he felt as if his head might just fly right off his shoulders and he had to concentrate hard on maintaining what little control he had left. A wave of need stronger than anything he could ever imagine threatened to swamp him and when he finally found the strength, he caught her hands in his to stop her tender assault.

"Honey, I don't want you thinking that I don't like what you're doing because believe me, I sure as hell do." His voice sounded like a rusty gate hinge and he had to clear his throat before he could finish. "But I'm hotter than a young bull in a pen full of heifers and I'm not going to last any longer than a June frost if we don't slow down."

Wrapping her arms around him, she smiled. "I love your quaint country sayings, even if I don't always understand them."

He laughed, releasing some of the tension that held him in its grip. "One of these days, we'll have to sit down and I'll give you a crash course in cowboy lingo. But right now I have other, more pleasurable activities in mind."

With his hormones better under control, Travis lowered his head to kiss her at the same time he parted her legs with his knee and moved over her. He'd wanted to go slow, wanted their lovemaking to last. But the two-hour ride back to the city in the limo had taken its toll. By the time they'd arrived at his hotel, he and Fin were both aroused to the point of no return and taking things slow wasn't an option.

He gazed down at the woman in his arms, the woman who was carrying his child. He didn't think he'd seen a more beautiful sight than the passion glazing her emerald eyes and the soft, welcoming smile curving her lips. "Show me where you want me, Fin."

The blush of desire painting her porcelain cheeks deepened as without a word she reached down and guided him to her.

As he eased into her and her supple body took him in, his chest swelled with an emotion he wasn't ready to identify. He felt as if he'd found the other half of himself, the part he'd been missing since the death of his wife. Trying not to think about it, or what it could mean, he set a slow pace and concentrated on bringing them both the satisfaction they needed.

The feel of her surrounding him and the motion of their bodies as they rocked in perfect unison had them racing toward completion. All too soon, he felt Fin's feminine inner muscles tighten around him a moment before she found her release.

Determined to ensure her ultimate pleasure before he found his own, he thrust into her deeply and watched her eyes widen a moment before she came apart in his arms. Gathering her to him, he let go of his rapidly slipping control to join her. His body shuddered as he gave up his essence and he was certain he felt fireworks light up the darkest corners of his soul.

His breathing harsh, Travis closed his eyes and buried his face in the cloud of her dark auburn hair. He had no idea where they would go from here or how they would work out raising the child they'd created together. But he knew as surely as he knew his own name, he was going to do everything in his power to find the right answers.

And if he had his way, he'd not only be a part of the baby's life, he'd be a big part of Fin's life as well.

The following Friday afternoon, Fin sat in her office listening to Chloe fill her in on the current projections from the accounting department and the latest EPH gossip. She was normally interested in anything that could help her push *Charisma* over the top and make her the new CEO when Patrick retired. But for the past few weeks, she'd been thinking less about her fashion magazine and more about a tall, ruggedly handsome cowboy from the wilds of Colorado.

When they'd parted ways the morning after Jessie and Cade's wedding, they still hadn't arrived at any conclusions concerning the distance separating them or how they were going to handle it during her pregnancy and after the birth. In fact, they hadn't even discussed it after he'd kissed her in the back of the limo.

Her body tingled to life from just the memory of his masterful kisses, but it was the thought of their lovemaking that quickly had her insides feeling as if they'd turned to warm pudding. Their coming together might have started out as two lonely people finding comfort and physical release in each other's arms, but somewhere along the way it had changed into something far deeper, far more meaningful.

It was completely insane, considering they had nothing whatsoever in common except for the baby she carried and their love for Jessie. But Fin hadn't been able to think of anything but Travis's request that she come out to Colorado for a visit as soon as possible. And what surprised her more than anything was that she desperately wanted to go.

"Fin, have you heard a word of what I just told you?" Chloe asked. Her assistant's tone drew Fin back to the present.

"I'm sorry, I guess I was daydreaming," she apologized. She needed to get a grip on herself or she could kiss winning Patrick's contest goodbye. "What were you saying?"

Chloe's exasperated expression indicated that Fin had missed something the young woman had thought was extremely significant. "I said that you still have a good chance of beating out Shane for the CEO position." Chloe's expression changed to one of excitement. "Word around the accounting department water cooler is that *Charisma*'s numbers have closed the gap and at the rate we're going, we'll pull ahead of *The Buzz* just before the deadline."

"Really?"

A month ago, Chloe's information would have been the best news Fin could have received. It would have sent her into overdrive to make it happen and she had no doubt that it would have. But now?

She wasn't sure whether her lack of enthusiasm was due to her pregnancy and the fact that the job of CEO would keep her from devoting as much attention to her child as she knew she would want to do, or if it was the discovery that since Travis returned to his ranch, she'd been more lonely than ever before. But either way, it was clear that her priorities had changed and she was no longer as driven to be named Patrick's successor as she once had been.

"Fin, what's wrong with you?" Chloe asked, clearly confused. "I thought you'd be doing the happy dance over the news."

Smiling at her executive assistant, Fin shrugged. "I am quite pleased to hear that *Charisma* is doing so well. And I hope with all my heart that we win."

"But?"

"That's it." Fin handed a stack of ad copy to the woman and motioned toward the door. "Put these on Cade's desk with a note for him to look over them as soon as he and Jessie return from their honeymoon."

She could understand Chloe's confusion as she scooped up the stack of papers and quietly left Fin's office. But that couldn't be helped. Fin wasn't about to reveal to her executive assistant, or anyone else for that matter, that she was just the same as conceding the race for CEO to Shane.

With her decision made, she swiveled her chair to gaze out at the western side of the Manhattan skyline. She really would like to win the competition, but not because she coveted Patrick's title. If *Charisma* did pull ahead of *The Buzz*, she had every intention of declining the position. But winning would certainly prove to Patrick that she wasn't quite the disappointing failure he'd always thought her to be.

Quite content with herself for the first time in years, she relaxed and thought about her lack of plans for the weekend. Her OB/GYN had advised that getting the proper amount of rest was essential to the health and well-being of both her and the baby. And for the past week, she had cut back on the hours she spent at the office. But the thought of rattling around in her huge apartment by herself for the entire weekend was extremely unappealing.

Nibbling on her lower lip, she wondered how Travis intended to spend the time. He had told her that he hoped she planned to visit the Silver Moon at her earliest convenience.

She turned her chair to face the desk, then typed a quick search into her computer. When the information she wanted appeared on the screen, she reached for the phone and dialed the number for the airlines.

When the booking agent answered, Fin's heart skipped a beat and she couldn't believe the level of excitement coursing through her as she made her request. "I need to reserve a first-class seat on the first available flight from New York to Denver, Colorado, please."

Seven

Parking his truck in short-term parking at the Denver airport, Travis impatiently checked his watch as he started walking toward the terminal. He'd been tied up in a traffic jam on the interstate while the authorities cleared away a fender bender and the longer he'd had to sit there, the more he'd realized how much he'd missed Fin since leaving New York.

It didn't matter that it had only been a few days since he'd said goodbye to her at his hotel the morning after Jessie's wedding or that they barely knew each other. It felt as if it had been an eternity since he'd seen her. And when she'd called this morning to see if he had plans for the weekend, he hadn't been able to tell her fast enough that he didn't.

He refused to think about why he was so anxious to be with her again or why he'd been as irritable as a grizzly with a sore paw since his return. All that mattered was the three days they'd have together on his remote ranch. Alone.

As soon as his housekeeper, Spud Jenkins, heard that Fin was on her way, he'd suddenly remembered that he had plans to visit his brother's family down in Santa Fe. Travis knew the old geezer had made up the excuse. Spud and his brother had been on the outs for well over twenty years. But Travis hadn't bothered to point that out to the old cowboy.

The truth was, he needed time alone with Fin to figure out what was going on between them. And he wasn't just thinking about how they were going to manage his role in her pregnancy and, later on, the raising of their child.

When he entered the baggage claim area, he spotted Fin immediately as she waited for her luggage to tumble out of a chute and onto the revolving carousel. Damn, but she looked good in a pair of jeans and that oversized tan sweater.

It was the first time he'd seen her in anything but dress clothes or formal wear and he wasn't the least bit surprised that he found her attractive in more casual attire. Hell, it didn't matter what she wore, she knocked his socks off every time he saw her.

Dodging a couple of teenagers with battered backpacks and an older woman pulling a suitcase big enough to hide a body in, he walked over to wrap his arms around Fin and lift her to him. He kissed her like a soldier returning from war and when he finally set her on her feet, they were both left gasping for some much-needed air.

"I don't remember you greeting me like this the first time I came for a visit," she said, her voice sounding breathless and sexy as hell.

He felt like a damned fool, but for the life of him he couldn't stop grinning. "We didn't have a history then, sweetheart."

She laughed as she reached for a medium-sized bag that had just come down the chute. "Your definition of history is knowing each other for a month?"

Shrugging, he reached down to take hold of the luggage before she could lift it from the carousel. "If you want to get technical, what happened yesterday is history."

As they walked through the terminal, her sweet smile sent his blood pressure up a good fifty points. "I suppose you have a point."

When they reached the automatic doors at the

exit, he shook his head. "Wait here out of the cold, while I get my truck."

"You don't have to do that," she said, taking a step forward. "I don't mind walking. I'm used to walking a lot and I'm sure it's not that far."

"It's pretty cold out there and you're not used to the altitude." He dug his truck keys from the front pocket of his jeans. "It might not be good for you or the baby."

She looked at him as if he might not be the brightest bulb in the chandelier. "Travis, being pregnant isn't a disability."

"I know that." Planting a kiss on her forehead, he smiled and shook his head. "But you're in my neck of the woods now, honey. And if I want to be a gentleman and take care of you while you're here, I'll damned well do it."

Fin snuggled into the crook of Travis's arm as they sat on the leather sofa in front of a blazing fire in the big stone fireplace in his living room. She loved the cozy feel of the Silver Moon ranch house. From the rich wood and leather furniture to the colorful Native American accents, it was warm, inviting and felt exactly the way a home was supposed to feel. Something her apartment was sorely lacking.

When she returned to New York, the first thing

she intended to do was call an interior designer to have her apartment redecorated. The ultramodern, museum look wasn't in the least bit child-friendly and she wanted a comfortable, relaxed place like the Silver Moon ranch house for her baby to call home.

"I'll give you a quarter for your thoughts," he said, resting his head against hers.

"I thought that was supposed to be a penny for your thoughts," she said, feeling more relaxed and at peace than she could ever remember.

"Inflation, sweetheart." He drew her a little closer and kissed the top of her head. "I've heard that even the tooth fairy is having to pay a buck a tooth these days."

She leaned back to look up at him. "What was the going rate when Jessie was growing up?"

"Fifty cents." His smile made her tingle all the way to her bare toes. "At least it was until she learned the fine art of negotiation."

"You're kidding."

"Nope." Chuckling, he shook his head. "One time, when I went to get her tooth from beneath her pillow and leave a couple of quarters, I found a note for the tooth fairy."

Curious to hear more about what Jessie had been like as a child, Fin asked, "What did the note say?"

"Something to the effect that since it was a little

farther back in her mouth and because she used it for chewing, she thought it was worth at least seventy-five cents."

Laughing, Fin shook her head. "She didn't."

"She sure did." He grinned. "The tooth fairy laughed so hard, he damned near woke her up."

"Did she get the seventy-five cents?"

"No, that tooth netted her a cool five bucks." He shook his head. "I figured the note alone was worth that much."

"You're a wonderful father," Fin said when they stopped laughing.

He shrugged, but she could tell from the sparkle in his incredible blue eyes that her comment pleased him. "I did what I thought was best." He kissed her cheek and placed his hand over her stomach. "The same as I'll do with this baby."

Emotion filled Fin's chest and she had to swallow around the huge lump that formed in her throat. "I'm so glad you're my baby's father."

His tender smile increased the tightness in her chest. "*Our* baby. Remember, we're in this together, Fin."

She couldn't keep a lone tear from sliding down her cheek. "Thank you."

He looked taken aback. "For what?"

Reaching up to cup his lean cheek with her hand, she smiled. "For being you."

Her stomach fluttered with anticipation at the slow, promising smile curving his firm male lips. He was going to kiss her and, if the look in his intense gaze was any indication, more.

When his mouth covered hers, Fin surrendered herself to the moment and the overwhelming sense of belonging that she'd come to associate with being in Travis's strong arms. Never in her entire existence had she felt more wanted or cherished than she did when he held her, made love to her.

It didn't seem to matter that they'd only known each other a short time or that they had very little in common. She'd never felt anything as right or as real as she did when she was with him.

Her heart pounded hard against her ribs. Was she falling in love with him?

She really didn't have a lot of experience at being in love, so she wasn't certain how it was supposed to feel. She'd been positive that she loved Jessie's young father, Sebastian Deveraux. But that had been a long time ago and she suspected every fifteen-year-old girl was convinced that she loved her first boyfriend. Unfortunately, in the years since, she'd concentrated all of her energy toward building her career instead of personal relationships and she had nothing else to compare to the way she felt about Travis now.

As his lips moved over hers, coaxing her to open for him, encouraging her to respond, she abandoned all speculation and gave herself up to the delicious sensations beginning to course through her. She could analyze her feelings once she'd returned to New York.

When he slipped inside to tease her inner recesses, sparkles of light danced behind her closed eyes. But as he stroked her tongue with his it felt as if a starburst lit the darkest corners of her soul. The hunger of his kiss, the taste of his passion, sent heat surging through her veins and made every cell in her body tingle to life.

Shivers of delight slid up her spine when she felt his hand slip beneath the bottom of her sweater to caress her abdomen, then come to rest just below her breast. Restless anticipation filled her when he paused his exploration long enough to unfasten the front clasp of her bra. She needed to feel his hands caressing her, wanted his moist kisses on her sensitive skin.

The hard muscles of his arms suddenly bunched as he lifted her, then stretched them both out on the long couch. She reveled in the rapid beating of his heart and the hard ridge of his arousal against her thigh where their legs tangled, but when he created a space between them to cover her breast with his large palm, her own pulse began to race and a moist heat began to gather at the apex of her thighs.

Needing to touch him as he touched her, she unsnapped his chambray shirt to trace the steely sinew of his broad chest and abdomen. The light sprinkling of hair covering the thick pads of his pectoral muscles tickled her palms and she marveled at the exquisite differences between a woman and a man. But when she traced his flat male nipple with the tip of her finger, the tiny nub's puckered reaction was much the same as when he touched her breasts.

His groan of pleasure thrilled her and as she continued to memorize every ridge and valley, she decided Travis's body was perfect in every way. Taut and unyielding, his muscles held a latent strength that belied his gentle touch and contrasted perfectly with the softer contours of hers.

"There isn't enough room on this damned couch to kiss and taste you the way I'd like," he said, nibbling the hollow beneath her ear.

His low drawl and the promise of his words sent quivers of excitement shimmering through her. "It is rather restrictive, isn't it?"

"Damn straight." He sat up, then pulled her up

beside him. "Let's find a place with more room to move."

"That looks inviting," she said, eyeing the colorful Native American rug on the floor in front of them. She shrugged one shoulder at his questioning expression. "I've never made love in front of a fireplace."

A slow smile began to appear on his handsome face as he glanced at the rug, then back at her. "It does look fairly comfortable, doesn't it?"

Before she had the chance to agree with his observation, he was easing them onto their knees on the floor. "I'm going to love the way your body looks in the glow from the fire," he said, switching off the lamp at the end of the couch.

With nothing but the muted light from the fire, the room suddenly became incredibly intimate, and as his smoldering gaze held her captive, he slipped his hands beneath her sweater to slowly push it upward. Raising her arms to help him slip it over her head and toss it aside, she slid the straps of her bra down her arms and handed it to him. His sharp intake of breath and the darkening of his blue eyes, made her insides quiver and her breathing grow shallow.

"I've dreamed of you like this every night since that evening in your apartment." His deep baritone, rough with passion, and his appreciative look sent a honeyed warmth flowing through her veins.

Pushing his opened shirt off his broad shoulders and down his muscular arms, she smiled as she dropped the garment on top of her clothing. "And I've dreamed of you." She placed her hands on his chest. "I've wanted to touch you like this again."

He cupped her face with his hands and kissed her deeply, letting her taste a hungry need that matched her own. "I intend to touch and taste every inch of you, sweetheart. And when I'm finished, I intend to start all over again."

As he nibbled his way down her neck to her shoulder, then her collarbone, Fin's head fell back as she lost herself to the delicious sensation of having his lips on her skin. But when his hot mouth closed over her tightened nipple and he flicked the bud with his tongue, she trembled from the waves of pleasure flowing through her and the empty ache of need beginning to form deep in her lower region.

By the time he finally lifted his head, she felt as if she'd melt into a wanton puddle at any moment. "This isn't fair. I want to kiss you like this, too."

"What do you say we get the rest of these clothes off?" he asked, standing up, then helping her to her feet.

Once he'd finished stripping both of them and

they knelt facing each other on the rug in front of the fire, he took her into his arms. The feel of skin against skin, his male hardness pressed to her female softness, sent tiny currents of electrified desire to every part of her.

"You feel so damned good," he said roughly.

Delightful shivers of excitement coursed through her at the passion in his voice. "I was just thinking the same thing about you."

The sultry quality of her voice amazed her. She'd never thought of herself as a sensual creature, but with Travis it seemed all things were possible.

When he lowered them to the rug and gazed down at her, the heated need and the promise of complete fulfillment she saw in his eyes sent hot, dizzying desire flowing to the most feminine part of her. As his mouth covered hers and he slipped his tongue between her lips the pulsing ache in her lower belly increased and she gasped from the intensity of it.

But when he trailed kisses down to the valley between her breasts, then beyond, her breath caught. Surely he wasn't going to…

"T-Travis?"

Raising his head, he gave her a look that caused her heart to skip several beats. "Do you trust me, Fin?"

Incapable of speech, she could only nod. No other man had ever made love to her the way Travis was doing now and heaven help her she never wanted it to end.

As his lips blazed a trail down her abdomen, she closed her eyes and tried her best to remember to breathe as wave after wave of heated pleasure washed over her. But when he gave her the most intimate kiss a man could give a woman, the sensations threatened to consume her.

"P-please…I can't stand…much more."

He must have realized the depth of her hunger, because he moved to gather her to him, and gazing down at her, tenderly covered her lips with his. His callused palm smoothed over her skin with such infinite care, it brought tears to her eyes and she felt branded by his touch.

Her body trembled with longing as he slid his hand down her side to caress her hip, then her inner thigh. But when he cupped the curls at the apex and his finger dipped into the moist folds to stroke and tease, spirals of sheer ecstasy swirled through her. The feelings were so intense, she couldn't have stopped her body's reaction if her life depended on it.

Arching into his touch, she fought for sanity as waves of excitement flowed through her. "P-please—"

"Does that feel good, sweetheart?" His low whisper close to her ear only added to the sweet tension gripping her.

"I…need…you."

In answer to her broken plea, he spread her thighs with his knee and rose over her. She felt the tip of his strong arousal against her, but instead of joining their bodies, he commanded, "Open your eyes, Fin."

The blaze of need in his dark blue gaze took her breath. He was holding himself in check as he slowly, gently pressed forward to fill her completely. He remained perfectly still for several long seconds and she instinctively knew he was savoring the moment, savoring her.

When he pulled his lower body away from hers, then thrust forward, time stood still. He set a slow, rhythmic pace that built her excitement faster than she'd ever dreamed possible. The heat spiraling throughout her body burned higher and brighter with each stroke and she wrapped her arms around his broad back to keep from being lost.

But all too soon, the delicious tension inside of her let go and wave after wave of fulfillment washed over her. Her moan of satisfaction faded to a helpless whimper as her body relaxed and she slowly drifted back to reality.

Only then did she hear Travis groan, then felt

him shutter as the spasms of his release overtook him. When he buried his face in the side of her neck and collapsed on top of her, Fin tightened her arms around him, holding him to her in an effort to prolong the feeling of oneness she had with this wonderful man.

As his breathing eased and he levered himself up on his elbows, he gently brushed a strand of hair from her cheek. "Are you all right?"

Smiling, she cupped his strong jaw with her palm. "That was, without a doubt, the most incredible experience of my life."

His low chuckle as he rolled to her side and gathered her to him sent a fresh wave of heat coursing through her. "If I have my way, it's just the first of many incredible experiences we're going to have this weekend."

A shiver of delight streaked up her spine. "I'm going to hold you to that, cowboy."

"I'd rather have you hold *me* to *you*," he said, brushing her lips with his. "And while you're holding me, we're going to have another one of those incredible experiences."

She felt his body stir against her thigh and her own body answered with a delicious tightening in the pit of her stomach. Wrapping her arms around his shoulders, she smiled. "I'm holding you against me."

His promising grin caused her heart to race. "Honey, I'm about to amaze both of us."

And to her delight, he did just that.

Holding Fin as she slept, Travis stared at the ceiling above his bed and tried to figure out what was going to become of them. They were treading in an area that could very well spell disaster for all concerned.

If it was just between the two of them, the stakes wouldn't be nearly as high. They could explore what was happening between them and if it didn't work out, they could go their separate ways with a minimum of fuss.

But it wasn't just the two of them. There was Jessie and the baby to think about. Whatever happened between him and Fin affected them as well.

Fin had told him up front that she wasn't good at relationships and he'd told her the truth when he'd said he wasn't looking for one. And he hadn't been.

After his wife died, he'd been sure that he'd never care for another woman the way he had for Lauren. But he was beginning to think that he might have been a little hasty in that assumption.

From the minute he'd laid eyes on Fin, he'd been drawn to her like a bee to honey. And apparently, it had been the same for her with him. Her first visit to the ranch was proof of that. They hadn't been able to keep their hands off of each other. But was great lovemaking enough of a base for a long-term relationship?

The way he saw it, they only had three things in common—Jessie, the baby Fin was carrying and an insatiable need for each other. Other than that, their lives were about as different as night and day.

He was country from his wide-brimmed Resistol hat to the soles of his Justin boots. His life was hard, grueling hours of work spent outside in all kinds of weather, and at night he slept with nothing to listen to but the crickets and an occasional coyote howling off in the distance. And he was much more comfortable in a honky-tonk where the music was loud, the beer was cheap and wearing a new pair of jeans and a clean shirt from the local Wal-Mart was considered dressed up than he'd ever be putting on a suit to go to a Broadway production or some trendy nightclub.

And as foreign as his life was to Fin, her life was just as foreign to him. She lived and worked in a city that never slept. Hell, how could it? With taxis honking and sirens blaring all the time, it was no wonder people were up around the clock. And that was just the tip of the iceberg.

Day in and day out, she worked in a climate-controlled office where the only time she felt the warmth of the sun on her face was when she stood close to the window, and every piece of clothing she owned had some famous designer's name stitched into the label. Even the jeans she'd been wearing at the ranch had some guy's name plastered across the back pocket.

When Fin stirred in her sleep, he tightened his arms around her and pressed a kiss to the top of her head. On her first visit to the Silver Moon, she'd mentioned that she loved the wide open space, but after a while the novelty would wear off and she'd go stir-crazy from missing the hustle and bustle of New York. He had no doubt, he'd be just as unhappy if he had to live in a crowded city.

As he felt sleep finally begin to overtake him, Travis closed his eyes and wondered how they were possibly going to share the raising of a child. Kids needed stability and permanence, not being bounced back and forth between two entirely different worlds.

As he drifted off with no more answers than he'd had before, his dreams were filled with images of sharing his life on the Silver Moon with a green-eyed, auburn-haired woman and child.

Eight

"What do I do first?"

Smiling, Travis handed Fin the keys to the old truck he used for hauling hay. "Put the key in the ignition and your right foot on the brake."

"That's simple enough," she said, doing as he instructed. "What's next?"

Fin's pleased expression caused his chest to tighten. He couldn't get over how excited she was at the prospect of learning to drive and he wouldn't have missed teaching her for anything in the world.

"Turn the key toward the dashboard. When you hear it start, let go of the key."

When the truck's engine fired up, she beamed. "I can't believe I'm actually going to do this."

"I think that's what you said last night when we—"

"You have a one-track mind, cowboy," she interrupted, laughing.

Feeling younger than he had in years, he grinned. "It's incredible, as well as amazing, wouldn't you agree?"

"Your mind or last night?"

"Both."

When she took her foot off the brake, the engine died. "What happened?"

He gave her a kiss that left them both needing resuscitation and when he finally raised his head, she gave him a look that was supposed to be stern, but only made her look more adorable. At least, to him.

"Back to business, cowboy. You're supposed to be teaching me how to drive."

"You have to keep your foot on the brake until you put it in gear or the engine will die."

She frowned. "This is going to start getting complicated, isn't it?"

"Not at all. Before you know it, it'll be second nature to you." He pointed to the ignition. "Put your foot back on the brake, start it up and take hold of the gearshift. Then, without taking your foot off the brake, pull the shift slightly forward and then down until the little indicator on the dash lights up the 'D'."

"Done," she said, looking more confident as she followed his directions.

"You're doing great. Now lightly step on the gas feed." He'd no sooner gotten the words out than she stomped on the gas and the truck shot forward at what seemed like the speed of light.

"This is fun."

"Holy hell!" They spoke at the same time.

It had been ten years since he'd taken Jess out in the same pasture for her first driving lesson, but he remembered it as if it were yesterday. They'd raced across the field and barely missed running off into a small pond.

As the truck bounced across the pasture, Travis tightened his shoulder harness. It seemed that mother and daughter were similar in more ways than just their looks. They both had a foot made of pure lead.

"You might want to take your foot off the front bumper and slow down a little, honey," he said, pulling his hat down tight on his head. He felt like he had in his younger days when he'd ridden broncs in the local rodeo.

When she eased off the gas a bit, Travis breathed

a little easier. The pond had been filled in a few years ago, and even though the pasture was wide open and there was nothing Fin could crash into, he was still glad the horses were safe in their stalls in the barn.

"I should have learned to drive years ago," she said, her cheeks flushed with excitement. "This is a lot more fun than having a driver take me where I want to go."

"I've created a monster," he groaned. His stomach clenched into a tight knot just thinking about her trying to drive in New York City traffic. "You aren't thinking about getting a license and a car, are you?"

"Hardly. There isn't enough room in the city for all the cars now. And parking is an absolute nightmare." She gave him an indulgent look. "I'll limit my driving to the Silver Moon and this pasture."

His heart stalled, then took off at a gallop. She was talking as if she'd be visiting the ranch quite frequently and that pleased him to no end.

"That makes me feel somewhat better," he said when she turned the truck in a tight circle and headed back the way they'd come. As they barreled toward the barn, he decided the horses might not be as safe as he'd first thought. "When you put your foot on the brake, give yourself plenty of room. These things don't stop on a dime."

Apparently, she took him at his word because in the next instant, Fin planted her foot on the brake and the truck skidded to a bone-jarring halt. "I suppose there's a trick to making a smooth stop," she said, frowning.

Reaching over to the steering column, he turned off the key and put the truck in Park. "We'll work on that the next time," he said, thanking the good Lord above for whoever invented antilock brakes.

She surprised him when she unbuckled her shoulder harness, then leaned over and wrapped her arms around his neck. "Thank you, Travis."

"For what?"

"I'm learning all kinds of incredible things this weekend," she said, giving him a smile that sent his temperature skyward.

He grinned as he pulled her close. "Is that so?"

The impish sparkle in her emerald eyes as she nodded fascinated him. "Some of what I learned was particularly amazing."

Lowering his head, he kissed her soundly. "What do you say we go back to the house for a while?"

"Did you have something in mind?" Her whispered words in his ear had him harder than hell in about two seconds flat.

Nodding, he unbuckled the shoulder harness, got out of the truck and walked around the front to slide in behind the steering wheel. "I want to show you something."

She grinned. "Is it incredible?"

He started the truck and, putting it into gear, laughed as he drove toward the house. "Honey, prepare yourself to be downright amazed."

"Have you given any thought to our situation?" Fin asked as she and Travis prepared dinner together. She was supposed to return to New York tomorrow morning and they still hadn't discussed anything about the baby, let alone made a decision.

"A little, but I haven't come to any conclusions," he said, tending to a couple of breaded steaks he was frying in a big cast-iron skillet.

"Me, either." Cutting up vegetables for a garden salad, she thoughtfully nibbled on a sliver of carrot. "I think it's only fair that we have equal time with her."

"Or him." Travis gave her a grin that sent her pulse racing. "There's a fifty percent chance the baby is a boy."

"True."

She turned back to the task at hand before her hormones diverted her attention from the subject. It seemed that with nothing more than a look or a touch, she and Travis gave in to the electrifying passion between them and found themselves in each other's arms.

Slicing a cucumber, she arranged the circles on top of a bed of lettuce. "I don't think we'll have much of a problem with equal time until he or she reaches school age."

He chuckled. "You're ahead of me. I can't think past how I'm going to juggle being in New York for your visits to the obstetrician and here, too." He arranged the steaks on two plates, then spooned milk gravy over the tops. "It gets real busy around here in the spring and summer."

"What's it like here in the spring?"

She loved hearing Travis talk about the ranch. From everything she'd seen and heard, it had to be one of the most tranquil places on earth.

"After the snow melts, everything is green." He smiled. "Then, when the wildflowers start to bloom, there's all kinds of colors mixed in."

"It sounds absolutely beautiful."

He nodded. "With the snowcapped mountains in the distance it looks a lot like the postcards they sell at the tourist places over in Colorado Springs."

"I'd love to see it," she said, unable to keep the wistful tone from her voice.

When he slipped his arms around her waist from behind, she leaned back against his solid frame. "If you'd like, after the baby comes, I'll take you on a trail ride up to some of the upland meadows."

Turning to face him, Fin put her arms around his shoulders, raised up on her tiptoes and kissed his cheek. "I'd love that, Travis. But I still haven't learned to ride a horse."

"And you're not going to until after the baby's born." He shook his head. "I'm not willing to take the chance of you falling. It might cause you to lose the little guy."

It was completely ridiculous, but his statement caused her heart to squeeze painfully. She knew this would be his only biological child, and therefore as important to him as it was to her. But was the baby the only one he was worried about?

It was an undeniable fact that they were extremely attracted to each other physically. That was the reason they found themselves in their current set of circumstances. But was that as far as it went for him? Was the baby the only one he cared for? And why was she suddenly obsessing over it now?

"Honey, are you all right?"

"I'm a little tired." She stepped back from his embrace. "If you don't mind, I think I'll skip dinner and lay down for a nap."

Fin could tell her sudden mood swing confused him, but that couldn't be helped. She needed time to think, time to sort through her feelings and try to understand why it was suddenly so important that the baby wasn't his only concern.

Wanting to get away from him before she did something stupid like burst into tears, she hurried down the hall and started up the stairs. But she suddenly had the strange sensation of flying a moment before she landed in a heap on the hardwood floor.

As she lay there wondering what on earth had happened, a sharp pain knifed through her left side, taking her breath, causing her to draw her legs into a fetal position. Her pulse thundered in her ears and as the room began a sickening spin, she felt herself being drawn into a fathomless black abyss.

She thought she heard Travis call her name, but the beckoning shadows refused to release her. As she gave in to the mist closing around her, her last thought was of losing the baby she wanted so desperately and the man she'd come to love.

Seated in the waiting area at the emergency room, Travis was about two seconds away from tearing the hospital apart if somebody didn't tell him something, and damned quick, about Fin's condition. When he'd brought her in for treatment, they'd run him out of the examining room and he hadn't been allowed back in there since.

He let out a frustrated breath and scrubbed his hands over his face. When he'd heard the loud thump in the living room, followed by an eerie silence, his heart felt as if it had dropped to his boot tops. He'd called her name as he started down the hall to see what happened, but at the sight of her crumpled body lying at the bottom of the stairs the blood in his veins had turned to ice water and he was pretty sure it had taken a good ten years off his life.

"Mr. Clayton?"

When he looked up, a woman in a white lab coat stood at the swinging double doors leading to the treatment area. Jumping to his feet, he walked over to her. "What's going on?"

"I'm Doctor Santos, the on-call OB/GYN," she said, shaking his hand.

"Is Fin going to be all right?" he demanded. If she lost the baby, he'd mourn. But if it came down to her life or the baby's, there was no choice. He wanted the best care humanly possible for Fin.

Smiling, the doctor nodded. "Ms. Elliott cracked a rib when she fell, but I think she and the baby will both be fine. She's healthy and the pregnancy seems to be a normal one, so I don't foresee any problems."

"Thank God." The degree of relief he felt was staggering and his knees wobbled as if they'd turned to rubber.

"She'll need to be on bed rest for the next few days and I wouldn't advise traveling for a couple of weeks. But after that, if she doesn't experience any more problems, she should be able to resume normal activities." The woman scribbled something on the chart she held, then she looked up and her brown-eyed gaze met his. "And it would be best to refrain from sexual intercourse until she goes back for her next prenatal check."

"Can I see her?" he asked, anxious to see with his own eyes that Fin was okay.

"She's getting dressed now," Dr. Santos said, turning to go back through the swinging doors. "You might want to go get your truck and bring it around to the patient pick-up area."

He frowned. "You're sending her home? Shouldn't you keep her for observation or something?"

It wasn't that he didn't want to take Fin back to the ranch. He did. But he wanted the best care possible for her.

"Relax, Mr. Clayton." The woman's dark eyes twinkled. "Believe me, she'll get a lot more rest at home than she would here. And of course, bring her back if she experiences any further problems."

Five minutes later, when he parked outside of the doors designated for discharged patients, a nurse pushed Fin in a wheelchair out to the truck. Once he had her comfortably settled on the bench seat, he slid in behind the steering wheel and started the thirty-mile drive back to the Silver Moon.

"Did the doctor tell you that I'm going to have to extend my stay with you?"

Fin's voice sounded weak and shaky and it just about tore him apart. She was one of the strongest women he'd ever met and it took a lot to bring her down. But he had a feeling that she was shaken more by the thought that she could have lost the baby than from physical pain.

"I wouldn't mind if you wanted to spend the rest of your pregnancy on the Silver Moon," he said, taking her hand in his.

She gave him a tired smile. "That would be nice, but I need to get back to the magazine."

Her words were like a sucker punch to his gut and a definite wake-up call for him. Of course, she'd want to get back to that damned magazine and the contest for CEO of her dad's publishing company. Jess had told him that Fin lived and breathed *Charisma*. She was the first one in the office in the morning and the last one to go home at night.

He'd lost a lot of sleep speculating on whether

anything could ever come of the attraction between them. It looked as if he'd just gotten the answer.

"Ooh. That doesn't feel good at all," Fin said, holding her side as she rose to her feet and took a tentative step toward the dresser. She'd known that moving around was going to hurt, but she hadn't realized how much.

Sitting on the side of Travis's bed for the past several minutes, she'd been trying to work up the courage to walk over and get her purse. She'd needed to call the office and talk to Cade. He was going to have to assume her duties for the next two weeks and keep *Charisma* on track to win Patrick's contest. Even though she had no intention of accepting the position, she wanted to win and prove to Patrick, once and for all, that his daughter wasn't a complete disappointment.

"What the hell do you think you're doing?"

Travis's booming voice made her jump and the movement jarred her sore ribs, causing them to hurt more. "I need my cell phone."

"Why didn't you ask me to get it for you?" Placing the bed tray he carried on top of the dresser, he helped her back to bed. "Is it in your purse?"

"Yes." As she reclined against a mountain of pillows, she took shallow breaths until the ache in her side receded. "I need to call the office and have Cade take over for me until I get back."

He handed her the purse. "Isn't this his and Jessie's first day back from the honeymoon?"

Nodding, she dug around in the bottom of the bag for her cell phone. "What a thing to come home to. He's still basking in the glow of being a newlywed and I'm going to tell him he has to put his nose to the grindstone and not look up until I get back."

Travis chuckled. "Jess might not take too kindly to that, either."

"I can almost guarantee that she'll stay at the office with him." Laughing, she held her side. "Even laughing hurts."

His teasing expression changed immediately. "Are you sure you're all right? No other signs that something else could be wrong?"

"None," she said, shaking her head. She concentrated on the phone in her hand so he wouldn't see the disappointment she felt at his concern for her pregnancy and not her.

She could feel his eyes watching her for several long moments before he finally cleared his throat and hooked his thumb over his shoulder toward the dresser. "I'll take your breakfast back to the kitchen and keep it warm for you. Let me know when you get off the phone and I'll bring it back up."

"Thank you," she mouthed as Chloe answered on the other end of the line.

While her assistant went through the spiel of which office she'd reached and whom she was speaking to, Fin watched Travis glance her way once more as he carried the tray from the room. She could tell he wasn't happy that she was conducting business instead of resting, but he was wisely keeping quiet about it.

"Chloe, it's Fin," she said, interrupting the young woman.

"Where are you? Why aren't you here at the office? Is everything okay?" The rapid-fire questions were typical Chloe.

Smiling, Fin answered, "I decided to take a weekend trip to Colorado."

"Ooh, you went to see Jessie's father, the cowboy, didn't you?"

"Yes." She listened for a moment as Chloe gushed about how handsome Travis was and how thrilled she was to hear about the baby before Fin interrupted. "Is Cade in his office?"

"He and Jessie arrived an hour ago, disappeared into his office and they haven't been seen since." Chloe giggled. "You know how newlyweds are."

Fin winced. She hated having to be the one to break up their bliss, but this was a business call. She needed to speak to him as his boss, not his new mother-in-law.

"Transfer this call to his office."

"When are you coming back, Fin?" There was an excited edge to Chloe's voice and Fin could tell her assistant had something she wanted to share.

"Probably not for a couple of weeks."

Chloe gasped. "You're kidding, right?"

"Unfortunately, no." Pinching the skin over the bridge of her nose, she tried to ward off the tension headache that threatened. "Now, ring Cade's office for me." She'd put just enough firmness in her voice to let Chloe know that the social part of her call was over.

"Cade McMann." From the slight echo, Fin could tell that he was using the speakerphone.

"Cade, it's Fin. I have something I need you to do."

"Do you need me to come down to your office?" he asked.

Fin sighed. "It wouldn't do you any good. I'm in Colorado."

"You're with Dad at the ranch?" Jessie asked excitedly.

"Yes."

"How long have you been there? Are you staying for a while?" Jessie's excitement seemed to be building.

"Three days. And yes, I'll be staying for the next two weeks."

"Two weeks!" Cade's voice forced Fin to hold the phone away from her ear. "With the competition as tight as it is you're not going to be here?"

"First of all, calm down and listen." When it came to *Charisma*, taking charge and getting results were second nature to her. "You'll be acting editor-in-chief until I return at the end of the month, Cade. Don't let anyone slack off on the push to bring profits up. Have Chloe give you a daily report of what she learns from the accounting department. And go over all ad copy with a fine-tooth comb to make sure it's in order before you send it to production."

"Anything else?"

"Call me every day and let me know how we're doing." She paused. "I don't have to tell you how much I want to win this competition."

"No, Fin. You've made it clear from the start how important this is." There was a long pause and she could tell he was trying to figure out how to word his next question.

"What?"

She could almost see him blow out a frustrated breath. "You haven't taken a vacation in years. Why now? Why couldn't it have waited until January after you've won the CEO position?"

"Believe me, I'd be there if I could."

"Fin, what's wrong?" The concern in her daughter's voice touched her as little else could.

"I'm fine, sweetie. Honest." Explaining what had happened and the doctor's advice, she added, "But I'm not so sure about your dad."

"He's hovering, isn't he?" Jessie guessed. "He doesn't like not being in control and when something like this happens, he always makes a big fuss."

"That's an understatement. He's waiting right now for me to get off the phone so that he can bring me breakfast in bed."

"You do realize he's going to drive you nuts?"

Looking up, Fin watched Travis walk into the room with the bed tray laden with every kind of breakfast food imaginable. "He already is, sweetie."

Nine

Travis cautiously watched Fin walk over to the couch and sit down. He'd tried to get her to take another day to lounge around, but she'd pointed out that the doctor had told her to take it easy for a couple of days and it had already been four since her fall. He hadn't liked it, but he'd reluctantly agreed to her being up as long as he was in the same room with her when she got up and started moving around.

She'd given him a look that would have stopped any of her male coworkers dead in their tracks. But it hadn't fazed him one damned bit. She was on his turf now, not some corporate boardroom where she said "jump" and the people around her asked, "How high?"

"Travis, will you please stop watching me like you think I'm going to fall apart at any moment?" She shook her head. "Aside from my ribs being sore, I'm as healthy as one of your horses."

He shrugged. "You don't look like a horse."

"Thank you." She frowned. "I think."

"Miss Fin, would you like for me to fix you somethin' to eat or drink," Spud asked, walking into the room.

"No, but thank you anyway, Mr. Jenkins," Fin answered politely.

"Well, anything you need, you just give me a holler," Spud said, giving her a toothless grin. "I'll see that you get it."

"I appreciate your kindness," she said, smiling.

Travis eyed the old man as he walked back into the kitchen. Fin had charmed his housekeeper's socks off the first time she'd visited the ranch, and when Spud learned she'd be staying with them for a while, he'd been happier than a lone rooster in an overcrowded hen house.

"I think there's something I need after all." She rose to her feet before Travis could get across the room to help her off the couch.

"Where are you going?" He pointed toward the stairs. "If you need something from the bedroom, I'll get it."

Shaking her head, she walked over to the coat tree by the front door. "I'm going outside for a breath of fresh air."

"Do you think that's a good idea?" he asked, following her.

He knew better than to try to talk her out of it. If there was one thing he'd learned when he was married, it was never tell a woman she couldn't do something. It was a surefire way to get a man in hot water faster than he could slap his own ass with both hands.

Holding her jacket for her, then shrugging into his own, he tried a different angle. "The temperature has dropped a good ten degrees since this morning and we've had a few snow flurries. You might get a chill and shivering would probably cause your ribs to hurt."

"Give it up, cowboy. You and Mr. Jenkins won't let me do anything and I'm going stir-crazy." She smiled. "Now are you going to stand here and argue, or are you coming with me?"

Resigned, he reached around her to open the door. "As long as we're going outside, we might as well check on the horses and see that they have hay and plenty of water." At least if they were in the barn, she'd be sheltered from the wind.

Her green eyes twinkled merrily and she looked so damned pretty, he felt a familiar flame ignite in the pit of his belly. "We're returning to the scene of the crime?"

Laughing out loud, he nodded. "Something like that." He didn't tell her, but be hadn't been able to go into the barn one single time since that night and not think about her and their lovemaking.

"How is the colt?" she asked as they walked across the ranch yard.

He didn't even try to stop his wicked grin. "You actually remember there was a colt?"

"You're incorrigible, Mr. Clayton. Of course, I remember the colt. That's the reason we went into the barn that night in the first place." Her smile did strange things to his insides and reminded him that he hadn't been able to make love to her in what seemed like a month of Sundays. "I'll bet he's changed a lot in the past month."

"All babies, no matter what their species, grow faster in their first year than any other time," he said, nodding. Pushing the barn door open, he waited for Fin to step inside. "When Jess was a baby, she grew so fast there were times I could have sworn she changed overnight."

"Unfortunately, the only memory I have of Jessie as an infant was seeing the nun carry a small bundle away," Fin said, walking up to the over-sized stall where he kept the mare and colt. "Patrick gave them strict orders that he didn't even want me knowing whether I'd had a boy or a girl. But one nurse told me I'd had a perfect little girl before she left the delivery room with Jessie."

Travis's chest tightened at the thought of Fin having to watch her baby being taken away, of never knowing whether she would see her little girl again. "You'll get to watch this baby grow up from the moment he's born, Fin." Slipping his arms around her, he held her close. "We both will."

Nodding, she remained silent and he figured she was struggling to hold her emotions in check.

It just about tore him apart to think of anything causing her such emotional pain and he knew right then and there that he wanted to spend the rest of his life making sure that she never knew another sad moment.

He took a deep breath, then another as the realization spread throughout every fiber of his being. There was no more doubt and no more denial. Whether they came from two different worlds or not, he'd fallen in love with Fin.

It scared the living hell out of him to think that

she might not feel the same. But he knew beyond a shadow of doubt that he had to lay his heart on the line and take that chance. Whether they lived on the Silver Moon or in New York, Fin and the baby were more important to him than taking his next breath. And he had every intention of telling her so.

Lowering his mouth to hers, he gave her a kiss that threatened to buckle his knees and had them both breathing heavily by the time he raised his head. Then, releasing her, he took a step back to keep from reaching for her again.

"As soon as I finish feeding the horses, we're going back to the house for a long talk, sweetheart."

"Cade, are you sure about this?" Fin asked, pacing the length of the living room. "*Charisma* is tied in the competition with *The Buzz*?"

When she and Travis returned from the barn, Spud had informed her that her cell phone had, as he put it, "chirped like a cricket with four back legs" about every five minutes since she'd walked out the door. After checking the caller ID, she'd immediately phoned the office to find out what was so important that Cade had called her four times in less than thirty minutes.

"Chloe heard it first when she was on break this morning. Then Jessie overheard someone from accounting talking about it in the hall." Cade paused. "I'm trying to get the official word on it, but from all indications we've made up the difference and we're in a dead heat with Shane and *The Buzz*."

The information should have excited her beyond words. But as Cade's news sunk in, she found that, although she was proud that it looked as if the hard work she and her team had put into making *Charisma* number one was paying off, it wasn't nearly as important to her as it would have been three weeks ago.

"As soon as you get the information confirmed one way or the other, I want you to call me." She glanced at Travis, standing ramrod straight across the room. He was watching her closely, his expression guarded. "I have to go now. Give Jessie my love."

When she closed the phone and set it on the end table by the couch, Travis nodded. "I take it that your magazine is doing well in your father's competition?"

"At this point, we're holding our own," she said, nodding. "With a little more work, I have no doubt that we'll pull ahead and win."

She watched his broad chest expand as he drew in a deep breath. "Then you'll take over as CEO of your dad's company in January?"

"That's the way Patrick has it set up," she said,

careful to be as noncommittal as possible. She hadn't told anyone that, in the event she won the competition, she'd step down in order to spend as much time as possible with her child.

Travis shook his head. "You didn't answer my question."

Should she tell him that it was no longer as important to her as it had once been? Should she admit that her priorities had changed and she wanted nothing more than to be his wife and their baby's mother?

"I…that is…we—"

She snapped her mouth shut as she struggled to find an answer. It wasn't in her nature to lie. But she wasn't certain she was brave enough to tell him the truth, either.

Would he believe her if she admitted that she'd only used *Charisma* all these years as a substitute for the family she really wanted? How could she put into words, without risking the humiliation of a rejection and a broken heart, how she felt about him? What if he wanted the baby, but not her? What would happen if she told him she'd fallen hopelessly in love with him and wanted to abandon her cold, lonely apartment overlooking Central Park to live with him and their child on the Silver Moon Ranch? Could she survive if he didn't feel the same?

He took a step toward her. "Fin?"

She gave herself a mental shake. What was wrong with her? She was Fin Elliott, a fearless executive who could face any challenge set before her and come out the victor. Why was it so hard for her to find the courage to tell the man of her dreams how she felt and what she wanted?

As she stared into his incredible blue eyes, she knew exactly why she was finding it difficult to express herself. Travis was far more important to her than *Charisma* or the CEO position at EPH had ever been or ever would be.

But when she opened her mouth to tell him so, Travis shook his head. "Before you say a word, I have something to tell you."

"I have something to say to you, too," she said, wishing that he would take her in his arms and give her the slightest indication they were in the same place emotionally.

"You can have your say, after I've had mine." He pointed to the couch. "You might want to sit down. I'm not very good at stuff like this and it could take awhile."

Lowering herself to the leather couch, she held her breath as she waited for him to tell her what was so important to him.

"When Jessie first talked about trying to find you, I was dead set against it."

Fin felt certain that her heart shattered into a million pieces and she wasn't entirely sure that she'd be able to draw her next breath for the devastating emotion tightening her chest. "I…didn't know. Jessie never said how you felt about our meeting."

"I was dead wrong and she was right not to tell you." He rubbed the back of his neck as if to ease tension. "You've got to understand, Fin. I wasn't sure you'd be all that receptive to meeting a daughter you gave up for adoption all those years ago. You were extremely young and some women want to forget something like that ever happened to them." He gave her an unapologetic look. "And from the minute my wife and I adopted Jessie, I dedicated my life to protecting her from anything that would harm her physically or emotionally."

Fin swallowed hard. Jessie couldn't have been placed with a better family than the Claytons. And although it had been the hardest thing Fin had ever had to do, Jessie had fared far better having Travis for her father than she would have with Fin raising her alone.

She could understand his reasoning, but it still hurt to think that if Jessie had listened to him, they might never have met. "You were afraid I'd reject her," Fin whispered brokenly.

He nodded. "I spent many a sleepless night

before Jess called to tell me how happy you'd been when she finally told you who she was."

Tears filled Fin's eyes. "I loved and wanted her from the moment I discovered I was pregnant."

"I know that now." He smiled. "In fact, the first time I laid eyes on you, I knew you were nothing like what I'd feared you would be."

"Really?" she asked cautiously.

He sat down on the raised stone hearth in front of her. "Instead of a corporate executive with a killer instinct, you were warm, personable and sexier than sin."

She almost choked. She'd never associated herself with the word sexy. "Me?"

"Honey, you've had me turned wrong side out ever since I first laid eyes on you."

His laughter warmed her, but she tried not to let her hopes build. Sexual attraction was one thing, but he hadn't mentioned anything about loving her.

"I don't think there's ever been a doubt for either of us that we share an irresistible chemistry," she said, nodding.

"But we've had some huge problems from the get-go," he said, his expression turning serious. "You live in New York and my life is out here in God's country. Your career is glamorous and impressive as hell." He shrugged his wide shoulders. "I'm nothing more than a rancher, leading a simple, uncomplicated life. I couldn't see anything coming of the attraction between us."

Her heart sank. Was he trying to tell her all the reasons that a relationship between them wouldn't work? That he wasn't even willing to give them a fair chance?

His gaze dropped to his loosely clasped hands hanging between his knees. "Then we put the cart before the horse. We discovered that I'd gotten you pregnant before we'd even really gotten to know each other."

She swiped at an errant tear as it slid down her cheek. "You see our baby as a problem?"

"Hell no." There was no hesitation in his adamant answer. "I couldn't be happier about our having a child together." He stood up and walked over to where she sat on the couch. "But what I'm not happy about is trying to juggle time and distance in the raising of him."

"Or her."

"Right." He dropped down to one knee and took her hands in his. "I've never done anything half-assed in my entire life and I'm not about to start now. I don't want to be a part-time dad any more than you want to be a part-time mother."

Her heart skipped several beats. "What are you saying, Travis?"

"I want us to get married, Fin," he said seriously. "I want both of us to be full-time parents and raise this baby together."

He'd talked about wanting their baby and his desire to be with the child, but he hadn't mentioned anything about loving and wanting her. "I…don't know what to say."

He leaned forward and gently pressed his lips to hers. "'Yes' would work for me, honey."

She had to clear her suddenly dry throat before she could get her vocal cords to work. Being Travis's wife was what she wanted more than anything, but not without his love.

Touching his cheek, she shook her head. "Unfortunately, it doesn't work for me."

Ten

Travis felt like a damned fool. He'd laid his heart, as well as his pride, on the line and Fin had just the same as stomped all over them.

Releasing her hand, he took a deep breath and stood up. In all of his forty-nine years, he'd never dreamed that he could hurt so much and not have something physically wrong. Gathering what was left of his dignity, he squared his shoulders and met her gaze head-on.

"Well, I guess all there is left to do now is figure out who gets the baby on holidays and where he—"

"Or she."

He nodded. "Or she will spend the summers."

Suddenly needing to put distance between them, he turned toward the door. "Let me know whatever you think is fair and I'll go along with it."

"Hold it right there, cowboy." Fin's hand on his arm stopped him cold.

Her touch burned right through his shirt and the pain in his chest tightened unbearably. Glancing down at her soft palm on his arm, then back at her beautiful face, he wanted nothing more than to take her in his arms and try to convince her that they belonged together. But he'd never begged for anything in his life and, God help him, he'd never been tempted to do so—until now.

"You've had your say, now I'm going to have mine." Her green eyes sparkled with determination and he loved her more in that moment than life itself.

"What do you want from me, Fin? I offered marriage and you turned me down."

"That's just it." She rose to her feet, then pushing him down on the couch, she planted her fists on her slender hips as she glared down at him. "You didn't ask me to marry you. You offered."

Damn, but she was gorgeous when she pitched a hissy fit. But as her words sank in, he frowned. "It's the same thing."

"No, it's not." She started pacing. "There's a big difference. Huge even."

He noticed that Spud had walked in to see what all the commotion was about. But one quelling look from the incensed female giving Travis hell had the old geezer retreating back to the safety of the kitchen as fast as his seventy-plus years and arthritis would allow.

"Did it ever occur to you that I might want a marriage proposal that sounded more personal and less like a business merger?"

He frowned. "I didn't mean for it to sound like—"

She held up her hand. "Save it. I'm not finished." Looking every bit as commanding as he knew she had to be in the boardroom, she narrowed her pretty green eyes. "It's all or nothing with me, cowboy. I want it all. Marriage, a cozy home and this baby. And maybe one or two more."

The tightness in his chest eased a bit. "I can give you all of that."

"Yes, you can." Pausing, her voice softened. "But can you give me what I need most of all?"

The tears in her eyes caused a tight knot to form in the pit of his stomach. He couldn't bear to think he'd caused her to cry.

Rising to his feet, he walked over and took her

in his arms. "What do you want, sweetheart? Name it and it's yours."

"I want you to want me, as well as the baby. I want to be your wife. I want to share your life here on the Silver Moon." Her voice dropped to a broken whisper. "I want…your love, Travis."

If he could have managed it, he would have kicked his own tail end. He might have been proposing marriage, but he hadn't bothered to tell Fin how much she'd come to mean to him, how he loved her and needed her more than he needed his next breath.

Holding her close, he lowered his mouth to hers and gave her a kiss filled with the promise of a lifetime of everything she wanted. "I'm sorry, honey. I told you I wasn't good at this stuff." Using his index finger to tip her chin up until their gazes met, he smiled. "I love you more than you'll ever know. I have since the minute I first saw you."

"Oh, Travis, I love you, too. So very much." Wrapping her arms around his waist, she laid her head against his chest. "I was afraid you wanted the baby, but not me."

He kissed her silky auburn hair. "I never again want you to doubt that I want and love you. You own my heart, Fin Elliott. The baby is an extension of that love." Leaning back, he smiled. "Even though

I don't deserve you, will you do me the honor of being my wife, Fin?"

"That's more like it, cowboy." She gave him a watery grin. "Yes, I'll be your wife."

He felt like the luckiest man alive. "I promise to spend the rest of my life making sure you don't regret it, sweetheart. But are you sure you want to live here on the ranch? What about your career? Your apartment in New York? Won't you miss them?"

"No." She placed her soft palm along his jaw and gazed up at him with so much love in her eyes it stole his breath. "When I was a child, my dream in life was to have a husband and family. But after Jessie was taken from me, I made *Charisma* my baby. I nurtured it and watched it grow. But it's time to let my 'baby' go. I've raised her to be a strong force in the fashion industry. Now it's time for me to step back and let someone else guide her while I devote myself to my first dream."

"You won't miss New York?" he asked, still unable to believe that she wanted to give up life as she knew it to marry him and raise their child under the wide Colorado sky.

She shook her head. "I belong here with you on this beautiful ranch." Her smile caused him to go weak in the knees. "I want to raise our children here in this wonderful place. I want to make love with you every night in that big bed upstairs. And I want to sit with you on the swing on the front porch and watch our grandchildren playing in the yard."

He would have told her that he wanted all those things, too, but he couldn't have forced words past the lump in his throat if his life depended on it. Instead, he showed her by placing his lips on hers and kissing her with all the emotion he couldn't put into words.

When he finally raised his head, he smiled. "Who do you think your dad will appoint as editor-in-chief at *Charisma*?"

"I'm not sure." She grinned. "But he'd better do it soon because other than occasional visits to see Jessie and Cade and the rest of the family, I'm not going back."

"How do you think your dad will take the news?"

Fin nibbled on her lower lip as she thought about her father. She'd held a grudge against him all these years, but it truly had been a waste of spirit and energy. It hadn't brought her baby girl back to her. Only time had taken care of that. And if she were perfectly honest with herself, she wouldn't have met the love of her life and had a second chance at motherhood if Patrick hadn't insisted that she give Jessie up for Travis and his wife to adopt.

"Why don't you give him a call?" Travis asked, as if reading her mind.

She sighed. "I'm not sure what to say."

"Start by saying hello." He led her over to the phone. "The rest will take care of itself."

As she dialed her parents at The Tides, Travis disappeared into the kitchen and she knew he was giving her the privacy he thought she needed for the difficult phone conversation. She loved him for it, but he needn't have bothered. She didn't intend for there to be any secrets between them.

"Hi, Mom." Fortunately, instead of the maid answering the phone, her mother had picked up on the second ring.

"Finny, 'tis good to hear your voice." The sound of her mother's Irish lilt caused Fin to smile. Maeve had always been the glue that held the Elliott clan together, despite their share of problems.

"It's good to hear you, too." After exchanging a few inconsequential pleasantries, Fin asked, "Is Patrick home from the office?"

"Yes, dear. He returned from the city about an hour ago."

Fin closed her eyes as she gathered her courage. "Could I speak with him, please?"

When her mother handed the phone to Patrick, his booming voice filtered into her ear. "Hello, Finola."

Taking a deep breath, she forced herself to bring up the subject that had driven them apart over twenty years ago. "I want you to tell me the truth, Patrick. Have you ever regretted forcing me into giving Jessie up for adoption?"

His sharp intake of breath was the only sound she heard from him for several long, nerve-wracking seconds. When he finally spoke, there was a gruffness in his voice that she'd never heard. "I thought I was doing what was best for you at the time, Finola. But in hindsight, it was quite possibly the worst decision I've ever made."

Patrick's admission that he'd been wrong was the last thing she'd expected him to say. "You never told me."

There was a short pause before he spoke again. "I never knew how to tell you how sorry I was that I put my pride and concern for social appearances ahead of your happiness."

"In all fairness, I don't think I ever gave you the chance," Fin said, admitting her own part in the rift.

"I'm—" he stopped to clear his throat "—glad that we've finally got this out in the open, lass."

His use of the pet name he'd called her when she was a little girl caused tears to pool in the corners of her eyes. "I am, too, Dad."

"I…love you, Fin. Can you ever find it in your

heart to forgive me?" The hitch in her father's voice sent tears streaming down her cheeks.

"Yes, Dad. I forgive you."

There was a long pause as if they both needed time to get used to the fact that they'd finally made their peace with the past.

"I'm going to marry Jessie's adoptive father," Fin said, breaking the silence.

"Does he make you happy, lass?" Patrick's voice held a fatherly concern that she knew for certain she'd never heard before.

"Yes, Dad. He makes me very happy."

"I'm glad you found him. He seems like a good, hard-working man. And he did a wonderful job raising Jessica." Her father surprised her further when he added, "I also think it's wonderful that we'll have a new grandchild soon."

"You don't know how much that means to me, Dad," she said, meaning it.

"How are you going to juggle time at the office with a new baby?" he asked, giving her the perfect opportunity to tell him the second reason she'd called.

"I'm not even going to try." She took a deep breath as she prepared to end her career and kiss the CEO position goodbye once and for all. "Effective immediately I'm no longer the editor-in-chief of *Charisma*."

"Are you sure that's what you want?" From the tone of his voice, she could tell her father already knew the answer.

"Yes, Dad. I want what Mom always had—time to be with her babies."

"I can't fault you for that, lass."

"Dad, there's one more thing."

"What's that?"

"I think Cade McMann would be an excellent candidate for my position. He knows the magazine inside out and he has fantastic instincts. You can trust him and his judgment to keep *Charisma* on the right track."

"And he's part of the family now," her father said, sounding thoughtful.

After telling her parents again that she loved them and that she'd see them at the New Year's Eve party they were holding at The Tides, she hung up the phone and went in search of Travis. She felt more at peace than she had in twenty-three years and finally ready to start the rest of her life.

"You look absolutely beautiful, Fin."

Smiling at her daughter, Fin asked, "Is your dad ready?"

"I think he's going to wear a hole in the floor from pacing so much," Jessie said, laughing as she finished with the tiny buttons at the back of Fin's wedding dress. "Cade and Mac have both threatened to tie him down and Spud offered to supply the rope."

Fin laughed. "He asked me two days ago if we couldn't just elope."

Tears filled Jessie's eyes as she nodded. "Dad loves you so much. We all do."

"And I love all of you." Fin gave her daughter a watery smile. "Here we go again. We're both going to ruin our makeup if we don't stop crying."

Dabbing at her eyes with a tissue, Jessie smiled. "I'm just so happy for both of you."

Fin hugged Jessie close. "I'm happy for all of us. I have a beautiful daughter, a wonderful son-in-law and I'm marrying the man I love."

"It's time, Aunt Finny."

Looking up, Fin smiled at her niece. Marriage to Mac Riggs definitely agreed with Bridget. There was a sparkle in her eyes and a glow about her that hadn't been there before she met the tall, dark-haired sheriff of Winchester County.

"We'll be right there," Jessie said, hugging Fin again. "Let's go take pity on Dad before he has to have the floor resurfaced."

As Fin followed the two young women down the stairs of the Silver Moon ranch house, her heart skipped a beat when she saw Travis, standing straight and tall in the tuxedo he'd worn for Jessie and Cade's wedding. When she'd asked him what he was going to wear for their wedding, he'd just smiled and told her not to worry about it.

When he met her at the bottom of the steps, she touched his handsome face. "You said your tux would hang in the closet, never to be worn again."

He grinned. "Do you remember what you told me when the kids got married?"

"I said you looked handsome and—" her cheeks heated and she smiled as she realized why he'd worn the tux "—incredible."

His low chuckle sent waves of longing throughout her entire body. "That's right. And since the doctor gave you a clean bill of health yesterday—"

"You wanted to amaze me?" Fin asked, laughing delightedly.

"Honey, I intend to amaze both of us tonight after we're alone." The promise in his blue eyes made her tingle from head to toe. "But right now I want to make you mine."

She smiled at the man she loved more than life itself. "I am yours, Travis. For now and always. Never doubt that."

"And I'm yours, sweetheart." He gave her a kiss so tender, she thought she might melt into a puddle right then and there. When he raised his head, he offered her his arm. "Let's mosey on over to the fireplace and let Mac make it official."

And as they took the vows that made them husband and wife, Fin looked forward to an amazing future filled with love and happiness beneath the wide Colorado sky.

* * * * *

BEYOND THE BOARDROOM

BY
MAUREEN CHILD

Maureen Child is a California native who loves to travel. Every chance they get, she and her husband are taking off on another research trip. The author of more than sixty books, Maureen loves a happy ending and still swears that she has the best job in the world. She lives in Southern California with her husband, two children, and a golden retriever with delusions of grandeur.

For my husband, Mark, because really, all of my books should be dedicated to him. I love you, honey!

One

"Okay then," Rachel Adler said, keeping her voice pitched to be heard over the thumping of running feet and the hum of the treadmill. "I've got you booked for dinner with Tawny Mason tonight at eight."

"At Une Nuit?" Shane Elliott asked, reaching for his water bottle, tucked beneath the cord at the head of the machine.

"Where else?" Rachel muttered with a little shake of her head. Why in heaven would he even ask? she wondered. Hadn't she been taking care of every detail of Shane's life for four years now?

"Good." Shane took a long drink of water and Rachel's gaze locked on the bobbing motion of his Adam's apple. Seriously, even the man's *neck* was sexy.

When he'd finished off the last of the water, he wiped sweat from his face with the towel looped around his neck and tossed Rachel the empty bottle. "And call ahead. Have Stash order in some flowers for, um..." He waved one hand in a silent attempt for help.

"Tawny," Rachel provided dryly as she set the empty bottle down on the floor beside her. For heaven's sake, the man couldn't even remember his date's name.

Plus, he knew as well as she did that Stash Martin, manager of Une Nuit, never missed a beat when getting the Elliott family table ready. There would, she knew, be flowers, champagne and some delicious appetizers just waiting for Shane and Tawny.

Tawny.

What kind of woman named her daughter Tawny? A stage mother, hoping for a starlet daughter? Or had the woman taken one look at her newborn baby girl and decided...future bimbo?

"Right." Shane nodded. "Tawny. She says her mother named her for the color of her eyes."

Rachel rolled her own green eyes.

Shane grinned at her and Rachel's stomach did a quick dip and spin.

If she could have managed it without looking like a complete idiot, she'd have kicked her own ass. Honestly. Why was it Shane Elliott who could turn her insides to mush with a simple smile?

The first three years she'd worked with the man, everything had been fine between them. They'd had a good working relationship and Shane even appreciated Rachel's sometimes quirky sense of humor, when most of her previous employers hadn't. Then she'd had to go and ruin the whole thing by falling for him.

For the last year she'd suffered silently, wanting him every day, dreaming about him at night, all the while knowing that he thought of her only as Good ol' Rachel.

Idiot.

"What do you think?" he asked, clearly oblivious to her thoughts. "Roses?"

"Huh?" She blinked, shook her head and reminded herself to concentrate on the moment. "Right. Flowers. Roses are boring."

"Really?"

"Trust me."

"I always do," he said, giving her another of those smiles that had the power to zap an unwary female at twenty paces.

She couldn't do this much longer, she thought. Couldn't keep working with him every day and dying a little more every day. Couldn't set up his dates with other women and imagine him in bed with every one of them. Couldn't keep wasting her life away waiting for the wrong man to wake up and stumble on her.

Sighing, Rachel flipped through her memo book, scanned the notes she kept on the legions of Shane's women and found what she was looking for. "Tawny prefers daisies."

"Sure, I remember now. Such a simple girl."

"Simple*ton*, you mean," she muttered again, keeping her voice low enough that her boss's running feet would drown out the comment.

"What was that?"

"Nothing." She automatically handed him the second bottle of water she'd brought with her to the executive area of the company gym on the fifth floor.

"Rachel, what would I do without you?" he mused, not really expecting an answer.

But oh boy, could she give him one. Rachel was Shane's right hand at *The Buzz,* one of the magazines in the Elliott family empire. As a weekly entertainment magazine, *The Buzz* covered all the new movies, did interviews with up-and-coming directors and fawned over whichever actor or actress was the current hot topic. And as editor in chief of *The Buzz,* Shane did his best to keep on top of everything going on around him.

Of course, when she'd first come to work for him, he hadn't been so involved. Instead he'd tried to avoid the office as much as humanly possible. But slowly, Rachel had convinced him to enjoy his job more.

Back then, he'd resented being pulled into the family business. But Rachel had seen just how good he was at not only handling the day-to-day running of the magazine but at dealing with people and managing disasters. She'd eventually convinced him that he was meant to run this business.

And he'd really come into his own over the last

several months—ever since his father, Patrick, had kicked off a competition among his children.

Old man Elliott had determined that the best way to name a new CEO of Elliott Publication Holdings was to see who was willing to work hardest to earn it. At the end of the year the editor in chief of whichever one of the magazines showed the most proportional profit growth would become Top Dog.

And *The Buzz* was the front-runner.

Shane's father was due to announce the winner any day now.

Patrick was a sneaky old man, in Rachel's opinion. Nice, sure, but sneaky. He'd found a way to make his grown children admit just how much they wanted to succeed. By pitting them against each other, he'd been able to sit back all year and watch them discover themselves.

And there had been plenty of discoveries, she thought, remembering all of the turmoil over the last year.

"Did you put that call in to Fin for me?" Shane asked, breathing hard as he picked up the pace on the treadmill.

"Yes," Rachel said, flipping back a page in her memo book. Smiling, she read off, "Fin says and I quote, 'Tell Shane he needs to get away from the city and smell some fresh air. Come to Colorado and I'll teach him to ride a horse.'"

Shane laughed. "A month on a ranch and she's Annie Oakley?"

Rachel chuckled along with him. She couldn't

help it. Shane's twin sister had been sad for so long, it was good knowing that she was finally happy. She'd reconciled with Jessie, the daughter she was forced to give up for adoption so many years ago. She was married to a man she was clearly nuts about and her newly discovered pregnancy was the icing on the cake. "She's happy."

"Yeah," Shane said, his running steps slowing a little as he thought about the sister he was so close to. "She really is. But damn, I miss having her around."

His eyes narrowed thoughtfully as he stared straight ahead, out the bank of windows overlooking Park Avenue.

"I know," Rachel said. "But she'll probably come back home for Christmas."

"Christmas." He shut off the treadmill, stepped neatly to one side and used his towel to wipe his face again. "It's December, isn't it?"

"All month," she agreed.

"Have I started shopping yet?"

"No."

"Damn." Grabbing the second bottle of water, he chugged down the liquid, then handed off the empty bottle. "No time to worry about it now, though. I'm gonna grab a shower, then I'll see you back in the office in half an hour. I'd like to take a look at the new copy for the magazine before it heads out to production."

"Right." Rachel winced as she thought about one column in particular that he'd be going over.

As if reading her mind, he turned and called back, "The new Tess Tells All column was turned in on time, right?"

"Oh, yeah. She's very dependable."

From across the room, Shane winked at her. "Just like you, Rachel."

She watched him disappear into the men's locker room and as the door swung shut behind him, she whispered, "You have *no* idea."

A few hours later, Shane listened with half an ear as his art director, Jonathon Taylor, laid out plans for next summer's Fourth of July edition even as snow flurries dusted the windows. On a weekly magazine, they usually operated months in advance. And the specialty editions required even more in-depth planning.

Jonathon really thrived on the rush of trying to outdo himself with every holiday issue. And damned if he didn't pull it off most of the time. Right now Jon was in the midst of describing, with wildly waving hands, his salute to patriotism, centering on celebrities dressed in red, white and blue. Not original, but knowing Jon, it would be great.

Sandy Hall, the managing editor, was practically frothing at the mouth. No doubt she had a complaint or two about the money Jonathon was budgeting for his blowout edition.

And Shane would have to listen to both sides and make a decision. Used to be that he hated being here, listening to all of the day-to-day drama of the magazine's inner circles. Now, though, he was enjoying himself.

Amazed him to admit it, but there it was. He'd been getting a charge out of running *The Buzz* for months now. Surprisingly enough, Shane realized he was pleased. Proud, even, of how well *The Buzz* was doing. He'd gone into this contest with halfhearted enthusiasm. But as the months had worn on, Shane had found himself being swept up into the competitive spirit. Nothing an Elliott liked better than a contest.

"So—" Jonathon was wrapping up his speech "—I figure if we shell out top dollar to a few of the biggest celebrities, the rest of 'em will come along, too. Nobody wants to feel left out."

Before Shane could respond, Sandy stood up, brushed her short blond hair back from her eyes and narrowed her gaze on Jon. "And if we pay top dollar for a handful of celebs, who's going to offset that expenditure?"

"You have to pay to play," Jon said smugly, shooting a glance at Shane as if knowing he'd back him up.

And he did. "Jon's right, Sandy," he said, holding up one hand to keep his managing editor's temper in check. "We get the right people into that issue, the advertisers will line up to be a part of it. Plus, we'll sell more copies."

"The budget's already stretched pretty thin, Shane," Sandy said, sneering at Jon's gleeful chortle.

"Bull." Shane stood up behind his desk, swept the

edges of his jacket back and stuffed his hands into his pockets. "You know as well as I do that the profit margins are way up. We're beating the pants off the rest of the Elliott magazines. And we're going to keep doing it. And the way we're going to keep doing it is by *not* cutting corners."

Jon slapped one hand to his chest and bowed his head as if in prayer. "Brilliant, my king, brilliant."

Shane laughed at the dramatics, but hey, it was good to be king.

"You're only saying that because you won," Sandy pointed out.

"Sure," Jon said, grinning at her now that he'd made his point.

"Before the bloodletting starts up again," Shane interrupted, looking from one editor to the other, "has either of you made any headway on the job I gave you?"

Jon and Sandy looked at each other, shrugged, then turned back to Shane.

"Nope." Sandy spoke first, clearly reluctant to admit that she'd failed. "I've talked to everyone I know and *nobody* has a clue about this woman's identity."

"I second that," Jon said, obviously disappointed. "Our little Tess is like Spider-Man or something, keeping her secret identity so secret, there's not even a whisper of gossip about her."

Just what Shane hadn't wanted to hear. Damn it. Tess Tells All was the most popular column in his magazine. They'd picked up thousands of new readers thanks to the anonymous woman's talent for being both funny and insightful.

Seven months ago *The Buzz* had carried the very first of the mystery woman's columns.

The response had been immediate. Calls, e-mails, letters, all from people who wanted to read more from Tess. But the woman was untraceable. She faxed her monthly column in from a different location in the city every time and her checks were sent to a PO box and then forwarded to yet another.

As well as *The Buzz* was doing, Shane knew it would be doing even better if he could just talk this woman into writing a weekly column. But she hadn't answered any letters he'd sent and all other attempts at communication had failed.

Making him one very frustrated man.

"Fine," he said on a sigh. "Never mind. Just keep looking for her." Then he sat down behind his desk, waved one hand at them dismissively and picked up the latest column by the mysterious Tess. He didn't even look up when his co-workers left his office.

He read every issue of *The Buzz* before it was laid out for production and eventual printing. The only way to keep a handle on what his magazine was doing was for him to stay involved. From the ground up.

But reading this particular column was always a pleasure. He leaned back in the black leather chair and swung around until he was facing the snow-dusted bank of windows overlooking Manhattan. He smiled ruefully as he read.

Tess says, the secret to surviving your boss is to never let him know you understand him. The poor guy's got to have a few illusions.

My boss thinks he's mysterious. Right. About as mysterious as a pot of chicken soup. The man, like all others of his gender, is so very predictable.

Just last week, I set up two "first dates" for him. At the same restaurant, with the same meal, the same wine. Only the names of the women were changed. Mysterious? Hardly.

I juggle his women just like I juggle his business meetings. The man has made me a good enough juggler that I could be making twice as much money working at a circus—and hey, the co-workers wouldn't change that much!

Shane chuckled. Tess was good, but he felt sorry for her. Working for a man like that couldn't be easy.

When it comes to business, though, he's at the top of his game when everything around him is falling to pieces. Which, I suppose, is why I'm still here after all this time. Despite having to run the man's social life, I do enjoy being at the top. I like being the right hand woman—even if sometimes I feel invisible.

Invisible? Shane shook his head. How could a woman like Tess go unnoticed by anyone?

Maybe it's the time of year that's got me thinking about my life. Sure, you're reading this column sometime in March, but as I write this, it's December. Snow's falling outside, turning Manhattan into a postcard. Wreaths are up on the shop windows, twinkling lights are everywhere and people are ice skating in Rockefeller Center.

The old year is winding down and a new one's getting ready to roll. And I have to ask myself if I really want to maintain the status quo. Is this all there is? Do I really want to keep working for a man who treats me like a well-trained dog? Toss me a treat every now and then so I'll keep running and fetching?

He frowned, wondering why the tone of Tess's column had suddenly changed. Usually she was funny, lighthearted. Making jokes about her boss and underlining, apparently, how every other assistant in the country felt about his or her job.

When he read the next line, he sat up straight in his chair and scowled at the page.

Wonder what he'd do if I quit?

Quit?

She couldn't quit. Hell, her column was too damn popular for her to quit working. If she walked away from her job, she wouldn't be writing this column anymore and where did that leave *The Buzz*?

The truth is, my boss probably wouldn't even notice I was gone until his dry cleaning went unclaimed or until he had to make his own reservations for dinner with the latest wide-eyed blonde. So why'm I still here?

I think we all know the answer to that.

I've let him become too important to me.

I spend more time living his life than I do living my own.

Shane really didn't like the sound of this.

What do you readers think? Should I give it up and stop torturing myself? Should I finally realize that he's never going to look up and notice me? The real me? Should I accept that all I'll ever be to him is an excellent assistant?

Shane grumbled and finished reading the column with a snarl on his face.

The answer to that question is no. The time has come to leave my job and move on to something else while I still can. To all of you assistants out there—all of you who've written to me over the last several months, telling me your own stories—I guess this is goodbye.

Goodbye?

By the time you read this, I'll probably be long gone. I'll miss you guys. I'll miss this column. Heck, I'll miss the boss, too.

I wish you all the best of luck with your own bosses and I'll never forget any of you.

Two

Shane hit the intercom button and when Rachel answered a second later, he snapped, "Come in here for a minute, please."

A moment later the double doors opened and Rachel stepped in, carrying a steno pad. "What's up?"

"Did you see the Tess Tells All column for March?"

"Yeeesss…" One word came out in four distinct syllables.

"So you know she's thinking about quitting her job?"

Rachel took a deep breath and turned her back on him for a second. Deliberately she schooled her features into a politely interested mask. Deciding to quit her job hadn't been an easily reached decision, but she knew it was the right one. Asking her readers for their votes had merely been a way of breaking the news about that decision.

Quietly she shut the door then walked across the thick red carpet toward his desk. "I read it. What's the problem?"

"The problem?" Shane dropped Tess's column onto his desktop and stood up. "She's too popular with our readers, that's the problem. She can't quit her job. We need her column."

Rachel wondered if Shane would be this concerned when she turned in her resignation. And if he were, would that change her mind? No. She had to leave EPH. Had to get out into the world and find someone else to care for. Hopefully someone who would care for her in return.

She shook her head as she sat down in the black leather armchair opposite his desk. Taking another deep breath, she steadied her voice. "I doubt this is a whim. She's obviously done a lot of thinking. Probably some soul searching. People don't just walk away from a good job without a lot of thought."

Which she knew for a fact, since she'd spent the last five months talking herself into doing just that.

He narrowed his gaze on her. "Do you know something you're not telling me?"

"Why would you think that?" Oh, good one, she told herself. Stall without actually lying.

She blew out a breath and tucked a loose strand

of honey-blond hair behind her right ear. She worried her bottom lip and said, "Honestly, Shane, I don't see how you're going to keep her from quitting her job when you don't even know who she is."

"We have to find out."

Rachel tucked her pad against her chest and folded her arms over it. "Haven't you had people working on that for months now?"

"Yes," he muttered, then turned toward the bank of windows. Staring down at the snow-covered street eighteen floors below, he added, "I can't understand how she can stay so hidden. Hell, you'd think her *boss* would recognize himself in her articles."

Rachel mmm-hmmed. "You would, wouldn't you?"

"How could he not?" Shane wondered, more to himself than to her.

"It's surprising, all right," Rachel said dryly. She knew darn well Shane had read every one of the articles she'd written as Tess. And yet, here he stood, completely clueless.

He glanced at her and Rachel caught the glint in his clear green eyes and recognized it. He'd had the same look in his eyes when this competition with his brothers and sisters was just getting started. Shane Elliott simply did *not* lose well. But this time, he was going to have to deal with it.

"Do you know something about Tess you haven't told me?"

She paused just a fraction of a second, then shook her head firmly again even as she skipped around his question. "She faxes those columns in from all over the city. No one knows where the next one's coming from."

He stared at her for a minute or two longer. Long enough to worry Rachel just a little. Good thing he couldn't read her mind. Although, if he *could* read her mind, she wouldn't have to quit her job, because he'd *know* that she loved him and then he'd either be pleased about it or fire her.

"Right," Shane said. "Right." Walking back to his desk, he slid Tess's column into the manila envelope with the rest of the layout for the March issue. Handing it to her, he said, "Get these to production for me, will you, Rachel?"

"Sure." Glad to be on safer ground, she asked, "Anything else?"

He dropped into his chair, braced both arms on his desk and said, "Just find the mysterious Tess. If she's looking for a new job, we'll give her one."

Rachel turned and left the office and when she'd closed the door behind her, she leaned back against it. Hah. Shane wanted to offer Tess a job? Ironic? Oh, yeah.

She walked past her desk and on down the hall toward production. She glanced to either side of her as her heels sank deeply into the rich scarlet carpet. It was going to be hard to leave this place. It was familiar. Comfortable.

Maybe *too* comfortable, she reminded herself.

The gleaming glass and chrome offices on either side of the wide aisle were bustling with sound as the staff of *The Buzz* worked on various tasks. Phones rang, someone laughed and the scent of coffee floated on the warm air drifting from the central heating system.

Rachel smiled at Stacy, the receptionist, as she strolled through the main waiting area. The walls were a clean, pure white, and the art on the walls mostly enlarged, chrome-framed covers of *The Buzz*. The effect was startling, but eye catching. The idea was to make this floor look up to the minute, fresh. Exciting. And it worked.

Every floor of the EPH building had its own color scheme and was decorated according to whichever magazine it was trying to promote. Rachel was probably prejudiced, but she'd always thought the eighteenth-floor home of *The Buzz* was the nicest.

Rachel kept walking, tossing a glance into the small meeting rooms as she walked, smiling in at one or two of the people she passed. The photography lab door was closed and she smiled wryly. Ferria—no last name—was notoriously territorial about her office. Even Shane had a hard time getting past the lead photographer's doorway.

At Production, Rachel stepped through the open door and handed over the manila envelope to the head man's assistant, Christina. Fiftyish, Christina was a single mother of four boys who took no crapola off of anyone—least of all her boss. Her snow-white hair was cut into extremely short layers that hugged her head and highlighted bright blue eyes.

The older woman pushed her silver wire-framed glasses up on her nose and grinned. "I'm thinking about heading out to Lucci's Deli for lunch. Want to join me?"

"Love it," Rachel said, realizing that Christina was only one of so many people she'd miss when she left. "I'll meet you at the elevator at twelve, okay?"

"Excellent."

Walking back to her desk, she felt almost as though she were already saying goodbye. Her gaze swept over the familiar fixtures and faces and she hugged the electrical hum of activity close. She was really going to miss this place.

She loved her job. Loved working for Shane and feeling as though she were a part of something special. Working on a weekly magazine, there was always something happening. An air of excitement, urgency that she would probably never find anywhere else.

But she knew she had to go.

She couldn't stay at *The Buzz*, working with Shane every day, loving him as she did. It was just too hard. Too hard to make his dates for him, to see him look at every other woman in the world with more interest than he would ever show her. So whether she liked it or not, it was time, Rachel thought, that she left EPH.

Both she and her alter ego Tess were going to quietly disappear from Shane's life.

And there was nothing he could do to change her mind.

By seven o'clock, most of the magazine's employees were gone. Shane walked through the empty office and listened to the sound of his own footsteps on the carpet. Only a few of the overhead lights were on, splashing the shadows with occasional bursts of light. The reflected lights shone against the black expanse of windows and mirrored Shane as he walked toward the elevator.

During the day, this office thundered with the noise of productivity. People laughing, talking, computer keys clicking, phones ringing. But at night…it was like a house emptied of its children.

Quiet to the point of spooky.

He passed reception, where an acre of desk sat dead center of a waiting area. Twin couches in matching shades of white faced each other across the expanse and on the far wall, the elevator gleamed dully in the overhead light.

Sighing, Shane stabbed the up call button and waited impatiently for the elevator to arrive. If he hadn't answered that phone call from his father a few minutes ago, he'd have been pushing the down button and heading for home to get ready for his date with… He frowned. What the *hell* was that woman's name?

Shaking his head, he pushed that question away to concentrate on another one. Why did his father want to see him? And why now, after the business day?

Patrick Elliott was a hard man. Always had been. More focused on building an empire than a family, over the years he'd become a stranger to his own children. Shane's mother, Maeve, was the glue that held the Elliott family together. Hell, *she* was the only reason he and his siblings were still speaking to Patrick.

The elevator opened in front of him and he stepped inside with all the enthusiasm of a man heading to a tax audit. Generic Muzak filtered down all around him, but he did his best to ignore it. He punched the appropriate floor button, and as the doors slid shut again, Shane let his mind drift back over the years.

In all the memories he had of growing up, Patrick was no more than a blurred image on the fringes of his mind. Until one memorable year.

He and his twin, Finola, were the youngest of the Elliott children. And, since they'd been born nine years after their brother Daniel, Shane and Fin were even closer than twins usually were. Growing up, they'd been each other's best friend. They'd fought each other's battles, celebrated each other's victories, and shared the hurts and pains that came along.

And maybe, Shane told himself, that was the main reason he just couldn't bring himself to get close to his father now. Patrick was trying to make up for his failures as a parent and slowly, each of the Elliott kids was coming around. But Shane held back—because he'd never been able to forgive the old man for what he'd put Fin through when she was just a kid.

He leaned back against the cool, slick chrome of the elevator wall and closed his eyes, remembering. Shane could see Fin as she'd been at fifteen, beautiful, trusting, with bright green eyes filled with anticipation. Until she'd made the mistake that Patrick wouldn't countenance.

She'd become pregnant by the son of another wealthy family, and neither side wanted their children getting married for the sake of a child they hadn't planned.

Though their mother had cried and sided with Fin—something none of the children knew until recently—Patrick had been adamant about saving the family's "good name." He'd shipped Fin off to a convent in Canada with as much feeling as a man who dropped off an unwanted puppy at the pound. No one had been able to reach Patrick. The old man never backed down from a damn thing if he believed he was right—and he *always* believed he was right.

Fin was forced to give up her daughter at birth and Shane would never be able to forget her pain, her misery. Just as he was pretty sure he'd never be able to completely forgive Patrick for causing it.

The elevator dinged as it reached the executive level of the EPH building and the doors slid open with a whoosh.

"Might as well get this over with," Shane muttered and walked into a very different atmosphere than the one found on the eighteenth floor. On the twenty-third, the carpeting was subdued, the walls a soft beige with cream trim and the furniture was elegant antiques. Even the air smelled different up here, he thought, more…rarified, he supposed.

But then, that's what Patrick had always been concerned about. How things looked. The perception of the Elliott family. Which was why it had taken Fin too many years to reconnect with her long lost daughter.

At least *that* had come around and turned out well. Now that Jessie was finally where she'd always belonged—with them—Patrick had at last accepted and welcomed the girl. And the pain Shane had seen in Fin's eyes for too many years was finally gone.

Knowing Fin was so happy had made dealing with Patrick easier than it used to be.

Shaking his head, he wondered where all the philosophical thoughts were coming from. Hell, he was wasting time. He still had to get home and change for his date with…what was her name?

Grumbling, he knocked briefly on the closed door to Patrick's office and waited.

"Come on in."

Opening the door, he stepped into an elegantly appointed office and looked directly at his father, seated behind a mahogany desk fit for a king.

At seventy-seven, Patrick Elliott looked at least ten years younger than his age. Still had most of his hair, though it was completely gray now. Tall, with squared shoulders and a defiant tilt to his chin, the old man continued to look like he'd be able to take on the world, if necessary.

Shane walked across the office and dropped into a burgundy leather club chair opposite his father's desk. Absently he noted that the chair was built to be lower than Patrick's desk, leaving whoever sat in it at a disadvantage. That was his father, though. Never miss a trick. "What can I do for you, Dad?"

Patrick leaned back in his chair, braced his elbows on the padded arms and steepled his fingers. "In a hurry, are you?"

"Not really." Of course he was, but if he admitted as much, Patrick was contrary enough to slow this meeting down. Crossing his legs, Shane rested his right ankle on his left knee and idly tapped his fingers against the soft leather of his shoe.

Nodding, the old man said, "That's all right. I am in a hurry. Your mother's got us tickets to some play or other."

Shane smiled. "A musical?"

Patrick shuddered. "Probably."

This time Shane dipped his head to hide a broader smile. His parents were sharply divided on the theater. His father hated it and his mother loved it. One thing he could give Patrick Elliott. The man was crazy enough about his wife that he'd actually suffered through seeing *Cats* twelve times.

"God knows what she's gonna make me endure tonight. But she's meeting me here in twenty minutes, so I'm gonna make this short."

"All right." Back to business, then. "Let's hear it."

Patrick leaned forward in his chair and gave his son

a broad smile. "The final reports are in. All of the profit margins on each of the magazines has been tallied."

"And...?" Shane's heartbeat quickened and a sense of expectation filled him. Hell, just a year ago, if someone had told him he'd care this much about being named CEO of Elliot Publication Holdings, he would have laughed himself sick.

Now?

Hell, he wanted that position more than he cared to admit. And even more, he wanted to *win* the competition his father had instigated.

"Congratulations," Patrick said.

Shane let out a breath he hadn't realized he'd been holding. "Yeah?" He grinned and stood up. "Thanks."

The old man stood, too, and held out one hand. Shane grabbed it and gave it a shake.

"You did a good job, son."

A surprising zip of pleasure shot through Shane. Apparently, he thought wryly, no one outgrew the need for approval from a parent. Even one who'd been as absent from his children's lives as Patrick.

"Appreciate it," Shane said, reeling in his thoughts as they careened wildly through his mind. CEO. It meant a world of responsibilities that only a year or so ago he would have done anything he could to avoid. Weird how a man's life could change.

He couldn't wait to tell Rachel. All the work they'd been doing for the last few years had finally culminated in winning the grand prize.

"I'll make the official announcement at the family

New Year's party," Patrick was saying as he came around the edge of his desk. "But I wanted you to know now. You earned it, Shane."

"Damn straight I did," Shane said, still feeling the hum of excitement. Gratification. "But I couldn't have done it without my staff. The people at *The Buzz* have worked their asses off this last year. Especially Rachel, my assistant."

The older man nodded, pleased. "I'm glad you realize that no man succeeds alone."

Shane slanted his father a look. "Oh, I know it. I'm just sort of surprised that *you* know it."

Patrick sighed and shook his head. "A man reaches a certain age and he gets to know all sorts of things, Shane. Things he should have realized a long time ago."

"Yeah, well," Shane said, suddenly uncomfortable. "Better late than never, I guess."

"I suppose. At the first of the year, I'll clear my stuff out of this office and you can move in."

"Seems strange. Thinking about me, working up here."

"Seems damn strange to me, too, son," Patrick said, wandering across the room to stare at the plaques and framed awards EPH had won over the years. "I'm so used to coming here every day," he murmured, "I can't really imagine *not* working."

"Hell, I can't even remember the last time you took a vacation."

The older man glanced over his shoulder at Shane. His eyes flashed with something that might have been regret, but it was gone so fast, Shane couldn't be sure. And even if it was regret, he told himself, what did it change?

"I made mistakes," Patrick admitted, turning around now to face his son. "I know that."

Shane stiffened slightly. He didn't want to head down Memory Lane with his father. Especially since those memories would no doubt douse the feeling of victory still rushing through him. Over the last year, Patrick had made a sincere effort to get to know his children. But the bottom line was, one good year didn't offset a lifetime. "Dad—"

"I know. You don't want to talk about it. Well, neither do I." Shoving both hands into the pockets of his well-tailored dark blue suit, the older man said, "But I can't help thinking about it. I can't rewrite the past, though I wish to hell I could. All those years, I focused on my work. Building a legacy for you and your brothers and sisters."

"And you did it."

"Yes, I did. But along the way," he said, his voice suddenly sounding tired, "I missed what was really important. It all slipped out of my reach and I let it go. Did it to myself. No one else to blame."

"There doesn't have to be blame," Shane said quietly. "Not anymore."

"Wish I believed that," Patrick whispered and he suddenly looked every one of his seventy-seven years. "But the mistakes I made are the point of this conversation."

"Meaning?"

"Meaning don't do what I did." He pulled his hands from his pockets and waved his arms to encompass the high-rise office, the awards and the incredible view from the bank of floor to ceiling windows behind his desk. "Right now, being in charge looks great. The challenge. The fun of beating the others."

Shane shrugged.

"I know you, son," Patrick said, stabbing his index finger at Shane. "I know you thrive on the competition, just like a true Elliott. But remember, winning doesn't mean a damn thing if you've got nothing but the victory to show for it."

Three

Rachel opened the freezer door for the third time in a half hour and stared at her nemesis. It sat there next to a stack of frozen dinners and mocked her silently.

Her own fault. She never should have bought it. But she'd had a weak moment right after work.

Well, actually, she'd been having plenty of weak moments lately. Every time she thought about quitting her job and walking away from her only connection to Shane Elliott.

"It's the right thing to do," she muttered as icy fog wafted from the freezer to caress her face.

Her hand tightened on the white plastic door handle and she squeezed as if gripping a lifeline. She had to quit. She knew it. She'd only been postponing the inevitable because she hadn't wanted to leave EPH until Shane had won the competition between him and his siblings.

"Well, that excuse is gone. You've helped *The Buzz* do so well in this last year that he's *bound* to win. What've you got left?" she asked herself, knowing damn well there wasn't an answer.

She shivered, and reached into the freezer, her fingers curling around a small carton covered in ice crystals. "Fine. I surrender. We both knew I would or I wouldn't have bought you in the first place."

When a knock sounded on her front door, she backed up instantly, leaving the carton where it was and slammed the freezer shut. She ran both hands over her wavy blond hair, released from the tidy French twist she kept it in while working. Then she automatically smoothed the gray skirt she still wore and shuffled out of the tiny galley kitchen in her pink fuzzy slippers. As she walked, she glanced at the pineapple shaped clock on the wall.

Eight o'clock.

Great.

Shane would be just sitting down to his first glass of champagne with Tawny the wonder girl. Glad she'd reminded herself of *that.* Oh, yeah, it was definitely time to quit her job.

She passed her overstuffed sofa on the way to the door and absently straightened a bright blue throw pillow. Rachel's gaze flicked quickly around her West Village apartment in approval. Only a one bedroom, it was plenty big enough for her. Plus, it was a family neighborhood, with a deli on one corner and a small grocery store on another.

In the five years she'd lived here, she'd transformed the old apartment into a cozy nest. She'd painted the walls a soft, French country lemon-yellow and done the trim in pale off-white. The furniture was large, overstuffed and covered in a floral fabric that made her feel as if she lived in a garden.

Natalie Cole sang to her from the stereo on the far wall and from downstairs, came the tempting scent of her neighbor Mrs. Florio's homemade lasagna. With any luck, Rachel thought, scuffing her slippers over the hardwood floor, she'd be getting a care basket of leftovers in the morning. Mrs. Florio, God bless her, thought Rachel was far too skinny to "catch a nice man" and took every opportunity to fatten her up.

Smiling to herself, Rachel looked through the security peephole and sucked in a gasp as she jumped back, startled.

Shane?

Here?

He knocked again.

She took another peek and watched as he leaned in toward the fisheye lens and grinned. "Rachel, come on. Open up."

Quickly she gave herself a once-over. Still in the yellow silk blouse and gray skirt she'd worn to work, she suddenly wished she was dressed in sequins and rhinestones and on her way out the door to meet…*anybody.*

"How do you know I'm here?" she demanded. "I could be out on a hot date." Sure. In an alternate universe.

"You're talking to me," he said, still grinning into the peephole. "So you're there. Now, you going to let me in or what?"

In the four years she'd worked for Shane he'd never once come to her apartment. So what in heaven would bring him here now? Did he somehow sense she was going to quit? Was he trying to undermine her decision?

"This is so not fair," she muttered as she quickly undid the chain, then twisted first one, then another dead bolt locks. Finally she turned the knob and opened the door.

Shane didn't wait for an invitation; he crowded past her into the living room, then turned around to look at her. In one hand, he held a bouquet of lilacs—Rachel's favorite flower—and in the other a huge bottle of champagne.

Stomach jittering, Rachel closed the door and leaned back against it. "What're you doing here, Shane?"

"This is a nice place," he said, glancing around at the apartment.

"Thanks."

"Wasn't easy to find," he added. "Had to go down to personnel and look up your records to get your address."

Her stomach did another wild twist and flip and she swallowed hard. "And why would you do that?"

"So I could bring you these," he said, handing her the lilacs.

The heavy, sweet perfume reached for her and Rachel just managed to keep from burying her nose in the blossoms and enjoying the thrill of Shane bringing her flowers. But there was something else going on here and she had to know what it was.

"Shane, why are you bringing me flowers?" she asked, silently congratulating herself on the steadiness of her voice. "Aren't you supposed to be at Une Nuit giving Tawny a bouquet of daisies?"

"Tawny!" He slapped the heel of his hand against his forehead. "*That's* her name. Why can't I remember that?"

"Good question," Rachel said. "Maybe because there are too many Tawnys, Bambis and Barbies in your life to keep them straight?"

He slanted her a look and then smiled and shrugged. "Maybe." Sweeping his gaze around the room again, he started for the kitchen, talking over his shoulder as he went. "Anyway, don't worry about what's her name. I called Stash. Told him I couldn't make it and to give…"

"Tawny," Rachel provided as she followed him into her kitchen.

"…right. Told him to give Tawny whatever she wanted on the house and to offer my apologies."

"So you stood her up."

"Had to," he said, setting the champagne bottle down onto the counter and shifting a look at the white cupboards. "Champagne glasses?"

Still clutching her lilacs, Rachel pointed with her free hand. "Just wineglasses, sorry."

He shrugged again. "That's fine." Then he opened the cupboard door, reached two glasses and set them on the counter.

This was too hard. Now that she'd seen him here, in her place, she'd never really be able to get him out again. She'd always be able to pull up the memory of him standing in her living room, rooting through her kitchen. Heck, she'd probably never be able to look through the peephole again without seeing his smiling face looking back at her.

"You shouldn't be here," she blurted, fingers tightening around the lilacs that must have cost him a small fortune.

Springtime flowers in the dead of winter? And she was sappy enough to really enjoy knowing that he'd remembered *her* favorite flowers even when he couldn't remember Tawny's.

His fingers on the wire cage of the bottle top, he paused to glance at her. His gaze swept her up and down, from her tousled hair to the tips of her furry slippers. Slowly a smile curved his mouth. "Why? You really do have a hot date?"

Straightening up a little, she said, "I was planning on spending the night with *two* guys, actually."

"Yeah? Who?"

Rachel sighed. It was pointless to pretend, since she wasn't exactly dressed for going clubbing. "Ben and Jerry."

Shane grinned as he started working on the champagne cork again. "This'll be better."

"I don't know," she said, moving past him to grab a cut glass vase from another cupboard. She glanced at him as she filled the vase with water. "It's *chocolate* ice cream."

"Not nearly good enough for the occasion."

"Which is?" she asked, stuffing the lilacs into the vase and giving them one last, lingering caress.

"We're celebrating." The cork popped, slamming into a cupboard before bouncing to the floor, and Shane held the bottle over the sink as champagne frothed and foamed out the neck. As he filled both of the heavy green glasses to the rim, he looked down at her, winked and teased, "Ask me what we're celebrating."

A jolt of excitement sizzled inside her. "What're we celebrating?"

"We did it, Rachel," he said, setting the bottle down and handing her one of the glasses. He picked up his own then clinked it against hers. "We won the contest. I'm the new CEO."

That single jolt of excitement burst into a fireworks display of pleasure that lit up her insides like the Fourth of July. "Shane, that's great."

It was. It really was. Even though it was now official and Rachel knew she'd be leaving, she was just so damn happy for him. He'd worked hard for this and really deserved it. That he was so pleased about it only went to show how much he'd changed in the last few years.

"I know," he said, taking her elbow and leading her out of the kitchen into the living room. He steered her onto the couch, said, "I'll be right back," and went back to the kitchen to retrieve the champagne.

He set the bottle down on the glass-topped coffee table, then sat down beside Rachel on the sofa. She watched him over the rim of her glass while she took a huge swallow. Bubbles filled her nose, her mouth and apparently, her mind.

Watching him, Rachel wanted to reach out and smooth back the lock of dark hair lying across his forehead. She curled her fingers around the stem of her glass to keep from doing just that. Instead she settled for looking at him. Shane had always been a good stare. The man was simply gorgeous.

Shining moss-green eyes, strong chin, wide smile and broad shoulders. He was the stuff that dreams were made of. Rachel should know. He filled her dreams almost nightly.

"You know," he was saying, "when my father broke the news to me a while ago, all I could think about was that you should have been there to hear it, too."

She took another gulp of champagne, hoping to ease the sudden dryness in her throat.

"You're the real reason I won, Rachel."

A happy little glow dazzled her insides, but she deliberately squashed it. "That's not true, Shane. You worked hard for this. You deserve it."

"Maybe," he said nodding, running the tip of his

index finger around the rim of his glass. "But even if it's true, I couldn't have done it without you."

"Oh, absolutely," she agreed smiling.

So much easier to keep this conversation light and teasing, as she always did. So much better for her equilibrium if she didn't start fantasizing about Shane throwing himself at her feet, proclaiming his love and begging her to marry him.

Oh for heaven's sake.

She took another big drink of champagne and didn't complain when Shane reached for the bottle and topped off her glass and then his own.

"We'll be moving into my father's office at the first of the year."

You will, she thought silently, wishing she could stay. Wishing she could be a part of his life. But it was just getting too painful.

"I'm guessing you'll want to redecorate," she said wryly.

"Oh, yeah." His grin was devastating. All the more so since he seemed to be oblivious to the power he wielded. "I can't stand the antique thing, but the glass and chrome look doesn't seem right for up there, either."

"I guess not," she said, as the music playing shifted from a drum pounding dance rhythm to something slow and sultry.

"This means a big raise," Shane said, leaning back into the sofa cushion. "For both of us."

"Uh-huh." A raise would have been nice.

"And a bonus," he said, "if you can locate our

mysterious columnist and convince her to keep writing for *The Buzz*."

"Shane—"

"I know," he interrupted, "we haven't been able to find her, but she's out there somewhere, Rachel."

"And doesn't want to be found." Oh, she really didn't want to be found.

"Yeah, but I've been thinking," he said, refilling their glasses again.

Rachel looked at the bubbles in her wineglass and told herself to stop drinking it so quickly. Already, her mind was a little fuzzy and her vision blurred just a little bit. Should have eaten that ice cream, she told herself.

She shook her head and told herself to pay attention as Shane kept talking.

"Tess said she's quitting her job. So I'm thinking, what if we just hire her to work for us?"

"She does," Rachel argued and wondered why her tongue suddenly felt a little thick. "She writes a column for *The Buzz*."

"Yeah, but if we made her a *staff* writer, she could call her own shots. Do advice, gossip, whatever." He jumped to his feet as if unable to sit still beneath the onslaught of too many ideas. "The readers love her, Rachel. She's funny and smart and that comes across in her column."

She almost said thank you. Catching herself just in time, Rachel frowned at her champagne and leaned forward to carefully set her glass on the coffee table. A buzz was good. Drunk was not.

"Why is this so important to you, Shane?"

He turned around to look at her. Taking a long gulp of his wine, he shook his head. "Not sure. All I know is she's good and I'm not going to let her slip away."

"I don't think you have much choice."

He smiled at her and something warm and liquid slid through her veins, leaving a trail of fire that seemed to be burning right through her skin.

Oh, boy.

"That's where you're wrong. You're my secret weapon, Rachel."

"Me?"

"You've got more contacts in the city than the mayor. You can find out who Tess is and where we can find her."

"Oh, I don't think so."

Setting his glass down on the table, Shane reached for her and pulled her to her feet. She swayed a little, but he steadied her fast.

"Rachel, you can't quit on me now."

Quit? How'd he know she was going to quit? She stared up at him and, just for a minute or two, lost herself in the green of his eyes. "Did you know," she whispered, "you have tiny gold flakes in your eyes?"

The smile faded from his face and his hands on her arms gentled, his thumbs rubbing against her silk blouse. "I do?"

"Yes," she said, leaning in even closer, tipping her head back to keep her gaze locked with his. "I never really noticed before, but…"

"Your eyes are green, too," he said, his voice

almost lost under the slow pulse of the music. "Soft green. Like summer grass."

Her pulse quickened, her heartbeat jangled wildly and a swirl of something hot and needy settled in the pit of her stomach. And Rachel was loving every minute of it.

His hands slid across her back and dropped to her waist. She felt the heat of his touch right through the fabric of her blouse and she wondered absently if his handprints were branded on her skin.

She hoped so.

"Rachel," he whispered, his hands moving on her back again in long, languorous strokes that fanned the fire simmering inside her into hungry flames. He took a breath, held it as his gaze moved over her face as if he'd never seen her before. As if she were the most beautiful thing on the planet. Then he released that pent-up breath and said, "I'd better—"

Go.

He was going to leave.

Already he was releasing her, taking a small step back, putting a small slice of safety between them. And suddenly Rachel knew she couldn't let this moment pass. Let him leave without at least showing him once just how she felt.

"—kiss you," she said, finishing his sentence the way she wanted it to be. She went up on her toes, slid her arms around his neck and tipped her head to one side. He watched her, not moving. She felt the tension in his hands. She was pretty sure time itself stood still for one amazing moment.

Then she laid her mouth over his and put everything she had into the kiss she'd been daydreaming about for a solid year.

Four

For a fraction of a second, Shane was too surprised to react.

He caught up quick.

Rachel's lips were warm and soft and the taste of champagne clung to them, giving him more of a rush than drinking the expensive wine itself had. He pulled her tighter, closer, wrapping his arms around her and squeezing as he devoured her mouth.

Random thoughts flashed through his mind like fireflies winking on and off on a hot summer night.

Rachel.

He was kissing Rachel.

And it felt good.

Right.

Her mouth opened under his tender assault and his tongue swept inside to taste her more deeply. To feel her heat, to claim…something.

Something he couldn't name but knew was within his reach. Something that he'd never thought to find.

Fin had long teased him about the right woman being there under his nose for four years, but he'd never really considered that she might be correct. His twin had hinted that Rachel Adler could, with a little effort on his part, be much more to him than a fabulous assistant.

But he hadn't listened. Hadn't really believed that Rachel and he would be able to…connect so completely. So amazingly.

Her hands slid up his back and he wished to heaven he'd taken his suit jacket off when he arrived. He wanted to feel her small, capable hands with their short, neat nails on his skin.

That thought jolted through him with the impact of a crashing meteor.

Then a ball of fire settled in the pit of his stomach and stretched out tentacles to every corner of his body. Heat radiated from him and fed the raw, raging hunger clawing at his insides.

He tore his mouth from hers and ran his lips down the length of her neck. "Sweet. So sweet."

"Shane." His name, on a sigh of sound that rushed through him with the force of a category 5 hurricane.

Her hands tangled at the back of his neck, fingers twining through his hair, nails scraping his skin.

Sensation boiled within and Shane had to fight for air.

He'd never known such an overwhelming desire. Such a demand from his body.

Such all consuming *need.*

He slipped his hands beneath the tail of her silk shirt and smoothed his palms over her back. Her skin was more tantalizing than the silk. Smoother, softer. He sucked in air like a dying man and licked the pulse point at the base of her throat.

She gasped and tipped her head to one side, silently inviting more of his attention. He gave it to her. As his hands stroked her back, he nibbled at her throat and covered that pounding pulse point until he could taste her need for him throbbing with every beat of her heart.

"Rachel," he murmured against her skin. "I'm not sure what's going on here, but I want you."

"Oh good," she said, sighing again and leaning into him more completely. "That's very good. I want you, too. Now, okay? Does now work for you?"

He smiled and lifted his head to look down into her passion-glazed eyes. His smile faded in a new burst of hunger. "Yeah, now works for me in a big way."

He looked around the room, as if expecting a bed to magically appear. If it didn't, he was thinking the couch would do. Plenty long enough. And if she didn't like the couch, then the floor. Or standing up against a wall.

Something.

Soon.

He had to have her.

Had to bury himself inside her and feel her heat taking him in. Had to watch her eyes blur and feel her breath catch. Had to see a climax shatter the cool green of her eyes.

"Bedroom," she said, lifting one hand to point. "Through there."

"Right." He didn't waste time. Couldn't. Sweeping her up into his arms, he crossed the room in a few long strides and kicked the partially ajar door wide-open.

A double bed with four heavy posts sat against one wall, its mattress covered by a floral quilt. The curtains were open and through the lacy sheers, a streetlight shone from outside, illuminating the softly falling snowflakes drifting past the glass.

They were three stories up. No one was going to be peeking in at them, so Shane left the curtains open to the pale wash of light. He wanted to see her. Wanted to watch her.

He carried her across the room and set her on her feet. She staggered slightly and Shane smiled. He knew how she felt.

Everything was just a little off center.

"You're not changing your mind, are you?" she asked.

"Not a chance," he whispered and reached for the top button of her blouse. In less than a few seconds he had them all undone and was pushing the silk down her arms to let it fall onto the floor.

"That's good," she said, swallowing hard and nodding. "Really good."

Shane nodded back at her. "How about you? We can still stop."

"Are you kidding?" she asked and stepped into the circle of his arms, wrapping her own arms around his neck and hanging on. She looked up into his eyes and said, "No one leaves this room until we're absolutely through with each other."

He gave her a quick grin. This was the Rachel he knew and admired. Sure of herself. Confident. "I learned a long time ago that it pays to listen to my assistant."

Then he kissed her again and quickly worked the hooks at the back of her bra. The fragile lace parted and she twisted in his arms, freeing herself while simultaneously pushing his jacket off his shoulders.

Shane felt the same urgency pounding inside him and worked with her. In a couple of minutes, they were both naked and tumbling onto the mattress. The quilt was cold against his skin and the fabric felt old and soft. The antique bed creaked and groaned under their combined weight, but neither of them noticed.

In the wash of light streaming through the windows, Shane looked his fill of her. Full breasts, narrow waist and rounded hips—she was built with curves in all the right places, as, in his opinion, all women should be. He ran his hands over those curves, tracing every line with his fingertips until she was writhing beneath him, her breath coming fast and furious.

As her need peaked, so did his. He felt every one of her thundering heartbeats as if it were his own. He touched her and she shivered. He stroked her and she sighed. She lifted one hand to drag her nails across his chest and he felt each gentle scrape as if it were a flaming arrow.

"Yes, yes," she whispered, "you feel so good, Shane." She turned into him, parting her legs for his questing fingers.

His heartbeat jumped, his breath caught. He slid one hand down, down across her rib cage, over her abdomen and past the juncture of her thighs. She jerked in his arms and tried to close her legs.

"Rachel?"

"I'm too on the edge. It's coming. And I don't want it to," she breathed shakily. "I want this to last. I don't want it over so fast."

"It's not over," he assured her, his voice tight, scratching past the knot of need lodged in his throat. "We have all night. Now let me take you."

She clutched at his shoulders as his fingers dipped lower to find her depths. She was hot, damp, ready for his touch. He watched her as he slid his hand lower, caressing her intimate folds.

She gasped and stiffened in his arms at that first molten contact. "Shane!"

Her climax hit her hard, shaking her from head to toe. She tipped her head back into the mattress, bit her bottom lip and, keeping a death grip on his shoulders, shuddered as her body erupted from within.

More aroused than he'd ever been in his life, Shane watched her as she rode the crest of pleasure, shaking, trembling in his grasp, her fingers clutching at him. Mouth dry, pulse hammering, he bent his head and took her mouth as she gasped for air. He wanted to feel that again. Feel her body exploding for him, *because* of him. He wanted to hear her gasp and scream his name.

Her body still shuddering, he took her up again, pushing her high and fast. Sliding first one then two fingers inside her as his thumb stroked the very core of her, he stroked her inside and out.

Rachel dragged in air, knowing it wasn't enough. She might never get enough air again. Her brain was melting, but that was probably because her body was on fire.

The first orgasm had hardly finished shimmering through her when Shane had her on the climb toward number two. And now that she knew how good it was, she couldn't wait for it to happen again. Her body hummed and sizzled. Her blood felt as if it were boiling. Her limbs were weak and energized all at once.

She twisted up closer to him, loving the feel of his skin against hers. The soft curls of dark hair on his chest felt like silk, and the muscles beneath his skin felt like steel. His body was hard and strong and, right at the moment, as necessary to her as the breathing that just wasn't working quite right.

Her mind numbed out, short-circuited from the

onslaught of sensations rocketing through it. She couldn't think, could barely see, and it didn't seem to matter. All that mattered was that he not stop touching her.

His hands moved on her and she opened her legs wider, loving the feel of him on her, *in* her.

He took her mouth again in another kiss and she knew that breathing was no longer an option. But who needed air when she had Shane? His tongue mated with hers in an erotic dance that sent shock waves of need and desire sliding through her system.

His breath brushed her cheek and she moved toward him, somehow trying to burrow into him. She hooked her left leg over his hip and groaned when his fingers dipped deeper inside her.

"I've gotta be in you," he whispered, tearing his mouth from hers to bury his face in the curve of her neck. His whiskers scratched her skin as he licked and tasted his way across her throat and down to her collarbone.

"Oh, yeah, inside me. That's good. That sounds good to me, too."

"Protection," he muttered thickly, dipping his head to bite her neck.

His teeth stroked her fevered skin even as that one word he'd said sailed through her brain and came to a dead stop.

"Protection. Yeah. Okay." And her without a single condom in the house. She couldn't let him leave. Couldn't *not* feel his body within hers. She had to have him. *Now.* Struggling to breathe and think and speak at the same time, Rachel finally found the words she needed. "I'm on the pill. I'm good if you're—"

"Clean as a whistle," he assured her.

"Me, too. Good for us."

"Oh, yeah, excellent for us," he whispered, moving over her, settling himself between her up-drawn thighs. "Best news I've ever heard."

She nodded. "Right there with you."

And then there was no more talking. This was too important for talk. Too important for thought.

Too damn important period.

His body pushed into hers and Rachel's breath caught. She arched up, meeting him, opening for him, welcoming him in deeper, harder. He was so big. So hard.

So wonderful.

He rocked his hips against hers, filling her, engulfing her with sensation. Then he took her hands and, capturing them in his, held them down at either side of her head. She tried to move and couldn't. Then she realized she didn't care about moving. She only wanted to feel.

He stared down into her eyes as he withdrew and advanced, his body lighting hers up like a fireworks show.

Every hard, solid inch of him filled her and when he pulled free of her body only to slide himself home again, Rachel groaned. This was all she'd ever dreamed of, wanted, and more.

As Shane's body drove hers toward completion, she realized that she never could have imagined this. Nothing in her experience—all right, her experience was pretty limited—could have prepared her for this. For the clamoring feelings, the mind-shattering explosions, the frantic, demanding need.

He looked down at her and she stared up into eyes that were green and gold and dark with passion. His generous mouth tight, his jaw locked, he stared into her eyes as if he couldn't have looked away if his life depended on it.

Music poured into the room from the stereo in the living room; the quilt beneath her felt cool and soft. And in the pale light, Rachel burned this image of Shane on her mind so that she would always have it with her.

He kept a tight grip on her hands, pinning her to the bed. Her hips rose and fell with him to the rhythm he set, and when electric sparks began in her bloodstream, she raced with him toward the release she knew was waiting just out of reach.

"Shane?" she called his name aloud. Had to say it. Had to hear it. Had to convince herself that this was real and not just another of her lonely dreams.

"Come for me," he said, his voice a rumble in the dimly lit room. "Come for me again. And then again."

With a shriek of bone-deep ecstasy, she did. Clinging to him as her body exploded into a fiery burst of sparks and color, she was only dimly aware when he called her name and followed her into the void.

A kaleidoscope of colors was still revolving behind her closed eyes when Rachel felt Shane roll off of her and to the edge of the bed. "What?"

She forced her eyes open and looked at him. Just one look was enough to make her body start humming again, ready for another go. Apparently, though, Shane was finished.

"You're *leaving?*"

He looked at her and gave her a grin that weakened her knees enough to make her grateful she was lying down.

"Just going to the living room. For the champagne."

"Ah. Good idea."

"Yeah," he said, leaning down to plant a quick kiss on her mouth. "Seems I'm just full of good ideas tonight."

She watched him leave the room and couldn't complain about the view. He even had a nice butt. But a second later, Rachel closed her eyes again and shifted lazily on the quilt her grandmother had made more than fifty years before. She winced at that thought and rolled off the bed. Quickly she pulled the quilt back and draped it over the foot of the bed, then lay down again on the clean, lavender-scented sheets.

Every inch of her body felt used up and happy.

But just as she acknowledged that fact, her brain started clicking along, demanding to know what she was going to do next. How could she sleep with her boss? How tacky was that? And how could she ever look at him at the office again without imagining that great butt?

Stop it. She didn't want to think.

Not tonight.

Heaven knew there'd be plenty of time for thinking and torturing herself later. For the moment, she only wanted to enjoy what she was feeling.

Icy cold trickled onto her breasts and her eyes flew open.

She looked up, directly into Shane's eyes and her heart thudded in her chest. "What're you…"

He drizzled a little more champagne onto her breasts, then set the bottle down onto the nightstand beside the bed. Climbing in beside her, he said only, "I was thirsty."

Then he bent his head to take first one of her nipples, then the other, into his mouth. His tongue twirled around and around the rigid, sensitive peaks and Rachel groaned as he suckled her. Her fingers curled into the sheet beneath her and she held on tight as her world rocked crazily from side to side.

He lapped at her, nibbled her flesh with the edges of his teeth and then suckled her again. She felt each drawing tug of his mouth straight to the heart of her.

Her body lit up again and when he lifted his head, she wanted to weep for the loss of his mouth. She drew in a deep gulp of air and blew it out again in a rush.

"Still thirsty," he quipped and grabbed the bottle. Carefully, he poured the frothy wine atop her breasts, down her rib cage and let it pool in her belly button.

Rachel shivered, but not because the champagne

was so cold. No, she was only surprised it didn't boil on contact with her skin. "Shane…"

"And a sip for you," he said, lifting her head from the bed and holding her as he tipped the mouth of the bottle to her lips. She took a long drink, easing the dryness in her mouth before she raised up and kissed him. She tasted him, the wine and passion.

And she wanted more.

"Are you ready?" he asked, easing her down and setting the bottle back on the table.

"Oh, I think so," she said, reaching for him.

He shook his head, caught her hands in his and said, "Then find something to hold onto."

He lowered his head to her breasts again and Rachel took his advice. Reaching back, she grabbed hold of the headboard and clung to it like a life rope tossed into a stormy sea. He sucked at her nipples, then moved down, licking the champagne off her skin as he went. Across her ribs, down over her abdomen and into the tiny pool of wine in her belly button.

She sucked in air, groaned out his name and held on even tighter. Her skin was on fire. Heat coiled inside and threatened to burst free. She felt every single nerve ending alive and hopping and oh, she hoped it never stopped.

He shifted position, moving to kneel between her legs, and Rachel smiled, eager for him to enter her again. Eager to feel the race to completion crowding in on her one more time.

But he had another surprise for her. Scooping his

hands beneath her bottom, he lifted her hips off the bed and smiled at her.

Her stomach did a quick somersault.

"Shane—"

"Hang on tight, Rachel," he whispered deeply. "This ride's about to get bumpy."

Five

His mouth covered her and Rachel groaned, his name sliding from her throat on a whisper of wonder. She watched him take her, couldn't look away. She concentrated on the feel of his hands on her behind, the lush sensation of his mouth, the hush of his breath.

Outside, the wind tossed snow against the frosted windowpanes. But inside, she was half surprised not to see steam rising from the bed.

Again and again, his lips and tongue worked her flesh, firing her blood, fuzzing her brain. She couldn't think. Couldn't remember *ever* thinking.

She was simply a mass of sensation. Her nerves stretched to the breaking point and hovered there as the tension in her body built and screamed through her, demanding release. Demanding satisfaction. Demanding his body inside hers.

Now.

"Shane," she managed to croak despite the tightness in her throat. "I want— I need you in me. Please."

He set her down and moved to cover her. "I need that, too," he whispered and wrapping his arms around her waist, he held onto her as he rolled onto his back.

And Rachel was straddling him, looking down into his eyes, feeling herself drowning in a sea of gold-flecked green.

She moved on him and Shane bit back a groan. In the lamplight pooling in through the windows, she looked like a goddess. Her honey-blond hair loose and waving about her shoulders, her breasts high and full, a knowing smile on her luscious mouth.

Something beyond lust, beyond desire quickened inside him. But it was forgotten in a new rush of need as she moved on him again. Swiveling her hips, she took him deep inside her body and sighed with satisfaction as she set a slow, steady rhythm between them.

He reached up, cupping her breasts and tweaking her nipples with his thumbs and forefingers. She sighed and that soft sound filled him with fire. He dropped his hands to her hips and guided her on him, helping her move.

Pushing himself higher and deeper inside her, he felt the first shuddering ripples of her climax wash through her. He saw her eyes glaze over, watched as her head fell back, and when she called his name,

Shane's body erupted and he jumped into oblivion, holding her close as he fell.

Rachel woke up a couple of hours later. She opened her eyes and found herself staring at the floor. Clinging to the edge of the mattress, she was cold and realized that not only had Shane hogged the bed, he'd also stolen all the blankets.

A sign?

Sliding off the bed, she hurried to the closet, threw it open and grabbed her robe. With the thick, dark green terry cloth wrapped around her, she tied the belt at her waist and looked at Shane, sprawled across her mattress. Torn between the glow of having been well loved and already worrying about how in the hell she would ever be able to look him in the eye again, Rachel chewed at her bottom lip. Her mind raced with possibilities and consequences.

None of them pleasant.

She wasn't an idiot.

She knew darn well that the hours they'd spent together in her bed wouldn't mean to Shane what it had to her.

Sure, they'd made something magical between the two of them, but he wasn't in love with her. She knew that.

What she didn't know was why he'd—

Stop.

Rachel shut her brain off, refusing to continue wandering down the twisted paths her mind kept showing her. It was too late to turn back the clock and prevent this night from happening, even if she wanted to. Which, to be honest, she didn't.

Turning her back on Shane, she slipped from the bedroom and walked quietly through the darkness. She paused in the living room long enough to turn off the stereo, then continued on to the kitchen, moving through a silence so loud it was deafening.

There, she moved around the familiar space, not needing a light. She filled the coffeepot with water, set it back on the hot plate and filled the basket with a few scoops of dark, rich Colombian coffee grounds. She hit the button and stood in the shadows as the coffeemaker hissed and gurgled, scenting the air with an aroma that was both comforting and familiar.

She stared out the window and nearly hypnotized herself watching snow drifting past the glass. Her body still hummed with satisfaction and yet…she couldn't settle. Couldn't enjoy even the memories of what she and Shane had shared. Because she knew that with the morning light, everything between them would be changed.

Forever.

What she *didn't* know was what to do about it.

Rubbing her hands up and down her arms against a chill she felt right down to her bones, she walked back to the bedroom, opened the door quietly and stood on the threshold. He was still sleeping, so Rachel indulged herself and watched him unnoticed as he slept.

Something inside her turned over and she realized that sleeping with him had only intensified her feelings. And she wondered what in the heck she was supposed to do now.

How could she look at him again, knowing what it was like to be in his arms, and pretend she didn't want it to happen again?

How could she face him at work and *not* remember his kiss, his body wrapped around hers?

"You're watching me."

His voice rumbled from the shadows and she jumped. "Didn't know you were awake."

He rose up and braced himself on his elbows. The quilt covering him slid down his broad, naked chest and puddled at his hips. She couldn't see his eyes in the dark, but she felt his gaze as surely as if he'd reached out to touch her.

Oh, she was in such deep trouble.

"I smelled the coffee."

Of course he did. He hadn't been reacting to some secret sense telling him she was nearby. They weren't *connected* on some higher emotional plane, for Pete's sake.

She swallowed regret and grimaced at the bitter taste. "It's ready if you want some."

"Sounds good."

Well, isn't this nice and stiff, she thought. Any more polite and there'd be icicles hanging in the air between them. But she didn't say that. What would be the point? She only nodded and left, knowing he'd get up and follow her.

It took him a few minutes and when he walked into the now brightly lit kitchen, he was dressed, his suit coat slung across one shoulder hooked on his index finger. He laid the jacket down over the back of a chair, then took the coffee mug she offered him.

"Thanks."

"You're welcome." How very dignified they were, when only a couple of hours ago, they'd been all over each other.

"It's good," he said after taking a sip.

Rachel tugged at the collar of her robe, feeling at a real disadvantage with him in his suit and her…well, naked under a layer of terry cloth. To occupy herself, she reached for her own coffee cup and folded both hands around it. Taking a long sip, she let the heat shoot through her before she spoke again.

Then, keeping her voice light despite the ball of lead settled in the pit of her stomach, she said, "So when does everyone else get to hear the news about your big win at EPH?"

He studied the surface of his coffee. "My father's going to officially announce it at the New Year's party."

"But word will get out to the family long before then."

"Probably," he agreed, a half smile on his face.

"You're looking forward to your brothers and sister finding out."

"Of course. And you should, too."

She leaned back against the edge of the counter. "Why's that?"

"Because we're a team, Rachel," he blurted, then let his voice trail off and his gaze drift back to his coffee.

Awkwardness rose up and sat between them like an ugly troll waiting to be recognized.

So Rachel did.

"We're not a team, Shane. I work for you."

His gaze snapped to hers. "Yeah, but—"

She set her coffee down on the countertop and stuffed both hands into the pockets of her robe. Her bare toes curled on the cold floor. "What happened between us tonight—"

"Was a mistake, I know," he said and Rachel's jaw dropped.

"Well, that was honest."

He set his coffee down on the small table, pushed his hands into his slacks pockets and started pacing. A few steps to the counter, then a few steps back again.

"It was my fault," he said, his voice gruff, laced with an emotion she couldn't identify. "And it shouldn't have happened. Damn it, Rachel, you *work* for me—"

"That's right," she said firmly, fighting back the quaver wanting to sound in her voice. "I *work* for you—but I make my own decisions. And last night was as much about *my* choices as yours."

He blew out a breath. "Fine. We both decided. But I should have been the one to back off."

A choked laugh shot from her throat. "Oh, yes. The big strong man should have found a way to save the little woman from herself. Is that it?"

His features tightened up and the muscle in his jaw twitched. "Damn it, that's not what I meant."

"I'm not so sure." Heck, she wasn't sure of anything at the moment. All she knew for a fact was she wanted him out of her house before she did something really stupid like cry.

Oh, wouldn't that be the cherry on top? Sleep with your boss then cry about it in front of him. Hey, atta girl Rachel, she told herself. Keep doing dumb stuff.

God, this conversation was even harder than she'd thought it would be when she was simply dreading it.

He glanced at his wristwatch, then to her. "Maybe we shouldn't try to talk about this now."

She nodded stiffly. "Maybe not."

"I should probably go."

"Good idea." Go already, she screamed inwardly. Hurry it up before the tears start.

God, she felt like an idiot.

But she'd brought this on herself. She was the one who kissed *him.* Heck, after that, of course he had to have sex with her. Turning her down would have been embarrassing. How much kinder to just sleep with the poor little lonely assistant.

A pity romp.

Great.

What every girl dreams of.

He picked up his jacket and shrugged into it. Straightening the collar and lapels, he looked at her and oh God, she saw concern in his eyes.

Concern. So close to sympathy.

To pity.

"I'll see you at work later?"

She lifted her chin, and forced herself to speak

past the knot in her throat. "Sure. I may be a little late because—"

"Doesn't matter," he interrupted. "Take your time. In fact, take the morning off. Come in this afternoon."

He was in no hurry to face her at work, was he? "Fine. I'll see you later."

He nodded and looked for a second as if he wanted to say something more. Thankfully he thought better of it and walked away. When he left the apartment, he closed the door quietly behind him. And Rachel was alone.

Again.

Shane tried to keep his mind on the job, but it wasn't easy. For one thing, every time he passed Rachel's empty desk, he remembered why she wasn't there.

Of course, if she *had* been there, it would have been even harder to walk past her desk. What an idiot he was. What had he been thinking?

He hadn't been thinking at all. Just reacting. To some really incredible feelings. To the press of Rachel's mouth to his. To the rush of holding her in his arms. He muttered an oath, pushed one hand through his hair and told himself to stop remembering. To stop reliving those hours with her.

He might as well take a vow to not breathe.

Restless, Shane pushed away from his desk and turned to stare out the windows. Snow was still falling, with more predicted. On the street far below him, people were rushing down sidewalks, oblivious to the cold. Twinkling lights lined the storefronts and he imagined the street corner Santas were doing a booming business.

It was the end of a long year. His family was closer than they'd ever been and he'd earned the CEO position at the company. By rights, he should be celebrating right now. Instead he felt as though he'd lost something important.

"Crisis! Crisis!"

Shane spun around to face Jonathon Taylor as he gave a perfunctory knock and hustled into the office. "What's wrong?"

"Oh, only the end of my Fourth of July spectacular, that's all." Jonathon lifted both hands dramatically into the air before letting them fall to his sides again.

Good. Business. A chance to concentrate on something besides Rachel. Folding his arms across his chest, Shane watched as the other man paced frenetically around the office. "What happened?"

"My queen," Jonathon moaned theatrically, "my star of the issue—Leticia Baldwin—"

"Ah…" Shane walked back to his desk and sat down. Letty Baldwin, the latest of America's sweethearts. A young actress with talent as well as beauty. "She won't do the article?"

"Oh, she'll do it," Jonathon pouted as he dropped into the chair opposite Shane's desk. "But she's going to be seven months pregnant when it's time to do the photo shoot. Can't exactly use the red, white and blue bikini theme I had in mind. This is just a disaster, Shane. She was my centerpiece. My star. My—"

"—queen, yeah I get it."

He slumped lower in his chair, his spine becoming an overcooked noodle. "I'm shattered."

Shane laughed.

Jonathon glowered at him. "I'm so happy to amuse you."

"Sorry," Shane said, lifting both hands to appease his friend. "It's just that I really needed this little crisis of yours, that's all."

"At least one of us is happy."

"Jon," Shane said, leaning back in his chair, "does Letty Baldwin still want to do the issue?"

"Oh, definitely. Her agent's convinced her that it would be good exposure. And it would, of course."

"Then do it now."

"What?"

"The photo shoot," Shane said slowly, patiently. "Set it up with Ferria and Letty's people. Do the shoot now and just sit on the pictures until the issue's ready to go to press."

Jonathon's features smoothed out as he thought about it. "We could, couldn't we?"

"As long as she agrees, I don't see why not."

"Sandy will throw a fit," Jonathon mused, and seemed to enjoy the idea. "She's already shrieking over the expenses for this quarter."

"I'll handle Sandy," Shane assured him, making a mental note to call his managing editor and smooth over any ruffled feathers.

"Brilliant," Jonathon shouted and bounded from his chair, rubbing his palms together. "This, my king, is why you're in charge."

As Jonathon left, Shane could only wish that all of his problems were so easily solved.

Six

Rachel carried a cup of coffee into Shane's office and braced herself before meeting his gaze. She needn't have worried. After stalling around for three hours, she'd finally come into work, only to be so busy she hadn't had to face Shane all afternoon.

Until now.

Every day at four-thirty, he had a cup of coffee while going over the day's reports, bringing himself up to speed on the different divisions and setting up appointments for the following day. It was a routine. One she'd long since become familiar with.

In fact, over the last few years, she'd come to enjoy this last half hour of the workday. It gave her a chance to relax with a man she both loved *and* liked. Of course, today there'd be no relaxing.

She felt as though every nerve in her body was strung tight and plugged into an electrical outlet.

He looked up as she entered and gave her a distracted smile. "Come on in, Rachel."

She carried the cup of coffee to him and set it down on his desk. Tension arced between them with all the dazzling light and power of a lightning strike. She could almost hear the sizzle in the air.

"How are you?"

"I'm fine, Shane," she said, lying through her teeth. But damned if she'd slink around the office. "And you?"

He reached for the coffee cup, but instead of picking it up, he trailed the tips of his long fingers over the curved handle. Rachel's gaze locked on the movement, and in an instant, her body lit up as she remembered the feel of those fingers on her skin.

Okay, this was going to be a touch more difficult than she'd thought.

"Worried," he said finally and she shifted her gaze to his.

"About…?"

He scowled at her. "About *us,* Rachel. About our working relationship."

She felt a warm flush of embarrassment move through her and she could only hope it wasn't blazing on her face. This was so not fair. She'd dreamed about Shane for over a year, had imagined what a night with him would be like. And now those dreams had become nightmares.

All she had left was her pride and she was going to cling to it with everything she had. "Our working relationship doesn't have to change at all, Shane," she said and hoped to heaven she sounded more sure than she felt.

"Is that right?" He stood up, pushed the edges of his suit jacket back and shoved both hands into his slacks pockets. "So, everything is normal."

"That's right."

"Then why haven't you ragged on me once about work?"

"Excuse me?"

"Normally you'd have come in here carrying that memo pad that's practically stapled to your hand," he pointed out. "And you'd be reading me the list of meetings to go to, warning me about which ones I couldn't duck. Any other day, you'd be standing there telling me who to call, when to do it and what to say."

Rachel sniffed, a little irritated that he knew her so well. But then, they were a team, weren't they? A well-oiled machine. It wasn't *his* fault that she'd fallen in love with him and changed everything. "I'm so very sorry. I had no idea I was that bossy."

He pulled one hand free of his pockets and waved at her. "Bull. Of course you did." He came around the edge of his desk and started toward her. But he stopped a few steps short, as if he couldn't quite trust himself to get too close.

Oh, you're dreaming girl, she told herself. It

was probably more like he was afraid his too aggressive assistant would jump his bones again if he wandered too near.

God help her, he was probably right.

"But that's why we've always worked together so well," he was saying and Rachel shut down her brain and opened her ears. "You keep me focused on the job and I give you somebody to nag."

"Very nice," she muttered.

"And now it's ruined," he snapped.

"Maybe that's for the best."

"Like hell it is," Shane said grimly. "How the hell can I get anything done when I can damn well *feel* the tension between us?"

Okay, she'd made up her mind earlier to be aloof. Distant. To do what she could to pretend that last night had never happened. But now that Shane had pried the lid off this particular can of worms, why should she try to jam the lid back on?

"You're not the only one, you know. Forgive me," she said, "for being just a little on edge. It's not every day I have to face my boss after he's seen me naked."

Shane winced. "I could say the same."

"Yeah," she agreed, "but from my perspective, this is just a little bit harder."

"How's that?"

She laughed shortly and felt the sound scrape against her throat. "This is a cliché for God's sake. Employers have been diddling with their secretaries/assistants for generations!"

"Diddling?"

"Don't you dare smile at me," she shot back. "Diddling is a perfectly good word."

"You're right," he said and took one cautious step closer. "But don't you lump me in with some sleazy guy who makes a habit of sleeping with his secretary."

"Assistant."

"Fine. Assistant." He shoved one hand through his hair and Rachel remembered how soft his thick, dark brown hair was. How it felt streaming through her fingers. She swallowed hard.

"My point," he continued, his voice hardly more than a growl, "is that what happened between us shouldn't have happened at all."

"Yes," she said tightly, "I believe you covered that this morning with the whole 'mistake' thing."

"Well, wasn't it?"

Her hands at her sides, she curled her fingers into her palms and squeezed until she felt the indentation of every nail digging into her skin. *Mistake?* No doubt. Did she regret it? She certainly should. But she couldn't honestly say she did.

She'd wanted him for so long how could she possibly regret having him? Even if it meant having to deal with the messy repercussions.

Watching his face, trying to read the maelstrom of emotion in his eyes, Rachel said, "Of course it was."

Was that disappointment flashing across his eyes? If it was, it was gone almost immediately.

He nodded, blew out a breath and said quietly, "At least we agree on that."

"Yay us."

A half smile quirked the corner of his mouth then disappeared again. "The question is, can we work past it? Can we just forget about what happened and go back to the way things were?"

"I don't know," she said honestly after a long, thoughtful pause. "I'd like to think so."

A small thread of panic jolted through Shane as he watched her. He'd called their time together a mistake. But he didn't regret it. How could he? He'd never experienced anything like what he'd found with Rachel.

He'd been thinking of nothing *but* her for hours. And now that she was standing there in front of him it took every ounce of self-control he possessed to keep from grabbing her and kissing her until neither of them was able to think.

But that wouldn't solve a damn thing. It would in fact, only make a weird situation even more uncomfortable.

"Rachel, I don't want to lose what we have. Our friendship."

"I think that ship has sailed, Shane." Her mouth curved sadly.

"I don't accept that."

Her green eyes filled with tears and he held his breath, hoping to hell they wouldn't fall. He was a dead man if she started crying. Nothing in this world could bring a man to his knees faster than a strong woman's tears.

As if she heard his panicked thoughts, she blinked quickly, furiously, and kept her tears at bay.

"You have to, Shane," she said, with a slow shake of her head. "If we hope to salvage this working relationship, we both have to accept the facts. We're not friends. We're not lovers. To be honest, I'm not sure what we are anymore."

After work, Shane was too irritable to go home alone and not in a good enough mood to call a friend. That last conversation with Rachel kept rewinding and playing in his mind and he couldn't quite seem to settle with it. Things were different between them now and he didn't have a clue what to do about it.

It had been a long time since he'd let his groin do his thinking for him.

Now he remembered *why.*

If he hadn't given in to his own desires the night before, everything in his world would be running great. He'd won the competition in the family, *The Buzz* was gaining strength every damn day and he'd finally realized that he was doing *exactly* what he should be doing.

He stepped out of the EPH building into a face full of wind-driven snow. Shrugging deeper into his overcoat, he squinted into the wind and glanced around. The sidewalks were crowded, as usual. Manhattan streets were never quiet. Cabs carried customers, buses belched along the street and a police squad car, lights flashing, siren whining, fought to get through the congestion.

He loved it.

Loved the noise, the hustle, the rush of life that pulsed in the city like a heartbeat. Stepping out onto the sidewalk, he fell into step with the crush of people instantly surrounding him. You had to keep up when walking these sidewalks. Move too slowly and the crowd would knock you down and kick your body to the curb, all without losing step.

Smiling to himself, he realized he was in the perfect frame of mind for walking in Manhattan.

He wasn't sure where he was going, he just knew he didn't want to go home. God knew there were plenty of women he could call for company, but that thought left him a lot colder than the melting snow sliding beneath his coat collar.

Hands in his pockets, he let his gaze drift while his mind raced. Strings of twinkling lights lined the front windows of the shops he passed, and the combined scents of hot chocolate, steaming coffee and hot dogs poured from a street vendor's cart. He came to the end of the block and while he stood waiting for the light to change, he glanced in the front window of Hannigan's.

A bar that was too upscale to be called a tavern, but too down to earth to be classified a club, Hannigan's offered cold beers and friendly conversation. Sounded a hell of a lot better than going home alone.

Shane marched to the door, pulled it open and was slapped with a blast of warmth, coated with laughter and the jangling beat of Irish folk music.

He shrugged out of his coat, hung it on the rack by the door, then made his way through the tangled maze of tables and chairs.

The hardwood floors were gleaming, a fire danced in the stone hearth on the far wall and behind the polished mahogany bar, a gigantic mirror reflected the faces of the patrons.

Shane pushed through the crowd, made his way to the bar and leaned both elbows on the shining top. When the bartender worked his way down to him, he said quickly, "Guinness."

In a few minutes, the practiced barman was sliding over a perfectly built drink, with a thick layer of cream colored foam atop dark, rich beer. Shane picked up the glass, took a sip and turned to look at the crowded room. His gaze slid across a few familiar faces; after all, everyone who worked in the neighborhood ended up in here at one time or another.

At a booth in the back sat a man more familiar than the rest. Shane headed that way, deftly avoiding a waitress with a laden tray. He tapped on the tabletop, waited for his nephew to look up at him in welcome, then slid into the booth opposite him.

Gannon Elliott was a big man, with black hair, sharp green eyes, and in the last year or so, a ready smile. At thirty-three, Gannon was only five years younger than Shane. The two had grown up more like brothers, though Gannon was his nephew, the son of Michael, Shane's oldest brother.

"Didn't expect to see you in here, Gannon."

The other man shrugged. "Erika wanted to do some Christmas shopping," he said, sliding his half full glass of beer back and forth on the tabletop. "Hannigan's sounded like a better idea to me."

"Christmas shopping." Shane slumped back against the red leather booth. "Haven't started that yet."

"My suggestion?" Gannon quipped, lifting his glass for a long drink. "Get married. Turns out women *like* shopping."

Shane smiled, both at the ridiculous notion of getting married and at the change in his nephew. Only a year ago, Gannon would still have been at work, staying late into the night. More like his grandfather Patrick than any of Patrick's kids were, Gannon had lived and breathed the family business.

Until Erika.

"What about you? Why are you sitting here having a drink with me?" Gannon took another swallow of his beer. "Why aren't you out with that Hollywood girl…what's her name, Amber or Brownie or something?"

Shane frowned, thinking about the woman he was supposed to have had dinner with the night before. He *still* couldn't think of her damn name. But if he'd only met her as planned, none of that mess with Rachel would have happened and he wouldn't now be sitting in the middle of a mess.

"What is that woman's name?" he muttered. "Never mind. Anyway, I wasn't in the mood."

Gannon laughed. "*You?* Not in the mood for a gorgeous woman? You feeling all right?"

"Funny." He took a sip of Guinness and savored the taste.

"Didn't mean it to be funny," Gannon said, studying him now through shrewd green eyes. "Something going on? You should be happy as hell. Heard you won the CEO position."

Shane's gaze snapped to him. "Who told?"

Someone at the bar laughed loudly and the music changed, drifting from a ballad in Gaelic to a jittering rhythm that even had Shane's toes tapping in time.

"Hell," Gannon laughed, "who *doesn't* know? Everyone in the company pretty much had it figured out a few months back. When those third-quarter profit statements came in, it was clear no one was going to be able to catch you."

Pride rippled through Shane, but it didn't do a damn thing to ease the knot of something else tightening in his chest. "Thanks. It was a team effort, though. We *all* made it happen. Everyone at *The Buzz* worked their asses off."

"Which begs the question again," his nephew said. "You should be happier than hell right now. Why aren't you?"

"Long story."

"Do I look busy?"

Shane chuckled. "No, you don't." He nodded, paused for another sip of beer, then said, "Okay, but before we get into the sad, sad story of my life… How's your mom doing?"

Gannon's mother, Shane's sister-in-law Karen,

had been battling breast cancer for the last year. And after a double mastectomy and a debilitating round of chemotherapy, the family was hopeful that she'd beaten the cancer.

Gannon blew out a breath and smiled. "She's doing good. Great, in fact." He signaled the waitress by holding up his empty beer glass, then shifted his gaze back to Shane. "Dad's at her side round the clock. It's pretty amazing to see, really. They've…rediscovered each other, I guess you'd say. And even with the cancer threat hanging over us all, they're so damn happy, it's ridiculous."

"I'm glad."

"Yeah," Gannon said wistfully, "me, too." When the waitress brought him a refill and took away his empty glass, Gannon turned his gaze on Shane. "So, now that we've covered Mom, what's going on with you?"

Shane really didn't want to get into it with his nephew. But who the hell else would understand? Gannon and his wife, Erika, had started out working together—and had an affair. It had all blown up in their faces of course, but they'd finally found their way back to each other and now seemed happy as clams.

Whatever the hell *that* meant.

"Before I get into that," he said, easing into an uncomfortable conversation, "when you and Erika first started your…"

"Affair?"

"Okay." Shane nodded. "Was it hard to work together? Was it…clumsy? Awkward?"

Gannon scraped one hand across his face. "It

wasn't simple," he finally said. "But we both knew what we were doing. We both *chose* to have the affair. Even though it ended badly."

"So you didn't have trouble working together once you'd had sex?"

"If you mean could I keep from imagining her naked, then no. But we managed. For a while." He frowned to himself.

Shane knew what he was thinking about. Gannon was one of the most private men Shane had ever known. The idea of people gossiping about him was anathema to him. The minute talk had started up in the company about his affair with Erika, he'd called it off. Erika had quit soon after and it hadn't been easy for Gannon to talk her into coming back once the Elliott family competition had started last January.

It hadn't been easy, but Gannon had finally realized just what Erika meant to him. And now they were married, and already a week overdue to become parents for the first time. "How's Erika holding up?"

"*She's* doing great," Gannon admitted. "I'm the one who jumps every time she makes a sound. But the doctor said if she hasn't delivered by next Monday, he'll induce. Thank God."

"That's good. Good." Shane nodded, then said under his breath, "I think I've done something really stupid."

"Rachel?"

"Is that a good guess or is there already talk?"

"No talk." Gannon took a drink. "It's just that Fin used to tell me all the time about how perfect Rachel was for you only you were too dumb to see it."

"Ah," Shane mused, "good to be loved by your family."

"Hey, we love you even when you're stupid."

"Small consolation."

"So," Gannon continued, "I'm guessing that things are not really rolling right along now that the situation with Rachel's…changed."

"You could say that." He shook his head and stared up at the pierced tin ceiling. "Hell, Gannon, I don't even know what to say to her anymore. I keep thinking about last night and—" He shut up fast, but it was pointless, since his nephew already understood exactly what Shane was feeling. Been there, done that.

"Don't use me for a template, Shane," Gannon said tightly. "I almost lost Erika, so I'm sure as hell not the one to give you advice."

Shane took a long, deep drink of his beer, then set the glass down again carefully. "Yeah, but you *loved* Erika. Even when you were being an idiot, you loved her."

"You don't love Rachel?"

Love?

He'd never really thought about love. Always been too busy just having a good time. But in his bones, he knew damn well that Rachel was different. She wasn't just another woman in a long string of unremarkable relationships.

But love?

Shane sighed and signaled the waitress. "Damned if I know."

Seven

Ben & Jerry's was a sad substitute for sex with Shane.

But, since it was all Rachel had, she indulged. Curled up on the couch, with the TV muted and showing some old black-and-white movie, she dug her spoon into the chocolate chunk ice cream. One bite after another slid down her throat despite the huge knot lodged there.

"Idiot," she muttered, pausing to lick her spoon. If she had any spine at all, she'd be out tonight, doing some Christmas shopping. Getting on with her life. Forgetting about Shane.

Apparently, though, her spine was pretty much a wet noodle.

She glanced around the room, sighing. But for the

three Hollyberry scented candles burning in a twisted metal candelabrum on top of the entertainment center, there were absolutely no decorations up. This just wasn't like her.

Ordinarily Rachel was a real Christmas nut. Nothing she liked better than dragging out all of the boxes filled with her Christmas goodies. Stuffed animals, three crèches, hand knit stockings she'd made during her knitting phase, silk garland and the wreath she'd made the Christmas before.

But no. She couldn't get her mind off her troubles long enough to care about the most magical season of the year.

"Just pitiful," she murmured and dipped her spoon back into the carton for another chunk of chocolate.

When the phone rang, she ignored caller ID and all but lunged for it, desperate to hear a voice other than her own. That feeling lasted less than ten seconds.

"Honey," her mother cooed in a voice pitched to carry over fifty thousand screaming fans in Yankee Stadium. "I'm so glad you're home!"

"Hi, Mom." Rachel swallowed fast and instantly took another bite of chocolate. She loved her mother, she really did. But every year about this time, Celeste Adler started in on the "you're not getting any younger" speech. Her mother was bound and determined to get her older daughter married and "settled." Rachel's younger sister, Rita, had been married two years and the "perfect" daughter was already pregnant. With twins.

So basically, even if Rachel got pregnant right this minute, Rita would still outdo her.

Pregnant.

For just an instant, she allowed herself a brief, tantalizing dream. One night with Shane and a baby to remember it by. Wouldn't that have been something? She sighed and took another bite of ice cream. No way. Her birth control pills were way too effective. Other women might have an accident, but Rachel wouldn't. Even her body was a rule follower.

"Rita had an ultrasound this morning and she let me come in with her and ohmygoodness—" that last was crammed into one breathless word "—it was the most exciting thing ever. You know, Rita's husband Jack is just the most wonderful man."

Rachel rolled her eyes. Jack would never be simply *Jack.* His full name from now unto eternity would be *Rita's Husband Jack.* Poor man. But then, she told herself as she crunched quietly on an extra big chunk of chocolate, no one had held a gun to his head. He'd dated Rita for two years. He knew exactly the kind of whacko family he was marrying into.

Not whacko in a bad way of course. She loved them all. But did she really need to hear a speech every year about how she was all alone? Thanks, no.

"He gave me a big hug and called me Grandma right there in the doctor's office, isn't that the sweetest thing?"

Suck-up, she thought, but said only, "Yep. Jack's a keeper."

"Oh my yes, and I just cried and cried. I'm so emotional about my girls, you know."

Rachel's spoon scraped the bottom of the carton and she frowned. Darn it. Only a couple bites left. She should have been more prepared. She knew darn well that her mother called every Wednesday night without fail. She should have stocked extra ice cream.

"I know, Mom."

"And Rita's thinking of naming one of the babies after me, if one is a girl, that is."

Great. Just what the world needed. Another Celeste.

"That's nice." Rachel tucked the phone between her neck and her shoulder and shifted a look at the television screen. *It's a Wonderful Life* was playing. Of course it was. It had become almost more of a tradition than Midnight Mass.

While her mother talked, Rachel concentrated on George Bailey's trials and tribulations. As he stood at the top of the bridge looking into the icy river, Rachel completely understood why he was considering the leap.

"So, honey, anything new to tell me?"

Rachel froze, silently thanking God that her mother was safely tucked up in her house in Connecticut. If Celeste was looking right at her, she could use her motherly psychic powers and know exactly what her daughter had been up to.

That was one humiliation she didn't have to suffer through, anyway.

"Nope," she said after way too long a pause, "same ol', same ol'..."

"Uh-huh, that's nice, dear. Did I tell you that Margie Fontenot's grandson Will is coming to town for Christmas this year?"

Oh God. She knew what was coming. Another fix-up. Frantically Rachel scraped at the ice cream carton, hoping for more chocolate—which she now so desperately needed. "Really?"

"Oh, yes," her mother continued excitedly, "he's a *doctor,* you know."

Oh man, Celeste's Holy Grail.

Hook a doctor for poor Rachel.

"That's nice," she said ambiguously, scrambling off the couch, clutching the empty ice-cream carton and spoon. Hustling into the kitchen, she tossed the carton into the trash, the spoon into the sink, then turned to the pantry. While her mother oohed and aahed over Margie's fabulous grandson, Rachel scrounged for cookies. Preferably *chocolate* cookies.

She settled for a stale Pop-Tart.

Taking a bite, she leaned against the counter and closed her eyes. Only have to hang on a few more minutes, she assured herself. Celeste's calls never went longer than ten minutes. Long distance charges, *donchaknow.*

"Anyway, honey," her mother said, then muttered, "oh Frank, go watch TV. Rachel knows I'm only trying to help." When she came back again, she said, "Your daddy says hello, honey."

Rachel smiled in spite of everything. God bless her father. Always trying to reel his wife in when her latest matchmaking attempt kicked in. "Hi back."

"She says hello. Yes," Celeste added, emphasizing the word with impatience, "I'll tell her to check her door locks."

Rachel grinned and chewed a rock-hard, cold toaster pastry. Her mom was only interested in romance or the promise of one. Her father, on the other hand, installed a new lock on Rachel's door every time they came to the city. Pretty soon she was going to have to buy an extra door to accommodate them all.

"Check your locks."

"Already done."

"Thank heaven." Celeste lowered her booming voice and Rachel knew it was because she was trying to avoid having her husband overhear. "Anyway, honey, we're giving a little party the weekend before Christmas this year. Nothing special. Just a few friends."

"Like Margie?" Rachel guessed, barely containing the helpless snarl as she tore off another chunk of dry Pop-Tart.

"Of course, honey, you know how fond I am of Margie," her mother went on, picking up speed as she finally reached her destination. "And of course, since Will is here in town visiting, he'll be attending, too. Won't that be nice? I just *know* you two will have so much in common."

Rachel sighed. "Where's he live?"

"Phoenix, I believe."

Well sure, Rachel thought. She lived in Manhattan and worked at a magazine. Will was a doctor living in Phoenix. So much in common it was uncanny. Almost eerie. Must be Kismet.

God, the pity just kept on coming. It was her own fault, though. If she hadn't spent so much time thinking about Shane, maybe she could have met someone else by now. Someone she actually might have a future with. She took another bite.

"Mom…"

"Now, don't you get your back up, young lady," her mother said, clearly hoping to disarm Rachel before she could get a head of steam going. "It's Christmas. It's a time for having friends and family together and we're *going* to be together. Understood?"

Rachel's chin hit her chest.

If she were George Bailey at this moment, she'd be jumping off that bridge. And if stupid Clarence saved her sorry butt, she'd just have to kill him.

But as much as she might like to refuse her mother's invitation, they both knew she wouldn't. She'd never missed Christmas with her family and she wasn't going to start now. "Understood, Mom. I'll be there."

"That's my girl," Celeste cooed again, gracious in victory. "So, would you like me to e-mail you a picture of the twins in utero?"

"Sure," she said. "Why not?"

After all, once those twins were born, they were going to take a lot of heat off of Rachel.

"I'll do that right away, honey. But first I have to call your sister and make sure she's all right."

"But you just saw her this morning." Rachel

frowned at the magnetized grocery list stuck to the refrigerator. Picking up a pen, she scrawled CHOCOLATE in capital letters and underlined it half a dozen times just for emphasis.

"Pregnant women need taking care of," her mother assured her.

"Okey dokey, then," Rachel said with a sigh. "Say hi to Rita for me."

"I will. Now good night, honey, and your dad just said for you to check your locks again. We love you!"

With those final words ringing in her ear, Rachel heard her mother hang up and then listened aimlessly to the dial tone humming frenetically. She loved her mother, but after one of these phone calls, Rachel always felt a little disappointed in her own life.

Or rather, her *lack* of a life.

Christmas time and the only romance in her future was a setup fixed by her *mother.*

Stabbing the power button, she turned the phone off and carried it and what was left of her stale treat into the living room. Once there, she curled up on the couch again and turned up the volume on the movie.

And if a few tears escaped and rolled silently down her cheeks, who but she would know about it?

Shane stood outside Rachel's apartment door and asked himself again what the hell he was doing there. He should have just gone home after leaving

Gannon in the bar. But instead, he'd found himself heading for Rachel's.

Which said exactly what?

That he was still uncomfortable with the way they'd left things at the office? That he still felt like a sleazy boss for having sex with his assistant? That he simply wanted to see her again?

Yes, to all of the above.

It wasn't a good idea, though, and he knew it.

And even as that thought shot through his brain, he lifted his hand and knocked on her door.

"Shane?" Her voice was muffled. "What're you doing here?"

He glanced up and down the hallway, then directly into the peephole he knew she was watching him through. "I wanted to talk to you, Rachel."

"About what?"

He didn't hear any locks turning and she sure wasn't opening the door.

"Do you think I could come inside?"

"Why?"

He blew out a breath, leaned into the peephole and said, "Because I don't want to have this conversation in the hallway."

"Fine."

At last, he heard the distinctive sounds of a chain being dragged off and several dead bolts clacking. When she opened the door, he stepped inside before she could change her mind.

"What do you want, Shane?"

He glanced quickly around the room, took a sniff

of Christmas-scented air, then turned his gaze on her. Her blond hair was loose, waving over her shoulders. She wore a white cut-off T-shirt and pale green sweatpants that hung low on her hips, baring several inches of flat, toned belly. She was barefoot and her toes were painted a dark, sexy red.

A blast of heat and need shot through him, rocking him to his bones.

She still had the door open, one hand gripping the knob as if for support. Her wary gaze was locked on him and Shane nearly regretted coming over here. Nearly.

"Afraid to close the door?" he teased. "Worried about what might happen?"

She slammed it shut. "No."

Turning her back on him, she walked to her sofa, sat down in one corner of it and drew her knees to her chest. Focusing her attention on the television set, she proceeded to ignore him. Completely.

What kind of twisted guy was he that he was enjoying this?

He took a seat on the sofa, too, but watched her instead of the TV. "I just thought we should talk."

"Ah," she said, not taking her eyes off the old movie on the television, "because it went so well earlier today."

"No, because it didn't."

She sighed, tightened her arms around her updrawn legs and said, "Shane, there's absolutely nothing left to say, you know?"

"We can't just leave it like this, Rachel."

Finally she shifted a look at him and he saw her eyes, green and soft, and felt a ripple of something warm move through him.

"I know," she said quietly. "I've been thinking about it all night."

Shane's insides fisted. He had a feeling he wasn't going to like what was coming next. The expression on her face warned him that whatever she was thinking, it wasn't pleasant. Still, he'd never been a coward. "And what did you come up with?"

"There's really only one thing to do."

"Yeah?" Wary now, he kept his gaze fixed on hers and saw regret flash quickly across the surface of her eyes. He braced himself and even then, he wasn't prepared for what she said next.

"I'm turning in my two weeks notice."

Eight

"What?"

It did Rachel's heart good to see how shocked he was by her resignation. But it didn't change anything. In the last couple of hours, she'd done a lot of thinking.

She'd sat through George Bailey's problems, watched the resolution and cried when Clarence got his wings. But somewhere during her movie marathon, she'd come to grips with what she knew she had to do.

Her heart ached, but there was simply no other reasonable option. If she stayed at *The Buzz,* working with Shane, she'd never be able to move on with her life. She'd always be in love with him. No other man would be able to compare to him, so she'd end up alone and watching old Christmas movies in the dark by herself.

So as painful as this was, there really wasn't any choice.

"What're you talking about?" Shane demanded, jumping to his feet and glaring down at her. "You can't quit."

"I just did." She met his gaze squarely and hoped he couldn't read on her face the misery she was feeling.

"This is your solution? Running away?"

"I'm not running, I'm sitting."

"If that's a joke, I'm not smiling."

"Neither am I," she said, unfolding her legs and pushing off the couch. Starting to feel just a little bit cornered, she made a move to walk into the kitchen, but Shane's hand on her upper arm stopped her in her tracks. She stared down at his hand for a long couple of seconds before lifting her gaze to his.

He let her go, jammed his hands into his pockets and muttered, "You can't quit on me, Rachel. Not because—"

"You can't even say it," she said with a slow shake of her head. "Because we had *sex,* Shane. And I think it's a pretty good reason to quit."

"I don't." He pulled his hands free of his pockets, scooped them both through his hair, then let them fall to his sides. "Damn it, we're a team. We work great together. You really want to throw away four good years because of one night?"

No. What she *wanted* was to have more than one

night, but she couldn't very well tell him that, now could she? Just as she couldn't tell him that it would be impossible for her to pretend indifference to him now that she knew what it was like to be in his arms. How could she arrange his dates with other women when her own heart would be breaking?

"No." One word, firmly spoken. "You don't need me, Shane. You won the competition. You're the head honcho now."

"Which means I'll need you even more."

"No, it doesn't. You're just *used* to having me there. You'll survive." She wasn't entirely sure she would, but that was her problem.

"Don't do this, Rachel."

"I have to."

"I won't accept your resignation."

She smiled. At the core of him, Shane Elliott would always have a healthy ego. "That won't stop me."

"What will?"

"Nothing."

He stepped in close. So close that the scent of his cologne reached for her, dragging her in closer for a deeper breath. She closed her eyes. If she looked up into those green eyes of his, she'd be lost. If she saw his mouth only inches from hers, she wouldn't be able to resist taking another taste of him.

His hands dropped onto her shoulders and she felt the heat of his touch slide deep within her.

"I won't stop trying to change your mind," he warned, his voice deep, ragged.

"I know that."

His hands tightened on her. "Look at me."

"I'd rather not," she admitted.

He sighed. "I came over here tonight to— I don't know. Apologize for last night?"

She winced.

He stroked one hand over her hair, his fingers sliding through the silky strands. "But now that I'm here with you again, an apology is the last thing on my mind."

"Shane—"

"Open your eyes, Rachel."

She did and instantly felt swamped by the emotions churning in his gaze. Her stomach dipped and rolled, her heartbeat jumped into a fast gallop and a curl of something warm and delicious settled low inside her. "Shane, this isn't a good idea."

"Probably not," he allowed, lowering his head infinitesimally.

She licked her lips, heard her blood humming in her veins and knew without a doubt that if she let him kiss her, she was only asking for more trouble. Being with him again would only make their inevitable parting that much harder.

And yet…

She'd wanted more than one night with him. This was her chance. This was her chance to have *him* seduce *her.* The night before had been her idea. Tonight, Shane was the one taking charge. Showing her how much he wanted her.

And if she couldn't have his love, then tonight, she'd settle for being wanted.

He kissed her and Rachel leaned into him, giving herself over to the glory of his mouth on hers. To the solid strength of him towering over her. To the feel of his hands sliding down her back and beneath the waistband of her pale green sweats.

His big hands cupped her bottom and pulled her tight against him. So tight that she felt his erection, hard and thick, pressed into her abdomen. Swirls of longing, of need swept through her like the ripples on a pond after a stone's been thrown in. Over and over again, sensations crested, fell and rose again.

She moaned and twisted her hips against his. In response, he pulled her even more tightly to him, grinding his mouth against hers. His tongue claimed her, mating with her own in a wild, frenetic dance of desire that pulsed in the air around them both.

Rachel's fingers dug into his shoulders and she held on for all she was worth. Her knees wobbled and the world tipped slightly off-center. But she didn't care. Nothing was more important than the feeling of Shane's arms around her, his body pressed to hers.

Laboring for air, Shane broke the kiss, stared down into her eyes and gave her butt a squeeze. "Yes?" he asked, his voice broken with need.

"Oh, yes," she said and leaped at him, wrapping her legs around his hips and hanging on as he started for her bedroom.

One corner of her brain couldn't believe she was

doing this again. Compounding one mistake with another exactly like it couldn't be the right thing to do. But then again, if she was quitting her job anyway, she might as well make the most of the time she had with the man she loved.

Reaching down between their bodies, she slid one hand down to the zipper of his slacks and when she pulled it down, he sucked in air like a dying man trying for one last gasp. Her fingers curled around the hard, thick length of him and he tucked his face into the curve of her neck. His teeth and tongue worked at her flesh as if the very taste of her meant life itself.

Rachel saw stars exploding behind her eyes. Every square inch of her body felt alive with sensation and almost too sensitized. And she wanted more.

Now.

"Can't wait," he muttered thickly and stopped just outside her bedroom door. He set her on her feet, dragged her clothes off and tossed them to one side, then lifted her again.

"No waiting," she agreed, wrapping her bare legs around his waist and hanging on.

He turned quickly, braced her back against the wall and when she rose up slightly in his arms, Shane pushed his body hard into hers. Rachel groaned as he filled her. Her body stretched to its limits to accommodate him, she bore down hard, taking him even deeper inside.

Bracing one hand on the wall to her side and one

hand on his shoulder, Rachel helped all she could, but Shane didn't need assistance. He took her weight and held her easily, lifting her up and down on his length until they were both tortured with a burning, fiery need that sizzled between them.

Again and again, he withdrew only to plunge into her depths one more time. His breathing was ragged, his eyes glazed. Rachel's heart pounded until it was nothing but a deafening roar in her own ears.

Shane couldn't think. Could hardly see. All he could do was feel. And what he was feeling was even more intense than anything he'd experienced the night before.

Most of the day, he'd tried to convince himself that the night with Rachel hadn't been as amazing as he remembered it. Now he knew that for the sad lie it was.

Rachel took him to places he'd never imagined. Made him feel things he'd thought himself incapable of. Made him want more.

Her body surrounded him, her mouth opened on a sigh and her eyes closed as the first wild, frantic pumping release jolted through her. He watched pleasure claim her for as long as he could and then finally, he allowed himself to follow after her.

She hung limp in his arms and Shane was grateful for the wall at her back. Otherwise, they'd both be lying in a puddle on the floor.

"You okay?" he whispered.

She chuckled. "I'll let you know when I get feeling back in my legs."

He smiled. "I hear that."

"Shane—"

He dropped his head to her shoulder. "Let's not start the 'mistake' talk again."

"Why not?" she asked quietly. "Seems appropriate."

He lifted his head and looked down into her eyes again. Strange, he'd never really noticed what a beautiful shade of green her eyes were before last night. And now he couldn't seem to tear his gaze away.

"I didn't come over here tonight to do this."

"I know that," she said and shifted position slightly.

That small movement was enough to wake his body up and stir fresh desire. He hissed in a breath and tightened his hold on her. "But I'm not sorry we did it."

She leaned her head back against the wall and inhaled sharply as he pushed his hardening body into her again, setting off a fireworks display of sensation. "No," she admitted, "I guess I'm not, either."

"Glad to hear that," he said tightly, pushing them away from the wall and starting for the bedroom again. "Because I don't think we're finished."

She shivered and lowered herself onto his length as hard as she could. "I think you're right."

He walked right up to the bed, reached down and dragged the quilt back, then fell onto the mattress, still fully clothed and deep within her body.

Rachel laughed and he noticed a tiny dimple in her right cheek. He'd never noticed that before, either.

"Maybe you should get undressed first," she said, then gasped when he rocked his hips against hers.

"After," he muttered and rolled to his back, taking her atop him where he could watch her. "I'm not stopping now."

"Good idea." Smiling, she reached for the hem of her little T-shirt and whipped it up and off, tossing it into the shadows of the small room. Then, watching him, she covered her breasts with his hands and twisted her hips on him, creating an unbelievable friction that stole his breath.

Riding him, she took him places he'd never thought to go and couldn't wait to visit again. The bed beneath him was soft and smelled of lavender. The woman above him was amazing and her scent was soap, shampoo and woman.

Like a man possessed he guided her hips, steering her into a mind-numbing rhythm. She was the only thing in the world he could see. Feel. And all too soon, an explosion burst up between them, leaving his body shattered, his bones shaken and his heart quivering.

Two hours later, they were naked, lying in a pool of white, thrown through the windows from the streetlights outside. Rachel stared at the ceiling and listened to Shane's ragged breathing.

Her own heartbeat was racing and her body was still sizzling when she acknowledged that once again, she'd been an idiot. But how could she possibly have turned him down, when all she'd been able to think about since the night before was being with him again?

Despite how wonderful her body felt, her heart

was aching. By giving in to the urge to be with him, she was only setting herself up for more pain.

This had to stop.

"You're thinking," he murmured.

"Aren't you?" she countered.

"No." He turned his head on the pillow to look at her. Reaching out, he skimmed one hand across her bare belly and Rachel shivered. "When I'm with you I don't want to think. Don't want you to, either."

She sighed now. "*Not* thinking is what got us here in the first place."

"Exactly."

Eyes closed, she savored his touch for a second or two, indulging herself. Oh, she wanted him to take her again. Wanted to take *him* again. And because she wanted it so badly, she rolled out from under his touch and slid off the bed.

Now that her blood wasn't on fire, she could think more clearly. And though it broke her heart to admit it even to herself, she knew that being wanted would never be enough for her.

She wanted love.

She wanted family.

And she would never get that from Shane.

He blew out a frustrated breath and pushed himself up onto one elbow. "Rachel—"

"Shane, this just can't keep happening," she said, turning to find her clothes, then snatch them up off the floor. In the pale wash of light, she pulled her T-shirt on, then struggled into her sweats, hopping first on one foot, then the other. When she was finished, she picked up Shane's clothes, too, and tossed them at him.

He grabbed at them then dropped the pile onto the bed beside him. "You know, maybe there's a reason we keep ending up here."

Impatient with both herself and him, she huffed out a breath and shook her hair back from her face. "Oh, there's a reason all right. Neither one of us can be trusted."

He gave her a weary laugh. "You may have a point."

A stab of something cold and lonely poked at her insides but Rachel fought to ignore it. She wouldn't let him see what his simple statement had done to her. Instead she said, "This is why I had to quit, Shane. Why I *still* have to."

Muttering darkly, he rolled off the bed and stood up to get dressed. As he stepped into his clothes, he argued with her. "What we've had with each other has nothing to do with work."

"Of course it does." She planted her hands on her hips, lifted her chin and continued. "You know how it was today. We could hardly talk to each other."

"Didn't seem to have any trouble tonight."

"That—" she waved her hand at the bed "—is *not* talking."

He tossed his suit coat onto the rumpled mattress. "Rachel, you're making too big a deal out of this."

"And maybe you're taking it too lightly."

Shane pushed one hand through his hair and yanked while he went at it. The pain shooting through his skull was a small, but welcome distraction from the woman making him nuts. "What do you want me to say?"

So much, she thought, but didn't say. Oh, she wanted it all. She wanted him making love with her and *being* in love with her. But since she couldn't have one, she wouldn't have the other.

In the moonlight, his green eyes flashed with annoyance and something else she couldn't quite identify. Maybe it was just as well.

If nothing else, she at least knew that her decision to quit her job and move on had been a good one. Now all she needed was the courage to go ahead with the plan. Somehow, somewhere, she found the strength to straighten her spine.

"I want you to say you accept my resignation," she whispered.

He grabbed his jacket and shrugged into it. Tugging at the lapels until it hung right, he just stared at her for a long moment. Rachel held her breath and counted the seconds as they ticked past as steadily as a heartbeat.

Finally, though, Shane nodded. "If it's what you want."

Want? No.

Need? Yes.

"It is. Thanks."

"Right." He nodded, looked uneasily around the room, then focused his gaze on her again. "I'd better go. I'll see you at the office tomorrow?"

"I'll be there."

* * *

Long after Shane was gone, Rachel sat at her computer. Her fingers flew over the keys, as her eyes blurred with tears she refused to shed.

One last Tess Tells All column.

One more time, she'd write down her feelings for her boss. One more time, she'd pour out her heart and mask it with humor. And one more time, she'd watch Shane read it, chuckle at Tess's cleverness and never see himself in the words.

Nine

A few days later, Rachel was wishing she'd just quit her job outright.

Working with Shane and maintaining a stoic, distant attitude was harder than it sounded. He was polite, courteous and completely unreachable. She should have been glad that he was apparently as determined as she to not let their own desires erupt again.

Instead she was only irritated.

Wasn't this hard on him at all?

Shaking her head, she scrolled down the list of RSVP responses to the annual Elliott Christmas Charity Ball. Making notations on who had and hadn't responded yet, Rachel lost herself in the work. It was the one thing she could depend on now. And if this year's ball was going to be the last one she arranged, then by heaven, it was going to be the very best one anyone had ever seen.

Every year, EPH sponsored a charity extravaganza, raising money for women's shelters and children's hospitals in the city. And for the last four years, Rachel had been integral to the planning and execution of the ball. She kept track of invitations, caterers, musicians, decorations. She arranged for Santa to appear at the party for the children who would be attending and she made sure that Santa had exactly the right present for every child.

This was one job she was really going to miss when she left the company.

"Hey," Christina said. "Earth to Rachel."

She blinked and looked up at her friend. Christina's silver-framed glasses were riding low on her nose and her bright blue eyes were fixed on Rachel.

"I'm sorry. What?"

"Honey," Christina said, lowering her voice and bending down to lean both hands on Rachel's desk, "you have something you want to tell me?"

"What do you mean?"

The older woman took a quick look around, assuring herself that no one was close enough to overhear. Still, she lowered her voice another notch. "A new Tess Tells All column just left Production for the boss's office."

"Really?" Rachel tried to look surprised. "I thought that last column was it for her."

"Apparently she had one more in her," Christina said, narrowing her eyes thoughtfully, "and it was a beauty."

Rachel lowered her gaze, picked up a stack of files and busily straightened them as if clean edges meant her life. "Why're you telling me?"

"Nice try," her friend countered. "But you forget. I've got years of experience dealing with kids trying to hide things from me."

"Christina…"

"You're Tess."

"Shh!" Rachel looked around now and when she was sure they were alone, she stood up, motioned to Christina and headed for the break room. Her friend was just a step or two behind her and when they entered the empty room, Christina shut the door and leaned back against it.

"It's true."

Rachel grumbled a little as she automatically straightened the counter before grabbing a coffee cup and pouring herself some. "Yes. It's true. Happy?"

"Delirious. I've had my suspicions for a while now, but this column just confirmed it." Locking the door, she walked toward her friend, got herself some coffee and while she dumped several heaping teaspoons of sugar into the brew, she said, "I can't believe you didn't tell me."

"I couldn't tell anyone."

"I'm not just anyone."

"True," Rachel said, taking a sip of coffee. "And I wanted to tell you about me being Tess but—"

"Oh," Christina said waving one hand at her, "who cares about the Tess thing? I want to know why you didn't tell me you slept with Shane."

"Oh God." Dragging a chair out, Rachel fell into it and set her cup on the table.

"Talk, sweetie. I want details."

"No details. Please. I'm trying to forget them myself."

"Damn. That bad?"

Rachel laughed at the disappointment on her friend's face. "Hardly. That *good.*"

"Ooh. So why the long face?"

"Because everything's changed now."

"That's good," Christina said, then frowned. "Isn't it?"

"I quit my job."

"No, you did not."

"I had to," Rachel said, cradling her coffee cup between her palms, savoring the heat radiating through her. "I can't work with him now. It's just too hard."

"That's bull and you know it." Christina sighed and leaned back in her chair. "Quitting solves nothing."

"It gets me away from him."

"Honey, you'll *never* be able to get away from him. You'll keep on loving him even if you wander off to Timbuktu."

"Well, there's a happy thought," Rachel muttered. "Anyway, my resignation is in and so are a few applications I've managed to drop off on my lunch hour the last couple of days. There are lots of magazines here in the city," she continued, wanting to steer their talk away from Shane. "So it's not like I'll never see you again or anything."

"Damn straight on that," Christina said, giving her a tight smile. "But here's a question for you. What do you think Shane's going to say when he sees this column?"

Rachel laughed miserably, picked up her coffee and took a sip. "He's read dozens of 'em so far and hasn't recognized himself. Why should this time be any different?"

Christina picked up her own coffee cup and smiled at Rachel over the rim. "Oh, didn't I mention that part? You screwed up in this one. You actually referred to Tess's mystery boss as *Shane.*"

Rachel's cup fell from suddenly nerveless fingers and hit the tabletop with enough force to send waves of hot coffee washing over both women.

Shane had been fielding phone calls all morning. From agents of minor celebrities hoping to make a splash in *The Buzz,* to heads of major corporations wanting to talk product placement. Normally he would have fobbed off most of those calls to the proper departments.

But for the last few days, he'd been doing everything he could to keep busy. Even if it meant getting back into the trenches. The plan was to keep himself so preoccupied he wouldn't have time to think about Rachel.

It wasn't working.

She was always there, right at the edges of his mind, waiting for a quiet moment to pop in and torture him. Damn it, he'd managed to work with Rachel—closely—for four long years. In all that time, he'd never looked at her as he would any other wildly attractive woman.

She'd just been there. Like an extension of himself. Part of his office, his work world. And in the last year, since his father had kicked off this ridiculous competition, she'd been the one to give him a kick in the can when he needed it. Hell, she was just as responsible as he for *The Buzz* winning the competition. Maybe more so. Because Rachel was always on top of things. She'd kept his life running smoothly for four years and he'd never even noticed her beyond being grateful for the help.

How the *hell* could he have been so blind?

How could he not have noticed her eyes, her mouth, her sense of humor, her legs, her agile mind, her breasts, her loyalty, her behind?

And why was he noticing all of that *now?*

Muttering darkly, he stalked across his office when the phone started ringing again. But this time, instead of answering, he let it ring and walked to the bank of windows behind his desk.

When the phone stopped ringing, he smiled grimly only to turn and frown at the quick knock on the door. Before he could call out for whoever it was to leave, the door swung open and Rachel was there.

Her blond hair was pulled back and twisted into

some sort of elegant braid she usually did. But now he'd seen it hanging loose and waving around her face and that was how he pictured her. In his mind's eye her plain, pale green business suit was replaced by a skimpy T-shirt and a pair of green sweats.

Oh man, he was in deep trouble here.

"You okay?" she asked, frowning at him.

"Fine." Or at least, he would be if he could shut off his brain. "What is it?"

Before she could answer, another woman sailed past Rachel into his office and demanded, "What makes you so crabby, I'd like to know?"

"Mom," he said and felt a smile warm his face.

Maeve Elliott was a tiny woman physically, but her personality made her seem larger than life. She'd married Shane's father when she was a nineteen-year-old seamstress in Ireland. And, though Shane could take exception to the way Patrick had ignored his children from time to time, the old man had always treated his wife as if she were the most priceless treasure on the planet. Which, Shane admitted silently, she was.

He came around the desk, enfolded her in a quick, tight hug, then stepped back to look at her. Impeccable as always, she wore a Chanel suit of icy-blue and her nearly all-white hair was swept up into an intricate knot on top of her head.

"So," she said, eyeing her son, "my question stands. Why so crabby, Shane?"

He frowned and shifted a look at Rachel, still standing in the doorway. "Just…busy."

"Then I won't keep you long," his mother said, half turning to motion Rachel into the office. "I just wanted to stop and tell you the news!"

Rachel came closer and Shane swore he caught a whiff of her scent. Just enough to tantalize. To tweak his memory of their last night together. To remind him there wouldn't be any other nights like it.

He bit back a scowl and focused on his mother, practically vibrating with energy. "What is it?" he teased. "Win the Mrs. America pageant, did you?"

"Ah, you were always the smooth one," she said, laughing. "No, no. Much better news. Our Erika's had her baby. A beautiful little girl she is, too. I'm a grandmother!"

"That's terrific," Shane said, meaning every word.

"Wonderful," Rachel added, smiling. "How's the new mom doing?"

Maeve smiled even wider. "Erika's doing just fine. It's Gannon who's having the breakdown. Poor love. Apparently being a witness to his wife's labor has left him flattened."

"Did he faint?" Shane asked, hoping for some good ammunition to tease Gannon with in the future.

"Of course not," Maeve said with a sniff. "It's just very hard seeing someone you love in pain."

"Yeah," Shane said, slanting a look at Rachel only to find her gaze on him. "It must be."

A second or two of silence stretched out between them and hummed with energy until even Maeve was affected by it. As she looked from one of them to the other, one perfectly arched brow lifted slightly. Delicately she cleared her throat until she had her son's attention again.

"I'll let you get back to work now, Shane darlin'," she said. "I'm just on my way to see your father and force him to take me to lunch."

Shane tore his gaze from Rachel and scrambled for equilibrium. Blowing out a breath, he took his mother's arm and said, "Why don't I join you? You can tell me all about the new Elliott."

"That would be lovely," she said, lifting one hand to touch his cheek. Then she turned to Rachel. "Would you like to accompany us as well, Rachel?"

"No," she said quickly, with a shake of her head. "I'll, um, just stay here and get a few things finished."

"Shame," Maeve said thoughtfully, then walked from the office, her son and Rachel right behind her.

With Shane gone for at least an hour, Rachel did something she'd never done before in all the four years she'd worked at *The Buzz.*

She rifled Shane's desk.

"For pity's sake, where would he put the blasted thing?" She yanked open the first two drawers in his desk, quickly thumbed through the folders and looked under the books and magazines stored there.

Nothing.

The bottom file drawer yielded no happier results.

She zipped through the stacks of folders atop his desk, her fingers flipping through the pages as her gaze swept the printed pages. But the new Tess column was nowhere to be found. Which left only one possibility.

Her gaze drifted to the locked drawer on the bottom left of the big desk. There was no way for her to get inside it. And if she *did* lose her mind and try to pick the lock, Shane would notice and then the jig would be up, anyway.

"How could I have been so stupid?" she wondered aloud and just managed to keep from thumping herself in the forehead with the heel of her hand.

Shane would read the column, know exactly who wrote it and would probably fire her on the spot. Of course, since she'd already resigned, it wouldn't carry a lot of weight. But oh, God. The embarrassment quotient was just too high to think about!

Mentally she raced back over the other columns she'd turned in for publication. All the times she'd talked about her boss in less than stellar terms. All the times she'd complained about his too active social life.

Her toe stopped tapping against the floor and her mouth dropped open. And the last column, where she'd admitted to feeling too much about him.

"This is a *disaster.*"

Dropping her head into her hands, she wished for a hole to open up under her feet and swallow her.

By the time Shane returned from lunch, tension bubbled inside him like a thick, poisonous brew.

Luckily enough, Rachel was gone from her desk, probably taking a late lunch herself. Just as well. He was in no mood for yet another stiff, polite exchange of empty pleasantries.

Especially after spending the last two hours dodging Maeve Elliott's questions.

God knew he loved his mother, but there was nothing the woman liked better than digging into her children's lives. Whether they welcomed it or not.

He'd been able to dodge her thinly veiled questions about his and Rachel's relationship—but just barely. And if his father hadn't insisted on talking about the company, Maeve wouldn't have given up until she'd pried every last ounce of information from him.

He stepped into his office, closed the door behind him and gratefully went back to work. At his desk, he unlocked the bottom drawer, pulled out the latest columns sent to him by Production, and leaned back in his chair to flip through them.

When he found the Tess column, he smiled to himself, put the other articles aside and started reading. After the first paragraph, he was frowning. At the second, he was muttering to himself.

And by the third paragraph, the words were blurring beneath the red haze covering his vision.

Heart jumping, stomach twisting, temper spiking, Shane crumpled the edges of the paper in his fists and forced himself to keep reading.

Sex with the boss is never a smart move,

Tess wrote,

> but in my case, it was imbecilic. I've spent the last year or more writing about how hard it is to work with a man who never sees you as anything more than an especially fine tuned piece of office equipment. But now that Shane actually has seen me—naked of all things—the situation is completely untenable.
>
> So here's a word of warning for all of you assistants out there. When the boss smiles and says "Let's celebrate," remember that celebrating usually means hangover.
>
> Or worse.
>
> For your own sakes, if the boss starts looking too good to you…run.

"Rachel," he muttered thickly, staring at the page in front of him as if he still couldn't believe what he'd read. "All this time, it's been her. All this time."

He swallowed hard, choking back the knot of fury in his throat. When he thought he could speak without growling, he snatched up the phone on his desk and punched in a number.

"Circulation and archives."

"This is Shane Elliott."

"Yes, sir," the female voice snapped out, and he could almost see the woman jerking to attention in her chair.

"Get me a copy of every one of our magazines that contains a Tess Tells All column."

"Oh, sir, I just love that column."

"Great," he muttered, thinking now about all of the people who'd read every word Rachel had ever written about him. Hell, people all over the *world* had been laughing at him for more than a year.

And he'd wanted to give the mysterious Tess a raise!

"I want those copies here in thirty minutes."

"Yes, sir."

Shane tossed the receiver back into the cradle, gave up on trying to rein in the temper nearly strangling him and started reading the most recent column again.

Ten

When Rachel came back from lunch, she was feeling a little better. She'd done a little Christmas shopping, wandered through the windy, cold streets and lost herself in the crowds.

Hard to keep feeling sorry for yourself when you're reminded that you're simply one cog in a very large wheel.

Now, back at *The Buzz,* she was simply determined to survive the rest of her two weeks notice and then move on with her life. Smiling at the people she passed, she headed right for her desk and noticed Shane's door standing open.

As she glanced inside, she saw that he'd been watching for her. And he didn't look happy.

"Everything okay?"

"Not really," he said, waving one hand at her. "Would you come in here please?"

A quick twist of apprehension tightened in her belly before she made a titanic attempt at smoothing it out. *Oh, God. He saw the column.*

Her brain raced, coming up with explanations, excuses, *anything.* She'd had a glass of wine at lunch, knowing that this confrontation would be headed her way. Now she wished she'd had two.

She paused long enough to deposit her purse in the bottom drawer of her desk, then steeling herself, walked into Shane's office and closed the door behind her. "What's going on?"

A brief, hard smile crossed his face. Standing up, he walked around the edge of his desk. Then folding his arms across his chest, he sat on the corner of the desk and watched her through narrowed eyes.

Rachel now knew how a rabbit felt staring down a snake. Fire flashed in his eyes and a twitch in his jaw told her he was gritting his teeth. No point in pretending ignorance any longer, she thought, and spoke right up. "You've seen the article."

"Not even going to try to deny it?"

"No."

"So you *are* Tess."

She smoothed the fall of her skirt, then clasped her hands together at her waist. Her fingers tightened until her knuckles went white. "Surprise."

"I can't believe this." He shook his head in disgust. "I don't even know whether to be insulted or flattered that you've been writing about me all these months."

"I didn't mean for you to find out like this."

"You mean," he corrected, pushing off the desk to stalk across the room toward her, "you didn't mean for me to find out at all."

"Well," she hedged, "yes."

He walked a slow circle around her and Rachel turned slowly, keeping her gaze fixed on him. "Did you enjoy watching me trying to find out ways to identify you? Did you get a laugh out of lying to everyone here? Lying to *me?*"

She huffed out a breath and mentally scrambled for the right thing to say. But she kept coming up empty. "I wasn't trying to lie to you, Shane."

"Ah, so that was just a happy side benefit."

"I don't know why you're making such a big deal about this," she said, deciding to go on the defensive. "You *loved* those columns."

"Yes," he snapped, coming to a fast stop. "When I thought they were written about some nameless, faceless *jerk.* I *don't* love finding out that *I'm* the jerk."

She held up one hand. "I never called you a jerk."

"You might as well have," he countered, spinning around and walking back to his desk. He picked up a thick manila file and waved it at her. "I've been going over all the old columns. And now that I think about it, I believe I'm more insulted than anything else. You made me look like a fool."

The knot of tension inside her started to loosen and

with it, came a burst of outrage. "I did not. All I did was write about the day-to-day job of working for you."

"And about the women I date."

In her own defense, she pointed out, "I wouldn't have had to write about that if you hadn't put *me* in charge of buying your make-up gifts, your break-up gifts. Ordering flowers. Making reservations for you and the Barbies, Bambis and Tawnys of the world."

"Tawny," he muttered. "That's her name."

"You're the one who dragged me into your social life, Shane, so you're hardly in a position to complain about it now, are you?"

"You're my assistant. Who the hell else would I ask to do all that stuff?"

She hitched one hip higher than the other, folded her arms under her breasts, cocked her head to stare at him and offered, "Oh, I don't know…*yourself?*"

He tossed the folder onto his desk and the columns inside scattered across the gleaming surface. "If you hated your job so much, why didn't you just quit?"

"I did," she reminded him.

"I mean before," he blustered, throwing both hands high. "If I'm such a bastard to work for, why did you stay this long?"

Rachel dropped the angry pose, walked forward and dropped down into one of the twin chairs opposite his desk. Looking up at him, she said, "You were never a bastard to work for. And I enjoyed my job. I just got…"

"Jealous?" he asked.

"No." She jumped to her feet again. "Not jealous, just—I don't even know what. I started writing those articles as a way to vent my frustration. And hey, apparently there are a lot of admins in the city who know just what I'm talking about."

"Yes, but—"

"You said yourself only last week that Tess Tells All is the most popular column in the magazine. You wanted to find her. To offer her—me—a weekly column. You wanted to give her a huge raise and bring her—me—on staff." She watched him and noted the relaxing of his jaw muscles and the tension dropping out of his squared shoulders. "So what's changed, Shane? Only the fact that you found out who Tess really is."

"That's plenty," he snapped.

"From your point of view, I guess so," she acknowledged. "But you have to admit that you laughed at my columns as hard as anyone else."

"That was before. Now…" He turned from her and walked to the windows. Staring out, he said, "You wrote about our nights together."

She swallowed hard and met his gaze when he looked over his shoulder at her. "Yes."

"Why?"

She shrugged and knew that wasn't an answer. But she wasn't sure she had one to give him. "I don't really know."

"I think I do," he said, turning back to face her again. "I think you wanted me to find out that you're Tess."

"Oh, I don't think that's it," she said, shaking her head slowly.

Shane walked toward her and noted that she took a half step back, as if trying to keep a safe distance between them. Wasn't going to work. He'd had time to think about this. Time to reread her columns with a clear eye.

"You wanted me to know, Rachel. Otherwise you never would have made the mistake of putting my name in the most recent article."

"That was a mistake."

"A Freudian slip."

"Oh, please," she said, backing away as he got closer.

"You wanted me to know because you don't want to quit your job. You don't want to leave *The Buzz*. You want your own column. You want to stay here. With me."

She laughed shortly. "I already turned in my resignation, Shane. And you accepted it."

"Reluctantly."

"Whatever. The point is, it's done."

She glanced around the room, keeping from looking at him, avoiding meeting his gaze. Shane actually enjoyed watching the usually unflappable Rachel display telltale signs of nervousness.

"No, it's not," he said. "I don't want you to quit, Rachel. I'm willing to offer you the same deal I was going to offer your alter ego."

Finally she looked at him. "You *want* me to keep writing about you?"

"No," he admitted. "But you're very talented. You're funny. And our readers love your columns. I'm guessing you could find something else to write about. Life in Manhattan. Interviews with other admins. Anything you want."

She thought about it for a long moment and Shane found himself wishing to hell he could read her mind, since nothing of what she was feeling was visible on her features.

"Well?" he prodded, anxious for her answer.

"Tempting," she admitted, backing up again. "But no. Thanks for the offer, but I'm leaving *The Buzz,* Shane."

Speaking up quickly, he offered her more money. Up to twice her present salary. Her eyes popped, but still she shook her head.

"It's not about the money and it's insulting to me that you're acting as though it is."

"You want to talk insulted?" he countered hotly. "You've made me a laughingstock all over New York for the last year."

Her lips thinned into a grim slash. "If you hadn't behaved like an idiot, I wouldn't have had so much ammunition."

"Oh, that's perfect."

"Look, Shane," she said, making a heroic attempt at controlling her temper. "You have the CEO position you wanted, but I can't be around you anymore. I just can't do it."

Disappointment gathered in his chest, warred with anger and tightened until he could hardly draw a breath. "Because of what happened between us."

"Partly," she said, nodding. "We can't just go back to our old working relationship, Shane. We can't pretend we didn't…"

Hell no, he couldn't pretend nothing had happened between them. Every waking minute she was there, in his mind. Every time he closed his eyes, he saw her. Felt her. Tasted her. She haunted him and he knew that even if she left, her memory would stay with him. Always.

"So let's just leave things as they are and part friends, all right?"

His gaze locked with hers, he tried to find some way to change her mind. To make her stay. He knew damn well that without her, he might never have won the competition with his siblings.

And he couldn't imagine trying to run all of EPH without Rachel's advice and common sense and humor. Damn it, she couldn't just walk out.

But she did.

She left him standing there staring at her back as she walked away.

The next couple of days, Rachel buried herself in the preparations for the big charity event that EPH sponsored every year. The rich, the famous and the infamous would gather in the ballroom atop the Waldorf-Astoria and donate enough money to keep several children's shelters running for a year.

She already had the flowers arranged for and the

caterers and band. Then she spent half the morning on the phone with security experts, lining up the extra guards they'd need on the doors. Running her finger down her list, she made several check marks and only frowned once.

Santa.

She still needed a Santa.

The one she'd used the year before was already booked and she couldn't hire just anyone to hand out gifts to children. Flipping through the phone book, she looked up several numbers for casting agents in the city. Somehow or other, she'd find the perfect Santa.

Her last job for EPH was going to come off perfectly even if she had to work herself to death to make sure of it.

When her phone rang, she reached for it automatically. "Shane Elliott's office."

"Ms. Adler?"

"Yes." Frowning, she sat back in her chair.

"This is Dylan Hightower at *Cherish* magazine."

"Oh." She straightened. *Cherish* was a celebrity homestyle magazine she'd applied to just last week. Good news. When she left EPH, she wanted to be able to go right into a new job.

"I wanted to call you and explain why we're unable to offer you a position."

She blinked, stunned. She was *perfect* for the job of executive assistant to the editor-in-chief. Her computer skills were excellent, matched by her organizational abilities and her work ethic. "I see."

"No, I don't believe you do," Hightower said

abruptly. "And frankly, I'm only calling to warn you that publishing is a very small business. Liars don't go undiscovered for long."

"I'm sorry?" Her stomach was spinning.

"You should apologize for wasting my time, Ms. Adler. I checked with your references and I have to say I was shocked when Shane Elliott told me the real story behind your leaving your present position."

"He did." Temper boiled and bubbled in the pit of her stomach and she was forced to take deep, even breaths to steady herself out. "What exactly did Mr. Elliott have to say, if you don't mind my asking?"

"Not at all. He informed me that you were quite possibly the worst assistant he's ever had. And the fact that you're not a team player and actually go out of your way to foment dissension in the ranks…" He paused for breath. "Let me just say that your reputation is less than stellar."

The edges of her vision went a blurry red. She could hardly speak she was so furious and it took all she had not to slam the phone down on Mr. Fabulous Hightower.

"I understand," she finally managed to say.

"I hope you do," he retorted and hung up.

Still clutching the phone, while a dial tone buzzed in her ear, Rachel shifted a look at Shane's closed door. Inhaling sharply, she slapped the phone into its cradle and stomped across the floor toward it. She didn't bother to knock, just shoved it open, slammed it shut behind her and advanced on her boss with blood in her eye.

"Rachel?"

"How *dare* you?" She slapped both hands on his desk and leaned in toward him. "How dare you submarine my chances at a new job."

"Now wait a—"

"Mr. Hightower just called to explain personally why he wouldn't be hiring me."

Shane's gaze snapped to one side and he scrubbed one hand across his face. "Oh."

"Yeah, *oh*."

He looked at her again, but couldn't quite meet her eyes. "Now, Rachel—"

"I can't believe you did that, Shane. My God, are you really that petty?"

He jumped to his feet. The cityscape stretched out behind him, snow falling softly against the windows, blurring the edges of his silhouette. The silence in the office was profound.

"It wasn't that. It was—"

"What, Shane? What could possibly have been the motivator for you to tell people lies about me?" She pushed up from the desk, folded her arms across her chest and tapped the toe of her shoe against the carpet. "Four years I've worked for you and in all that time have I ever screwed up?"

"No."

"Fomented dissension in the ranks?"

"No."

"Then why?" she asked, shaking her head and

looking at him like she'd never seen him before. And indeed, this side of Shane was a mystery to her. Never before had she seen him so embarrassed. Ashamed.

He blew out a breath, shoved both hands into his pockets and rocked back on his heels. "I thought if I could slow down your job search you might change your mind about leaving."

"By lying about me. Amazing."

"A bad idea. I see that now."

"Well, congratulations," she snapped. "A breakthrough. You're finally willing to admit that not everything in the known universe is about Shane Elliott. Other people have their little lives and problems, too."

"Rachel, I'm sorry, I—"

"Forget it," she said, stepping back from his desk but keeping her eyes on him, as if expecting him to stab her in the back again. "It's a lesson learned, that's all. I'm sure I'll grow from the experience."

"Damn it…"

"You can have personnel send me my last check, Shane. I'm leaving now."

"You can't. You gave me two weeks notice."

She'd reached the door. Snaking her arm behind her, she turned the knob and pulled it open. "If you can lie," she said quietly, "then so can I. Goodbye, Shane."

Eleven

The dining room at The Tides, the Elliott family home, was elegant but warm. Deep burgundy walls, with cream colored trim and crown moldings gave it an old-world feeling. A polished to perfection walnut table that could easily sit twelve stood on a thick Oriental carpet. Original oil paintings dotted the walls and a hand carved buffet sat against the far wall.

When Patrick and Maeve Elliott hosted dinner parties, this room sparkled with fine crystal and fragile china. But Shane remembered all the years growing up in this house and he could almost hear the memory of his brothers' and sister's voices echoing off the walls.

The estate was palatial—seven thousand square feet of turn-of-the-century home, surrounded by five acres of meticulously cared for grounds, situated on a bluff overlooking the Atlantic Ocean in Long Island. And though the house could be intimidating to visitors, to the Elliott children it had simply been home. And a great place for spur-of-the-moment games of hide-and-seek.

The roar and hush of the nearby sea pulsed in the background, almost making the old house seem alive. Shane loved this house. But at the moment, he wished he were anywhere but there.

"Your Rachel is certainly a lovely girl," Maeve said, taking a tiny sip of white wine.

Shane snapped his mother a warning look. "She's not *my* Rachel and yes, she is."

"I sensed a bit of—"

"Mom."

He should have tried to get out of dinner tonight. But to do that, he'd have had to come up with a damn good explanation and at the moment, Shane just wasn't up to it.

Hell, even *he* couldn't believe how he'd sabotaged Rachel's attempts to leave EPH. It had seemed like a good idea at the time. Downplay her abilities, make her seem a little less employable and maybe she'd stay with him.

He hadn't meant to— Damn. Yes, he had. He *had* meant to screw things up for her. So what did that make him? A bastard? Or a desperate bastard?

Either way, he'd lost her.

She'd gathered up her things and walked out of the building right after leaving his office. And for the rest of the day, walking past her empty desk drove needles of guilt into his skull, making his head ache and his temper spike.

He could still see the expression on her face when she'd faced him down just a few hours ago. Shock, betrayal, fury. If he could have, he would have kicked his own ass. He never should have given into the temptation to sabotage her job search.

His own fault. He'd let Rachel become too important to him over the years. She'd become such a part of his day, he could barely imagine *not* having her there.

That thought irritated him more than a little and he scowled to himself.

"Fine, fine," Maeve said, having another sip before setting her glass down on the linen draped table. "Far be it from me to interfere in my children's lives."

Shane snorted a laugh and his mother's eyes narrowed on him.

"Well," she pointed out, "if you and your brothers and sisters would talk to me about what's bothering you, I wouldn't have to pry now would I?"

"Ah, so it's our fault."

"Darlin'," she said, a soft smile still curving her mouth, "I can plainly see that there's something bothering you. Won't you tell me?"

For a moment or two, he considered it. Just unloading on his mom. Then he thought about how

Maeve would react when she discovered what he'd done to Rachel and thought better of it.

"I spoke to Rachel this afternoon," his mother said into the silence.

"Really? About what?"

"The charity ball," Maeve reminded him. "She wanted to say that despite the fact she no longer worked for you, she would continue to oversee the preparations."

"Ah." Of course she'd do that. Rachel was the most responsible human being he'd ever known. She took her duties seriously and once she'd given herself up to a project, she never quit.

Not even when she had more than enough reason to.

"Idiot," he muttered, rubbing his eyes in an attempt to ease the headache pounding behind them.

"Aye," Maeve said, the Irish accent she'd never quite lost dancing in her tone, "apparently you are, dear. Would you like to explain to me why you've fired that lovely girl?"

"I didn't fire her."

"She quit?"

"Yes."

"Why?"

He slanted Maeve a look and wished he hadn't. He was thirty-eight years old, the newly crowned head of a Fortune 500 company and one steely glare from his mother could completely cow him.

Thankfully he was saved by an interruption.

"What're you two talking about?" Patrick asked

as he walked into the room, heels clicking on the marble floor, and took the chair at the head of the table.

"Not a thing, my love," Maeve said, patting his hand. But the look she sent Shane told him that this wasn't over.

"Hmm." Patrick wasn't convinced, but he was willing to let it go. Focusing his gaze on Shane, he asked, "Before dinner arrives, why don't you tell me what your plans are for the company?"

"Patrick," his wife said, "can't we have a single meal without discussing business?"

"No," Shane said quickly, eager to talk about anything but Rachel. If he could keep his mother's mind off of that subject, he just might be able to get through dinner and escape before she could corner him again. "It's fine. Actually I'd like to get Dad's opinion on a few things."

Maeve picked up her glass of wine and took a sip, focusing her gaze on her son. Shane pretended he didn't feel that hot stare and concentrated instead on his father.

The next week was a blur of activity.

Even though Rachel was now officially unemployed, she was busier than ever, coordinating the charity function. Keeping in touch with the event planner at the Waldorf, Rachel had her finger on every hot button.

Nothing was getting past her; she wouldn't allow it. If this was going to be her final task for EPH, it was going to be one that people would be talking about for years. She'd arranged for a ten-foot pine tree to be delivered and professionally decorated. There would be a champagne fountain, a chocolate bar and enough hors d'oeuvres to keep even the most famished guest satisfied.

Every table at the event would boast its own tiny tree, complete with twinkling lights, and garlands of holly and mistletoe would be wound around the perimeter of the elegant room.

This ball was going to be organized smoother than a military coup. There wouldn't be a single hiccup.

She took a bite of her maple scone and shifted a look out through the window of the coffeehouse at the street beyond. Dark clouds hovered over the city as if waiting for just the right moment to dump another few inches of snow on the already slushy streets. People were bundled up, colorful scarves wound tightly around their mouths and necks. And the wind whipped down the high-rise canyons, snatching up trash and twirling it through the air.

Made her cold just looking out at it. So she turned back to the paperwork spread out over the table in front of her and got back down to the business of running a charity event.

Her cell phone rang and Rachel rummaged in her oversized purse for it. A perky little tune played louder as she grabbed it, and a few of the patrons in the coffeehouse glared at her. "Hello?"

"Honey, how's it going?" Christina's voice came across in whispered concern.

Rachel leaned back in her chair, picked up her latte and took a drink. She'd only spoken to her friend once since leaving EPH and Rachel had really missed her. "It's going *great*."

"Uh-huh."

"Really." She put every ounce of conviction she possessed into her voice, but clearly it wasn't enough to convince Christina.

"Oh sure, I believe you."

"Fine," Rachel muttered, shooting a glare at a bearded man hunched over his laptop. What was up with him? He was allowed to type and clatter but she couldn't have a conversation? Honestly, some people.

Focusing on her friend, Rachel said, "I'm working myself to death to keep from thinking about Shane."

"That's what I figured. So if you're still so nuts about him, why'd you quit?"

"What other choice did I have?" she demanded a little too loudly and glared right back at the Beard. Lowering her voice, she said, "I couldn't stay there after—"

God, she couldn't even think about those nights with Shane. It was hard enough to lie there in her bed and remember him lying alongside her. To imagine the hush of his breath, the sweep of his hands on her body, the taste of his mouth on hers.

She took a gulp of hot coffee and burned her mouth. Good. Nice distraction.

"Okay," Christina said, "sex with the boss would make things a little…sticky."

"Yeah, just a touch. But it's more than that, too."

"You mean it's because you love him?"

Rachel winced. "Oh God. *Yes.* I do. And it's hopeless and pitiful and ridiculous and all of the above at once." She shook her head and trailed the tip of her index finger around the circumference of her coffee cup lid. "He's never going to see me like that. Never going to love me back. How could I stay there?"

"I guess you couldn't," Christina said on a sigh. "But I really miss you around here."

"Miss you, too. Heck, I miss my *job.* I was good at it, you know?"

"I know." There was a long pause and then Christina lowered her voice so much Rachel could scarcely hear her. "Would it help to know that since you've been gone, Shane's been miserable?"

Instantly Rachel cheered right up. "Really? His new admin isn't working out?"

"Doesn't have one."

"No way." Surprise made her voice a little louder again and this time Beard actually lifted his index finger to his mouth and warned, "Shhh." Rachel sneered at him.

Shane hadn't hired someone to take her place? Why not? She'd been gone a week. And heaven knew the man couldn't keep track of his own appointment schedule. He needed someone highly organized or he'd never get anything done. And that thought brought a small smile to her face.

"It's weird. Your desk sits there empty," Christina

said, "like the elephant at the cocktail party that nobody wants to talk about."

It shouldn't have made her feel better that Shane hadn't replaced her, but it did. She should be letting him go, getting on with the life she'd promised herself to find. But how could she, when every other minute Shane's face kept popping up into her mind?

"So who's doing all the work if he hasn't hired somebody?"

"No one. That seems to be the problem."

"Oh boy."

"Exactly. And he's not a happy camper these days. Shane's got every department head hopping. Jonathon even threatened to quit yesterday!"

"No, he didn't."

"Oh, yes, he did and Shane backed off quick. I mean, he's crabby, but he's not stupid. If he lost you *and* Jonathon, he'd really be up the proverbial creek. And to top it all off, Shane slams his office door so often, the doorjamb's coming loose."

For a moment or two, Rachel indulged herself, pretending that it was *her* he missed. But in reality she knew better. Right now he was angry because she hadn't fallen into line with his plans. He was feeling a little ashamed of himself for ruining Rachel's job opportunity and he was, no doubt, frustrated because his office life wasn't running as smoothly as usual.

"He'll survive," Rachel said firmly, "and so will I. I hope."

"You hang in there, honey," Christina said. "How about you and I meet for dinner tonight?"

"I'd really love to," Rachel assured her, "but I can't. I have to go to my folks' house for the annual What's Wrong with Rachel holiday discussion."

"Man. You just can't catch a break, can you?"

Actually she *did* catch a small break.

Another storm was rushing toward the city, so to avoid having to drive in a blizzard Rachel made her excuses and left her parents' house early.

Not nearly early enough, though.

She flipped on the rental car radio and tuned it to a soft rock station. The windshield wipers slapped against the glass, keeping time with the rhythm of the song. Nearly hypnotized, Rachel started talking to herself, more to stay alert than anything else.

"A podiatrist. *This* is the dream doctor Mom wants me to hook up with?" Okay, he was a perfectly nice man and not too bad looking in that "probably has back hair" kind of way. But could the man *be* more boring?

"Feet. That's all he talked about all night—feet." Rachel was willing to admit that in the grand scheme of things, feet were a fairly important body part. After all, they made walking a lot easier. But she now knew way more than she'd ever wanted to know about corns, blisters, calluses and warts.

"That's it, Mom," she swore and slapped one hand against the steering wheel. "No more fix-ups. I absolutely refuse."

Her cell phone rang and she reached one handed into her purse, on the passenger seat. Keeping her eyes on the road, she didn't even look at the screen, just opened the phone and said, "Hello?"

"Rachel."

Chills swept up and down her spine, ran along her arms, across her knuckles and back up to swirl in a happy little clog dance in the middle of her chest. God, would the sound of his voice always have that effect on her? "Hello, Shane."

He smiled at the sound of her voice, even though it was less than welcoming. Ever since leaving his parents' house, Shane'd been thinking about Rachel. Hell, he hadn't been able to get his mind off of her all week. Every time he passed her empty desk, he was reminded again of what an idiot he was.

The nights were the worst, though. He glanced around his apartment and found no pleasure in the stark, designer furnishings. White couches, hardwood floors and a lot of glass and chrome, much like the offices at *The Buzz*. His home had all the warmth of a dentist's office. And, at the moment, about the same appeal.

He kept remembering being at Rachel's place. A small, cozy place that she'd made warm and friendly. He could see her, all curled up in one corner of the couch, her blond hair lying loose in soft waves. He heard her laughter and remembered the passion in her eyes.

He couldn't stop thinking about carrying her into her bedroom and how she'd looked in the pale glow of the streetlight shining through the window. He couldn't seem to sleep without tasting her again, reaching for her, like a blind man fumbling for a life rope he knows is there, but can't find.

During the last week, he'd been forced to admit to himself just how important Rachel really was to him. And the question Gannon had asked him a couple of weeks ago kept replaying over and over again in his mind.

Do you love Rachel?

He'd spent so many years avoiding that particular word that now a part of him recoiled even at the thought of it. But the more he missed Rachel, the more he was forced to acknowledge that maybe love had sneaked up on him.

Maybe.

But how was a man supposed to *know?*

The only way he could think of was to get Rachel to come back to work at *The Buzz,* so that they could spend more time together. And then maybe what he was feeling would start to make sense to him.

He walked across the living room of his spacious apartment overlooking Central Park and stopped opposite the terrace doors. Behind him, a fire roared in the hearth, in front of him, a storm was blowing in off the Atlantic, threatening to shut the city down this time.

And he was oblivious to everything but the woman on the other end of the line. He held the phone to his ear in a white-knuckled grip and asked, "Is this a bad time, Rachel?"

"Actually…"

He'd only said that to be polite, so he spoke up

fast. Couldn't risk her hanging up on him. He figured it was best if he went straight to the point. "Rachel, you've gotta come back to work."

"What?"

"I mean it. The place is falling apart, nothing's getting done."

What he didn't say was that it wasn't just work that concerned him. The real problem was *him.* He couldn't think anymore. Without seeing Rachel every damn day, it was like part of his life—the most important part—was gone.

"Not my problem anymore."

He slapped one hand on the icy glass of the French doors and tried to keep his voice calm, steady, without betraying any of the panic he was beginning to feel. It wasn't easy. "Damn it, Rachel, without you there, nothing works right. Nothing is what it should be. I need you, Rachel."

For some reason, something his father had said to him just a couple of weeks ago came flying back into his brain. *Winning doesn't mean a damn thing if you've got nothing to show for it but the victory.*

The old man was right, he thought. Without Rachel to share things with, the victory he'd won over his brothers and sister was an empty one.

There was a long pause where all he heard was a radio playing softly. He stared out at the swirling snow and noted the lamps and the blazing fire behind him reflected in the glass. He waited what seemed like forever for her answer and when it finally came, it wasn't what he wanted to hear.

"You don't need *me,* Shane," she said, her voice sounding sad and weary. "I really wish you did. But what you need is a good admin. There are plenty of them in New York. Find one."

"Rachel, wait—"

"Goodbye, Shane."

Twelve

She wasn't coming back.

Shane scrubbed both hands across his face and blew out a shaky breath. He looked around his office and tried to find the excitement, the old sense of pride being here used to give him. But there was nothing.

Nothing at all.

The work went on.

The world went on.

But nothing was the same.

Rachel was gone.

And he didn't know how to fix it.

When the phone rang, he almost ignored it. God knew he was in no mood to talk to anyone. But the shrill rings sliced into his head, accentuating the headache already pounding behind his eyes. So he grabbed it and snarled a greeting.

"Well, Merry Christmas to you, too," a familiar female voice said.

"Fin." He sighed, plopped down into his desk chair and spun around so that he was facing the windows and the cold, dark world beyond the glass. Outside, the sky was gray and heavy. New York had been getting quite the winter this year and it looked as if it was going to keep right on snowing through Christmas.

Christmas. Only about ten days away and he still didn't have any shopping done. Another example of just how much he missed Rachel. She'd have made damn sure he got out to the stores.

Pitiful, he thought. He couldn't even Christmas shop without Rachel in his life.

Just pitiful.

"So," he said, "you coming home for Christmas?"

"I don't think so," Fin answered. "I sort of want to start our own traditions this year. But I'll definitely be there for the New Year's party."

Disappointment flared briefly to life inside him. He hadn't realized how much he'd been looking forward to seeing his sister again.

Shaking his head, he forced a smile into his voice and asked, "So how's life in the Wild, Wild West?"

Fin laughed again and Shane saw her in his mind. His twin. His best friend. Like a younger version of their mother, Fin was short and slender with auburn hair, green eyes and a few gold freckles across her nose. Her smile could light up a room and he was grateful that lately, his twin had had so much to smile about.

Fin might be living on a ranch in Colorado these days, but clearly their connection was still strong. She'd chosen just the right time to call him.

"You really need to get out of Manhattan more often, Shane," she said, still chuckling. "You know, we really don't have gunfights in the center of town and desperadoes hardly ever hold up the stagecoach anymore."

"Cute," he said, nodding, "and the ranch was a great place to visit but I think the West Village is about as west as I really want to go."

His sister sighed a little. "I know you're not the outdoorsy type, Shane, but I know you enjoyed yourself."

The Silver Moon ranch, just outside Colorado Springs, was mainly a cattle ranch, but according to Fin, her new husband ran quite a few horses, too. Enough to make her happy anyway.

And it wasn't as if his city born and bred sister was roughing it. She and her husband, Travis Clayton, lived in a huge, two-story log home, surrounded by tall pines and open spaces. Shane had seen for himself how happy she was there. And that was good enough for him.

"I did. And I'll come back," he promised. "This spring. In the meantime, how're you feeling?"

"Good," she said, a little less enthusiastically. "I could live without the morning sickness, but otherwise, I feel great."

Shane smiled. "I'm glad. And damn, it's good to hear your voice."

"Yeah," she said wryly, "you sound thrilled."

"Been a bad couple of weeks," he admitted, leaning his head against the chair back.

"Not the way I hear it," she said. "You made it, Shane. You're the new CEO. This is a good thing."

Should have been, he told himself. Now it didn't mean a thing to him. How could it when the woman who'd helped him win the damn thing was gone?

His silence must have told her there was something wrong.

"So do you want to tell me what's going on?" she asked.

"I wouldn't know where to start," he admitted.

"Most people say start at the beginning," Fin said and he heard the smile in her voice. "I say start with what's upsetting you and work backward."

"Upset?" he repeated. "Small word for what I'm feeling." Hell. What *was* he feeling? He couldn't ever remember experiencing this kind of emotion. The feeling that his chest was too tight. That his heart was empty.

That he might never be *warm* again.

"Talk to me, Shane."

"It's Rachel," he blurted. "She's gone."

"What do you mean gone?"

He frowned at the phone. "How many things could I mean?"

"She quit?"

"Yeah." He bit the word off and tasted the bitterness of defeat.

"Why?"

He rubbed his mouth, closed his eyes and said, "Because I'm an idiot."

Fin chuckled. "She's known that for a long time, but she just now quit, so what else happened?"

"We—" He caught himself and shook his head. "None of your business, Fin."

"Well, *yahoo,*" she crowed. "It's about time."

"What?"

"You slept with her."

"Like I said, none of your business." And why was his twin, the one person in the world who should be on his side at all damn times, so excited by his misery?

"So did you tell her you love her?"

He sat up like a shot and noticed the horrified expression on his reflection in the windowpane. "Who said anything about love?"

"Oh, Shane, I love you, but you really *are* an idiot."

"Thanks for calling," he snapped.

"For Pete's sake, everyone but you has known for at least a year that Rachel's nuts about you."

"What?" If that was true, why hadn't he known about it? Why hadn't someone told him? Hell, why hadn't he *noticed?*

"And you feel the same way."

He shook his head firmly, decisively. "I'm not in love."

"Really?" his sister prompted. "Then why don't

you tell me how you're feeling now that Rachel's gone?"

He scowled and his reflection glared back at him.

"Be honest," she said and her voice softened in sympathy.

"I feel like hell," he finally said, admitting what he'd been keeping inside for too long. "Nothing feels right without her here. Nothing's working. I can't work. Can't think. Can't sleep. Damn it, Fin, I wasn't looking for this."

"No, you weren't. You just got lucky."

"I'm *lucky* to feel this bad?"

"No, Shane," she said on an impatient sigh. "You're lucky to have the chance at something amazing. Most people never find what you have. Don't blow it."

He shook his head, as if he were going to try to deny his sister's words. But he couldn't. "I already *have* blown it. Fin, she won't talk to me. Won't see me."

"Then it's up to you to find a way to make it happen."

"Easier said than done."

"Nobody said it would be easy. Nothing worth having comes easily, Shane." A long pause and then her voice dipped even lower. "Trust me on this one. I know."

Fin had gone through so much in her life to reach the happiness she'd finally found, he knew she was speaking from experience. But just because she and Travis had found each other didn't mean that he and Rachel were destined to find the same thing.

Did it?

Was Fin right?

Was it all so simple after all?

Was this overpowering emotion nearly choking him *love?*

"Shane," Fin said quietly, and he focused on the sound of her voice, "for too long, I was living only for the company. I forgot about actually having a life. But now, I've got a wonderful life, with a man who loves me. I've found my daughter and I have a new chance at being a mom."

"I know and I'm glad for you—"

"I want the same kind of happiness for you, Shane," she said, interrupting him neatly. "Don't let Rachel get away. Don't miss your chance at love."

When he finally hung up with Fin, Shane was thoughtful. Everything she'd said played over and over again in his mind, as if the words were on a permanent loop. Love. Rachel. Chance at happiness.

The silence in his office pushed him to leave it. As he wandered through the deserted hallways of *The Buzz,* his footsteps echoing in the quiet, he felt the underlying pulse of the business his father had built. Everything that he himself was now responsible for. And weirdly, he felt both fulfilled and empty.

This place was where he belonged, but the woman who belonged *with* him wasn't there.

And without Rachel, he knew suddenly, none of this was worth a damn. Fin was right. If he didn't act quickly, do *something* to convince Rachel to take a chance on him again, he'd end up just like his father—a lonely man with more regrets than anyone had a right to.

Patrick Elliott loved his wife madly, but he'd so buried himself in the business he'd created, that he'd missed much of the life they could have had. He'd been a stranger to his children and a phantom presence in his own house.

Shane didn't want the same kind of life.

He didn't want to be a man whose only happiness lay in the profit margins of his business. He wanted to be happy. To love and *be* loved.

He wanted Rachel.

Now, all he had to do was convince her that she still wanted *him.*

The Waldorf-Astoria hotel was decked out in all its grandeur for the Elliott Charity Gala. Towering floral centerpieces sat atop gleaming tables that lined the marble foyer where elegantly dressed attendees mingled, enjoying appetizers and champagne.

Crystal chandeliers shimmered with quiet light and led the guests along the marble hallway toward the elevators that would take them to the grand ballroom. Upstairs, the long, narrow room was ablaze with strings of white lights. A DJ stood along one wall, playing a selection of Christmas music that had feet tapping and a few couples twirling on the dance floor.

In one corner of the room, a gigantic blue spruce tree stood proudly, its limbs bowing under the weight of lights and ornaments. At its feet were dozens of gaily wrapped packages awaiting the crowd of children here representing those this fundraiser would be assisting.

Rachel smiled and nodded to those she passed as she listened with half an ear to the voices coming across the earpiece/microphone she wore. Keeping everything running smoothly was enough of a task that she didn't really have time to think about Shane. Or the fact that he wasn't there.

She'd missed him desperately the last week or so. Missed going into work every day and seeing him. Missed teasing him and hearing him laugh. Missed working with him and sharing the victories and defeats of running *The Buzz.*

And every night, alone in her bed, she missed the feel of his arms around her. Missed the sound of his breath in the darkness and the heated touch of his hands on her body.

She closed her eyes and swayed slightly under the onslaught of memories rushing through her. Rachel's heart ached as her gaze swept the crowd, searching for the one man she most longed to see. But he wasn't there and in the ocean of people, she might as well have been alone.

Two hours later, the DJ began playing "Here Comes Santa Claus," and the gathered children erupted in excited cheers.

A voice in Rachel's ear said, "Santa's here, and hey, it's a good one."

"Excellent," she answered and followed the

crowd as the people slowly moved toward the decorated Christmas tree and the "throne" that had been set up for Santa.

Then the man himself stepped out from behind a panel of velvet curtains and paused midstage for a hearty belly laugh. His voice rolled out across the room and sent a chill straight up Rachel's spine.

Her heartbeat quickened and her mouth went dry as her gaze locked on the tall man in the red velvet suit. The red hat, white wig and beard, bushy eyebrows and rectangular glasses perched low on his nose did a good job of disguising his true identity.

But Rachel would have known him anywhere.

Shane.

She wove through the crowd, excusing herself, apologizing, but never stopping. Her gaze on Santa, she headed straight for him. And halfway there, his gaze found hers. She felt the power of his stare slam into her and for the first time in more than a week, she felt wholly, completely alive again.

"Merry Christmas," Santa shouted, his gaze still on Rachel.

The children shrieked and clapped and the gathered adults got into the spirit of the thing, too. Women in diamonds, men in designer tuxes smiled along with the kids, enjoying the thrill of the moment.

Rachel stopped alongside Santa and looked up into Shane's beautiful green eyes. She didn't want to make too much of his being here. Of his playing Santa. Of the quickening jolt of her heartbeat.

But how could she not?

How could she not hope that somehow, someway, they might find each other in the magic of this night?

"Santa's got some work to do," Shane whispered, "but once the presents are distributed, you and I have to talk."

"Shane…"

His eyes actually twinkled. *"Santa."*

She nodded even as one of the kids moved in close and started tugging at her hand. "After, Santa."

Shane grinned and immediately bent down to scoop up the little girl who was staring at him as if he held the answers to all of the universe's questions. Perching her on his hip, he tapped her nose with the tip of one finger and said, "Now, let's see what Santa's got especially for you!"

For an hour, Rachel worked side by side with Shane. His laughter rang out and inspired hers. The kids were awed and touched and thrilled with the gifts the Elliott foundation had purchased specifically for them. The real magic of Christmas hummed in the air as the crowd began singing along with the carols pouring from the stereo.

Outside, the snow started again and turned the ballroom into a picture postcard. And when the last of the children's wishes had been satisfied, Santa took Rachel's hand and pulled her backstage.

"You were wonderful tonight," she said, taking a cautious step back from him even as her heart urged her to move in closer. "The children loved you."

Shane pulled off the hat, wig and beard, then carefully took off his glasses and set them aside before turning to Rachel. "I've never had so much fun," he admitted. "And it's all because of you."

"What?"

"You, Rachel," he said, reaching for her, dropping his hands onto her shoulders and pulling her slowly toward him. "I played Santa tonight because I knew you'd be here. Knew you'd like it. And I hoped you'd give me a chance to say what I should have said a long time ago."

"Shane…" Her throat felt incredibly tight. As if air were just too thick to penetrate it.

"Just listen," he said quickly. "Please."

Rachel nodded because she simply couldn't speak. She locked her knees to keep herself upright and stared into his beautiful eyes.

"I miss you, Rachel," he said, his voice gruff, raw. "I miss seeing you every day. Miss hearing you laugh. Miss the way you nag me into doing what needs doing."

She found her voice at that. "I don't nag, I—"

"You do," he interrupted, "and I need it, God knows. Nothing is right with me, Rachel. Since you left, there's no light. There's no laughter. There's no…anything."

"I miss you, too, but—"

"No," he said quickly, pulling her even closer, tipping her head back until she was staring straight up into his eyes. "No buts, Rachel. Just the simple truth. Without you in my life, I've got nothing worth having."

She swallowed hard and let the tears crowding her eyes begin to fall.

"I love you, Rachel," he said, his fingers digging into her arms as if holding on to her meant life itself. "I think maybe I've always loved you. I just never knew it until you were gone." He bent his head, kissed her gently, lightly, then said, "You're everything to me, Rachel. You make me want to be a better man. A man who deserves you."

Her heart thundering in her chest, Rachel could hardly believe she was hearing him say all the things she'd dreamed of hearing. Her soul lit up like Christmas morning and hope for a future filled with love swept through her.

"If you let me," he said, hurrying on as if unwilling to stop talking long enough to hear her answer, "I'll spend the rest of our lives proving to you just how much I love you."

"What are you saying?" The words squeaked out of her throat. She was pretty sure what he was getting at, but she wanted no mistakes. No misunderstandings. Not about this.

"I'm proposing, Rachel!" He dragged her tightly against him and wrapped his arms around her, holding her in place. "For God's sake, haven't you been listening?"

Rachel laughed and nodded. "Yeah. I really have. But I don't think I've heard an actual question yet."

He gave her a brief smile. "I'm getting to it. This isn't easy for a man, you know. What if the woman you're asking says no?"

She smiled back at him. "Just a chance you're going to have to take, I guess."

"Well," Shane said, "a very wise woman I know told me recently that nothing worth having comes easily."

"I like her already," Rachel said, loving the feel of Shane's arms around her, there in the dark. From the room beyond, Christmas music drifted on the air and conversations came muted, as if from a distant planet.

"Yeah," he said, "me, too. But this is about us."

"Us," Rachel echoed. "I like the sound of that, too."

"Glad to hear it," Shane said, lifting one hand to smooth her hair back from her forehead. "Marry me, Rachel. Let me marry you."

"Yes."

His smile was quick and broad. "Just like that?"

"Just like that," she said, nodding. "Although, I'm not going to work for you anymore."

His smile faded abruptly. "Why the hell not?"

"Because," she said, "I'm going back to school. I always wanted to be a teacher. I think I'd be a good one."

"I think you'd be a great teacher," Shane said, dipping his head for another quick taste of her. "I'll miss having you at the office, but as long as you come home to me every night, I'll be a happy man."

"I do love you, Santa," she said, going up on her toes to meet him for another kiss.

His glued-on, bushy white eyebrows wiggled expressively over his twinkling green eyes. "Then how about a sleigh ride?"

Epilogue

The tree was still up, the garlands and lights still twining around the great room at The Tides. And with all of the Elliotts gathered at the family home for New Year's, the noise level was pretty impressive.

Shane wandered through the crowd, listening to snatches of conversation and smiling at the sudden bursts of laughter that shot up and flavored the air. He glanced across the room, caught Rachel's eye and felt again the punch of sheer joy that was a constant companion these days. With Rachel's love he could do anything. Face anything. And he looked forward to a future of loving her and the children they were already trying for.

The stereo was suddenly turned off and each of

the gathered Elliotts turned to look at the older man standing beside the roaring fire in the hearth.

"I think it's time for a speech," Patrick Elliott announced, lifting a glass of champagne to his family.

"Now, Patrick," his wife chided, "'tis no time for one of your long talks. The family's here, we should be celebratin'."

Shane watched as his father dropped an arm around his wife's shoulders and pulled her close.

"You're right, Maeve," Patrick said, "as always. But, the idea was for Shane to give the speech. As the new CEO of EPH, it's only fitting."

Around him, applause erupted and Shane grinned. Gannon slapped him on the back and gave him a shove toward the front of the room. Erika held their baby daughter as if she were made of spun glass and smiled up at her husband.

Tag had his fiancée, Renee, trapped under a ball of mistletoe and the lovely woman showed no signs of trying to escape. Michael stood beside the chair where his wife, Karen, practically glowing with her very short hair, sat enjoying the fun.

Shane kept walking, stopping long enough to snag Rachel's hand and drag her along with him. He grinned at Summer and her rock star Zeke, huddled with Scarlet and John, no doubt planning the double wedding that Maeve was already fretting over.

Outside the living room, the night was cold and moonlit, pale silvery light glancing off the mounds of snow, illuminating the grounds. Inside, warmth filled the gathered Elliotts and touched Shane more deeply than ever before.

Fin lifted a glass to him and gave him a wink. He grinned at her and her husband, Travis, who'd flown in from Colorado with Bridget and her husband, Mac, just for this traditional party. In a corner of the room, Daniel and Amanda were cuddling, ignoring everyone else. And to round out the crowd, Jessie and her husband, Cade, were talking with Liam and his fiancée, Aubrey, about their upcoming wedding at their Napa winery. Collen and Misty were cuddled up together, as if they were alone on an island. And Bryan and Lucy were kissing under the mistletoe. The family was together and happy. A great start to a New Year.

Finally, though, Shane was at the head of the room and as his parents stepped to one side, he pulled Rachel close against him. His heart swelled as she leaned into him.

"I'm a lucky man," he said, lifting his glass to the faces turned toward him. "I found the woman I was meant to love and the work I was meant to do."

"Hear, hear!" Gannon shouted and was quickly shushed by Erika.

"But," Shane continued, looking from one beloved face to another, "I think this year we all got lucky. When Dad started his little contest, I thought he was trying to drive a wedge between us." Shane glanced at his father and smiled. "I should have known better."

Patrick smiled and kissed Maeve.

Renee gave Tag a friendly slap and stepped out from under the mistletoe to listen.

"The Elliotts have come together this year," Shane said, lifting his champagne glass even higher. "We've rediscovered our family ties and forged the bonds that connect us one to the other, even tighter than they were before. We've passed our own tests, we've faced our fears..." He paused to nod at Michael and Karen. "And we've come out the other side. We've found love and we've found each other."

Liam whistled and Fin applauded.

"Old wrongs have been righted," Shane went on, with a nod at Fin and Jessie. "And the future stretching out in front of us looks bright."

"Well said," Patrick called out.

"To the Elliotts," Shane shouted, "together, we're invincible!"

And as the family celebrated, Shane pulled the love of his life into the circle of his arms. Together, they shared a kiss that promised a future filled with all the love and hope anyone could ask for.

* * * * *